THE HEART IS A LONELY HUNTER

THE HEART IS A LONELY HUNTER

❀

Bertrand E. Brown

iUniverse, Inc.
New York Lincoln Shanghai

The Heart is a Lonely Hunter

Copyright © 2005 by Bertrand Brown

iUniverse books may be ordered through booksellers or by contacting:

iUniverse
2021 Pine Lake Road, Suite 100
Lincoln, NE 68512
www.iuniverse.com
1-800-Authors (1-800-288-4677)

ISBN-13: 978-0-595-36178-6 (pbk)
ISBN-13: 978-0-595-80623-2 (ebk)
ISBN-10: 0-595-36178-1 (pbk)
ISBN-10: 0-595-80623-6 (ebk)

Printed in the United States of America

CHAPTER 1

❁

"C'mon Stacy, the party's supposed to start in fifteen minutes and I've still got to take these rollers out and do my hair. I really don't have time for you and your little Dear Abby routine right through here. So, if you don't mind, Miss Thang, would you please stop minding other people's business and concentrate on doing my hair and make-up. Boy, you let a sista get one semester of psychology under her belt and she thinks she can cure the problems of the world," Monica laughed.

"Whatever...I was just trying to help girlfriend out a little. This is supposed to be her night you know and instead of comin' in hear singin' *Joyful Joyful* or *Oh, Happy Day* she comes in lookin' like someone died and forget to include her in the will. I was just tryin' to lift her spirits a little," Stacy replied.

"Let me guess? Chad again?" said Monica.

"Who else? That fool could fuck up a wet dream at the Playboy mansion."

"Damn! I knew there was something wrong. What did that asshole do now?" Monica asked.

"Same ol' same ol'. Sylvia said he was supposed to pick her up at her dorm an hour ago and she ain't seen the boy yet."

"And she ain't going to. He's wit' that lil' freshman with the J Lo ass and real cute smile that lives right under me. Saw them going up to her room when I was getting off the elevator." Monica stated matter-of-factly.

"Uh uh." Stacy was shocked. "Did he speak?"

"Of course he spoke. He always speaks. He doesn't care. Hell, but then why not speak. Everybody in the dorm knows he's been seein' her. That's common knowledge. Chad's been hittin' that thing all semester. Shit, he's been up there so much that her neighbors nicknamed him 'the chef.'"

"Uh uh! Please tell me you're lying. Why do they call him that anyway?" Stacy asked.

"Would you lower your voice. You know Sylvia's in the next room," Stacy whispered

"But anyway, from what nosy-ass Annette and Sheila tell me, they can hear everything being that their right next door and the walls are so thin. And the way they tell it, it must be Miss Thang's first time getting some 'cause they say they can hear her hollerin' anytime Chad gets ta workin' that thang. And from what I hear she's down for everything. Said she 's even gotten to the point that she's instructin' Chad each and every step of the way now."

"But you still haven't told me why they call him the 'chef'," Stacy added as she rubbed the blush into the young woman's cheeks.

"Will you hush! You know Sylvia's in the next room and you're all loud and shit," whispered Monica. "Now hush and I'll tell you."

"Okay, okay. Go ahead."

"Well, from what Annette tells me, they gave Chad the nickname, 'the chef' because they say he's steady servin' up sista girl a new dish every week.

Annette said that on some nights he just stops by for five or ten minutes and gives her a little appetizer. Then at other times he tosses that poor girl's salad like there ain't no tomorrow. Said she loves it too. Annette said those are the nights the whole floor can hear her yellin' just beggin' him for more. Said she one time she stood right there in the hall half-naked and cried 'cause he didn't finish. I'm talkin' real tears too, girl.

Then they say there's other nights when he's got a little more time on his hands and brings her to a slow simmer before makin' the cream rise to the top. But they say the days they *really* hear her is on those weekends when Sill goes home. They say that's when he really gets ta cookin' and pulls out all the stops. Say he shakes it and bakes it and gets to blendin' it just right before he brings the whole damn thing to a boil with her screamin' and hollerin' and tellin' everybody all the secret ingredients and then when it's over and it cools, they say he chows down," Stacy said laughing hysterically.

"Oh, get the hell out of here. I know you're not saying what I think you're saying? You know sometimes I have to wonder why I listen to your crazy ass at all," Monica replied.

"I don't know how true it is 'cause Annette's a freak herself and probably has her ear pressed to the wall but ya gotta admit, it's funny and it sounds good and if you know Chad then you know anything's possible 'cause he ain't worth his weight in...So, it could very well be true. But there's one thing I do know.

He does spend an awful lot more time with her than he does Sill. That I do know. What I really don't understand is why she even bothers dealin' with his shit but then I guess we've all done the same thing at one time or another."

"No doubt. But you know, I can feel the tide changin', Stace. And who knows tonight may be the beginning of something new for all of us. The three of us have been together for four long years and none of us has met a man yet we'd wanna write home about."

"Ain't that the truth," Monica replied.

"Never know though. Like I said, tonight may be the start of something new for all of us."

"That's wishful thinkin' but I ain't even thinkin' about men tonight. This is our night. This is the night we celebrate four years of having the top sorority and the largest chapter in school history and nobody else can take responsibility for that but us. You, me and Sill. When we came on campus what did they have? Four members. Now what are we lookin' at? Close to a hundred members and fourteen more on line. We did that. We accomplished that shit. And we accomplished it without a single man's assistance. Now there's definitely somethin' to say about that. Who needs 'em. We can just as well do without 'em and all the drama an bullshit they bring to the table."

"*HELLO!*" Monica shouted. "Wait a minute, now. I feel everything you're sayin' but let's not get carried away. The brothas do have their usefulness."

Hearing all the yelling and commotion, Sylvia came running from the living room.

"Damn, I thought something was wrong," Sylvia said staring at her sorors.

"No, ain't nothin' wrong, Sill. How could anything be wrong on a night like this? In fact, things couldn't be much better especially with you being voted in for the fourth straight time. And who deserves the credit? Hello. None other than your campaign manager and brain trust. Thank you very much," Stacy said grinning.

"Yeah yeah! Here she goes pattin' herself on the back again, Monica."

"I know. She's so busy tootin' her own horn that by the time she gets finished doin' my hair the party will be over."

"Girl please! You ain't worried about nothin' but tryin' to get there before someone else steals your man," Stacy laughed.

"What man? Don't tell me you're still tryna push up on Zach. Girl you need to give that up. There's a line a mile long in front of you. Especially since they say the boy's going in the top ten of the NFL draft," Sill said feigning a smile.

"That's alright. You know what they say about the cream always risin' to the top. When he comes to his senses he'll recognize the fact that he's not going to do much better than moi." Monica replied.

"Whatever. I'm in no shape to say anything with that sorry man I'm stuck with. I just wish you more luck than I had with this piece of shit. But anyway, I'm going to go on ahead since I'm supposed to be the guest of honor or whatever and you two look like you're going to be here awhile," Sill said closing the bathroom door on her way out.

"Alright Sill, I'll be there as soon as I figure out how to fix this child's face. Ain't enough L'Oreal in the world to help her but she insists on me working miracles. Anyway, we'll be there in a few. Save us a plate," Stacy yelled.

"And a man," screamed Monica. "You know how I like 'em, Sill."

"Yeah, with all there limbs," Sill yelled back.

"Well, that's not a lot to ask, now is it?" Monica laughed.

"Don't take much does it?" Stacy said as the two women waited to hear the door close and bolt lock fasten into place.

"She seems awfully down doesn't she, Stace?"

"Wouldn't you be if you were in her situation? This is supposed to be her night and that stupid ass wannabe playa should be by her side, but no. Oh, the hell with Chad. He doesn't deserve this much conversation. What we need to do is make Sill's night a night to remember? After all, she's the first sista ever to be elected president four times in a row in the history of the chapter and besides that, you couldn't ask for a better friend. Sill's the shit but just because she's a little odd and ain't out there, this motherfucker ain't tryna give her no respect but let's make it a night she'll never forget.

Sylvia didn't know how long she'd been sitting there in the living room thinking, waiting for Chad to show up.

The least he could have done was call. Picking up the phone, she tried calling his dorm room again. Still no answer, Sylvia said goodbye to Stacy and Monica, grabbed her jean jacket and headed for the door.

Little whore is probably running the streets or up in one of the girl's dorms, chasing some little freshman that don't know no better. Sylvia thought about checking Van Sykes Hall, the girls' dorm adjacent to her own and one of Chad's favorite hangouts, then decided against it. If she found him, all hunkered up with some female then what? It certainly wouldn't be the first time. Besides, he'd just lie like he always did and after a week of not speaking, she'd end up taking him back until he did it again.

She kept telling herself that she didn't need this madness but in the end she always took him back despite the rumors and the snickering. Even those closest to her, her own sorority sisters, had spoken to her from time to time about Chad and his midnight rendezvous. How many times had they mentioned the fact that they'd seen Chad sneaking out of one of their dorms, shirttail hanging out of his pants, hair undone in the wee hours of the morning? It was nothing new. It was just the way he was. What she couldn't understand was why she stuck with him. They'd been together ever since they were sophomores and she had lost count of the times he had cheated on her.

Every time there was a new freshman class, he felt compelled to conduct the welcoming tour, which was comprised of him showing her the campus and she showing him her—.

Angry and oblivious to the world, Sylvia crossed the lush lawns of Tech's campus. On several occasions, she was sure she heard her name being yelled from a dorm window or from across the street. But not once did she turn around to see who was calling her. Brothers she had class with or who were simply trying to hit on her from time to time spoke in passing but she ignored them for the most part.

"Stuck up bitch," one of them remarked, as she passed.

It was starting to drizzle. Sylvia donned her pink and green, AKA umbrella and made her way past the crowd of young men who stood crowded under the eave of Smith Hall. She cringed at the thought of what was to happen next.

After four years, she still hated walking past the guys' dorm. The lewd remarks were bad enough when it was just one or two guys but they seemed to grow in intensity when they were in a crowd, showing off for each other. Surprisingly enough, they were not quite as obnoxious as they usually were. She thanked her lucky stars that she was at the tiny girls' college across the street. At least there, she wasn't subjected to this on a daily basis.

As the drizzle began to pelt the pink and green umbrella harder, Sylvia picked up her pace hoping to hit the student union before it came down in buckets. She wondered if Chad were downstairs in the lobby of her dorm waiting for her or calling her room. One thing was for sure. Wherever he was, she was sure *he* damn sure wasn't getting wet. That little bastard had probably forgotten all about their date, the party, and her being sworn in as president of her sorority. Sure, it was her third time being elected to the post but if it meant something to her, he could have at least shown some empathy, some damn concern and escorted her. The more Sylvia thought about Chad, the angrier she became.

Truth be told, there were simply too many guys on Tech's campus that were interested in her for her to be messin' around with this low life, thug. She wondered if there was something innately wrong with her. What was it that attracted her to thugs in the first place? Maybe, just maybe, her mother was right about good girls just naturally being attracted to bad boys. Sylvia wasn't sure about that. But one thing she was quite certain of at this point. She was tired of Chad and his flippant fuckin' attitude.

Hell, Chad could ruin a wet dream but she'd be damn if she was going to let him ruin her night? After all, the party was in her honor. And Lord knows she wasn't about to let him rain on her parade. She was going to party like she never had before. *Yessirree, buddy!* The ever so prim and proper, Miss Sylvia Shipp, always so damn correct, always the model citizen was finally going to let her hair down. It was time to let the world know who she really was. She was tired of playing the role while Chad and everyone else did whatever the hell they wanted. Wasn't it her sorors that were constantly telling her to do just that? *You need to go on and get yo' groove on, girl! Forget Chad!* Come on and go to happy hour with us. Meet some new guys, some nice guys for a change. And leave the losers and low-life's for the ho's and hoochies.

Apologetically, she would decline always citing homework or some prior commitment. The only time she did go anywhere other than to a meeting of this organization or that was when she crossed Lee Street and made her way onto Tech's campus to see Chad. And then all he did was keep her locked away in his dorm room until she grew tired of his constant pawing and feeling. When she declined his advances, he would leave her for hours with no explanation, only to return later that night high as hell or drunk as a skunk. All too often, he would pass out and she would have to find someone to escort her back to Bennett. Usually, Chad's roommate, Zachary, would assume the responsibility of walking Sill back to her dorm. And more than once, she had considered asking Zachary in after the long walk. However, she didn't think it was appropriate. And, though they were friends, it was obvious that Zachary had feelings for her. Besides that, Black people loved to talk.

For four years, Sylvia withstood the ugly, rumors and the never ending gossip that made its way between the campuses of the two schools. Hell, it was enough that she had to withstand the constant chatter surrounding Chad's late night liaisons. But now in her senior year, she was not about to let such an innocent event as Zachary walking her home at night escalate and evolve into any more than that.

Ever since her freshman year, Sylvia had done her able-bodied best to keep to herself, concentrate on her classes and her grades and for the sake of everyone involved to stay aloof. She was by no means unfriendly, just purposely distant and detached. Statuesque, she seldom wore anything provocative but was content with the subtle earth tones that blended in so well with her dark, brown skin.

For as long as she could remember, Sylvia had always been the focal point. And yet, she had never really grown accustomed to being the center of attention. In her attempts, to spurn the attention and move the spotlight from her, she'd gained the reputation of being pompous and pretentious. Yet, her sorors and a few close friends knew Sylvia to be just the opposite. Easygoing and down-to-earth was how they described her and criticized her constantly for being too nice, especially to that monster, Chad.

Now for the first time in four years, Sylvia had to agree with her sorors. She was *too* nice to Chad and not once did he act as if he appreciated her kindness. *Not once.* Instead, he acted as if she owed him the world just for being with her. To him, she was nothing more than a trophy that he had paraded on campus during their freshman and sophomore years when it seemed the *in* thing to do. Now she was old hat.

Fuck, Chad! Sylvia said aloud to no one in particular and anyone within ear shot. The two shots of *Courvoisier* she'd guzzled down in her dorm room while waiting for Chad were starting to hit her now while the warm gentle rain found its way around the umbrella and beat against her face. Getting closer to the union, she was glad for the rain that helped mask her burning anger that resulted in a river of tears.

Stopping briefly to wipe both rain and teardrops from her face, she quickly collected herself before joining the party already in progress. Promising herself that this would be a night to remember, Sylvia Shipp entered the student union to the applause and hugs of her sorority sisters. The inauguration ceremony itself took a little less than twenty minutes. When it ended, champagne bottles popped, corks flew and the artist better known as Prince screamed as only Prince can scream.

Out of the corner of her eye Sylvia saw Chad's roommate Zachary dancing with one of her sorors on the other side of the floor and seriously considered cutting in to inquire about the sudden disappearance of his roguish roommate then thought better of it and joined her partners for a drink. Hell, why should she ruin Zach's night by forcing him to lie for Chad's stupid ass anyway? It was, she knew, some unwritten male law that forced them to cover for each other no matter how wrong they were. She never understood it but chalked it up to being some macho thing. Anyway, that's just the way they were even though she knew Zach didn't particularly care for Chad or his antics. They just happened to be thrown together when they were freshman and had come to know each other well enough to know that neither of them wanted to go through learning anyone else so they remained together for the past four years and managed to stay out of each other's way as much as possible. And since Chad was seldom there that just made it that much easier. But it was a known fact that they were as opposite as day and night. Yet, neither would give the other up in a hail of gunfire despite their misgivings about each other. So, there was really no need to ask. Besides that, Zachary looked like he was torn up. Sylvia had seen him drunk before but never like this. He could barely stand. Chuckling to herself, Sylvia grabbed the bottle of *Hennessey* off the table, found a corner of the union not occupied and guzzled freely hoping to reach the same plateau.

Her thoughts drifted. How could she have denied herself for so long? For four long years, she had relinquished all notions of pleasure, seemingly, content to live on the outskirts of campus life. But wasn't this what every woman wanted? To be wanted, loved, appreciated and more than anything, accepted?

An hour later and still no Chad in sight, Sylvia found herself gyrating slowly to the sounds of Will Downing. Never had she been this drunk or felt this good. She was movin' now. Groovin'. Climbing on the now empty banquet table, she began a slow, exotic dance. Bottle in one hand, umbrella still in the other, Sylvia Shipp had the floor. Through the mist and drunken fog of liquor, Sylvia could hear the steady rhythmic chant of, "GO GIRL, GO! YOU GO, SILL! GO GIRL!"

For the first time in four years, there was no whispering, no snickering. She felt good, real good, better than she ever had. For the first time she felt accepted and a part of it all and it felt wonderful. And what's more she not only *wanted* this, she *needed* this. She wondered how she could have possibly denied herself for so long. For four long years, she had relinquished all notions of pleasure seemingly content to live on the outskirts of campus life. But wasn't this what every woman wanted? To be wanted, loved, appreciated and more than anything to be accepted?

The shouts grew louder. "TAKE IT OFF! TAKE IT ALL OFF!" There was a crowd now but she hardly noticed. Tilting the bottle up she took another swig from the half empty bottle and unbuttoned her blouse. And the more she took off the more the crowd roared. Before long, she was down to her thong. The crowd of students was in a frenzy now, her sorors screaming louder than the guys. "TAKE IT OFF! TAKE IT ALL OFF, SILL!"

Then, not to disappoint, Sylvia Shipp began doing just that. Before she could bare her soul completely, she felt an arm reach out and grab her. There were no words, no arguments, nothing but the raucous boos of those who were dying to see the ever so prim and proper, Sylvia Shipp finally unveil.

She was so drunk that it wasn't until she was outside of the student union that she realized that she was in no other than Chad's arms. She could hear him ranting and raving but his words were a meaningless garble. What she did understand was that she had never seen him quite so angry. Not bothering to put her clothes on, Sylvia felt the cold chill of the rain trickling down her back. Chad threw her limp body in the car; bumping her head with such force that she was sure, she was going to pass out. *Damn, it hurt.* Not sure whether it was the bump or the alcohol, Sylvia ignored the pain.

For once, he was the one angry and she was glad. Maybe, just maybe, he did care after all. If he had been there in the first place, this would never have happened. She would have been right there with him, by his side, happy just to be spending time with her man, but no. As usual, he couldn't find the time to be with her. Of course, he couldn't let lil' ol' Sill, steal his thunder and be in the limelight for once. How could he take a backstage to a woman? Not Mr. Thang! Now he had the nerve to be angry. Sill laughed aloud at the thought, then passed out.

She awoke with a start. Never had she experienced such pain in all her life. She vaguely remembered the car ride she but she did remember Chad telling her over and over that this was a night she would never forget. He'd been angry, angrier than she'd ever seen him in the four years she had known him. She remembered little except for him calling her a cheap ho' but everything else was so blurred, so fuzzy now.

Suddenly embarrassed, she screamed at him to stop driving so fast and to take her home. And then she passed-out again. When she awoke, this time the pain was too much to bear and she wondered if they had been in an accident. God, how her insides ached. There were people crowded around her watching, staring, laughing. But how could this be? Wasn't anyone going to call an ambulance? And where was Chad? She hoped he was okay. Sill, felt her legs being lifted, then pulled apart and once again, she felt that same agonizing pain. She tried to scream but there were no words, no sounds, just pain.

Through the haze, Sylvia searched the room for a familiar face, to wake her from this nightmare but recognized no one. She was in and out of consciousness now but each time she awoke, there was another face staring down into hers. She smelled the stench of masculinity and cheap cologne and finally came the grisly reality that she was being raped.

With every ounce of strength she could muster, she fought, but there were just too many. No, this couldn't be happening. When she tried to scream, someone forced a washrag in her mouth. Unable to move and barely able to breathe, she lost consciousness. Still, she felt the penetrating pain not once but over and over and over.

CHAPTER 2

❀

Three days later, Sylvia Stanton regained consciousness in the Intensive Care Unit of the Christopher-Eliot Memorial Hospital. She awoke screaming. A nurse arrived quickly to increase the morphine drip from the I. V., which hung next to the bed. And though in pain most of the pain she felt was not of a physical nature. The medical team that admitted her diagnosed her as having suffered extreme trauma to the pelvic area and internal hemorrhaging. X-rays showed an inflamed uterus and ruptured ovaries but the full extent of the damage could no be determined from the X-rays alone.

Mr. and Mrs. Shipp stood anxiously awaiting word of their daughter's condition and though both were exhausted, they refused to leave their only daughter's bedside. The fact that they'd come to learn that date rape was not uncommon among young women did little to stem the shock they felt upon learning of their daughters' plight.

"Mr. Shipp, my name is Dr. Reid and I'm one of the members of the hospital's trauma team. It looks as though your daughter was in a pretty bad accident. I haven't really had a chance to thoroughly go over her charts but I see she's regained consciousness and that's a good sign. I also received her X-rays and can see that there's a fair amount of hemorrhaging around the ovaries but they're so much blood and swelling around them that at this time that the X-rays are in and of themselves, pretty inconclusive. Right now, the best thing we can do is just sit tight and wait until some of the swelling goes down. Right now she's stable and for the time being that's about as good as it gets."

Grimacing, Mr. Shipp put his arm around his wife's shoulders to comfort her. He was certainly hoping for the best but clearly expecting the worst. Dr. Reid continued: "What we may need to do is go in and do some exploratory surgery to see how extensive the damage is and to see if we can save the ovaries. If, however, we find that they're too badly damaged and cannot stop the bleeding then we may have to remove them. This would ultimately mean that Sylvia would not be able to bear children. Now, as time is of the essence and for fear of being blunt and perhaps in your eyes somewhat unfeeling I'm forced to cut through the chase and in lieu of proper protocol and good manners what I need from you two at this point is your consent for us to operate." Dr. Reid handed Sylvia's parents the necessary consent forms for their approval.

"We understand but is the operation safe, doctor?" Mr. Shipp inquired timidly.

"It's a pretty simple and a very common procedure, Mr. Shipp. I'm sure you're familiar with a woman having her tubes tied or a partial hysterectomy where the ovaries are removed. It's really no more than that. Actually, the operation is really no more serious than a child having his or her tonsils removed. The biggest factor in a situation like your daughter's is how well she will adapt—or perhaps I should say recover, knowing that she will never be able to have children.

Her recuperation will depend a lot on the support she gets from you guys but from what I've seen of the Shipp family, I'm sure she'll have more than enough support to pull her through. And, despite the trauma your daughter has suffered, she seems to be fairly strong and healthy so there really shouldn't be too much to worry about. However, with the internal bleeding, we do need to get started as soon as possible."

The doctor left quickly after getting the necessary signatures and the following morning, Sylvia was wheeled down to pre-op to be prepped. Mr. Shipp, in an attempt to mask his worry suggested that he and his wife grab a bite to eat at K & W Cafeteria across the street. Neither ate more than a few mouthfuls and soon found themselves heading right back to the hospital where they could do little but wait. It was almost four hours later when Dr. Reid entered the waiting room.

"Relax, relax Sylvia did just fine. We weren't able to save the ovaries but otherwise, she's fine. She's in recovery. They have her on the intensive care unit in Room 411, so we can better monitor her progress. But just as soon as she's stabilized, we'll move her to a regular room until she's ready to go home. You might want to wait before you go in and see her. She's in a pretty good deal of pain, so we've increased her morphine drip and she may be in and out of sleep," Dr. Reid said.

"Thank you, sir," was the best Mr. Shipp could offer as he extended his hand but there was no doubt he was profoundly grateful to the good doctor who had pulled his only daughter through.

As soon as the Shipps' stepped off the elevator on the fourth floor, they heard the screaming. Ignoring it, they made their way to Room 411. The screaming grew progressively worse until both Horace and Beulah Shipp came to the sudden realization that the voice they heard was not just some patient deranged and out of control obviously with more than a medical problem but as they grew closer, they recognized the voice as being their own daughter's.

Rushing into the room, they found a bevy of nurses and orderlies, shouting orders at each other. And in the middle of the melee, was Sylvia fighting with all her might and screaming at the top of her lungs. The head nurse shouted in turn at one of her subordinates.

"Increase the morphine flow!"

"It's already maxed, Samantha. Anymore and it'll kill her," the young nurse shouted.

"Hold her hands then, while I strap her down," an orderly screamed at no one in particular, as he grabbed one arm while another did his best to fasten the buckle on the strap. Sylvia's screams only seemed to grow louder when she was strapped down. And Mr. Shipp, never expecting anything like this, had all he could do to get out of the way and eventually backed completely out of the room in tears. And then just as quickly as it all started, it ended. The screaming, the lurching, the attempts to battle the nurses and orderlies all stopped.

Sylvia, spent and exhausted, closed her eyes, then opened widely and stared at the tubes, which seem to emerge from every open pore. The orderlies and nurses finally breathed a collective sigh of relief. Little did they know just how brief their respite would be.

For the next two days, the high-pitched screaming continued. Each time the nurses entered the room, Sylvia would begin screaming frantically. If they opted to change the sheets, she would scream. If they tried to check her blood pressure, she would scream until after the third day of her screaming bloody murder doctors, nurses and orderlies would move to the other side of the hall in hopes that she would not see them as they made their rounds.

Her parents' daily visits met with the same reaction. So taken back was Mr. Shipp by his daughter's behavior that he would peek in the room making sure to stay out of plain eyesight and then spend the remainder of the visiting time in the waiting room waiting for his wife.

Steadfast in her love for her daughter, Mrs. Shipp endured the screaming and yelling. She had even grown accustomed to her little girl being strapped down to the bed so she wouldn't—as the nurses so aptly put it—"*Wouldn't cause harm to herself.*" Mrs. Shipp laughed at this one. "Shoot, they're more worried 'bout Sill causin' harm to *them* if you ask me" she told her husband one day on the ride home from the hospital. Both laughed at that one. Sill would eventually calm down and Mrs. Shipp would then approach her daughter slowly, cautiously, so as not to alarm her. She would then take both of Sill's hands in her own and talk to her softly, gently about friends, relatives and the goings on in the world outside of Room 411.

Sometimes Sylvia would sit and stare out of the fourth floor window at nothing in particular. At other times, her eyes would become fixated at a spot on the floor or the unopened orange juice container on her lunch tray. At other times, she was content to simply shriek and yell at the top of her lungs for the duration of her mother's visits despite her mother's attempts to soothe her. This Mrs. Shipp could endure. What ate at her very soul was that not once in the last four days had her daughter spoken a word and what was worse she didn't seem to recognize her.

The screaming tirades against the hospital staff continued on a daily basis, and as Mr. and Mrs. Shipp concluded their visit on the fourth day following the operation, they were stopped at the elevator by one of Sill's nurses. "Mr. and Mrs. Shipp I presume? Dr. Reid is on his way down from his office. I think he'd like to have a word with you concerning your daughter." No sooner had she said that then Dr. Reid emerged from the elevator.

"Thank you, Susan," he said, winking at the young petite nurse with the bright red hair. "Good evening, Mr. and Mrs. Shipp. And how are you, today? Good. Good. I thought I might have a word with you concerning Sylvia's progress. Do you have a few minutes? Good, why don't we head down to the cafeteria? I'm starved."

The good doctor led the way down the narrow hospital corridors, nodding to this person and that, stopping occasionally to talk about his golf handicap, then remembering the Shipp's who trailed closely, an uncomfortable silence engulfing them, as they waited ever so anxiously.

"Oh, how rude of me," he would say before stopping again to discuss the idea of increasing a patient's medication, then off again, around another bend, before heading down another long and winding hallway. After what seemed forever, they reached the cafeteria where Dr. Reid held the door for the Shipp's. Both Mr. and Mrs. Shipp had had enough cafeteria food to last them a lifetime so when the doctor offered, they politely refused. By the time they were seated, Mr. Shipp was so wound up, so full of worry and anxiety, that he was certain that Sill was near death and was already regretting not having had the strength to endure his only daughter's screams. Still, what Dr. Reid told him next seemed almost worse than death. After tasting the healthy serving of Salisbury steak and licking, his lips in appreciation he turned to the Shipp's.

"Well, as you know the operation was a complete success. Sylvia's recovery is going as well as expected. She seems to be healing nicely. There is no excessive scar tissue forming around the incision and her vitals are back to normal. However, I am afraid that the trauma she's experienced has left some far deeper emotional scars than we could ever have imagined. From what I understand, she has not spoken since she's been here. This is not good. And the excessive screaming at first thought due to the operation is probably also due to the terrible ordeal she's just been through.

I'm really worried about her emotional stability. And as you know, if your minds not healthy then it can alter what and how your body heals. Presently, she's not eating. The nurses inform me that she hasn't eaten solid food in two days and that can't be good so I've recommended she be fed intravenously. Not eating suggests to me that she's not fighting. She's also made no effort to get up and walk around on her own or use the bathroom. We try to encourage this but she has not responded. In all honesty, I think Sylvia has lost the will to live."

Dr. Reid continued to eat, scooping up another forkful of mash potatoes and sweet peas before continuing. "Sure you won't have some? The Salisbury steak is better than my wife's and she's a pretty fair cook."

Both nodded no.

"In any case, I've met with my colleagues concerning Sylvia and the direction we need to go and the general consensus is that we let her continue her recovery under the care of Dr. Henrik Divac, who is our resident psychiatrist and who's located right next door in the psychiatric ward of the hospital. He is one of the premiere men in his field and if anyone can break through and release those inner demons that are plaguing Sylvia, it is he."

Mr. and Mrs. Shipp were stunned by this pronouncement. "A mental ward? Are you suggesting our daughter be placed in a—mental ward?" Mrs. Ship asked almost incredulously. "Are you saying our Sylvia's crazy?"

"Not by any means, not by any means at all would I ever consider suggesting that your daughter is crazy. *I prefer* not to even use the word crazy since it can imply so many things, none of which I think applies to Sylvia's situation.

What I am saying is that the trauma from the rape can cause a myriad of rather unusual side effects, most being psychological. And, as a physician and surgeon, I am not qualified to do much more than heal physical ailments. But what I'd really like to see is your daughter regain her previous form as quickly as possible."

But Mrs. Shipp hadn't heard a word the good doctor had said. She was still hung up around the idea of her daughter being placed in a facility that as far as she was concerned housed nut cases and crazy people.

"No, no, no! Y'all ain't puttin' my baby in no insane asylum!" Mrs. Shipp yelled as the tears flowed down the side of her face. "No! Hell no! Ain't nothin' wrong with my baby that some tender, lovin' care won't fix."

Mr. Shipp was horrified as well but had quickly come to the realization that there was little he could do to help his daughter who it appeared could hardly stand the sight of him. And, if they could help bring his little girl back to normal, well then, much as he hated her being in a mental institution, he had to agree to it, despite his wife's objections.

The following day, ranting and raving, despite the injection of Demerol, Sylvia Shipp was transferred to the psychiatric ward of the Christopher Eliot Memorial Hospital. To no one's surprise, neither Dr. Reid nor the staff appeared overly distraught when they learned of her departure.

Once admitted to the psychiatric ward, Sylvia's tirades grew in intensity as well as frequency. Therapy, which she took part in twice a day, did little to quell these disturbances. And special rules were set up just to alleviate some of the friction between her and the staff on duty. Male staff members, for example, were not permitted within ten feet of her unless there was a life-threatening emergency. This was for their own safety; however, as she quickly earned a reputation for attacking any and all the male staff that attempted to approach her.

One particular evening, she even went so far as to throw her tray of food at a female orderly who sported a crew cut and had a fondness for men's fashions. All in all, in the months following the operation, there was little improvement. Despite daily counseling and therapy the staff had yet to hear her utter an intelligible word.

If she was not staring off into space, her gaze usually remained fixed and distant. If, on the other hand, she did appear lucid it would come in short spurts before she would again begin screaming at the top of her lungs. At other times, she would scratch holes in her flesh in an attempt to get whatever it was that she thought was on her off of her.

On another occasion, a young man about her age, who was finishing his internship at a local university, was assigned to the ward, to accompany the psychiatric patients on their daily walk. Sylvia refused to walk on these daily outings content instead to sit in her wheelchair and collect different colored rocks and stones under the big oak tree. On this day however, she seemed much more enamored by the young intern. Out of the corner of her eye, she watched him as he made his way from patient to patient. When he finally caught sight of her in the distance he could not fathom the idea of someone so young and as beautiful as she being in a psychiatric unit. When he could no longer resist his youthful curiosity drove him to find out first-hand what could possibly cause such an attractive woman as she to be committed to such a dreadful place. Whatever the reason, he was naïve enough to believe that it had to have been a mistake of the grandest kind, perhaps a simple case of mistaken identity, or perhaps simply a faulty diagnosis.

Whatever the case may be, the best method of treatment in most instances was just a matter of exhibiting a heartfelt commitment to the patient and having a caring and empathetic attitude. Armed with these gleaming attributes, the young university intern approached the woman in the wheelchair gingerly. As he grew closer, she appeared to smile. He was sure now that someone, doctors, staff, someone had misdiagnosed her and probably had her committed out of pure jealousy because of her drop-dead good looks. Considering this, he walked over to the old oak tree abandoning everything he'd been taught at the university and much of what he'd been told by the hospital staff on duty.

Sylvia's smile brought newfound confidence to the young intern and he quickened his pace. He was now no more than five feet from her when the first rock struck him below the right eye. The second rock cut his bottom lip, knocking a tooth loose. When he dove to grab her hand in an attempt to stop the onslaught, he found himself locked in a grasp like he had never known before. And then came the burning searing pain as her teeth locked on to his earlobe. She swung her head back and forth like rabid dog in heat. He could feel his ear literally ripping apart in her mouth. When he tried to free himself, he found both his arms pinned to his sides. A wrestler in high school, he quickly realized amidst the excruciating pain he felt that he'd never in his life been put in a hold like this. It took two orderlies, a security guard and two nurses to finally untangle the two. When it was finally over, seven stitches were required to reattach the earlobe and close the gash in his bottom lip.

The nurses in the ward say that despite a sedative Sylvia grinned for the rest of the day. The young intern, on the other had, did not return and it was later learned that he met with his advisor the next day to change his major.

Following the incident with the intern, there was little change in her behavior. However, her ranting and raving grew less frequent as the days went on. And after a time, she even allowed the male staff to approach. The doctors believed her familiarity with the staff was the reason she no longer went off. She still had a fit when her father came to visit and, though this disturbed him greatly, even he could feel and hear the expectant tone of hope in the voices of the staff.

Mrs. Shipp, on the other hand, became increasingly unhappy and frustrated with both administration and staff. She saw little progress. And attributed Sill's less frequent tantrums to her withdrawing further and further into her shell instead of fighting to exorcise her demons. Hell, she was no doctor but she would rather see her daughter screaming at the top of her lungs than just sitting morose, vegetating. Of course, the staff preferred her comatose-like state. She was less work and that in turn made their jobs simpler. However, Mrs. Ship's complaints were becoming so frequent that the nurses joked about sending Sylvia home and admitting her mother in her stead.

One day, not long after, disgusted with the hospital the doctors and the staff in general Mrs. Shipp decided it was time for Sylvia to come home. Tired of making the daily jaunt to the hospital following a long tiring day at work she decided to use the month or so she'd accumulated for sick leave to stay at home and cater to her daughters needs. Mr. Shipp who had long ago grown tired of his wife's bitching and moaning concerning the hospital's deficiencies also agreed that it might be time for their daughter to be released.

Arriving at the hospital at a little after six that Tuesday evening, Mrs. Shipp was somewhat surprised to find her husband already there. Not only was he there but he had the unmitigated gall and the audacity to be standing and grinning right along with the rest of the staff. And that good for nothing Dr. Reid stood right next to him probably selling him that same ol' b.s. about the precarious nature of mental illness and how you couldn't put a time frame on recovery. It was bullshit. Pure and simple. Nothing more than insurance fraud. Fifteen hundred dollars a day and she still hadn't seen any improvement, nothing even closely resembling recovery. In fact, it appeared that if anything, Sill was growing worse. In her eyes, the time for idle chitchat was over. If she had to she'd choose her own home remedies to fix her little girl.

Moving closer to the crowded nurse's station, her anger rising, Beulah Shipp couldn't help but wonder what all the commotion was about. After all, her husband hardly ever came onto the ward to visit his daughter. He was always content to wait in the lobby or the cafeteria. The mere sight of him had the unnerving effect of sending Sylvia into an uproar and it was far more than he could tolerate. Yet, today, despite vehement objections at having their daughter discharged against everyone's better judgment, stood her husband. Approaching the nurse's station, paperwork in hand, she froze, dumbfounded.

In the midst of the crowd, stood Sylvia, chattering away with orderlies and interns. It was almost as if a former employee had come back to the hospital to visit. Beulah Shipp was spellbound. The moment Sylvia caught sight of her mother standing there she turned and rushed towards her. Hugging her tighter than she ever had before, she whispered into her ear.

"I believe it's time for me to go home now, mommy."

The ride home from the hospital would have been unusually quiet had it not been for Sylvia's constant chattering. It was almost as if she were trying to make up for lost time. She had no recollection of the events passed or at least chose not to speak about them. And her parents were so glad just to have her back in the fold that they dared not bring up the incident.

Before leaving the hospital, Dr. Reid had suggested that Sill continue counseling on an outpatient basis, fearing that if she suppressed the rape, there was a good chance it would show up eventually and perhaps cause a relapse. According to the good doctor, the rape had to be confronted. In due time, Sylvia would have to face the reality that she was the victim of a horrendous crime through no fault of her own. The Shipps on the other hand, were so eager to have their daughter back to her old self that they would have agreed to almost anything at this point but after the first couple of weeks at home, they were as convinced as Sill that the demons had passed. And each time she would come home from those damn sessions, she seemed so morose and distant, so removed from the family that they tended to agree with Sill about the counseling doing more harm than good. Bored out of her mind, it wasn't long before Sylvia started bringing up the subject of returning to school. Zachary had called several times to apologize and to keep her abreast of the happenings on both the campuses and she was glad for this.

Meanwhile, the district attorney and prosecutors sought to have criminal charges brought against the alleged assailants but were unable to gather enough evidence for a case and were forced to withdraw the allegations entirely and submit a formal apology to both the school and the alleged assailants. One parent who could not believe her son to be mixed up in anything so 'vile' even went so far as to having a lawsuit filed suggesting defamation of character against the district attorney's office.

Sill would later find out from the chief prosecutor on the case that Zachary was the only one who had charges filed against him. They were later dropped when the assailants learned that Zachary Phillips either would not or could not testify against them. From the chief prosecutor, who was given the unenviable job of closing the case, the Shipps learned of that terrible night.

"It seems Chad's roommate; Zachary Phillips came home quite drunk that evening to find there was a party going on in his room. When he entered, he found seven or eight young men in his roommate's bedroom, performing intercourse and fellatio on a female, seemingly against her will. Upon witnessing this it seems from all our accounts that Zachary Phillips, a star linebacker at the college and NFL prospect lost it completely.

Picking up a desk chair, Zachary broke the nose of one young man, the collarbone of another who just happened to be one of his teammates and came close to gouging the eye out of a third student. When he found out that it was Sylvia that had been raped, they say, he broke down in tears but still had the wherewithal to take her to the hospital where he stayed until she was admitted. He then went after his roommate Chad whom, thank God, he never found and whom we are still unable to locate. Lord knows what he would have done if he'd found him.

For several days after the incident, no one was able to locate Zachary but local police in Raleigh picked him up on a trespassing charge. It seems he went to his roommate's house expecting Chad to return home. When the boy's parents told Zachary that Chad wasn't there, Zachary parked his car across the street from the house where he waited for close to two days. The neighbors were scared stiff. Imagine a six foot five, two hundred and eighty-five pound man standing in front of your house for two straight days. In any case, they had him picked up for trespassing and he remained there until the Raleigh police informed the college who sent someone down to bail him out. By the time, we had a chance to question him it was pretty obvious that the school, the coach or an NFL scout had already gotten to him and scared the beegeezus out of the kid. Must have told him his NFL chances would be ruined if he mentioned anything about the incident. Everybody downtown in our office is sure that this was the case since none of the students he assaulted pressed charges and the trespassing charges in Raleigh were suddenly dropped. They suspended him from the football team and then quite mysteriously reinstated him. Therefore, it is our belief although we can't substantiate it that someone got to him before we did. He's a good kid though and we're certainly glad that he found Sylvia when he did. Otherwise, there's no telling what those drunken punks might have done. And it may be the closest thing to justice that we'll see."

There would be no criminal charges filed. And Sylvia was opposed to a civil suit against those involved and the university. Her lawyer was convinced that her suit against the college for not providing a safe environment was extremely winnable but she didn't want to face her attackers or rehash the entire rape scene again. It was enough she had to continue with the damn therapy which went over the same thing time and time again. Truth of the matter was that she was sick of the whole affair and wanted no more than to let bygones be bygones. After all, she was the victim and she was willingly to let it go. Hell, it was time to get on with her life and she just had too much living and too much catching up to do.

CHAPTER 3

✿

Out of sheer boredom, Sylvia grabbed the first job that came along and found herself at J.C. Penney's working as a part-time greeter and received so many compliments for her charisma that before long her supervisor recommended her for a full-time position in customer service. She gladly accepted the position since it allowed her no time to attend those ridiculous counseling sessions at the hospital.

Feeling better about herself and life in general, she hated being reminded about a situation that somehow had just happened. She missed school, missed her friends and her sorors but working full time kept her busy and before long, she had put together a small nest egg. She knew she was a burden on her parents. They had to double up now since there were three of them working and had only two cars so she made up her mind one day on the way home from work that maybe it was time for her to buy a new car. Heck, she wasn't paying any rent and Tech had offered her a nice out of court settlement in lieu of her not going forward with a civil suit so a car was not out of the question although she was sure her parent's would somehow disagree. They had suddenly become very overprotective but a car would certainly give her a sense of freedom. At least she *could go* even if the fact of the matter remained that she really had no place to go.

So on Friday, which just so happened to be payday, Sill stopped by the Ford dealership where her father bought his cars and was greeted by a very bright and very handsome young car dealer. It was the first time in Lord knows how long Sylvia had actually felt anything towards the opposite sex without feeling either guilt or some type of animosity towards them. Somehow, he was *different*. He didn't seem at all serious or preoccupied with selling cars. There was none of the high-pressure sales techniques employed by your typical car sales-men. In fact, at one point, Sylvia wondered if he were interested in selling her a car at all. But by the end of the day, Sylvia found herself sitting behind the wheel of a brand new royal blue, Ford Escort, complete with rear spoiler, sun-roof, CD player—and a date for the evening.

"No need for you to change clothes, Sylvia, the salesman said. You drive your parent's car. I'll follow you in your car and then we can shoot over to Ruby Tuesday's for a burger or something before we head to the movies. How's that sound?"

Peter Townsend was his name, and Sylvia was to say the least, smitten. He was bright, good looking and working on his Civil Engineering degree at Morehouse in Atlanta. When his grant did not show up on time, he was forced to take a semester off and ended up selling cars for his uncle to pick up a little extra cash until it was time to go back to school.

Mrs. Shipp loved Peter from the outset. She like her daughter found the young man to be both witty and charming. And she was certainly glad to see her Sill finally getting back into the swing of things so soon after her ordeal. A little more cautious, Mr. Shipp eyed Peter Townsend the entire time he was there as if he were an escaped convict on the lam. When the couple said their good evenings and prepared to leave Sylvia was sure that her father was going to follow them and felt almost compelled to take him into the den to reassure him that everything would be fine.

The evening turned out to be one of the best Sylvia had had in as long as she could remember. Off the car lot, Peter Townsend was quite different. He was actually rather quiet and unassuming content to listen to Sill babble on about her favorite music groups and college life. Not once during the whole conver-sation did he even bother to interrupt except when she paused to catch her breath or to laugh at one of her less than funny anecdotes.

Over the next few months, Peter Townsend and Sylvia Shipp became insep-arable attending movies and plays and going off for quiet dinners at quaint lit-tle out of the way restaurants. Peter Townsend was everything that Chad was not. Sylvia was quite sure of this when Mr. Shipp, always the evil ogre when it came to her choice of men finally gave Peter his blessing. He even got to the point where he would take Peter fishing with him for crappy on the weekends. Her parent's could hardly remember a time when Sill had been happier.

When Mrs. Shipp's transmission decided that it would only go in reverse it was Peter and his uncle who arranged the loaner. Two weeks later, her trans-mission still not fixed, Peter sold her the car at their cost. All was well, until

Peter now unsure of whether he should return to Morehouse or continue selling cars brought his dilemma to Mr. Shipp during one of their Saturday afternoon fishing excursions.

Both men had come to appreciate these outings. Content to sit on the muddy banks of No-Name Creek both men had come to the point where they enjoyed these outings more than either would admit. Neither was much of an angler although no one could tell Mr. Shipp that. He had every piece of fishing equipment one man could possibly own. And because of that, he often felt the added pressure to bring something home to account for his extravagant spending and long forays into the backwoods of North Carolina's Piedmont that often netted nothing but excuse after excuse and another reason to buy another piece of equipment that would end his fishing woes. But since Peter had become his fishing partner there was no need for excuses or to stop by Sam's and pick up a couple of catfish to bring home to Mrs. Shipp who planned her Saturday fish fries around her husband's catch.

Now that Peter was here, fishing was just a means of getting out of earshot of the women who bugged him with their constant idle chatter. Here out in the open air, men could talk in peace about the real goings on in the world. It was the good life. A couple of sandwiches and a twelve pack and right there next to No-Name Creek real men like Shipp and Townsend could solve the puzzle of the Middle-East, end starvation and other epidemics which plagued the world. Yet Horace Shipp, long accustomed to these unofficial cabinet meetings between him and his future son-in-law never expected the conversation that Peter Townsend was about to spring on him that particularly Saturday afternoon.

"Mr. Shipp, I've got something on my mind that's been kinda bothering me. Well, actually, it's not bothering me but it does present sort of a dilemma for me." As always, the young man chose his words slowly and precisely always making sure that what he said is what he meant.

"Mr. Shipp, I'm sure that by this time you're aware of how I feel about your daughter. If you're not then I gotta tell you that I am absolutely crazy about her. Sometimes it frightens me. Before I met her I had everything planned down to the millisecond. When my grant fell through last fall, I figured it to be just a minor setback, a temporary situation. Figured I'd be back in school by January, finish up my thesis and graduate in May. You follow me, sir?"

"Sure, son, but your calendar seems to be a little off considerin' that May is practically here and you have yet to go back. I'm sure you're aware of the fact that the longer you put it off, the harder it is to go back," Mr. Shipp observed, thoughtfully.

"That's what I'm trying to tell you, sir. Ever since I was knee-high to a grass-hopper, I've wanted to be an engineer, I've wanted to construct things It's kinda been my passion, my dream. It's been the driving force behind every-thing thing I do—everything I've ever done. Then along came this woman, out of the clear blue, and I gotta confess, sir, I can't tell which way is up anymore." The young man dropped his head, embarrassed by his own weakness.

Mr. Shipp cast the line out with the deftness of a seasoned angler. The two had been sitting on the muddy bank for close to two hours without so much as a nibble. He yanked the line back gently as it hit the water, then watched the tide carry the line and bait downstream. The tiny bob dipped under the crest of the wave as something tugged hard at the line.

"What the hell?" Giving the line a sharp tug, Mr. Shipp felt the fish grab the bait and the hook grab him. Smiling, he gave whatever it was on the other end of his line a little leeway and then another sharp tug, pulling the rod over his right shoulder just like he practiced out in the driveway. 'There, got him', he said to himself. Whatever it was was making a pretty fair go of it now.

"You got something there, sir," Peter yelled. "Gotta be a four or five pounder the way he's got that line stretched out."

"Get the net, Pete. Yes sir, looks like a fighter there. Pretty nice size one too, judgin' from the fight he's puttin' up," Mr. Shipp said.

The older man was doing his best to remain cool but soon found himself slipping; then sliding down the muddy incline to the water's edge. Yet, he refused to let go of the rod. The fish seemed to know that the old man had lost his footing and was off balance. Just as he was about to brace himself against the remainder of a hollow tree stump near the water's edge that fish jumped a good three feet straight up out of the creek and with every muscle and ounce of strength he had, dove straight back down into No-Name Creek, pulling Mr. Shipp and young Peter Townsend right on in, along with him. Peter had done his able-bodied best to grab the older man. No sooner had he arrived, net in one hand, trying to hold onto Mr. Shipp's yellow rain slicker than that monster of a fish hit the water like a torpedo from a German sub, pulling both of them in head first with him.

Both men climbed out of the creek drenched. Mud covered the pair from head to toe. Looking at each other, all they could do was lean back on the bank and laugh. Mr. Shipp held on to his pole throughout the whole ridiculous affair. But there was no longer a fish on the end of the line. At this point, there was nothing but memories. Alas, both men, muddy beyond belief, agreed that that was enough fishing for one day.

Sitting in Peter's Ford F-l50, the older man had to ask: "Pete, my boy, did you happen to get a look at the size of that joker?"

"Biggest large-mouth bass, I've ever seen in these parts," Peter answered. I wouldn't have believed it if I hadn't seen it with my own eyes. Do you want a beer? I believe there's two left. Yes sir, Mr. Shipp if you coulda reeled that one in, you could have probably had him mounted. Could've had something to tell your grandkids about. Hell, he had to have been close to eight-and-a-half—maybe even nine pounds. Boy was she a beaut!" the young man added. "Speaking of beauty, Mr. Shipp, I was trying to get your opinion on a rather perplexing problem that's arisen before you decided to take me swimming," the young man smiled, broadly, thinking of how he and Mr. Shipp were pulled into the creek. He was serious though the smile doing little to mask just how serious he was.

"Like I was telling you, I'm in love with your daughter, sir. I've already postponed going back to school once and the summer semester's right around the corner but I just hate to leave her. My uncle says I can continue working with him at the dealership. Hell, not to brag, but I'm outselling his top salesmen, guys that have been there fifteen and twenty years. There's a pretty good future there. I could probably have my own dealership in about ten or twelve years and you can't beat the money."

"Who are you tryin' to convince, Peter, me or yourself? Look, Sill's my only daughter and you are like a son to me. There is not a doubt in my mind that you love her and have nothin' but the best of intentions for her. Of this, I am sure. But you just met Sylvia. You've had the dream of becomin' an engineer your whole life. Don't let Sylvia or any woman defer your dream. If you do, you will always hold some animosity towards her. You will always wonder what you could have been, what life may have held if you had just followed your dream. I believe you can do pretty much whatever it is that you set your mind to, Peter, but the truth is that ten or twelve years from now you won't want to sell cars when you know you should be designin' them. C'mon, think about it."

Peter frowned and reflected for a moment before continuing "You're probably right, sir, but you know, someone like Sylvia doesn't just come along every day. The Sylvias of the world are once in a lifetime."

"That may be true, son, but neither do young Black engineers named Peter Townsend. Go ahead and get your degree, son. Trust me. If what you and Sylvia have is meant to be, then it will be," the old man regretted the words as soon as he said them but knew them to be true. "Now, when will you headin' back to school?

Peter sighed, "Guess I'll be leaving in about two weeks. I gotta give my uncle at least two weeks notice so he can hire someone and train them. Actually, it's gonna take me at least two weeks just to get up the courage to break the news to Sill."

"Don't you worry about Sill, Petey boy. You're not goin' to find a woman much more resilient than Sill. I don't know how close you two are or if she's told you but she's been through hell and back and still kickin' up a storm in the face of adversity. No, I don't think I'd worry about Sill too much."

As the F-150 turned into the Shipps' driveway, the two women emerged from the backdoor, the screen door slamming shut behind them. "What in the world happened to you two?" Mrs. Shipp asked looking at the mud-covered fishermen.

Sylvia was doubled over in laughter. Tears ran down both sides of her face. Never had she seen a funnier sight than her two favorite men covered up to their ears in mud. When she finally stopped crying, she grabbed the bucket of ice they usually carried their haul in. Digging through the ice, Sylvia dropped the bucket in the driveway and held up a fish no bigger than her thumb. "Please, please tell me this isn't all you two caught. Hey, mommy, it looks like Captain D's tonight or sardines." Sill was on her knees now. It was even worse when Peter retold the story over dinner. Sylvia had to leave the table and every time she would gaze at one of the men, she would burst out in fits of laughter. "God, how I wish I could have been there to see Peter trying to save you, daddy," she said, still grinning.

Peter met Sylvia later that evening after going home and showering. No one seemed to be in the mood for fish after the long trying day, so they settled on pizza from Amore's. After dinner, Mr. and Mrs. Shipp retired to the living room to watch reruns of the *Fresh Prince* and *Cosby* while the lovebirds found their way to the swing on the front porch.

"Sylvia, sweetheart, we need to talk," Peter said at last.

"*We* need to talk or *you* need to talk?" she asked.

"*We* need to talk, Sylvia. You know I have a semester left to finish my Masters and get my degree and I think I've put it off long enough. I've finished writing my thesis and now it's only a matter of me knocking out a couple of classes but I need to do it. The longer I put it off the harder it is to go back especially working with my uncle. Damn, the money's good. You know it will probably take me five or six years to make the money I'm making now. Anyway, I'd like for you to wait for me." There, it was out now. He'd said it.

"*Wait for you?* Peter you don't want to come back to this little one-horse town anymore than I want to. Elizabethtown has to be the armpit of the world. You didn't grow up here and I know you don't want to come back. I grew up here and certainly have no intentions of coming back so when you do get your Master's you'll be looking for a large cosmopolitan area where you'll be adequately compensated. Whereas I'm just looking for any place other than Elizabethtown where I can teach youngsters and, hopefully, make a difference in shaping their lives.

We've spent some beautiful months together, Peter, and you don't know how much you've meant to me but it's time for you to stop thinking about us and to start thinking about yourself and your future. How long have you wanted to be an engineer?"

Deeply disappointed, Peter dropped his head. She was sure he was crying. She wanted to herself, but knew she had to be strong for both of them. Still, Sill hoped that he would argue in his defense of their love, challenge their being apart, but instead, he agreed though reluctantly.

Two weeks later, Peter Townsend was no more than a memory. And Elizabethtown was even less than it had been before. For Sylvia, the pain she felt on that dark and rainy night outside Tech's Student Union building was back again. She wasn't really sure she loved Peter Townsend. She wasn't sure she had loved or could ever love any man again. However, one thing was for sure, she missed Peter. And, despite all the hullabaloo surrounding her good looks and charm and her being the most likely to succeed, she with all of these enviable attributes could not keep a man. She was like those colored girls in the play 'who considered suicide when the rainbow wasn't enough'. No matter what she did or didn't do, she just couldn't seem to keep a man.

CHAPTER 4

Once she was positive that Peter was returning to Morehouse there was really no reason to see him. She refused to answer his phone calls and refused to see him when he stopped by during the week prior to his leaving. Sylvia saw no reason to prolong the inevitable. But when he left she couldn't believe how absolutely dreadful she felt. She wanted to scream, and then thought of her parents and how much they'd been through already and felt muzzled. More than once, she considered taking the pills her doctor prescribed for depression but knew that there were not enough pills to cure what ailed her. Like so many sistas, she guessed she was destined to be unhappy and man less.

She continued working at Penney's and even took a few on-line classes to pass the time. And by September of the following year, she had received her Bachelor's in Education. Having been to Atlanta with the family on vacation, she fell in love with the city and immediately began sending resumes to the Fulton County Board of Education, seeking an elementary teaching position. Her dad teased her about trying to get closer to Peter but she was adamant in her denial. In the months, since Peter left her she'd come to the conclusion that all men were basically dogs and Peter Townsend was no better than the rest.

In fact, if anyone missed him it was daddy. No more fishing buddy, no more rolling in the mud, no one to chaperone crazy ass Sill. No one to make sure that she was in good hands and financially stable when he passed on.

Shit, come to think of it she hadn't heard from him since he'd been back at Morehouse. The only news she got was from Peter's uncle when she went in to have her oil changed or a tune-up. When Peter first left, she had the best kept car in Elizabethtown. Her own father made the comment at dinner one night soon after Peter's departure that, 'Sill was at the Ford dealership more than most of the mechanics.'

Yet, Peter never called, never wrote, and *never* even inquired from his uncle as to how she was doing. Sure, she had been childish when she heard about his leaving but if he loved her, *truly* loved her, he would have persisted. After all, wasn't it he the one that was constantly telling her that, *'Persistence overcomes resistance.'* But there had been little or no persistence on his part. She was angry at herself for falling for him in the first place, for once again letting someone get close enough to cause her pain. She was angry that he hadn't cared enough to continually pursue her. She was angry because, although she did not love him, she could not see him rejecting her. She was angry because to him she did not matter that much. And she was angry because no matter how angry she became, she knew deep down inside that daddy was right. She was going to Atlanta not to teach but to be near Peter Townsend.

On September 3rd, the Shipps drove down to Atlanta to help Sylvia move into her very first apartment. Both had grown accustomed to her being around again and neither was too happy having her move so far from home. Yet, they realized how far she had come in the last few months and knew it was finally time for her to move on. Reverend Scales had prayed for Sill during the benediction at last Sunday's service and Mrs. Shipp had all she could do to hold it together.

The last few months since Peter's departure was particularly hard on Sylvia as well as Mr. Shipp who seldom if ever went fishing anymore. Yet, they all knew that Sylvia had far too much to offer to waste away in Elizabethtown.

Dr. Reid, who had grown rather fond of his patient, made it a point to stop by the house the day before they were leaving to bring the addresses of some prominent therapists in Atlanta in case Sill needed someone to talk to. He hugged her when he left and Mrs. Shipp swore she saw a tear in the good doctor's eye. Hugging him, Mrs. Shipp felt compelled to apologize for not trusting his judgment more and then they all began crying in earnest. That is, except for Mr. Shipp, who saw the whole damn scene as one big charade. He had been out of sorts ever since Peter left and now that Sylvia was about to leave, he was downright cantankerous.

"Why the hell we got to go out there and get a U-Haul and spend money we don't have is beyond me," he said. "Hell, it ain't but a six hour drive down there. I could use the pickup and make a couple of trips down there while you ladies get the house in order. Don't make a lick a sense to spend a hundred and fifty dollars for that raggedy-assed, U-Haul and we got a truck sittin' right here in the yard. Don't make no sense at all."

Mrs. Shipp was not much better. "You're absolutely right, Horace. Didn't make a bit of sense to buy that damn pickup in the first place. What the hell you plan on haulin'. Here you are damn near sixty years old and you actin' like you done caught your second wind. What? You plannin' on startin' to haul coal or is it logs? No, wait! You fashion yourself as Fred Sanford and I guess I'm spozed to be Lamont. Do you know what your father told me when he bought this truck, Sill?"

Sill tried not to frown. She hated getting caught in the middle but knew her leaving had as much to do with the arguments as anything else.

"He told me that that thing out there in the yard would pay for itself. That's what he told me. And I swear, I've been watchin' it everyday and I ain't seen it get up and go to work yet," Mrs. Shipp stated matter-of-factly while Sill feigned a smile in amusement.

Despite his protests, Mr. Shipp drove the twenty-foot U-Haul down the highway with Sill and Mrs. Shipp taking turns riding with him. After what seemed like forever and a day, they finally found the Lake Spring Apartment complex Sill was to move into. She had been here only a week before to get a firsthand look, pay the security deposit, first month's rent and pick up the key but it was evening now and Atlanta appeared so different. Everyone seemed more relaxed, everyone, that is, but Sylvia who was positively ecstatic.

"Put the étagère over here, daddy. Mommy did you see the balcony? And look at the view. Ooh, I can't wait to decorate," she crowed.

The Shipps watched Sylvia bounce from one room to the next and were at last at peace. More than anything else, they like all parents were happy when their daughter was happy. Over the next couple of days, they managed to unload the huge truck with minimal help from outsiders other than one neighbor, a teenage boy who seemed taken by Sill. They spent the remainder of their time getting directions and getting lost as they traipsed from landmark-to-landmark and from restaurant to restaurant.

Sylvia never dreamed Atlanta could be so large or so cosmopolitan. Mrs. Shipp on the other hand, was fascinated by the sheer number of Black people in one place. And Mr. Shipp, po' thing, who refused to drive in the city was just happy to sit in the back seat of the tiny Ford Escort and let his neck turn from side to side and prayed that the Lord would bestow a photographic memory so he could remember every fine sista he saw, to take back to Elizabethtown with him. Lord, so many fine, fine, hammers. If only he were twenty again he thought to himself.

Sylvia couldn't recall ever enjoying her parents as much as she did those first three days in Atlanta. Sure they bickered but it was all in good fun. That's just the way old married couples do, she guessed, and only hoped to have what they shared after thirty-four years of marriage. Together they laughed and joked and ate then ate some more. And, for all intents and purposes they had a grand ol' time. When it came time for them to drop off the U-Haul and pick up their train tickets, it suddenly dawned on Sill that not only were they leaving but that she would be alone in a city that made Elizabethtown and Greensboro look like Andy Griffith's Mayberry. Her parents saw the growing apprehension when they mentioned their leaving and agreed to stay another day, which just happened to be Sill's first day teaching.

When she returned that day after her first day in the classroom, Mr. and Mrs. Shipp knew that their baby girl had found her niche and would be all right. Sylvia quickly found teaching to be a revelation, an eye-opener. For so long Sylvia had searched to find out exactly where she belonged, just how she fit into the whole scheme of things. But the first time she stepped in front of those twenty-six, grinning, eager third graders, there was no question as to her purpose in life. Sure, she'd been nervous but, closing the door to her classroom, she knew two things: These were now *her* children and her children were a reflection of her. That being the case, her children would be the best and the brightest. She vowed to defy the odds and take them where others had failed and written them off. Sylvia considered each tiny personality that stepped in her classroom each day hers. She didn't have time to blame the parents or the school system. She only had time to teach. And she felt that it was equally important to teach them how to be strong little African-American boys and girls, as it was to teach them how to read and write. With hugs and love and an occasional harsh word for some of her miniature wannabe street toughs, Sylvia Shipp soon had her third grade class eating out of her hand. And soon thereafter, she was not only the talk of the school but the talk of the neighborhood as well.

It was not at all unusual for the diminutive third grade teacher to be seen in the evenings long after the school day was over walking through some of Atlanta's most dangerous neighborhoods searching for the home of one of her students. If a child's attitude changed drastically, Ms. Shipp was ringing that child's doorbell to see what was wrong. If one of her children missed more than a day of school, Ms. Shipp was ringing the doorbell. And no matter how bad the neighborhood was said to be she had no fear. What was even more remarkable was that everyone knew her. Even the young thugs who hugged the corners in Atlanta's worst ghetto stopped their trade and spoke to her out of reverence. Most of them had younger brothers and sisters and it didn't take long before the word was out that there was a newcomer in the hood and she *cared*. Every now and then, a case worker from Social Services shuffled into the projects before daybreak and rushed to get the hell out of there by nightfall. But not Ms. Shipp whom they joked about before they got to know her.

"Bitch, sho' must cain't tell time. Either that or she ain't got no watch, yo," one young thug quipped to another as she exited Raul's building one evening.

"Must not, yo. Walkin' roun' *here* this time of night she sho' don't know what time it is," they laughed.

But Ms. Shipp didn't care about them or the crackheads they served. All she cared about were her kids. A week later, the same two thugs who had joked about her not knowing what time it was, nodded as she passed. "Evenin', Ms. Shipp." Somewhat surprised that they knew her name, she returned the nod.

When her supervisor became aware of her evening forays, he immediately called her down to his office to warn her about the dangers and the risk she was taking but she refused to take heed and continued her journeys, so committed was she to her students. If they weren't in school, then they couldn't learn, she reasoned. And unless they were terminally ill there was no good reason why a third grader should not be in school. Armed with her student's well being at heart, Sylvia spent her evenings scrupulously correcting papers and seeking new and creative ways to reach some of her hard-to-reach children. If a child wasn't learning, then she wasn't teaching and so it went. It didn't matter that the little Black children she taught were from single parent households or that her school district still hadn't received their books and Thanksgiving was just around the corner. She expected her kids to learn in spite of it all. And they did. Despite the odds, they learned. And they learned at a record pace. She made no excuses and found a variety of ways to motivate them to reach new heights each school day and they loved her all the more for it. At lunchtime, her colleagues remarked that she had more kids in her room than during her regular class period. The word was out that Ms. Shipp was out to make a difference and it wasn't long before the parents were there offering there help as well.

Mr. and Mrs. Shipp called almost nightly checking on Sill and were almost as excited as she was about her new found success. But they still worried and couldn't help but wonder if she were truly happy or if it were all a facade. Sylvia had little time to entertain their concerns. There was simply too much to do.

Never one to make time, she was late frequently. She blamed it on the drive in to the inner city which was always hectic. There always seemed to be an accident or a bottleneck no matter what time she started out. Once she got to school, she had virtually no time to prepare so she would usually begin her day by assigning her class a journal topic to start them off and give herself a chance to gather her thoughts and unwind from the long commute. She would teach until almost two-thirty then gather her belongings and start the savage trek home.

After picking up her dry cleaning, stopping at the supermarket and Office Depot for supplies it would usually be some time after five. Then by the time she took a quick shower and prepared herself something to eat there was little time to do anything other than check her kid's papers and go over the next day's lesson plans.

Too often, she found herself nodding off in her easy chair, exhausted, red pen still in hand. It was not until the weekend that Sill began to feel that something was amiss, that perhaps her life was anything but full and rewarding.

It wasn't until Friday afternoons, when her white colleagues discussed ticket prices for the upcoming Cher farewell concert, did she come to the realization that her whole life centered on a bunch of third graders. And if Friday afternoon's were bad, Saturday afternoons were the worst. Never one to sleep late, by the time Saturday afternoon rolled around Sill had changed the linens, washed and ironed her clothes for the week and cleaned her house despite never having any company. These were the times she dreaded most. Those dull, ordinary Saturday afternoons drove her crazy.

When she first arrived in Atlanta, it was nothing to curl up with a bag of those greasy ol' Wise Barbeque Potato Chips, some French Onion Dip, a large Pepsi and a good book but in time she found the dip going straight to her hips and herself in a rut. The five movies for five-day thing from Blockbuster didn't work either. There were no plots, no themes, and no storyline in movies anymore. Nowadays, everything was graphics and special effects. Aside from _A Beautiful Mind_, she couldn't remember the last time she'd seen a good movie and that was years ago. In the days and weeks that followed, Sylvia finally conceded, that she had always been lonely and a loner. Even with mom and dad, her sorority sisters, Chad…

Growing up out on Highway 46 in Elizabethtown, the houses were so far apart and the neighbors so few that she often had to find solace in waving at the passing cars. Her brother, David, was eleven years older than she was already driving and dating when she first came to recall him as a memory. Her best friend had been Pinky who was an imaginary person she'd made up. Pinky used to wait along with her each evening for daddy to come home from work. Then together she and Pinky would jump out from under the table to greet him when they could no longer wait for him to find them. She wondered and wondered if there had been something wrong with her as far back as Pinky.

When she reached high school, so desperate had she been for friends that she latched onto the first group of kids that looked to extend a hand in friendship. Of course, these were always the worst sort but she'd been so desperate for friendship that it hardly mattered. With them she found friendship and camaraderie as well as cigarettes and alcohol. Still, there was only so far she would stray from the nest so when they decided to go on their little shoplifting sprees, she would always find her way back home.

Casual sex was out of the question. In fact, she was still a virgin until those animals raped her. In her eyes, she was still a virgin. Probably would remain one the rest of her life. Hell, what was the point of having sex anyway? She couldn't have kids. Matter of fact the only person she had ever considered having sex with was Peter and he hadn't seemed the least bit interested. Sylvia never had understood that. Peter was constantly telling her how good she looked but he had never approached her other than as a complete gentleman. In fact, it was she who had to initiate or better yet, force him to kiss her at the end of the night or whenever they went to the movies.

After dating for a little more than two months, Sill actually wondered if her parents had engineered the whole thing. She then remembered that it was she who made the impromptu stop at the dealership on her way home from work that day. Their meeting was no more than coincidence at best. Then she wondered if her father had spoken to Peter and warned him about putting his hands on her. But if that were the case, and Peter was like the rest of the guys she knew he would have bolted then. And, Lord knows, the boy had all the money in the world. He was probably making more than the entire Shipp household combined so they couldn't be paying him off. Still, she had never run into a guy like him. Never. Sylvia smiled at the thought. Yep, Peter was definitely the man for her. She could marry Peter, never have to tell him what happened at school and not worry about how she'd respond since they'd probably never have sex. If she was frigid, she'd never know.

Sylvia laughed out loud then caught herself. Most people occasionally laughed aloud but Sylvia was always careful to catch herself She wouldn't even allow herself to daydream. She called it a waste of time. What she was really

afraid of was being lost in time and reverting back to the months she lost staring, daydreaming and laughing to herself.

"The hell with Peter Townsend," she said aloud, now angry that she had
given him the time of day and even angrier that she was talking to herself. "I've
got to get out of this house before I go stir crazy. I've got to find something to
do with my time." There it was again. She was talking to herself once again but
this time it didn't bother her quite as much.

This time she had devised a plan. She smiled. relaxing now she curled back
up on the loveseat and turned the television back on but left the volume on
mute. *There!* Now she had company in the house but the voices on the television could not distract her as her thoughts quickly returned to Peter and his
unusually low sex drive.

CHAPTER 5

Sill smiled as she remembered the warm night in April when the two of them were sitting on the rusty old porch swing in front of the house. Peter sure was old to be twenty-three, she mused. In many ways, he acted as old if not older than her father and daddy was in his sixties. Nothing made her father happier than to grab his pipe after the end of a long day and a good meal than to sit out there on that old, rusty swing and just let life pass him by.

Maybe that's what it was that attracted her to Peter. He reminded her so much of her father. Peter liked to sit there after an evening out and just listen to her go on and on about her co-workers at Penney's or her sorors. But on that particular evening, she was going to find out just what Mr. Man was made of. She remembered the night as if it were yesterday and began to smile at the thought as she remembered their conversation.

"Peter, you don't mind if I run upstairs and change do you?" Sill asked. "This skirt is killing me. I think I ate too much."

"No, not at all Sill. Go ahead. Take your time," he replied. He was used to Sill changing after a night out since he usually picked her straight up from work before she would have a chance to change.

"Do you want some popcorn or anything?" she asked as the screen door slammed shut behind her.

"No baby, I'm fine," he said, then added. "You can't possibly be hungry after the meal you just ate. I swear I don't know where you put the food, little as you are."

And he was right about that. Standing no taller than five-four in her stocking feet, she would always insist she was five-six. Whether five-four or five-six, Sylvia did not have an ounce of fat anywhere.

At one hundred and thirty-two pounds she was a knockout. Her cocoa brown skin looked as if it had been poured on, so rich was it. Her eyes suggested an Asiatic slant, uncommon in Southern Blacks. And her thin Roman nose also suggested mixed blood but her full lips countered any misconception of her African heritage. Sylvia's perfectly proportioned hips and round buttocks were in sharp contrast to her tiny waist and though they would never allow her to grace the cover of *Vogue* or *Cosmopolitan* magazine they kept heads turning. They weren't so large as to seem obscene but were just large enough to make a devoted husband walking with his wife do a double take. And her legs only made men beg for more.

Always subtle in her attire, Sill never wore a dress above knee length but the shapely calves that protruded from beneath her skirt suggested an abbreviated high school track career that only managed to firm what was already too firm. All in all, Sylvia Shipp had the power to make most men leave home without so much as a glance back. But not Peter.

Peter stopped daydreaming long enough to check his watch. It was already a quarter past nine and he had to get up and be on the lot by seven. He could smell the popcorn but still there was no Sill. And then, she appeared like a Black Scarlet O'Hara in <u>Gone With the Wind</u>. Sylvia stood before him wearing a red floral evening dress that stopped just above the ankles. Gone were the fashionably faded jeans and blouse with the Penney's badge. Gone were the panty hose that masked her golden, brown skin. Decked in red pumps that said I'm ready for anything, Sylvia watched Peter for any signs of an irregular heart palpitation. When she noticed no change in his demeanor, she immediately went to Plan B. "Popcorn, sweetheart?" she asked, turning to place the pitcher of lemonade on the wicker end table to her right. As she turned and readied herself for their long kiss goodnight, Sylvia made it a point to cross her leg purposely revealing much of her long chocolate thighs. And when Peter didn't notice she brushed her arm ever so gently against the bowl of popcorn. Popcorn scattered everywhere, Sill smiled.

"How clumsy of me," she said in her best Scarlet O'Hara impersonation. Bending down on one knee, Sylvia began picking up the kernels of corn as slowly as she could. Realizing that she would not allow him to leave without their goodnight kiss, Peter bent down to help her. Hearing him gasp and breathe heavily she dropped her head hoping he wouldn't see the smile now spreading across her face. Mission accomplished she whispered to herself.

Sylvia never liked the dress she now wore, always figuring it was too Southern, too debutante ballish. That night however, it was just what the doctor ordered. She'd worn it because it showed more cleavage than all her other outfits combined. And tonight she made sure that she wore no bra to cover her thirty-six double D's. Aside from that it had always been a size too large giving her plenty of room to move around inside. And when she knelt down to pick up the popcorn, she made sure the shoulder strap fell giving Peter a full view of her breasts, nipples and all.

"Sill, sweetheart, I've really got to run," he'd said, now breathless and almost panting. Before she knew it, she heard the modified engine of the F-150 crank up and the low roar as it headed down the road.

"Well, I'll be damned," Sill, said on the way into the house to get the broom. Her parents were sitting in the kitchen watching the news on CNN when she walked in and burst out laughing for no apparent reason. *What a chicken,* she thought. *Probably still a virgin. Poor little mama's boy, I guess we'll have to learn together.*

Sill thought of Peter's expression as he'd eyed her breasts, thought of him gasping and then broke out laughing again. Her parents looked at each other and then at their daughter.

"Are you OK, Sill," her father asked. They were always so worried nowadays.

"Yes, Daddy, I'm just fine," she replied somewhat sarcastically.

"Where's Peter?" her mother inquired.

"Now that's the person you should be asking about," Sill replied. "I bent over to pick up some popcorn I spilled and I guess he saw a little too much cleavage. Next thing I knew, Peter's up in the truck and flyin' out the driveway. I think the twins scared him away," she laughed, referring to her breasts. They all had a good laugh about Peter that night. Her father, glad that nothing more had transpired, called Peter a "good ol' boy" while her mother warned her about wearing something so provocative. Little did they know that Peter's rejection of her that night would stick in her craw, gnawing at her until she'd convinced herself that Peter Townsend was the man for her.

In reality, Peter Townsend was no more the man for Sylvia than RuPaul was but his rejection of her made him that much more appealing and she suddenly became obsessed with the thought of his making love to her.

On Monday morning, Sylvia parked her car at the bottom of the hill and made the long trek up to Community Elementary School 73X. Anyone that paid any attention at all had to notice that Sylvia Shipp had a new air about her, a new spring in her walk. Stopping at the local *bodega*, she grabbed a bagel with cream cheese and a large regular coffee. She often wondered why she made the long trek up the hill each morning for exercise and then nullified it all by eating such fattening foods as cream cheese and sugar-laden coffee.

Unlike most Monday mornings though, she was early. This gave her time to browse the tiny store and pick up a few dollars worth of penny candy for her kids, a newspaper and a couple of meat patties for her lunch. The *bodega* owner always made her feel welcome and had endeared himself to Sill from her initial visit. She could always count on him to throw in a *Corn Frito* or *a plate of arroz con pollo* that his wife made especially for her. When she was running late he would send one of his sons out to stand in front of the store with her breakfast so she wouldn't have to stand in line. *And there was always a line.* But there was no need for that this morning. This morning, she was not only on time, she was early. When he recognized her, he shouted out, loud enough for all his customers to hear: "*Tu te ve linda, hoy, Senorita Shipp.*" Whenever Mr. Ramirez became excited he would inevitable switch, going back and forth between his native Spanish and broken English. This usually happened when he was angry or one of the local drunks tried to shortchange Mrs. Ramirez around a bottle of wine, but not today. Most of the people in the *bodega* were Hispanic and all turned to see the young woman who commanded such attention. Mrs. Ramirez agreed."*Si, Senorita, muy bonita,*" she said. "Thank you, Mrs. Ramirez," Sylvia replied. Any other time Sill would have been embarrassed to no end. But not today. Any other time she would have been ready to crawl up under the counter but not today. No, this was just the response she wanted. Her kids greeted her with the same enthusiasm telling her that she looked 'really nice today', when she arrived in the schoolyard for first bell.

Sylvia had made it a point to call Mr. Cooper at home the previous night so he could arrange to have a substitute cover her class that afternoon. The disappointment showed in her students' faces when she informed them that she would be leaving early. Not since the first week of school had they been this unruly. She was almost afraid to leave them with the substitute. But after a good tongue lashing they appeared better but there was no question that her leaving left them feeling abandoned and unwanted. After hugging each and promising to be there bright and early Tuesday morning, she left. She understood their fear. She too felt abandoned at times but in a little while she would remedy those same feelings that had haunted her while in college, in her final days in Elizabethtown and for most of her life.

Mr. Cooper, who was usually rather close-lipped, looked wearily at Sylvia as she was leaving the school that fall afternoon. Suddenly fearful that he might be losing another promising young teacher, Mr. Cooper walked her to the front door of the school and held the door for her. She knew he wanted to ask her if she had an interview but was reluctant. The best he could do was to tell her she looked nice. A single, simple compliment from him was worth a thousand from anyone else. Well, almost anyone else. One more would make her day.

Sylvia stepped out of the blue, Ford Escort looking like she belonged on a fashion runway. The brown tweed, Christian Dior suit she had purchased the day before at the quaint little consignment shop downtown brought out a quality that even she didn't know she possessed. She didn't just look rich. She looked elegant.

Crossing the campus of Morehouse she was hardly oblivious to the stares. Smiling inside, she watched heads turn and slowed down to soak it all in. It had been several years since she'd walked across a college campus and never one quite as prestigious as this.

Morehouse, with its historical buildings, bookish profs and preppy students, was a far cry from Tech or the tiny little girl's college she'd attended. Well, just the fact that it was all male made it a far cry from Winfrey College but there was that elitist ambience of the intellectual bourgeois she'd become so accustomed to at Winfrey. She could feel it in the air. Bright, beautiful Black men from every walk of life crisscrossed the inner city campus the same way they would later cross the country, the world, making an impact as they went. There were some stares but the people here seemed far too sophisticated to punctuate the crisp fall air with catcalls and wolf whistles. Sylvia wondered why she hadn't thought about attending Spellman, which was right across the street. She was by no means elitist but Morehouse appeared to have a better class of people, of men. Never one to have regrets she quickly dismissed the thought and managed to find the School of Graduate Studies without too much fanfare. Once there, she inquired about a dear friend enrolled in the Civil Engineering Program. Over time, she explained to the admissions secretary, she had somehow lost contact with him but since she was now working in Atlanta, she thought she would look him up. His name, she informed the woman was Peter Townsend. For the first time since she entered the office the woman looked up from the jumble of papers that cluttered her desk.

"Oh, do you know, Peter?" she asked smiling. "Why yes, he's on our faculty. I believe if you hurry you just might be able to catch him. I believe he has a class in—." Again, she rifled through the heap of papers that made up her tiny desk. "Oh, yes, here it is. Professor Townsend has a class over in the Engineering Building, Room 203." Relieved, Sylvia thanked the secretary whose head dropped once again, lost in the jungle of paperwork before her.

In the Engineering Building, Sylvia found the elevator and stepped in. She was glad no one else was on the elevator and immediately took out her compact. She found that she was more than a little nervous and her hands trembled slightly as she attempted to put on her lipstick. The elevator came to an abrupt stop, making her stomach even queasier than it already was and for the first time since she decided on visiting Peter the possibility of him not wanting to see her loomed large. But it was too late now. Besides, she had nothing to lose though at that very moment she truly wished she were back in front of her third graders who always made her feel at home and wanted. And she *was* making progress with her lesson on adjectives although poor Angela was still having some problems. Sylvia's thoughts ended abruptly as the elevator came to an abrupt stop and the doors slowly opened.

Her nerves on edge, she considered taking the elevator back down to the main floor and heading for her car. If she hurried, she could be back at school before lunch was over. Her kids would be tickled. Yet, she had come this far. And what was it that she was constantly telling her kids'. *Nothing fails but a try.* Hell, what did she have to lose? Stepping out of the elevator and making her way down the dimly-lit hall, Sylvia checked the room numbers until she came to Room 203, where a crowd of students were just getting out. Sylvia stood across the hall waiting for the crowd to thin. Her heart raced and she could feel the beads of sweat forming on her nose. Two or three students still crowded around the young professor's desk in the front of the class when Sylvia slipped in and found a seat in the rear. He had yet to notice her and Sylvia aware of the perspiration opened her pocketbook and drew a *Kleenex* to wipe her nose.

A few minutes later, the classroom empty, Professor Townsend collected the remainder of his belongings and neatly assembled them in his attaché case. Still unaware of the shapely young woman in the back of the classroom, Professor Townsend closed his briefcase.

"Excuse me, Professor Townsend, I have a question," Sylvia said in an attempt to get his attention.

The neatly attired young professor's head snapped to the back of the room so quickly, Sylvia was sure he had whiplash.

"*Oh, my God! Sylvia! What—what in heavens name are you doing here in Atlanta? Oh, my God!*" He dropped his briefcase and barreled headlong into several desks in his haste to get to Sylvia who was now quite at ease and glad she'd made the decision to come.

Peter was ecstatic to say the least, hugging and squeezing Sylvia and forcing her to laugh out loud before regaining her composure. And to think, only a few minutes ago she'd seriously considered heading back to the car. "My goodness. You don't know how good it is to see you, Sill. You don't know how often you cross my mind," he said at length.

"I can tell from *all* the letters and phone calls I received," she replied rather sarcastically.

"Don't go there, Sill. Don't you dare go there. I tried calling you everyday before I left. Sometimes I'd call two or three times a day and you refused to speak to me or return any of my calls. What was I supposed to do?" he inquired, earnestly.

"Persistence overcomes resistance," Sylvia replied curtly.

"How much persistence is one man supposed to have, Sill? You really hurt me. So, when I got back here I did my level best to put you out of my mind and still I think about you and our summer together quite frequently. It was probably the best summer I've ever had. And Lord knows I regretted leaving. Gosh it's good to see you. C'mon let's get out of here," he continued.

Turning off the lights and locking the classroom door, Peter hugged Sylvia again before leading her to the front of the building where they chatted some more about the past summer, her move to Atlanta and her third graders.

"Where's your car, Sill? I have a prior engagement in about an hour but if you'd like we can grab some lunch later, that is, if you're free."

Sylvia wanted to tell him that she'd traveled close to three hundred miles to be with him and he's got the nerve to ask me if I'm free. She chuckled to herself Yeah, I'm free, she thought, but once I get my hooks into you this time Professor Peter Townsend, freedom will be little more than a brief memory to you.

"Yes, I'm free, Peter," Sill said. "I took the afternoon off to see some of Atlanta's more prominent landmarks," she lied. "You know, Morehouse and Spellman. Thought I'd look up a couple of my sorority sisters who are teaching over at Spellman."

"And to think, I thought the sole purpose of your visit was to come and see me," Peter teased, seeing through Sill's attempt at being coy and aloof.

"I hate you, Peter," Sill said, giving Peter a shove that sent him sprawling into the side of her car.

"How's the car holding up? My uncle tells me you're in every week having something done to it. *That* many problems, Sill?" Peter asked. He was grinning from ear to ear now.

"You dirty dog! And he never even mentioned a word. *Y'all ain't right,"* Sill said, feigning exasperation. Actually, she was relieved to know he had been checking on her.

Still, it had been more than seven months since she'd last seen him and that was more than enough time for any man to get over someone and find someone new. And in Atlanta, where the ratio of women to men was something like three-to-one, a bright, young, handsome engineer was a prize package that was surely in demand. But she was not ready for anything but good news, today. If he'd found another woman, he would certainly let her know. Yet, from what she'd gathered from the conversation so far, she was still the only woman in his life.

"Peter do you mind if I ask you a question," Sill asked, speculatively.

"Ask away, but first did I mention how stunning you look. You seem like you're growing more beautiful each time I see you," Peter said.

"Peter, please! Be serious for a change. I need you to put my mind at ease. That's really why I came here today," she grabbed his arm and leaned over the console, which divided the seat in the car.

"Go ahead, Sill."

"Peter, if I had insisted that you stay in Elizabethtown last summer, would you have stayed?" she asked, bluntly.

"I really don't know, Sill. I asked myself that very same question a thousand times and I've yet to come up with an answer. Morehouse has been good to me. I have ties here that aren't easily broken. A lot of people have invested a lot of time to make sure that I succeed. As much as I love you, Sill, I also have to consider the time and effort they've invested in me as well," he said.

"Did you ever consider marrying me, Peter?" Sill asked.

"No, but I considered pushing your father in No-Name Creek a couple of times and hooking up with you mother 'cause she's a much better cook," Peter laughed.

"Oh, no you didn't! Peter Townsend, you are despicable. I don't know why I love you."

As soon as she said it she wished she hadn't. It was too late now. The cat was out of the bag. Still, Sill wondered why Peter hadn't responded. If he told her that he loved her as well, they could have continued as if nothing had happened. Their relationship renewed, they could have started planning to build on what was already there. They loved each other. Of this, she was sure. So why couldn't he just commit? What was it that men were so afraid of anyway? Regardless, Peter Townsend had no choice. Now that she'd found him, she'd be damned if he was going to get away again.

In the weeks that followed, Sylvia could not believe that Atlanta could possibly have so much to offer. There were more parks and art galleries and every kind of restaurant and nightclub than she could ever have imagined. It was certainly the place to be if you were young, Black, aspiring and in love. Not that Peter had ever said that he was in love with her. His commitment or lack of was only a temporary situation, she thought. It was only a matter of time before she would have him wrapped around her little finger but for right now she was just happy to have him in her life once more.

To her surprise, he had changed little. Still, quiet and unassuming, he was just as happy sitting at home with her as he was hitting the local clubs or bars. That was, as long as she wasn't watching that damn *Lifetime* channel she had grown so fond of recently. Actually, he really didn't seem to have a passion for anything except engineering and spending time with her.

Every now and then, he would get caught up in some fervor of the moment and get the notion that he was a fisherman and force them to take that long-ass drive back to Elizabethtown to go fishing with her father. Mr. Shipp, tickled to death to see the two back together again after such a lengthy hiatus, would dig his fishing gear out of storage and the two men sometimes would disappear for the better part of the weekend.

Sylvia and her mother would use this time to catch up on all the latest gossip. Either that or they'd jump in Sill's Escort and ride to Myrtle Beach or Cross Creek Mall in Fayetteville where they'd shop 'til they dropped. Sill hated making the long drive from Atlanta to Elizabethtown and hated the idea of sharing Peter during her weekends off but didn't want to appear selfish so she rode along. Besides, she feared that if she chose not to go Mr. Independent would probably go anyway.

The only positive aspect of the whole affair was that they no longer had to bounce up and down in Peter's pickup. Upon receipt of his Masters, Peter promptly traded the Ford pickup in for a brand new Lexus. He still wasn't making the money to afford the luxury car but purchased it under the deferred payment plan with the assumption that he would be working in his field by the time the payments hit. The only reason he wasn't already working as an engineer in some firm and was teaching was because he was taking the place of one of the engineering professors at Morehouse who'd been diagnosed with colon cancer and was currently undergoing chemotherapy.

And although this bothered Sylvia, she refused to let on. All Peter talked about was getting out of Atlanta and going to New York or L. A. "That's where the money is," he would say. He was even considering Texas. Houston or Dallas. Not once while discussing his plans did he mention or include her. Either she had to infer that she was going or he simply had no intention of taking her.

Either way, there was no specific mention of her in his plans. Whether he knew it or not, she wouldn't have been able to leave anyway, even if she wanted to. When she accepted her teaching position, she signed a five-year contract, which absolved her of all of her student loans, with the agreement that she teach in a depressed area for five years. And, if she couldn't go, then he couldn't go. She'd come all this way to be with him and she hadn't come all this way to be abandoned by him again.

CHAPTER 6

❀

Fall soon became winter. And Peter remained steadfast in his quest to finish out the semester and to pursue his dream of being a civil engineer but he seldom mentioned it around Sill who became increasingly hostile when he talked of relocating. The last time he'd mentioned that he'd sent a résumé to Hoffman LaRoche in New Jersey she'd gone off the deep end. To this day, he didn't know why she grew so perturbed when he mentioned leaving but if that was going to be her reaction then from now on he would keep his plans to himself

In spite of his plans, Sill still enjoyed the time they spent together. She had never known anyone quite so thoughtful. He called her on her cell everyday without fail during her planning period at work. And, if for some reason she was having a particularly rough day, she could always expect flowers or a box of chocolates when she arrived home. When both the doctor and fireman cancelled at the last minute during the career day she planned for her students she was in tears. Twenty minutes later, Peter Townsend arrived with a nurse from the Morehouse infirmary and one of the campus cops to fill in.

And she hardly ever cooked anymore. She didn't have to. If he didn't bring dinner and she refused to order out then he made her get dressed and took her out to eat. Peter introduced her to foods so foreign; she couldn't even pronounce their names. He insisted that she try new things regularly. And when he felt she was homesick or needed to see her family, he'd arrive at six o'clock Saturday morning, pack her belongings, fix lunch and off they went. Yet, for some reason he still remained an enigma in her eyes. When he wasn't with her she had no idea where he was. And even after being together for three and a half months in Atlanta, she had never even been to his apartment. He always claimed that he was too embarrassed to take her to his 'hut' as he referred to it.

But what bothered her more than anything about Peter was his reluctance to sleep with her. More than once, they cuddled on the tiny loveseat in the living room watching television when he would begin nuzzling her ear. Soon she would find herself kissing him deeply, passionately, the ugly memory of Tech far from her thoughts. All she wanted at these times was for Peter to pick her up, walk her to her bedroom and make love to her. Yet, each time they reached this point Peter would find some excuse to bail out. She wondered if the word had gotten to Peter that she was soiled goods. Whatever it was, Sylvia had had enough. She was twenty-four years old and had never slept with a man of her choosing. Her sorors used to tease her before the incident that she was going to have cobwebs growing soon. Now she wasn't so sure they were wrong. But tonight, all that would end.

Sill arrived home from work exhausted. "Thank God it's Friday," she said to herself.

Running a piping hot bath, she knew she was going to have to hurry. Peter was due to pick her up in an hour. He never seemed to worry about her attire but tonight was different. Everything had to be just right. "No more excuses, Mr. Townsend," Sill said to herself. "Tonight we're going to see what you're really made of" Sill laughed as she stuck her foot into the bathtub. "Damn, it's hot," she said. No longer was she worried about talking to herself. In fact, tonight would not only bring a new facet to their relationship but would ultimately bring closure to the demons she so desperately had been trying to escape.

Sylvia grabbed the bottle of lilac beads and poured them into the tub before grabbing the glass of *Jack Daniels* that sat on the side of the tub. She drank the first shot slowly and then gulped down another three shots. An half an hour later, she stepped out of the tub smelling like lilacs and whiskey.

After drying off Sylvia pulled out the shopping bag from *Victoria's Secrets* grabbed the fishnet stockings, garter belt and black teddy with the tear away undies and dressed quickly. Now all she needed to do was step into the six-inch spiked heels when the doorbell rang. Wrapping her faded pink terry cloth robe around Sylvia headed for the door but not before putting the ice bucket with the champagne and two champagne glasses next to the bed for easy access. She then mixed three shots of *Jack Daniels* in a separate glass with just enough *Pepsi* to give it color and placed it on the living room table. Going to the stereo she turned on the CD player. She had just received the <u>*Body and Soul Collection*</u> of old school love songs in the mail. She'd ordered the CD's for just such a night and was sure that the sweet soulful sounds of Marvin and Teddy and Barry would certainly set the mood for the night she had in store.

"I feel sorry for you, Mr. Townsend. I don't know when you'll get a chance to see daylight again," Sylvia said to no one in particular.

No sooner had she started to relax, the doorbell rang again. "Right on time," she said to herself.

"Peter stepped into the apartment. Before he could speak, Sill put her hand to his lips and whispered seductively: "Come in Peter, but don't say a word." She took his jacket from him and hung it on the coat rack behind the front door. "I have a very special night planned for us but you have to promise that you won't say a word," Sill looked straight into Peter's eyes. "Promise?"

"What's this all about, Sill?" Peter asked. "I thought we were going out to dinner tonight."

"There's been a change of plans, Peter. I've planned a very special night for us. A night you won't forget and all you have to do is relax and go with the flow. The first thing I need you to do is to come in, sit down, take your shoes off and relax. That's not a lot to ask, is it?" Sill asked as she propped up the pillows behind him.

"Seems easy enough," he answered. "Would you mind passing me the remote," he asked.

"Sorry sweetie but there will be no time for television tonight. The only thing you need to be watching tonight is your Sill and that should keep you busy for quite awhile," Sill said smiling. Peter didn't realize just how serious she was, however. "Do me a big favor, Peter? Drink this while I freshen up a bit." Always game for a new adventure, Peter turned the glass up and took a huge swallow of what he thought was *Pepsi*.

"Good God Almighty! What are you trying to do to me?" Sill heard the remark and could help but laughed.

"Loosen up, Peter." Sill, tickled by his reaction refused to give in, "Just drink the damn thing. You promised me that you'd go along with the program and you're hedging already."

"Hedging? *What?* Should I let you kill me? That's straight liquor, sweetheart!" Peter was teasing but Sill was in no mood. Glaring at him now, she asked Peter: "Are you going to go along with the program or what, Peter Townsend? I've spent a lot of time and effort setting up this evening for you. The least you could do is play along." Sylvia said angrily.

"I didn't know it meant that much to you, Sill. I hope you can carry me home after I pass out in a drunken stupor girlfriend," Peter said before guzzling the remainder of the glass. "I just *hope* you can."

Sylvia was smiling, now. "Hold on, sweetheart, let me get you something to chase that with," she said, regaining her poise. A minute later, she was back with the ice bucket, champagne and glasses for them both.

"Go ahead Peter. Pop the cork. I'll be right back. Oh, and will you pour me a glass, too? Not too much though, I've got a long night ahead of me."

Sylvia returned to the bathroom locked the door opened the medicine cabinet and found the plastic casing with her diaphragm. It was the first time she'd used it and no matter how she twisted and turned the damn thing it simply refused to fit snugly. She'd been fitted for it before she left Elizabethtown. She'd practiced putting it in on numerous occasions when she was almost positive Peter was going to sex her but it had been all been a waste of time then. Now that she was sure it was going to happen the damn thing wouldn't fit. Not only wouldn't it fit it made loud popping noises that were embarrassing as hell. Hell, she couldn't get pregnant anyway but Dr. Reid had suggested she use it anyway as a contraceptive along with that nasty-ass gel. After another ten minutes of more twisting and shoving, Sill gave up on the idea and came to the conclusion that the gel and a prophylactic would just have to do. Besides, there was no doubt in her mind that as slow as Peter was, chances were good that he was still a virgin at twenty-seven.

"Did you pour me a drink, sweetheart," she called as she wiped the gel from between her legs.

"An hour ago," he replied. "What's the big surprise, baby?"

Sylvia, remembering that she'd left her shoes at the front door wrapped the robe around her waist and grabbed a Food Lion bag to put her shoes in. He obviously hadn't noticed them when he came in and she wanted everything to be picture perfect. She walked to the front door grabbed her shoes, threw them in the bag then returned to the bedroom where she greased her legs and feet with baby oil and eased into her fishnet stockings and heels. After dabbing a bit of Liz Taylor's, <u>White Diamond</u> perfume behind each earlobe and brushing her hair up in a bun looked into the mirror and smiled. She felt good knowing she was ready to make love as Betty Wright used to say, *"for the very first time."*

Dimming the lights in the bedroom and the hallway, Sylvia Shipp emerged from the darkness into the living room, radiant and glowing and ready for anything Professor Peter Townsend had to offer. This was her night. This was the night where all schools of etiquette would be dismissed early. This was the night she would rock Professor Peter Townsend's world and make him forget all notions of going anywhere without her. Tonight was the night Sylvia Shipp would make him hers or die trying in the effort.

After thirteen months of longing for this man Sill wasn't looking for good manners and proper protocol. She didn't want feels and foreplay. She wanted raw, unadulterated sex. *She wanted to know—needed to know—that Peter Townsend desired her physically as a woman.*

Up until now, the jury had been out but if it meant her getting on her knees to beg for his love then beg she would do. But she had to know.

It was immediately apparent the Peter was stunned, shocked beyond belief *"Oh my goodness! Damn, Sylvia!"*

"You promised not to say anything, Peter," Sylvia said, placing her finger to his lips in an attempt to silence him. Leaning over, she kissed him gently at first and then harder, pushing him backward onto the loveseat and unbuttoning his shirt. Smelling the sweet scent of masculinity, she grew savage in her desire, ripping the final two buttons when they refused to come undone as quickly as she desired. She wanted him now and decided that if he wasn't going to take the initiative then she certainly had no problem with showing him how that was done as well.

At that moment, Sylvia Shipp wanted Peter Townsend more than she had ever wanted anything in her entire life. *Anything!* Sylvia licked and nibbled at his chest as she made her way down to his belt buckle. She was hot now, fever-ish. Grabbing his belt buckle she pulled with no regard for the man and then straddled him when it took too long to unfasten the buckle and began grinding slow and hard and exotically against his genitals in hopes of arousing him. But if anyone was aroused by the lap dance now being performed it was she. Sylvia could feel the fire in her loins and all signs of an orgasm crying for release. It was no longer about Peter and she wondered if she'd really ever loved him or even liked him. She wondered if she was using him as revenge for what those animals at Tech had done to her. And then she laughed as she pressed even harder against his pelvis with every ounce of strength she could muster hop-ing, then praying that he would beg for her so she could administer the same thing that had been administered to her. She laughed although she hardly knew why and felt warm tears cascading down her cheeks at the same time. She tried to understand her feeling, tried to understand why she felt this about a man who obviously loved her. She thought of Dr. Reid suggesting that she con-tinue therapy and knew now that he was right about it not going away on its own but now was hardly the time to think about it. Despite the tears she felt a strange sensation, a warmth she'd never known before. And although it was all new to her she knew that she was on the brink of an orgasm. And no matter how she felt about the man beneath her at that very moment he was going to help her feel this thing that men felt was so goddamn important that it took twelve of them to hold her down and beat her to achieve. Sylvia laughed again then screamed out desperately as another warm rush descended over her.

"Help me, Peter!" she cried. "Oh, God, Peter, please help me. I think I'm coming. I don't know what to do. Take me now, baby. Show me. Oh please take me, Peter!"

The lap dance Sylvia tried to perform with the hopes of seducing Peter rendered her weak, almost helpless and Peter had yet to move or utter a word. Not noticing and not caring, Sylvia slid down to the floor and knelt between his legs. She was trembling with desire. Her hands shook but she managed to finally undo his buckle. As she reached for his zipper, he grabbed her wrists firmly.

"You promised me, Peter. You promised me that you wouldn't say a word," she protested. "The only thing I want to hear from your lips tonight is you calling my name and telling me how badly you want me. That is all I want to hear my love, that and nothing more," Sylvia said.

Peter sighed, looked into her eyes and said: "Sylvia, you are truly a beautiful woman. But before we go any further, throw your shawl around you, I'd like for you to take a quick ride with me. Don't worry about getting dressed there's really no need to get out of the car. Hurry now, I think it will answer a lot of your questions a lot better than I can."

Sylvia's loins were still aflame with hunger. She burned with desire but her curiosity forced her to put everything else on the back burner and she soon found herself, fishnet stockings and spiked heels, pulling up in the driveway of a palatial estate on Atlanta's perimeter. Peter stopped the car at the gate, fed several numbers into the gates security system and waited for the gate to slide open. A long black Mercedes stood parked in front of the arched front door. Peter parked the Lexus got out and opened the passenger door.

"Oh no, Peter, you told me that I wouldn't be getting out. *I can't be seen in public dressed like this*," she stammered. It was obvious that Peter wasn't taking no for an answer and held his hand out.

"You wanted answers, Sill. Come on let's see if we can't answers some of those questions I know have been eating away at you all of this time," Peter said as he led Sylvia to the large mahogany door.

Sylvia was prepared for the worst. She prayed that Peter hadn't set her up for a confrontation with another woman instead of just having the guts to tell her he was married. Sylvia wasn't given long to agonize. No sooner than they arrived at the door, it swung open and Sylvia drew a deep sigh of relief as an elderly white gentleman with more hair under his chin than on top of his pate greeted them.

"Dr. David Marchus, I'd like you to meet my good friend, Ms. Sylvia Shipp." Dr. Marchus grabbed Sylvia's hand, anxiously.

"Ms. Shipp, I'm truly honored to make your acquaintance. Peter has told me so much about you. He, however come close to describing such beauty as you possess. Welcome to our happy home," Dr. Marchus said. Then he turned to Peter, grabbed him, and kissed him deeply, passionately.

Stunned, Sylvia experienced a range of emotions. At first, shock, disbelief, nausea and then rage followed by a host of words that she had never used before in her life and then when she'd cursed him and vented and blamed him for every ill in the world today she ended the barrage the way she'd started. "Why you—you flaming faggot! You cocksuckin' bastard! Tell me you're not gay, Peter! Oh, Peter, please tell me that you are not gay. Please tell me that I haven't spent the last year and a half with some raving poop scooper. You're not even bi-sexual, are you? That's why you cringe every time I put my hands on you. You're one hundred percent slurpy, just as soft and sweet as you wanna be. Ain'tcha, boy? Lord! Lord! Lord! Someone please tell me where all the strong Black men have gone? No wonder you enjoyed going fishing with daddy so much. Probably just wanted to sit there and stare at his ass. Boy, if daddy knew this, he'd beat your ass straight. Just the thought of you two makes me wanna' puke."

Sylvia took a deep breath and just stared at the two men. Peter dropped his head. Dr. Marchus, unperturbed by the whole incident, pulled his pipe from the pocket of his smoking jacket, filled it with tobacco, lit it and then inhaled deeply before speaking, "I warned Peter about telling you Sylvia but it seems you have quite an influence over my friend here. He was sure that you would somehow understand his dilemma."

"*His dilemma,*" Sylvia laughed. "What dilemma? Oh, I'm sorry, please continue, Dr. Marchus. I'm sorry I didn't know that Peter was in such turmoil. How difficult it must be for poor Peter to get up each morning with such pressing issues," she said. "My God, how insensitive I must seem." Sylvia turned, fixing her gaze and her conversation on Peter. "I'm so sorry, hon, I just didn't realize the trials and tribulations, the sheer agony you must be going through each morning. What do you say to yourself? Here, let me see if I can put myself in your shoes, Peter, darling. Let's see if I can be a little more empathetic, a little more understanding," she said. "When you get up each morning and look in the mirror, I guess you must say this to yourself. "Let me see, Pete ol' boy, shall I go see my sweetheart this evening after work for a quiet candlelight dinner and some soft music. Perhaps I'll stay until the wee hours of the morning with a woman willing to cater to my every need. A woman whose body beckons me with it's every move. Should I make mad, passionate love to my woman, a woman most men crave to be with whose body exudes sensuality, whose every orifice is at my disposal? Then when it's over, sex her until she screams for me to stop. Should I fondle her breasts and she mine until we are both bathed in the heat of passion then enter her once more to complete our union. Hmmm. Decisions, decisions. Let me see. What are the alternatives? Perhaps I should go up to the big house and let some bald, wrinkled up old white man old enough to be my father, bend me over and stick his wrinkled-assed dick in my butt? Hardly a dilemma if you ask me." Sill laughed aloud at her own cynicism. In reality, she saw no humor, not to mention a dilemma.

"Sylvia, your depiction of what possibly could have been a rather breathtaking evening with Peter was eloquent. Your depiction of me, however, leaves a bit to be desired and at best is rather inconclusive, I'm afraid." Dr. Marchus said with little or no emotion.

Sylvia wanted blood not logic and interpretations of each discourse.

"Who is this fool, Peter?" Sylvia asked. Peter, his eyes still lowered, finally spoke: "Just listen, Sill. Please, give me a chance to explain."

"I wish you would explain but the only conversation I'm getting is from this stranger, excuse me, your friend or should I say *your* lover. Why the hell am I here anyway, Peter? Take me home this instant. Here I am with Victoria's Secret lingerie on and for what? There are no men here just little boys and faggots. Damn, Peter you could have at least gotten a good lookin' faggot," Sylvia laughed.

"You two are pathetic. Grandpa over there tryin' to look like Ricardo Montalban with his smokin' jacket on and you standing there lookin' like Tattoo. You two don't even make gay bashin' fun. Damn you both to hell! Just take me home," she was crying now but then caught herself abruptly. "What the hell am I crying for? I don't have any questions about my sexuality. I've always been very much a woman. See!" Sylvia dropped the shawl from her shoulders. "Is this what you want to be? A goddamn woman?" She was crying again and on the verge of hysterics. "Please take me home, Peter. Please! Just take me home!"

"Perhaps we should step into my study, Sylvia, maybe have a cup of tea and see if we can come to an understanding. Maybe we can resolve our differences. Communication is the key, you know," Dr. Marchus said with an air of authority.

Sylvia glared at him. "If you say another word to me Dr. Marchus or whatever the hell your name is I will knock the living shit out of you. Do you understand? Now Peter bring your punk-ass on or give me the keys." And with that said, Sylvia turned and walked out the door.

"Nice to meet you, Ms. Shipp, despite your misgivings about me," Dr. Marchus said.

Sylvia spun around as soon as she got outside the front door. If Peter even thinks about kissing that man in front of me again I'll beat both their sorry asses, she thought to herself. But there was no pretense of affection this time as both men walked to the door.

"You know Sylvia, I honestly believed from what Peter told me about you that you would be a bit more understanding. But I honestly can understand your hurt as a Black woman. Still, I somehow thought that with all the prejudice and injustice that Black people have endured...

Well, I guess I just didn't figure that you would be as closed minded as most. I must admit that I am sorry that there was no communication. Perhaps, if there had been some dialogue then you would have understood the dilemma that Peter is undergoing. Again, I am sorry. I'm sorry for Peter. He really does love you. He fought with the idea of asking you to marry him but I thought it best that he tell you that he had homosexual tendencies. He's a bit naïve, you know and he honestly believed that he could overcome his homosexuality if he were to marry you," the doctor said.

Sylvia shocked, turned to Peter. Was this true? Peter, obviously dejected by the whole turn of events sat in the car his head resting on his hands atop the steering wheel. The doctor continued, "He's struggled with this since he returned to school. I did no more than play devil's advocate. There is no doubt that I love Peter. Yet, at my age and in my infinite wisdom, I have come to learn that one cannot possess another and if Peter chooses to leave me there is nothing I can do to hold him. But if I truly love this young man I certainly wouldn't want to see him hurt. Should he be happier with you then I must bow out as gracefully as a jilted lover can. But I'd be willing to bet that had he told you of his homosexuality some years down the road it may have had a far more devastating effect on both of you than it would today. It is my belief that people should be up front with each other from the outset of any relationship. Peter agreed but was so afraid of losing you that he kept it a secret until now. I guess he knew you better than I after all. From all he told me, I continued to tell him that if you were as open-minded as he professed you to be that you would find some happy medium, some way in which you two could work this out.

He was so anxious to leave here and find somewhere to start over with you in a place where his past would not follow him, a place where you two could throw down stakes and settle down and raise a family. I actually grew jealous knowing that I wasn't included in his plans.

I so hated constantly hearing how absolutely gorgeous you were and what a fantastic teacher you were that I even went so far as to threaten to cut him out of my will. I have no children, no heir apparent and have amassed a small fortune all of which is bequeathed to Peter. Yet, it did little good to threaten him when it came to you my dear. So, what was I to do? I simply accepted the fact that you were now a part of our lives and Peter would be leaving when he could come to grips with the skeletons that plagued him. You know, Sylvia, I have considerable influence in the region due to my wealth I suppose. And when you first became a threat to my happiness, I had you investigated out of pure anger and malice."

"Why, you bastard," Sylvia shouted. "You son of a bitch!" The doctor ignored her.

"I was hoping to find some dirt, something to persuade Peter that you were not the person he thought you were. I hired a private investigator that learned of your ordeal when you were in college as well as your stint in the mental ward. By the time, I received the information I was so ashamed that I never told Peter. Knowing Peter, do you think either of these incidents would have changed the way he felt about you? I think not. That is one of the reasons he still doesn't know. And I'm pretty sure you haven't told him either. What if he were to ask you to marry him? Would you tell him that you are not able to bear children? I doubt it very seriously. Do you know why? Because after meeting you I'm painfully aware of one thing if nothing else. And that's that you are not half the woman that he is man. You're out for Sylvia and Peter's nothing more to you than a prime candidate for a husband and a meal ticket," the doctor said.

No, he didn't just go there, Sylvia thought to herself. This goddamn bearded, old geezer with an appetite for young Black men didn't just call me a 'gold digger,' did he? Sylvia was beside herself with anger but Dr. Marchus was hardly finished.

"You've go to admit, he's a helluva catch. Young, bright and good looking, Peter finished in the top five-percent of his class as an undergrad and came out first in the Master's program. I bet you didn't know that, did you?"

"No I didn't," Sylvia heard herself mumble in spite of herself.

"He's got companies recruiting him from as far away as Hawaii. But Morehouse was in a bind and was desperate to find a professor of engineering. When they couldn't find one, they asked Peter. So, he put off his career plans and took the position. He could have made twice what he's making here but he has this thing about giving something back to the community. Actually, I think he was waiting to see if he had exhausted all of his options concerning you. Anyway, after you guys got back together again he couldn't wait to leave. I know he wished he hadn't taken the teaching position now but he's committed to his students and the college. He had it all planned so perfectly. He was throwing out options to you, mentioning different cities hoping you would bite so he could get a feel for where you might want to relocate. Sure, he had his preferences but he wanted to go where he was sure you'd be most happy.

Once the school year ended, Peter was going to propose and start packing but from what he tells me you grew angry every time he brought the subject of relocating up. I'm truly sorry that things didn't work out between you two, and I'm not being facetious by any means but after meeting you I'm glad they didn't." Knocking the ashes from his pipe, the doctor turned and walked back into the house.

"Fuck you," was all Sylvia could manage as she made her way to the Lexus.

Peter was not there smiling or holding the door as she'd become so accustomed to. In fact, he hardly seemed to notice her as she wrapped her shawl around herself and closed the car door. She didn't care. The mere thought of him sleeping with that old geezer gave her the willies. It was revolting and to think she was willing to give herself to this faggot only an hour or so ago with no protection. *Hell, he probably had AIDS.*

The ride home seemed to take forever. When they finally did arrive Sylvia jumped out of the car without so much as looking back and Peter pulled away before she could turn the key in the lock.

"Why you bastard," she yelled after the departing car. "You no-good bastard!"

Once inside, Sill fell down on the very same living room sofa she had hoped would be the start of something beautiful and cried like a baby.

But by the time Monday rolled around, Peter was just another bad memory and she was back in front of her classroom doing what she did best, teaching.

"I'm young, bight and intelligent and most men find me attractive. I have my whole life in front of me. I hardly have time to look back or have regrets and I have twenty-six beautiful beaming faces that look to me for guidance and depend on me. I've got to keep pushing on, if not for me then for them. Besides I'm not sure that I ever loved Peter anyway." Hearing the sound of her own voice frightened her and it took her a few minutes to regain her composure.

She considered how she'd felt straddling him last Friday night and wondered if God himself weren't punishing her for using Peter or at least having ulterior motives. What was even more disturbing were the thoughts she'd had about the rape and the fact that she had all intentions of making Peter pay for something he had nothing at all to do with. But then again he was a man and they were all worthless in her eyes. Sylvia felt herself smile and knew immediately that she still had some unresolved issues and was frightened once more.

Searching for the business card Dr. Reid had given her the last time home and not being able to locate it she promised herself to find it when she got home that evening and set up an appointment. At least that's what she told herself.

The weeks following Peter's admission were uneventful. She seldom thought of Peter now, and after a week, she stopped checking her voice-mail to see if he had called. The only thing that really perturbed her was why she couldn't seem to keep a man. Why? Why? Why? She sighed wearily.

Well, whatever the reason there was no need to worry about that now. She had been neglecting her kids ever since she and Peter had gotten back together. Now it was time to get back in the swing of things and pick up the pace. The hell with men. She was through this time. After Peter there would be no more. From now on there could only be one man in her life and that would be her Lord and Savior, Jesus Christ. To hell with those roguish fools running around like dogs off their chains. The only man she would put her faith in from now on was the Lord.

Never again would she be subjected to the human frailties of love and sex. No longer would she feel compelled to look for happiness in another human being. No longer would she trust any man or allow him to jeopardize her emotional well being. For her those days were long gone.

CHAPTER 7

❀

The third grade class at Community Elementary School 73X made unbelievable strides with the re-energized Ms. Shipp at the helm. And by the time spring rolled into Fulton County, Georgia with its peach trees in full blossom, her class ranked behind only Mr. Oscevedo's in growth according to those damn standardized tests she hated so much. And there was good reason. She spent every waking hour finding new and creative ways to motivate her students to reach for higher goals. And it was paying off. The culmination of her efforts came during the annual spring concert when she had each of her students dress as slaves and recite a part of the Declaration of Independence.

Parents and teachers applauded her efforts for weeks afterward. Even the usually rather stoic, Mr. Cooper, seemed inspired by her students' efforts. Yet, and still, there was a void, an eerie emptiness in her life that she couldn't quite seem to figure out or to fill. She hated to think that she needed a man to be happy but that's the way it was beginning to look. She pulled out the card Dr. Reid gave her the last time she'd seen him and seriously considered calling the number of the therapist on more than one occasion. Each time she thought of the very painful and probing questions that he would inevitably ask she would neatly fold the tiny piece of paper up and place it back in her wallet. *No need to revisit old haunts,* she told herself.

Sensing something slightly amiss in her daughter during their weekly phone conversations Mrs. Shipp suggested Sylvia find a church if she hadn't found one yet. "Just place your troubles in the hands of the Lord, sweetheart," she would tell her apropos of nothing.

A devout Methodist, Mrs. Shipp, was a firm believer in the power of prayer and had become 'born again' during her daughter's protracted hospital stay.

She sensed Sylvia's loneliness but feared asking about Peter. Her maternal instincts told her the pair was no together any longer. But then it didn't take a NASA scientist to figure that one out.

The last time Sylvia came home, she was alone and didn't mention Peter's name once. The older woman had long ago learned not to pry into her daughter's private affairs knowing that if something was bothering Sill and she wanted to talk then she would in her own good time.

In actuality, Sylvia had been to quite a few churches since her move to Atlanta. She was just having difficulty finding one that fit her. Most of the Black churches she went to were no different from the ones in Elizabethtown where the preacher seemed enamored by the sound of his own voice. All too often she would walk away at the end of service still wondering what it was the minister was trying to convey.

At others, there was the typical ceremonial grunting and hollering that she so despised followed by a chorus of amen's. It reminded her of those old James Brown records her daddy used to be so fond of and that new girl. What's her name? The one who never said nothin' but baby, baby, baby. Oh, yeah. Ashanti! In any case, those churches always left her hungry, always wanting for more. She had even gone so far as entertaining the idea of converting to Catholicism after reading an article in the Atlanta Constitution about the growing number of Black Catholics in Atlanta. But after entering a small Catholic Church one Sunday morning and feeling every head turned to view the new arrival she had second thoughts. After all she was not there to be judged by her peers for her outward appearance. That's not what church was all about. Despite that, she still wasn't sure if she could be a part of a religion where the faithful didn't have enough respect to dress not so much for one another but for their God. As open-minded as she appeared to be, she was still shocked to find many of the parishioners in faded jeans and dirty sneakers. When she finally got past the dress code or lack thereof and the *horrible* singing coming from what was supposed to be a choir, the incessant genuflecting and shaking hands, the whole affair was over. She wasn't sure, after all the standing and kneeling if she was coming from Gold's Gym for her afternoon workout or if she'd just been the twenty-third customer through Burger King's drive through window. And just like dining at one of those fast food chains, she found herself still to be hungry five minutes later and struggling to remember what she'd consumed in the way of a message. That's what the Catholic Church reminded her of: A fast food joint, a gym and just about everything but God.

Some of her colleagues at school recommended she attend church with them. She thought better of this though after attending a Pentecostal service with one of her co-workers. Initially, she found the church service intriguing and the congregation warm in welcoming her but as the minister's message grew in intensity so did the congregation until he incited them to feel the work of the Lord at which time they began shouting and running and jumping from one end of the church to the other. It had all been a bit much to swallow. Never had she seen the Holy Spirit manifested in such a way. And although she had taken three years of Spanish in high school she had trouble deciphering the worshipers' language when they began speaking in tongues. She'd done her best to sit through the service but when they all started *runnin'* and *jumpin'* and *hoopin'* and *hollerin'* she found herself runnin' too. Only she didn't stop *runnin'* until she reached her car.

When she returned to school the following Monday, she was so embarrassed that she did her best to avoid the elderly teacher's assistant that had invited her. She hadn't meant for her leaving to be considered a personal affront but the woman was offended and it was several months before the two spoke again. Now she made it a policy not to attend the church of someone she knew despite their persistent claims that their church was unlike any other.

Sensing something amiss in her daughter's tone over the last month, her mother's phone calls increased. When Mrs. Shipp could not get a feel for Sylvia's sudden mood change, she informed her daughter that she would be coming to Atlanta to do some shopping and visit her relatives the following weekend.

Sylvia loved Atlanta, loved the feeling of living alone and loved the grind of teaching. However, the enormity of Atlanta could be overwhelming at times. As much as she hated to admit it she missed Peter's companionship, his calm demeanor and unassuming personality, his attentiveness and his kindness. And she had to force herself not to call him on several occasions. At other times she'd dial his number, wait for him to answer just to hear his voice before hanging up on him. She wondered if he had caller I.D. and really wished he'd call her back. But her wishes went unanswered and by the time the semester came to a close she so desperately missed Peter that she swallowed her pride and called Morehouse to apologize for being so shallow and closed minded and was shocked to find out that Professor Townsend had moved on weeks ago. So devastated by the news of Peter's departure that Sill seriously considered throwing in the towel and was actually lying across her bed with a bottle of Valium in her hand when she received the call from her mother informing her that she would be in town the following weekend. Sylvia wasn't sure exactly what she would've done if she hadn't received the call. But when she heard that her mother was coming she was thrilled.

Mrs. Shipp arrived at the Amtrak Station early that Saturday morning with enough boxes and bags to make Sill wonder if she'd already been Christmas shopping. In them, Sill found all of her favorite foods. There was baked and barbequed chicken, rice pudding, shrimp, salsa, pickles her mother had canned as well as a host of other goodies. Sill thought must have surely died and gone to heaven. They shopped most of Saturday afternoon after meeting her cousin and aunt at one of the local malls. By the time they finished shopping, Sill was completely exhausted. But she had to admit that it was the best time she had had in who knows how long. She found her cousin Laurie, a year younger than her and a graduate of Spellman currently working as a CPA in some downtown firm to be crazy and carefree with a great sense of humor.

The physical resemblance between the two young women was nothing short of remarkable. Sill wished now that she had taken her mother's advice and sought Laurie out when she first arrived instead of that pathetic wretch she'd been wasting her time with. They could have had a ball together. Sill remembered her only vaguely from family reunions and remembered her as being a snotty-nosed little brat who would never share her dolls but boy had time changed her. Not only did she favor Sill in looks, she sounded just like her when it came to men.

When they finally finished shopping it was agreed on by all that the women would meet at Sylvia's aunt's house for dinner later that evening. Sylvia, however, insisted on shooting back to her place to freshen up. And since she was still getting to know Atlanta, Laurie volunteered to ride with her so she could show her the way back to her mom's for dinner. It was an experience Sill would hardly forget. She never remembered Laurie being quite so talkative but what a difference a few years had made.

"Girl, have you been to Shaggy's?" Laurie asked as soon as they'd gotten in the car.

"No, I really haven't been anywhere since I've been here. Teaching keeps me pretty busy. I don't really have time to do too much of anything," Sill answered.

"*Girl, you've go to go to Shaggy's.* Tuesdays are the nights to go, girl. It's men's lockup. Ladies are admitted free until ten and, Lord knows you've got to see the men up in there. *Good God almighty! Talk about some fine ass men! Girl, they got it goin' on!* Walkin' around there in them little g-strings serving drinks. Hell, the first time I went was about two months ago on a payday. I cashed my check before I went. You know to have a little spendin' change so I could buy a drink or two. It was the first of the month, you know. The mortgage was due, light bill was overdue and they were just about to turn the cable off, so I was feelin' a little stressed. I was tellin' one of my girlfriends about my bills and this sorry-ass man I was dating so she suggested we try out this new club downtown, you know, to relieve the stress and shit, so I said sure why the hell not.

Girl, when I got there they dimmed the lights and this tall, fine thang walks up to me. Thought I was gonna pee right there and I ain't had the first drink yet. Tells me his name is Timothy or something another. I can't really remember 'cause all my attention was focused on that little ass piece of string tied around his waist and wonderin' how that little string could possible hold all of that delicious lookin' man I was seein'.

By the time Timothy had gotten my order, I'd ordered for everybody at the damn table just trying to keep him there. And not once did my eyes leave that damn string. I don't even recall his face but I can give you the length, width and diameter of that string and its contents. Girl, let me tell you. By the time the night was over, the mortgage was in default, I was at Family Dollar searchin' for some damn candles and on my knees up at the cable company beggin' for an extension." They both laughed out loud.

"Girl, you need to stop your lyin'," Sill was laughing so hard the tears rolled down her face. "So, what did you end up doing?" she asked.

"What do you mean *what did I end up doin'*? I got the damn candles, told Timothy I was goin' to treat him to a candlelight dinner, bought the nigga a value pack from Bojangles, you know, two pieces a chicken and a biscuit and sexed that boy til he was hollerin' for me to let him go. I hurt him so bad he tol' me he was goin' to use the john and ended up sneakin' out the back door. Shit, the hell if I wasn't goin' to get some of my tips back."

"Damn, if it's all that I may have to go," Sill said, tears still streaming down her face.

"Trust me, girlfriend, it's all that. 'Cept I never see Timothy anymore so don't expect to see him when we go," Laurie said.

"What happened? Did you end his career?"

"No, he's still there but he runs every time he sees me. Spends all his time in the back. But don't worry girl. There are plenty of Timothy's *up in dere.* They're not supposed to get personal with the customers but you rip a Benjamin in half and tell them to meet you later and they'll get the other half and trust me you don't have to worry about whether they'll get personal. Know what I'm sayin'? *Personal!* Hell, they ain't makin' much more than that in a night. So when you see 'em later and tell 'em that all you need is an hour or so of their time for a little undercover work you ain't goin' to get too many complaints, baby girl. Shit, I had one nigga wanted to give me a refund. Tol' me the pleasure was his. Let me tell you, girl. I rocked this boy's boots. He was still callin' me two weeks later tryin' to take me out to dinner and what not," Laurie bragged.

"I know you went?" Sill asked.

"Heck, yeah. Went to the Blue Marlin for some seafood that was out of this world. I don't know where this fool thought he was takin' me but he looked shook when I told him I wanted to go to the nicest seafood restaurant in Atlanta. I guess he thought he was takin' me to Red Lobster or something but I let the brotha know from the outset that this sista don't do chains," Laurie said matter-of-factly.

"When the waitress came askin' me what I wanted for an appetizer and pushin' this salad up in front of me, I pushed it right on back and ordered the Shrimp Scampi. She gonna' tell me Shrimp Scampi ain't considered an appetizer. I said it is today, sista girl. Then for the main course, I ordered a three and a half pound lobster with a baked potato and this witch is still pushing this salad. Anyway, the chef comes to the table. You know, when you order lobster at the Blue Marlin they push this big ol' aquarium up to the table and I knew that but I tol' the chef that there's no need to do that, I'd just go with him and look. See that way I can forget about bein' a lady and all that. Shit, I'm lookin' like I just stepped out of *Vogue*, anyway. I got this young boy droolin', just thinkin' about dessert.

Anyway, let me finish tellin' you about the chef and the lobster. I followed the chef over to the tank and get to lookin' at the lobsters. And, girl, they had some lobsters. Must have been a hundred of them just floatin' around. So the chef tells me to pick one. Well, the last time I was there, I let the chef pick the lobster and I ended up stoppin' by the Burger King on the way home. So I said to myself, I'm not goin' home hungry tonight. Where's your scale? I must have had the chef weigh twenty-five lobsters before I got a nice size one. Then, I told him to prepare another and put it in a doggy bag and hand it to me on the way out."

"No, you didn't!" Sill shouted, laughing.

"Oh, but I did. Girl, if you've been around this town as long as I have with these little po' ass Negroes tryin' to be playas, you'd better know the tricks of the game. See, the way I figure, if the boy wants to be with me badly enough and feels confident enough to be with one tough, professional Black woman, then he better not come half steppin'. Ain't no way I can eat out like this every night but I can when I want to with no help from anybody. So if you choose to be with me *I hope to God* you can carry your weight. Don't come tryin' to impress me and ain't got a pot to piss in or a window to throw it out of. Don't come pullin' up to me in no Cadillac Escalade tryin' to floss and you livin' *with yo' mama.* Know what I'm sayin'? Anyway, I go back to the table and listen to him talk about himself and how he's about to drop an album. So, I ask him what he does and of course, he's a music producer and at the moment he's in the studio producin' some chick's album. So, I'm like, yeah okay, 'cause every unemployed nigga in Atlanta claims to be a rapper and most of 'em can't read or write, let alone rap. But anyway, I'm listenin' while I finish up the shrimp and wonderin' how I can ditch this boy before he tries to make a power move at the end of the night. See, I'm thinkin' the whole time. Ya gotta stay one step ahead of 'em or you'll find yourself wrapped up in some shit you can't get out of.

Well, by this time I'm so full I have to go to the bathroom to let some out before I can put some more in. And just then I see the chef comin' with my lobster as I'm on my way to the bathroom. He smiles. I smile and that silly waitress is followin' him with the side orders so I stop her and tell her to bring me a bottle of wine. But on the way, I stop at the bar and order a double *Hennessey* on the rocks, throw that down on the way back to the table and tell the bartender to put it on the tab.

By the time I get back to the table, I'm feelin' no pain and I'm listenin' to my boy go on and on about comin' back from New Jersey where he just finished puttin' the finishin' touches on Kem's new album and now I know he's lyin' but I don't say anything, not a goddamn word. I'm thinkin' he can have his lies. I'm gonna have this lobster. Talk about somethin' good. By this time, I'm sippin' the wine, the *Hennessy's* hittin', pieces of shell are flyin' over to the next table, I'm dippin' that lobster tail in the butter and got lobster and everything else hangin' from my mouth. Shit, I'm havin' a goddamn ball and he's still runnin' his mouth tellin' these fantabulous lies about how absolutely niggariffic he is like he's the Second Coming or some shit.

Now it's about this time that I start thinkin' about dessert and this delicious looking hot-fudge brownie that I saw on the menu. So, I ordered that and figured I'd better keep this fool talkin' cause he sure ain't gonna be able to say anything when the bill arrives. Plus, I want to make him think that I'm really interested in what he's sayin' so he don't wanna whoop my ass when he drops me off and I don't give him any." Laurie paused to light a cigarette.

"So, go ahead, what happened?" Sill asked with baited breath.

"Well, I'm talkin' to him askin' him 'bout his producin' and all and then I get around to who he's produced and he starts namin' stars. I figured he'd bring up some no-name artists and tell me he was just gettin' his feet wet but no, this fool starts namin' names like Keith Sweat, Kelly Price, Jaheim, you know, the big names so I'm thinkin' to myself, this boy's a pathological liar if I ever did see one. Here he is dancin' in Shaggy's on Tuesday nights and drivin' this beat-up Toyota Corolla pickup and he's gonna tell me he's producin' megastars.

That's when it dawned on me that the fool was crazy. I lost my appetite right then and there and told him it was time to go. I said any nigga with this active an imagination is liable to do anything 'cause all the bricks ain't in the wagon. Now, I'm scared that when the check comes he's gonna make a scene right there but at least we're in a crowded restaurant so he won't be so apt to whoop my ass right there. When the check came, it was a hundred and thirty two dollars which really wasn't bad. But to be on the safe side I decided to head back to the ladies room just in case he needed some time and space to vent.

While I was in there, I figured he'd probably slip out the door when he saw the check so I started lookin' for my *Visa Card*. When I got back to the table, he was sittin' there like nothing had happened and on the tray was a twenty-dollar tip. Now I know I'm in trouble. I was so scared of what he was gonna do to me that I forgot my damn doggy bag with the extra lobster. Anyway, by now I'm absolutely positive the nigga's gonna' whoop my ass. I'm thinkin' he's probably just waitin' til we get in the car.

That's when I thought about taking a cab home or callin' one of my girlfriends to pick me up, you know, just to be on the safe side but I didn't want it to appear like I was afraid or had done anything wrong so I got in the car and he took me home."

"So, what happened then?"

"Well, when we got to my house the streets deserted. Half the street lights don't work anyway 'cause the drug boys bust them out and I'm thinkin' this is what he was waitin' for all along, some dark lonely stretch where he could bash my brains in with no one noticin'. But I didn't get out. I couldn't. I was frozen stiff. I just sat there, almost like I knew I had done wrong and was waitin' for my punishment. Then he leaned over. Girl, I thought I was going to pee on myself right then and there. But all he wanted to know was if I was goin' to invite him in. I kept thinkin' about the headlines of the next day's papers sayin' something like, *Unidentified Woman, Murdered and Dismembered in Own*

Townhouse," so I told him tonight isn't a good night, but call me around the end of the week and we'll get together. Then I thanked him for dinner, jumped out of the car and ran like hell up to the steps to let myself in.

Luckily, my next door neighbor was walkin' his dog so by the time he opened the car door to get out I was already in the house with the bolt lock on the door, honey," Laurie finished the cigarette and put it out in the ashtray, blew out the rest of the smoke and continued.

"All I wanted to do when I got in the house was kick back and relax. So, I grabbed a glass of wine, put on some Jaheim and called my girlfriend up to tell her about this crazy nigga I just went out with and I'm sittin' there chillin' sippin' my wine waitin' for her to pick up and fiddlin' with the CD when I see big as day, 'produced by Aaron Brown'.

Girlfriend, I dropped the wine and the phone. I just sat there and stared at the CD. I must have stared at it for about ten minutes until I heard my girl yelling over the phone, "Laurie? Laurie, are you there?" I picked up the phone. I don't even know if I told her I was goin' to call her back. I just hung it up. I had CD's everywhere. And sure enough he was on the Keith Sweat, the Kelly Price, the Luther, all of the one's he mentioned."

"No."

"Girl, I wanted to kick my own ass." Laurie said.

"I'm feelin' you there, girl. You run into a good man out here, you'd best scoop him up. What is it they say?" Sill asked.

"A good man is hard to find," Laurie said.

"Ain't that the truth. Either they're married or dead," Sill added.

"Shit, a few of the married ones I've dated seem like they're *dead*," Laurie said, smiling as she scrounged through her purse for another cigarette.

"Tell me you don't date married men, Laurie. At least not *knowing* they're married."

"Baby girl, this is Atlanta. Do you know what the ratio of men to women is here? A thousand to one. Hell, if he's married and looks in my direction and I like what I see, he's mine. He could be walkin' hand in hand in the mall with his wife and kids but the minute he glances in my direction then he's fair game. His marital status is *his* business. And if he ends up out here with me then she ain't doin' somethin' right at home. I'm not a home wrecker, Sill. I'm a homemaker. If he ain't happy there, then I promise that I'll make him a happy home here. She better just be glad that I'm not in the market for a full-time man. If I was I wouldn't send him home when I got tired of him. I wouldn't send him home at all. But honestly, I do try to stay away from married men but not because they're married. I stay away from 'em because I'm high maintenance and brothaman has got to be in great shape to keep up with me and ain't too many married men that I know can satisfy wifey and me too. What about you, Sill? Have you been datin'?" Laurie said.

"No, not really. I'm still trying to get over my last relationship," she confessed.

"Let me guess? Brotha either got locked up was gay or is messin' with that shit," Laurie speculated.

Sylvia dropped her head for a second. The thought of Peter was still painful and for some reason the memories and the hurt she felt seemed to be growing stronger instead of fading as time went on.

Laurie, sensing her cousin's turmoil interjected: "Okay Sylvia, here's the bottom line. It's something my daddy used to tell me before he passed on, God bless his soul. Daddy used to tell me to, 'never ever let another person live rent free in your mind for more than a minute'. I never understood what he was sayin' at the time but after meetin' my fair share of men, excuse me *dogs* that were pretending to be men and after being in a fair amount of relationships, I think I understand what he was tryin' to tell me.

You see, life is hard enough without lettin' someone else bring chaos and confusion into it and before you let that happen, you let them go. Life is just too short, girlfriend. And never but *never* dwell on the fact that this person had that much effect on your life that you're still thinkin' about a situation that's long gone. That's why I don't really have relationships anymore. What I have that serves me just as well is a good doctor who keeps me supplied with penicillin. See, the only thing I need from a man right through here is a good workout every now and then. And hell, I'd rather buy it straight up than to deal with all the bullshit of a relationship. Shoot, I give them a hundred dollars, check their health card, make 'em whisper they love me in my ear three or four times while they're sexing me and I'm good to go. And I'm not chinchy either. If a multiple orgasm comes into play, I just might tip 'em. But please don't call me afterwards. I'll call you in a month or so if I need some more. And that way, I don't have to entertain the silly games and constant bullshit. Now what's your story, Sill? C'mon, you can tell me. We're family. Besides, I'm nosy as hell and the suspense is drivin' me crazy."

"There's really nothing to tell, Laurie," Sill lied.

"Okay, well, at least tell me this. Was he messin' with drugs?"

"No, not that I know of but then there was a lot I didn't know. No, he was a professor of Civil Engineering at Morehouse," she replied.

"Then, he must have been married," Laurie concluded.

"No, he wasn't married," Sill said wishing the guessing game would stop.

"Then, he *had* to be gay," Laurie ventured, finally.

Sill dropped her head. They had been sitting in front of the apartment for a good twenty minutes and Sill saw no better time to get out than now.

"Help me grab the bags," she said as she popped the trunk. "I'll tell you about it later."

"That bad?" Laurie infused.

"That bad," Sill replied.

Laurie helped Sill grab the shopping bags and made their way into the apartment.

"Ooh girl, this is nice. I love the skylight and it's *so* spacious. You should see mine. If you hold your arms out and turn around, you can hit all four walls," Laurie said as she walked from room to room. "So, go ahead, tell me about Mr. Softee."

"There's really nothing to tell, Laurie. We dated for a year, maybe a year and a half and I found out he was gay. That's about it," Sill said.

"Did you love him?" Laurie asked.

Sylvia hesitated. "I'm not sure. You know I never really thought about it. He was just there and I pretty much figured he would always be there but I never really asked myself that question. And, when I found out he was sleeping with a man, I was so angry that I still didn't ask myself if I loved him. I do miss him, though."

"Well, did you sleep with him?" Laurie probed.

"No, we never slept together. Matter of fact, I was trying to seduce him one night and that's when I discovered it."

"So, you mean to tell me that you spent a year and a half with this fool and you never slept with him? C'mon Sill, fess up." Laurie couldn't believe what she was hearing.

"It wasn't like that, Laurie. The two of us did everything together. I mean everything. We just enjoyed being around each other," Sill said in her own defense.

"So, what you're tellin' me is that you broke up with him because he wouldn't sleep with you but he was your best friend," Laurie asked, incredulously.

"Yeah, I guess you could say he was my best friend. Do we have to talk about this?"

"No, not really. I can see it's still pretty painful but can I say one last thing?" Laurie asked. "Girlfriend, I'm not tryin' to sound like white people, tryin' to cover up their own prejudice when they say one of my best friends is Black. And I don't have a whole lot of gay friends so I really can't generalize but I have one friend who just so happens to prefer men over women and he's probably the best friend I've got. He's the sweetest person in the world and I'm not being factious when I say *sweet*. So, I could care less about what kind of sex he prefers 'cause Lord knows I got some kinky shit in me but I wouldn't trade his friendship for anything in the world. I'm sure it's probably different when you're in a relationship and tryin' to get your sex on but girl, good friends are hard to find and if you find one good friend in a lifetime you can count yourself lucky. Now, with that said, are you ready to go? I know momma's got the food on the table and I'm about starved."

Sylvia thought about what her cousin had said later as she showered and packed her overnight bag. Good friends *were* hard to come by. Again, her thoughts returned to Peter. Lord knows she had never had a better friend. She even considered calling Dr. Marchus under the pretense that her mother was in town and wanted to see Peter. Marchus would surely know his whereabouts and he would surely come then and perhaps they could resolve the problem. On second thought, maybe it would be better they wait until they were home before inviting him over.

Forty-five minutes later, Laurie and Sill pulled up at her aunt's home outside of Atlanta. Sylvia had never been to their new home and didn't know what her uncle had done for a living but he sure had provided nicely for his family before he died.

The house which sat back on several acres of land was palatial. Marble floors and crystal chandeliers met Sylvia as she entered the spacious home. A young, Hispanic woman about Sylvia's age answered the door, welcomed them and led them to the dining room where Mrs. Shipp and her sister were already dining.

"Well, nice of you two to finally join us," Sill's aunt said. "I hope Laurie hasn't been too bad of an influence on you."

"Not at all, we were just reminiscing, getting caught up," Sill replied.

Laurie kissed her mom and her aunt.

"What's for dinner? I'm starved," she confessed.

The evening turned out to be far more fun than Sylvia could ever have imagined. After a dinner in which Sylvia ate far too much, the four ladies played *Guesstures* and chatted until the wee hours of the morning. It seemed to

Sylvia that no sooner had she closed her eyes than the warm smell of bacon singed her nose. Laurie was already up and in the shower and Sylvia had all she could do to drag herself out of bed and into the bathroom when she heard her aunt's voice. "Church starts in thirty minutes. You ladies need to get a move on, if you expect to get breakfast and a good seat. Hurry up now. Laurie, you know how I hate to be late."

Sylvia finally found the main bathroom after opening what seemed like a thousand doors. There were rooms and more rooms. She hadn't seen the house in its entirety the night before but soon realized that she was in a mansion if there ever was one. Donning the navy blue *Christian Dior* suit she had purchased a few weeks ago with the hope of impressing Peter, Sylvia made her way down the stairs and met the approving eye of everyone there. Her mom and aunt were already at the door while Laurie waited impatiently in the car. Five minutes later, the four women arrived at John Wesley A.M.E. Zion Church's parking lot. She never imagined a church of this size and magnitude. There must have been a thousand cars in the parking lot alone. Once inside, she found there to be even more people than there had been cars. The church was enormous and Sill just hoped, no, she *knew* that this many people couldn't be coming to hear some illiterate jack-legged preacher hoopin' and hollerin' as she was so used to.

To her surprise, the minister was no more than thirty or so and not only was he eloquent in his delivery he was quite handsome as well. No one turned to see the newcomers; there were no hostile stares, no routine genuflecting, no hoopin' and hollerin'. There was nothing but a simple well thought out message on loving thy neighbor which not only addressed the congregation but spoke in terms of American as a country, a superpower and a leader being more tolerant of others in spite of their differences.

The young minister addressed the escalating violence in the Middle East and the war in Iraq. He questioned patriotism and religion and sought to ask the tough questions.

He asked the congregation if we were as a nation unpatriotic because we did not support the war in Iraq. He questioned the war fitting into the Judeo-Christian doctrine which this country was founded on. He concluded by asking the congregation, "If Jesus were alive today, would he be considered treasonous or unpatriotic for not supporting military intervention in Afghanistan or Iraq? For not supporting war?

And then he went on, "I have the Good Book right here in front of me. And in this book which governs most of our lives I am unable to find one passage, not one single reference, where it says that out Lord and Savior Jesus Christ condoned war. I can find passages where he grew angry. I'm okay with that. We all grow angry at times. After the initial shock of 9/11 I grew angry too. How many of you out there were angry and felt like your privacy had been invaded? Sure, you were angry. But let me digress for a minute. How many of you have ever been to the doctors and he tells you to jump up onto the examination table. After you get up on the table, the doctor takes this little hammer with a rubber tip and *pow,* he bangs you on the knee with it and your knee shoots straight out. No matter what you do to keep that leg from moving when the doctor hits that one spot there's nothing you can do to stop that leg from jumping out, from reacting. That's a natural reaction. I believe they call that a knee-jerk reaction. It's natural and there's nothing you can do to stop it. That's how anger is. It's a natural reaction to something or someone that offends us in some way. Many times we can't stop it. It's a natural reaction. But we do have the ability to think and reason and we must use these capabilities to determine how to react after the initial anger has subsided. It is at these times when we must ask ourselves, what would Jesus do? Now, my friends, I didn't want to steer you wrong so I spent the week searching the Good Book. And again, I cannot find one passage where our Lord and Savior Jesus Christ said it was alright to go to war and kill another man.

Now, I can find passages in the Old Testament where Moses descended from the mountaintop after having had some pretty meaningful dialogue with God the Father. During this dialogue the Father gives Moses some fairly stringent guidelines on what we are to do and what we are not to do. I believe they refer to them as the Ten Commandments. Let me read just a couple of them to you. The first one I'd like to read to you refers to the lesson we've talked about today and that is, *Love thy neighbor.* I'm not going to read the second part of that because some of us don't love ourselves so I'll be satisfied with love thy neighbor even if you don't love yourselves. The second commandment, which I think is equally as important however, and is in direct correlation with today's service is, *Thou shall not kill.* Now, the way I interpret the commandments is a little different than the way Moses may have.

In fact, I do believe that Moses may have had some trouble with the translation since from all accounts he was pretty shook up when he saw that bush burning and heard that voice calling out to him especially when he knew that no one had accompanied him up that hill. That's why I tend to think he may have had some problems with his interpretation.

You see it seems to me that a couple of the commandments are just a little redundant and I have never known the good Lord to be either long winded or redundant so it is my belief that Moses may have misinterpreted the message just a bit. You see if we love our neighbor as we love ourselves then there is no need for the commandment which says, *Thou shall not kill.* If you follow my reasoning let me hear you say *Amen,*" A loud raucous chorus descended upon the pulpit amidst laughter as the congregation shouted, "*Amen*" in unison. But he wasn't finished. "And therefore, if we as a nation who pride ourselves on our Christian heritage believe in these basic tenets better known as the Ten Commandments then we must find a way to love our neighbors in spite of the atrocities and we must a better answer than war to solve our differences. That is what I have learned from the teachings of our Lord and Savior, Jesus Christ. If you tend to agree can I get an 'Amen'?

Again there was a resounding chorus of 'Amens' from the congregation.

"In summation, and before we answer the broader questions I want each and every one of you, as you go through your week to ask yourselves while at work, or at school, or at home with your families to ask yourselves how you are treating the people next to you, closest to you, your neighbor. Ask yourself this and as the trials you incur in every day life descend upon you I want each of you to reflect on the life of our Savior and ask yourself what would Jesus do. Don't just slap the armband on your wrist or put the letters WWJD on the license plate of your car. *Live it!* Let it be the recurring thought as you go about your daily ventures. Make it a mantra. Repeat it throughout your day as you proceed from your homes to school or to the workplace. Ask yourself: What would Jesus do?" And with that the minister closed the book in front of him and nodded to the choir who broke into a lively rendition of <u>Joyful, Joyful</u> followed by <u>We Are the World.</u>

Sylvia smiled. She was moved by the whole experience, not deeply but moved nonetheless and walked away feeling a sense of renewal.

There was life after Peter she surmised. Here was Laurie extending a hand of friendship and a church and minister who breathed new signs of hope where all had been lost only a day or so earlier and Sylvia found herself feeling rejuvenated as she followed her cousin downstairs into the basement of the church. Here they found groups of people congregating in small clusters singing praises to the Lord while others gathered to discuss the sermon. Still, others busied themselves with the many pastries that crowded the banquet table against the far wall No sooner than Laurie hit the room she found herself surrounded by a host of adoring young men.

Turning to look for her cousin Laurie found Sill occupied by a rather congenial looking fellow. So this was Sill's type. He was tall and muscularly built and had a certain charm and swagger about him but Lord knows the brotha couldn't dress. Laurie had never seen him before but was glad that Sill had found someone to talk to and was not alone. There was nothing worse than being in a room full of people and not knowing anyone. What she didn't know was that Sill had fallen for the tall gentleman the first moment she laid eyes on him. And he her.

CHAPTER 8

❀

Three months later they were married. And though her parents accepted their daughter's choice they agreed that she didn't have that same sparkle in her eye that she'd had while dating Peter and both questioned her love for William. Mrs. Shipp believed that she was only marrying him to get about Peter. And Mr. Shipp had little or no opinion on the subject when he found out that William didn't fish.

In the beginning the union between the two was everything Sylvia could have asked for. It seemed obvious that they truly enjoyed each other's company and William Stanton—that was his name—had never been more ecstatic than he was with the vibrant and vivacious woman he'd chosen for his wife.

Not only was she beautiful and bubbly, she was bright and unbelievably sexy. And that made not only her made her more attractive to him but being that he was making significant strides climbing the corporate it made her a boon to him as well. The last thing he wanted to do was marry a nobody, who was content to remain a nobody with little or no aspirations of growing, and seeking new heights for herself. He hardly had to worry about that with Sylvia who after completing her Bachelors and teaching for a couple of years was insistent on acquiring her Masters in Education despite William wanting to spend some quality time with his newlywed before either of them embarked on any new endeavors.

When he finally convinced her to take off a year or two and concentrate on the house and their marriage she did so reluctantly and simply changed her focus from her own career goals to her husband's. Much to his surprise she was as adamant about his career goals as she'd been about her own. She insisted that he begin thinking about acquiring his own clientele instead of continually feeding the company's stockpile and receiving what amounted to a mere pittance in her eyes.

Loyal to a fault and lacking the insight, the intuition and self-confidence to move beyond corporate confines, of being little more than a company man, William Stanton was grateful for the opportunity at this stage in his career to just be working for such a distinguished firm as Hill and Morris. He could hardly understand his wife's not being thankful when he did his best to provide the best of everything for her. But the expensive and jewelry he purchased from Jacobs for her whenever he could usually went unnoticed.

For whatever reason, Sylvia hardly ever seemed to be impressed no matter what the price of an item and seemed to be just as content to don a pair of old faded Levi's and a sweatshirt as to throw on a Versace suit and a pair of Gucci loafers. The diamond studded necklace in the platinum setting he had custom made for her had all but wiped out his savings account and although she'd oohed and ahhed initially she'd only warn it one time and that was at his request.

He was soon coming to realize that what made most women happy had no effect on Sill at all. She was just as happy curled up in front of the fireplace at home reading a Zora Neal Hurston novel or a play by Wole Soyinka as she was stepping out to the opera or dinner at one of the plethora of hot new supper clubs springing up all over Atlanta's perimeter.

William, on the other hand felt more comfortable being out with Sill, sipping and mingling with a crowd than being cooped up in the house discussing some book or God forbid politics. All too often she tended to be all too knowing, too sensitive, too righteous but most of all, too damn liberal.

She was always preachin' and proselytizing and acting as if he was one of her students instead of her husband when the fact of the matter was she didn't make enough to make change let alone make a change.

Out in public amongst friends everybody loved him. And he could hold his own, diplomatically speaking. Always on cue, with a short funny well placed anecdote he had a great sense of humor and was never off color. And he'd learned to be cordial. Mingling and grinning even when he saw little humor in a remark his associates considered outrageously funny. William knew that that was essential to every marketing rep as well as a mainstay in the codebook for Black Republicans. Sometimes, even this became burdensome but it was still a far cry from sitting home with Sill on a Friday night discussing Baldwin's, *The Fire Next Time.*

At other times he had to sit and smile as he watched her devour book after book while he fought to remember the last book he'd read. Then other times lost in her own little world he wondered if she wasn't just a bit too bright and remembered the words of his daddy who proclaimed that too much book learnin' wasn't good fer nobody' and especially a niggra.

Yet, to be in her mere presence and to know that she was his and his alone, brilliant, untouched, and virginal was enough for William. To have her walk in and out of their library in her sheer silky lingerie feeding him late night snacks or to have her sit with her pretty legs propped up, her thick brown thighs cascading from beneath a violet or taupe tunic, firm pendulous breasts dangling from her camisole was enough to make William give praise to the gods. And though for some reason she had not been exactly receptive when it came to the act of lovemaking itself, William was sure that after some thirty odd years of virginity, the deflowering of this tree would certainly take more than the seasonal wind of a new marriage and so he accustomed himself with the occasional petting unless she had far too much to drink and then any slow refrain was gone and she was like an imprisoned tiger suddenly released from captivity, so ferocious was she in her response.

At first he had seriously thought she was frigid. But following one of ol' man Morris' dinner party he knew that even though she seemed to have some sexual issues, once he got past the wild laughter and the crying spells which all too often went hand-in-hand he had a wildcat on his hands. He had to admit that it scared him at first. The faraway look in her eyes was disturbing but anger she exhibited and the way she tore at his flesh made him wonder. Still, being little more than a novice himself when it came to sex he took it all in stride and only dreamed of the next time. He lusted after her nightly thereafter but to no avail.

In reality that was the only area in their marriage he really found lacking. It wasn't that she wasn't great in bed. When the mood struck her she could be a handful screaming and cursing and thrashing around until her energy expended she would orgasm in great leaping surges. Only problem William had was that it was so infrequent. Still, aside from her cold spells in the bedroom William was euphoric.

In the few years that had now passed since they'd been married he could honestly say that he was truly happy with every aspect of their marriage. Well, almost *every* aspect of their relationship. He had to admit that both he and Sill were adamant in their political views only she more grounded in hers. He was a part of that new wave of Black Republicans and not altogether confident in his political views. He at least knew it posed a change in what had always been and what he perceived as Blacks pandering to one party with little or no clout in the other.

Yet, aside from that, William loved him some Sill and as on every other night couldn't wait to get home to her.

She'd returned to teaching although third grade hardly provided the challenge she needed and so she'd transferred to the local high school and was positively ecstatic teaching ninth grade English. And aside from school she still stayed incredibly busy with the after-school program, the church advisory board, local charities and things of that nature. Yet, despite work and all of her extracurricular activities she always made sure that William was well taken care of.

She quickly became familiar with his favorite dishes and introduced him to the finer foods in an attempt to expand his tastes. She made sure that when they went out with his associates on business or just out together for a social gathering that she was the finest thing in the place and represented him well

At home, she made it her business to keep their marriage as new as their social life even though he really did nothing for her behind closed doors. But her mother had schooled her well. Telling her when she was younger never to believe the old adage that they way to a man's heart is through his stomach. 'That's a crock. Soon as a niggra's full he just' out dere looking fer somethin' else to whet his appetite. The key to a man, sweetheart, is to never let him get full but ta keep him wantin' fer mo' and the way you do that is to jes tease him. Let him lick the spatula and then tuck it way for another day.'

And no advice did Sylvia follow as well as she did this. Taking her mother's advice, Sylvia Stanton prided herself on being a bona fide tease in the bedroom and a queen in the living room. And in no time she had William panting over the plethora of nighties and costumes she would greet him with each evening. But seldom if ever did she do much more than whet poor William's appetite or let him lick the spatula. Never one to complain William followed the scenario with little or no complaints and continued to make inroads at work staying long after his co-workers were long gone. Always a firm believer that hard work and dedication was the key to success he found himself spending more and more time in the office and less time with Sill.

Not sure if this was what was bothering Sill or not William had noticed a definite change in her mood since he'd mentioned them starting a family. Each time the subject arose she would go into an uncontrollable rage and stop talking to him for days on end. It made no sense to William. Everyone that knew

Sill talked about the great rapport she had with her students. And it was the same at church where Sill had not one but three Sunday school classes and the kids simply adored her so he couldn't understand her not wanting children. Yet, if the discussion of children was responsible for the sudden divide between them then they didn't have to talk about his wanting kids or anything else that bothered her. It had already been three days since she'd uttered a word to him and three days was far longer than he could bear. Tonight when he went home he'd put an end to all the hostility and apologize before taking her out to her favorite Italian restaurant.

Arriving home that evening William found Sylvia on the loveseat, despondent. Her mascara had dripped black teardrops down her usually clear, cocoa complexion. Her hair was matted and collecting cotton by the minute. Her left breast dangled from the right side of her camisole. And for the first time since they were married, William could see Sill's mother. She had aged in that short amount of time or maybe he had just never taken the time to see her in this light. Always upbeat, moving, whistling or humming the latest tune by Sade, William knew something was now amiss. He had become accustomed to coming home to the pungent aroma of some new gourmet dish she was fixing or Sill, red pen in hand correcting papers with her favorite jazz or gospel radio station on, depending on her mood that day.

"Sill, are you okay?" William asked excitedly, his concern obvious.

Sylvia glanced in his direction but did not really acknowledge his presence. For the first time in their marriage, she did not try to mask the contempt she harbored for her husband. How often did she have to tell him that you didn't wear white pants in the middle of the winter?

"What's wrong, baby?" William was genuinely concerned and on the verge of panic now and Sill, not to make matters worse said matter-of-factly, "I fell down the stairs William. I think my ankle's broken."

"And you've been here like this all day? Why didn't you call someone?"

"William, if you knew the pain I'm in, you wouldn't ask such asinine question", Sill replied

Twenty minutes later, they arrived at Dr. Anderson's office. The good doctor took her right away. He was quite methodical in his examination and afterwards, much to Sill's relief, he determined that the ankle was not broken but severely sprained. Putting a soft cast on the ankle he informed her she could return to work when the pain subsided and gave her some extra strength Advil for the pain.

There was little in the way of conversation on the way home and William, now accustomed to her prolonged silences gave her her space. In obvious pain Sill remained bedridden that evening and the next day.

Two days later, William awoke to the smell of coffee and bacon. Her mood more upbeat than he'd seen it in sometime, Sill was heading out the back door when William entered the kitchen. She looked ravishing in her bright red dress and ruby red lipstick. This was the Sill that drove him crazy and made him proud in a crowd. Except for the blue cast that went from just below her knee to her foot, she seemed to have no recollection of the day before. William felt a sudden rise in his pajamas and reached for Sill who paid little attention.

"Grits and eggs are on the stove, bacon's in the oven," she said. "Gotta run, Sugar. Don't wanna be late." She gave him a peck on the cheek and was gone.

William poured himself a cup of Folgers threw a couple of slices of bacon on his plate, scooped up the grits before they got hard, placed a pat of butter on them and tossed his eggs on top. He had grown accustomed to Sill's fine breakfasts but tasted nothing this morning.

It was obvious that things had changed since he'd first met her six years ago. Sure, she cooked, cleaned, was the model homemaker, endeared herself to his clients in their home, at dinner parties and at formal functions but there had been little between them sexually for the past two years.

William wiped the grits from the corner of his mouth, swallowed the last sip of coffee and leaned back in the chair. He thought of their first year together and wondered what had changed. They'd spend every moment together that first year, hardly seeing or noticing the rest of the world. It had been work, Commuter's Cafe afterwards for a few drinks and then upstairs to the mezzanine for a few more rounds while Sill danced the night away. He didn't dance and had a hard time watching her dance the night away with the various faces but somehow rationalized it by knowing that at the end of the evening she would be leaving with him.

He'd begun to drink more and more since he met Sill in a vain attempt to mask his inferiority, his insecurity. Sure he'd graduated Morehouse *Magna Cum Laude* and president of his senior class but he never really felt a part of the campus social life.

Put him in ol' Doc Mayberry's English literature class and he could recite passage after passage from *Chaucer's Canterbury Tales* verbatim, but ask him about the importance of Malcolm and Martin and he hadn't a clue. Ask him about Langston or Zora or Nikki or Maya and…When the brothers got together on the yard to kick it about the Knicks chances this year he was truly at a loss.

He always considered himself an outsider and didn't date often. In fact, he'd only had one date while at the "House", as Morehouse was called, and that had been with a white girl who, after offering her assistance in preparing for a Statistics Exam, offered herself as well.

William, not too far from his home in Beaufort, South Carolina was smart enough to know proper protocol even if O.J. didn't. He still faced ridicule, on a daily basis, from what he termed the short-term frat brothers. These were the brothers he never met but felt he knew so well. Their first semester on campus was usually spent checkin' out the females, a forty ounce of beer in one hand a blunt in the other. Bob Marley or Sizzla blasting from the boom box until campus police showed up to disperse the gathering after many an accusation and much name calling. Academic probation usually followed along with a now much concerted, occasional visit to class. By the time summer school rolled around, they were history, sporting Morehouse caps and t-shirts in Philly, D.C. and other urban areas better known as home.

William couldn't understand these brothers and spent many a night discussing the situation with his roommate, Abdul, a pre-med student from Nigeria. "I just can't understand it. Given every opportunity to make something of themselves and they're still out here playing the fools. Then when shit doesn't happen and they flunk out they're the first ones to blame the White man."

His roommate usually concurred by stating, "In my country…"

One thing William did admire was the way the brothers dressed but he simply couldn't understand how they could afford the $150 Nikes and platinum chains on financial aid.

There was one brother in William's English Literature class known only as 'Black', who seemed to enjoy the class almost as much as William did but unlike William, Black was equally at home with the brothers on the yard in spite of his academic achievements. Black had the rather unique ability to balance a high G.P.A. as well as a stellar rep for bein' a down brotha on the yard and William admired him not only for this but for understandin' black folks and the way they thought. Black tried to explain the dilemma to William one day, after class as they walked across campus together. William was astounded by the number of people who spoke and seemed to know Black.

"What's up, Black?" "Ain't nothin' my brother, how you?"

Classes were changing and William could barely get a word in for the countless salutations. Made him feel good just being with the brother. For the first time in four years, other blacks nodded and spoke to him as well. He felt recognized and he liked the feeling.

On the way, they decided to grab a cup of coffee and finish their conversation. This ain't Beaufort, my brother. This here's *Hotlanta* so baby, when you come, you got to come correct. Know that ahm sayin'?"

It was obvious William didn't understand and was having a hard time trying to grasp what Black had to say. Black, realizing this broke it down in the following manner: "For four hundreds years, Black people ain't been given nothing but hard times and bubble gum. Then Mr. Charlie says he's fresh outta bubble gum. So what's left? Whatcha leavin' me? Nothin'! Nothing but hard times. We tried to do that Jesse Jackson thang. You know, keep hope alive, refusing to give up, refusing to quit, and we didn't. We didn't give up. We didn't crawl up in no hole and just go away neither. We jumped when we had to jump, shuffled when we had to shuffle, danced when we had to dance and did it better than anyone else considerin'. Then when Malcolm and Martin and Thurgood came along they gave us the opportunity. They opened the door, kinda like Berry Gordy and Motown. And along with that came some hope. And that's all we needed. We just exploded onto the whole national scene. Know what ah'm sayin', dog? This was our time to shine."

William was still at a loss.

"Whatcha sayin' Black? I mean what's the point? Black went on not the least bit discouraged by Williams' inability to grasp his meaning.

"It's kinda like ol' Doc Mayberry was sayin' when he was talkin' about Virgil and the Trojan Horse. You step out here in some soiled overalls, do you think anybody's gonna give you the time of day? You can be a financial wizard, my brother. I'm sayin'. You go down to Wall Street *without* a suit or tie, you're gonna come home the same way, unemployed. You've got a problem with the brothas wearing expensive gear and not havin' two pennies to rub together and that's because you're not understandin' the brotha's. Let me break it down for you. Black people know that the man ain't interested in what he's got inside, how bright he is or what he's capable of. They ain't really interested in that at all.

But Black people wearing expensive gear are like the Grecians who built that big ol' shiny horse to fool the people of Troy. You see we know that if they like what they see they may let us in the gate and then and only then can we begin to let them see what's on the inside.

It's the only way to win the war, my brother. This ain't Russia and you ain't Pushin. This here's America and ain't no such thing as merit before skin color.

Now I know that a lot of these brothers be wearin' a lot of expensive gear, and ain't nothing; on the inside but how else they gonna express themselves and put their best foot forward? And if they ain't got nothin' on the inside then they'd better at least shine on the outside. They just strugglin' like you and me brotha. Just tryin to put their best foot forward and present themselves in the best possible light they can. Can't blame 'em for that now can you, Will?" William smiled.

But he did. Blamed 'em for puttin' somethin' on instead of putting something in those empty heads of theirs and all they were doing was perpetuating the stereotype and making hard working brothas like him look bad. Not long after that he joined the Young Black Republican Party at Morehouse. There were a total of three other members, including his roommate and he was soon appointed the chapter's first president.

As William pushed himself back form the kitchen table and looked at the big screen T.V., which took up only a tiny corner of the rather spacious living room he thought of Black for the first time in years and laughed out loud. He needs to see me now he thought to himself.

William graduated Morehouse in the summer of '89 with a degree in Business and Finance and was soon employed by Hill and Morris in the fall as an account executive. He was promoted senior executive quicker than anyone else had in the history of the company and was given one of their largest accounts to add to his portfolio. There was no misconception as to why he was given this particular account and even though the annual commission from the Nigerian account alone put him his salary in the six figure bracket it also put him at odds with Sylvia who looked at him as simply a pawn in the whole scheme of things. To William it seemed like if there had been a turning point in their relationship in their marriage which had seemed oh so promising then taking that one account was the reason. That had to be it. That's when he first recognized the permanent change in attitude and he couldn't understand why his success bothered her so. After all, his success was her success as well. He just couldn't understand it.

Their first couples of years of marriage were picture perfect. Cezanne couldn't have created anything more lovely. When Sill wasn't involved in some school related function she spent a good portion of her time decorating the plush, Victorian styled home, while William spent the majority of his time working on streamlining his account presentations and studying market fluctuations. At night they'd sip hot chocolate, though Sill more often than not preferred a glass of Zinfandel before joining him in front of the fireplace and making small talk until the wee hours of the morning.

Between teaching, their new home, and being a trustee at the First Methodist A.M.E. Zion Church, Sill had her hands full. Problem was, when she finished her attempts at interior decorating and gotten well into the groove of teaching and into the rhythm of marriage, Sill was somewhat at a loss as to what to do next. What bothered her more than anything wasn't the idea of marriage or the marriage itself. It was the fact that somewhere in the deepest recesses of her heart and her soul she wasn't sure that she was capable of loving a man at all but and if she was one thing was apparent. William was not the man.

At first the idea of marriage so appealed to her that she figured that in due time she could learn to love him, but well due time had come and gone and she was no more sure about him now than when she said I do. If anything she was finding it increasingly difficult to even talk to him let alone have a relationship. The more she talked to William, the more she felt she'd made a huge mistake. Several times she found herself searching for some common ground, and more often than not, she found herself coming up empty. There was little question that she cared about William. What bothered Sylvia was the way in which she cared.

She often thought of the tiny Labrador puppy daddy brought home from work one day when she was a little girl. The first few months Sylvia and the tiny, black Lab had been all but inseparable. After that, the novelty worn thin; Sill walked and fed the puppy only because she had agreed to do so and, despite her appearance of grief, was actually relieved when she returned from school one cold, winter afternoon to find he'd been in an accident and daddy had to have him put to sleep,

Sylvia Stanton welcomed her return to work. The daily routine at West Lansing gave her a sense of worth, of well-being. And after missing a day it was especially rewarding. The concern from students and colleagues was overwhelming and reassuring to say the least. And although she no longer had third graders she still enjoyed the challenges that came with teaching.

Terrance Daniels, the first year teacher from New York, was the first to approach her. She'd noticed him out of the corner of her eye but had never had the opportunity to speak or welcome him to West Lansing. She'd always been too busy.

As he approached her she dismissed her students' inquiries concerning her accident and sent them scurrying off to their respective homerooms.

"Missed you yesterday. How's the leg, or is it the ankle?"

"It's the ankle and its fine" Sylvia stuttered" Just fine."

"Everyone was worried about you," he said, "We're certainly glad to have you back, Mrs. Stanton. I know your kids are also. Don't think they cared too much for your sub."

"Thanks, Mr. Daniels," she said. "It's only been a day."

"Some days can seem like a lifetime, Mrs. Stanton." He winked at her and hurried to his classroom, beaming.

Terrance Daniels had finally gathered the courage to at least speak to Mrs. Sylvia Stanton. The big question still remained in his eyes though. Could he hold his own with this beautiful Black woman?

Terrance had always been a tad apprehensive when approaching a woman of Sylvia's stature. He was sure at this point in his life that he'd overcome this nagging hang-up but here it was raising its ugly head again, dammit!

Sylvia Stanton was certainly no Halle Berry. No she wasn't even Lena Horne or Angela Bassett. In his eyes she was more of a Cicely Tyson. Simple black elegance. No doubt he'd dated more beautiful women in his life but Sylvia's beauty emanated mostly from within and in his eyes she was radiant.

The fact that she was a teacher mattered little. He'd dated teachers before or at least those who fashioned themselves as teachers. Most were non-descript dates making him almost glad he'd completed his schooling when he did and didn't have any children. Those he'd come into contact with lately made the old adage, 'When all else fails, you can always teach,' seem even more prophetic than usual.

Sylvia somehow was different though, having what Terrance deemed the most important quality of an effective teacher. She had a genuine love for her students, her 'babies' as she liked to refer to them. The feeling being mutual made her classroom more conducive to learning than most

Without giving it a second thought, without thinking he made it a point to meet her, during her planning period in the Staff Lounge. This meant giving up his usual third period cigarette in the back of the sixth grade hall. When he entered, she was sitting, leg crossed at the small round table, red pen in hand marking papers. Seating himself across from her he took it upon himself to break the uncomfortable silence.

"Been looking forward to talking to you for some time, Mrs. Stanton. The word around here is that you're a fantastic teacher. My kids all seem to agree."

"I've heard the same about you, Mr. Daniels. Not only do the children love you, it seems a good deal of the female teachers feel the same way. What have you been doing to these women, Mr. Daniels?" Sill asked, smiling broadly.

"I don't know what you're talking about, Mrs. Stanton. If anything I'm just trying to get the inside scoop on next year's Teacher-of-the-Year. The word is you're a shoo-in."

"Only if you stop teaching, Mr. Daniels,"

"I've done my best to pick up pointers here and there. I make sure to keep my eyes and ears open."

Terrance grinned widely now.

"So I've heard. My kids tell me everything. From what I've heard your interest tends to be more than just professional."

Terrance blushed. The flirtation continued, and she did little in the way of curtailing it, suddenly feeling very much at ease in his company.

"I guess I am guilty of trying to get to know you through your students," Terrance confessed finally."

"Why didn't you just come and ask me what you wanted to know. I'm forever telling my students continually that the only bad question is the one not asked."

"You're absolutely right, Mrs. Stanton, but you've got to be very careful about the kinds of questions you ask nowadays. Sexual harassment suits are running rampant."

"I'm pretty sure a handsome young man such as yourself hardly has to harass anyone,"

"Funny thing Mrs. Stanton, I feel at ease talking to most of my colleagues but in your case it's a little different. I'm not sure in your case my motives are above reproach. There's also the fact that you're married. Frankly Mrs. Stanton, there were times when I really wished it was an unhappy marriage." As soon as he said that he caught himself. He knew he'd crossed the line.

Sylvia Stanton smiled politely the way airline stewardesses and hostess often do, picked up her paperwork, checked her watch and headed back to her next class.

Now he wished he'd had gone for that smoke instead. Just before he was about to curse his own stupidity, Sylvia Stanton turned and stared at him. This time there was no smile. Terrance cringed in anticipation of what was to follow.

"Mr. Daniels, every rainbow does not have a pot of gold at the end and every marriage isn't a happy marriage."

Terrance was stunned He stood there unable to reply. Speechless. *Perhaps there was hope after all.* Feeling energized, Terrance's classes went exceptionally well that day. In fact, they went well for the next few weeks but he was no closer to luring Sylvia than he had been before their conversation.

A month and a half passed, Sylvia's cast was removed. Spry as ever she moved back and forth between classes almost always accompanied by an entourage of students and yet still managed to maintain Terrance's attention without so much as saying a word. When the school day ended at three fifteen Mrs. Stanton was the first one out the door. *Gone.* And when the one opportunity did present itself for Terrance to ask her out for a drink she hadn't even bothered to respond.

Months passed by and Terrance was no closer to knowing Sylvia Stanton than he'd been that day in the lounge. In fact, he felt he was losing not only ground but losing face as well. Days in the classroom grew longer, the monotony made him long for Easter vacation. He still saw her from time to time in passing. And at times, he caught himself staring at her and had difficulty averting his gaze.

On the home front, things had definitely taken a turn for the worse. Sylvia blamed herself for the problems, for the lack of communication. William, in turn, began spending more and more time at the office. Regardless of who was to blame it bothered Sill nonetheless. If William wasn't faithful that was no reason for her to take her vows any less lightly. After all, her commitment was not simply between her and William but more importantly between her and God.

In William's case, this was the first time in his career he'd actually felt the pressure of his workload. Everyone knew the decreasing profits in the Nigerian account were due in large part to the 1998 legislation forbidding the sale of ivory. However, the current Civil War and military regime were also factors putting a damper on potential monies and investments. He had other accounts. Sure. But the combined total did not come close to this one Third World account. This was his creation, his baby. Ol' Man Morris, one of the founders of Hill and Morris and Chairman of the Board had even taken the time to stop by Williams' office earlier in the week to discuss the account which was the company's third largest.

"William, it's been quite a while," he began. "How've you been? I've been meaning to stop by for some time now but with the misses receiving chemotherapy it's been kind of difficult finding the time. Certainly do miss being on the frontline though. Sometimes you get too comfortable sitting in the home office. You probably won't believe this but I really miss the selling, the different cities, the bickering—the challenge. The only thing I never cared for was the constant traveling. Nothing like being out there on the frontline, though. By the way, how's Sill? Doing well, I hope. Good! Good! Still teaching is she? Honorable profession. Doesn't get nearly enough recognition. I figured you'd have a couple of kids by now. Everything O.K. at home?"

"Fine, sir," William responded.

William wondered if the old man had gotten wind of his declining account. Was Morris, who made a fortune being able to read clients' strengths and weaknesses in a matter of half-a-heartbeat trying to get a feel for his account losses or was this just a social visit. William knew it wasn't. He really wished the Ol' Man would get to the point.

"You know; William, I started this agency forty-one years ago and believe you me, there were plenty of ups and downs but the most important lesson I learned in all those years came from my daddy. God rest his soul. At his best, he was nothing more than a backwoods dirt farmer. But Poppa used to always tell me, 'Plow to the end of the road son.' Wasn't 'til I was a grown man that I fully understood what he was trying to tell me. Well anyway, it's good to see you again, William. Give me a call from time to time son and let me know how you're doing. And be sure to give Sill my regards."

William got up to shake Mr. Morris's hand. But the Ol' Man did not rise. Instead he instructed William, "Sit down, son. Don't be in such a rush to get rid of an old man. This old man may be able to teach you a thing or two."

William eased back into his chair. Morris continued.

"You might want to consider taking a month or so to get away. Take Sylvia, fly to Nigeria and stay a while. Reacquaint yourself with your clients and relax. Lagos is a beautiful city, rich in tradition, yet as cosmopolitan as New York and London. I think you'll like it. I know I did. And don't worry about anything. I think we'll be able to hold the fort down until you get back."

William was at once both stunned and ecstatic. He hadn't expected this and he hadn't had a vacation, hadn't even thought about taking one since joining the firm close to seven years ago. No question, he needed one. And Sylvia would die! Africa! She would literally die! Ol' Man Morris rose from the chair. This time William followed his lead. Slowly he rose, breathing a deep sigh of relief. The two men shook hands and the meeting ended.

"You know, William, we didn't have this as an option when I was coming up. Fortunately, we're a little better off now, so take advantage of it and above all else, enjoy yourself."

William was elated. Seeing the Ol' Man exit the building, William hot on the Ol' Man's heels, kissed his secretary, Melinda on the cheek then headed out to tell Sill the news.

"I'll be out of the office the rest of the day. If there's anything urgent, text me," he told Melinda.

CHAPTER 9

Sylvia, deeply immersed in thought, rummaged through the West Lansing High School yearbook pictures again. Coming across a picture of Mr. Daniels, she was forced to smile.

'Handsome devil. If I wasn't married, I might have to give him a little taste', Sill whispered, giggling to herself as she took another bite of the pastrami and Swiss sandwich and sipped the Zinfandel. Turning up the volume on the stereo, she never heard William come in.

"Sill, how you doin' babe? How was school?" he asked her. Sill was still leafing through the yearbook. "Got some great news, baby."

"William, is that you? Goodness! You frightened me, 1 didn't hear you come in. I was in another world."

"Speaking of another world," William said, Ol' Man Morris dropped by my office today. Thought it would be a good idea if I got away—took a vacation—reacquaint myself with some of my clients. And then he dropped a bomb on me. Sill baby, it's an opportunity of a lifetime—a chance to see the world. You and me baby, all expenses paid. Know what a trip like that would cost?"

Sill interrupted William,

"Whoa, whoa! Slow down, William. You're rambling. Start from the beginning."

William took a deep breath and told her about the huge, fledgling overseas account and Morris' suggestion, which was really no suggestion at all. By the time he'd finished, he'd dressed it up to look like a goodwill tour. Sylvia instantly saw through the facade. This was one of the reasons that Ol' Man

Morris held Sill in such high esteem. She was sharp and he knew it. She was also tactful, but not tonight.

"William, let me ask you a question. How many other Black males are there at the agency?"

"Not tonight Sill, Okay? Not tonight." William was in no mood for her hard-nosed observations or a class on the racial injustices that plagued the poor and disenfranchised. "Just answer my question, William. How many African-American males are there with Hill and Morris not counting file clerks, mail boys and janitors?"

"C'mon, Sill, you know the answer to that."

"Answer my questions, William. Better yet, how many are there in management? C'mon, humor me. William, how many African-American are there besides you and how many Third World accounts do they have?"

"What's the point, Sill?"

"The point is they're using you. They're using you to do their dirty work. No longer can America just waltz into foreign countries and take what they want—especially Third World Countries. Colonialism is dead. Dead! Dead! Dead! So, now they send dumb, money-hungry Negroes to do their dirty work and call them ambassadors and envoys. But it's the same ol' story. Anyway, you want to dress it up; it's the same ol' story. It's exploitation."

"Call it what you want, Sill. I see it as an opportunity that may never come along again in life. It's exploitation when you vacation in Las Vegas or Miami, and put your money in the hands of the same people that are taxing the hell out of each paycheck if you really think about it. It's exploitation when you buy pack after pack of those cancer sticks knowing you're being targeted, taxed and terminated all at the same time." William smiled knowing he'd hit a nerve.

"C'mon, William, we've talked about this before. Look at Mike."

"Mike who?"

"Michael Jordan!!"

"Michael Jordan? What the hell are you talking about? What the hell does Michael Jordan have to do with you and me taking a trip to Africa?"

"Just humor me for a minute, William. I'm gonna tell you. Look! Jordan signs a contract with Nike for a few million and every little nappy headed little Black boy and girl runs out, buys a pair of sneakers so they can be like Mike. Meanwhile the good ol' boys at Nike are making billions. Billions! But who's looking at the bigger picture? It's time we started seeing the bigger picture, William. Don't you see what Ol' Man Morris is doing? Can't you see how they're using you? Vacation, hell. Tell the old man to send Jack Thomas and let you do Jack's bidding in Rio. See what he says. You and I both know that if it weren't for the anti-American sentiment and military regime in power you'd probably be down on the unemployment line with the rest of the outta work brothers. Morris pays you a hundred grand a year and makes how many millions from your account? Think about it, William."

Pouring himself a drink, William continued to listen listlessly. After all, he'd heard it all before.

"Look, William, if you can create and maintain one of the largest accounts for one of the largest, most prestigious import-export firms on the East Coast then you can certainly establish your own."

"Right, Sill." William sipped his drink smugly as Sill paid homage to his creative abilities and business acumen.

"Look at Magic."

"Magic who?"

"Magic Johnson."

"Oh, here we go again." William was teasing her now and enjoying it. Sill, so adamant in her views, hardly realized.

"Magic Johnson led the Lakers to the championship, I don't know how many times. A grown man running down the court in his boxers while millions watched. But Magic knew he was being used and grinned all the way to the bank. He was the one filling the Forum while owner, Jerry Buss was filling his pockets. But Magic was no Michael. He had the foresight and the common sense to get a piece of the pie. Now he's part owner of the Lakers.

He's got someone runnin' up and down the court for him now. And the sneakers he endorses are his own. He owns the company. Now everyone knows that Magic ain't no rocket scientist. Remember his talk show? But at least he has the good sense to realize his own self-worth. I said all that to say that there is no reason you shouldn't be looking for a piece of Hill and Morris, a partnership, William, or even better, your own firm."

William had heard enough.

"All that's fine until we hit hard times. I open my own company, the market changes and for the first time in your life you can't shop the way you want, the way you're used to shopping, then we'll see how all your liberal self-help principles stand up. Take away those T-bone steaks and taters you're so fond of and we'll see what those little tight-fittin' outfits got to hang onto. Take away the T.V., stereo, getting your hair and nails done once a week and you'll be one evil Black woman. All those little things add up. The washer, the dryer, and all the other things you take for granted now are all that separate you from all the rest of those old beat up nags with no money and no man. So don't tell me any-thing about Hill and Morris when you're steady reaping the benefits from them. The house you live in, the car you drive, the food you stick in your big ol' liberal mouth and settles on those big, broad liberal hips of yours are all the result of Hill and Morris, thank you very much." William was visibly shaking now but his anger did little to deter Sill.

"Wait just one goddamn minute, William Stanton," Sill was standing and on the verge of screaming now. "I have lived off of my own salary and it has been that little meager teacher salary that has paid for my car note and our food since we've been married. I took care of myself before I met you and will continue to do so when you're dead and gone. And as far as needing washers and dryers and fancy cars to boost my self-esteem, let me tell you one thing, since you wanna be 'lil Clarence Thomas. I have enough pride in myself that I don't have to buy a German-made car or Italian-made suits to feel good about myself. And as far as these liberal lips and hips are concerned, you didn't say a word last night when you were running around here panting like a dog in heat tryin' to get next to these ol' broad hips."

William was truly agitated. How long had it been since they'd slept in the same room, let alone the same bed? Her continual rejection was a source of much of his frustration, if not most of it.

"Damn, woman! I'm so tired of that ol' tired-assed sixties bullshit, I don't know what to do. You're the same type of nigga I went to school with that was in one semester and out the next. Steady talkin' that backdoor, back-alley, lib-eral bullshit. All of them niggas together didn't have a pot to piss in or a win-dow to throw it out of. Runnin' 'round campus talkin' 'bout how they wouldn't have been no slave. Picture that. If we'd all acted like that there wouldn't be any of us here now. Same niggas are back at home right now slavin' at McDonald's and still talkin' about what they gonna do and what they not gonna do. Simple ass, hypocritical niggas, talkin' about makin' some damn changes in the sys-tem. How much change you gonna be able to make, makin' five and a quarter an hour. And like it or not somebody's gotta still get out there and shuffle today so that our children can see a better day tomorrow. I do it for you and I do it for them goddammit. You better be steppin' and fetchin', and shufflin'too if you expect to be in a position to give somethin' back. Shit, talk is cheap.

How many niggas are out there reciting that liberal bullshit are actually in a position to give dollars? With all your ideas and lofty ambitious how many of your young and gifted students have you put through school? Hell, you can't even pay your own way! Sure, you prepare them but preparing them isn't paying their tuition. C'mon, talk to me, baby! What's your claim to fame? What? The best prepared college students at Mickey D's."

Sill had never seen William this angry before.

"All I'm trying to say is that-"

"You ain't sayin' nothin!" William, his rage and frustration obvious, cut her off. "You can't tell me a damn thing. Not a damn thing. Nothin'. At least nothin' I ain't heard before. I know what Black people had to endure in order to get where they are. I'm living proof. Tell me something I don't know."

"Look, William," she said, "I applaud your contributions to—what is it? The United Negro College Fund? But damn, so does George Bush and right now I don't see a whole lotta difference. Here you are siphoning millions of dollars from Lagos, from poor people so your ass can drive around in a brand new Mercedes. You're making close to a hundred grand a year. You donate five of that because your accountant tells you that you need a tax write-off and you've got the nerve, the gall, to think you've done your part. When in reality, you haven't done a damn tiling when you turn around and make a donation to the Republican Party. Shit! You've just negated any contribution you've made to the United Negro College Fund.

Hell, if my granddaddy knew I'd married a Republican and a Black Republican to boot he would turn over in his grave. How many of them are you altogether? Five? Doesn't that tell something? You might as well get a rope and just start hangin' the brothas yourself. You ain't any better than what's his name? The senator from your home state, what's his name? That Thurmond from South Carolina. Yeah, Strom Thurmond or that so-called black Lieutenant Governor from Maryland."

Logical, persuasive, cunning, Sill was in her element now. Never having seen him this angry, Sill reached for William's hand but this only angered him more.

"Look! If you really wanna do something, William, something for me, for the community then stop parading around here in your expensive car, and your extravagant home on the hill and your 'ready for every occasion' woman and your I-got mine-get-yours attitude that don't say nothin' except that I sho' is glad to be up on the hill wit' you good white folks. It's just sad. You are really sad, William.

And by the way since we're on the subject of things I'm tired of, another thing I'm tired of is you thinking that I belong to you, that I'm just another one of your possessions. Truth of the matter is, I'm good for you and if you haven't figured that out, just ask your lily-white counterparts down at the agency. They know it. They respect me even if they don't agree with my politics but they'll never respect you because they recognize you for what you are and that's a goddamn puppet. A fuckin' sell-out.

When you get to Nigeria and look into the eyes of some those that are less fortunate than you, ask yourself one question. Ask yourself, *'What price fame?'* Why, you're no better than the African who sold his brother and sisters into bondage for some damn trinkets."

Sill threw the pastrami sandwich down, marched into the kitchen, pulled out a tray of ice scattering it everywhere in her haste and anger and reached for the bottle of Jack Daniels. Empty, it dawned on her that she'd finished it days ago. "Silly, nigga," she muttered not really caring whether he heard her or not.

"What did you call me? Silly nigga?" William was livid "This silly nigga who takes care of your fat Black ass knows one thing. You're gonna pick up every bit of that goddamn ice you got all over the floor."

"Fat Black ass? Tell me! Please tell me you didn't say that. My ass wasn't too fat last night when you were trying to get next to it."

"Sill trust me. You're not all that you think you are, in or out of bed."

Sill not to be out done but knowing that she was wasting her time simply replied, "You know what they say, William. One man's garbage is another man's gold."

William was out for blood now and Sill realizing this regained her composure. After all, there was no reason to make matters worse. William was lost. Hopeless.

"I think its best we don't say anything else to each other tonight, William. This is obviously something that's been brewing awhile. Perhaps I'm just not what you need at this juncture in your life. Maybe your trip will do us both some good. It'll give us some time to think." Sill was sure William would reconsider taking Ol' Man Morris' offer now.

William, though thrown for a curve by Sill's latest barrage also managed to regain his composure.

"Look Sill, a lot of things were said in anger that probably shouldn't have been said, but let's not be hasty."

There was little question of William's love for his wife and the thought of separating on these terms was more than William bargained for. Repeating his travel plans, Sill was stunned by William's sudden stubbornness.

"You haven't heard a word I've said, William Stanton." And on that note Sylvia grabbed her keys, her pocketbook and was out of the door.

"Don't do this, Sylvia!" William pleaded. "Don't!"

Sylvia walked towards the garage door, backed the ten-year-old Ford down the long u-shaped drive way, through the wrought iron fence, ignoring William's desperate pleas.

In her rush to leave, she'd forgotten her cigarettes. Relieved and alone and realizing that she had absolutely nowhere to go, Sill stopped at the local convenience store grabbed a pack of *Newport's* and a *Pepsi* and made her way back to the car.

Sill thought of her last visit to the bank and the encounter with the ever so debonair Mr. Davis and immediately began the search for his business card. Finding it tucked away ever so neatly in the corner of her purse she paged the number printed on the front. Waiting for the call back, she realized she hadn't seen his son Stephan in school since last semester when classes were switched over. She tried calling Edwin again but there was still no answer. Her banker and real-estate broker Edwin was the divorced, single-parent of two of her brightest students and a fellow church member. Financially secure, he'd always made it plain that any time she came to her senses and had the good sense to leave William he'd be there to pick up the pieces.

Two teenage boys, sporting beginner dreadlocks and those baggy jeans she just couldn't get used to, be-bopped over to the phone. She started to head over to the phone to tell them she was waiting for a call and then hesitated. William would never have permitted this. A similar situation had occurred on their way to Maryland a few years ago.

William had driven around in circles for what seemed like forever in search of a phone booth because he refused to ask a young Black man how long he would be on the phone. "Too many crazy people out there. They'd just as soon shoot you as say 'hello'," he'd told her as they rode around in circles lost looking for an empty phone booth. She made it a point to pick up a cell phone the very next day but hardly ever remembered to bring it with her. She cursed William again to herself as she stepped out of the car and approached the young man. "Excuse me sir, I'm waiting for a call."

The teenager spun around with looks to kill. His scowl melted almost as soon as he glanced at Sill. "Lord, have mercy! You say you need to use the phone?" he questioned, looking at her up and down, devouring her with his eyes.

"Yes, sir, I'm waiting for a call."

The young man hung the phone up, almost immediately. "No problem, mommy. No problem at all. Anything else I can help you with?"

"Thanks but no thanks, poppy." Sill smiled at the boyish attempts at flirtation. She waited another five minutes or so still glancing at the young men, now just standing there waiting, laughing, as only idle young men do. Sill headed for the car. As she did, one of the young men remarked loud enough for her to hear. "If he could see what I'm seeing, mommy, he would be the one calling."

Sill smiled, self-consciously. In her haste to get out of the house or better yet away from William, Sill did little more than put on some lipstick. She still wore the sheer blue Danskin stretch pants, cut-off t-shirt and navy blue heels. Not in a million years would she have considered wearing an outfit like this out in public. It was just a little somethin' somethin' she threw on to keep his libido on high. She cursed William again before donning the navy blue blazer she kept in the back seat of the car to cover some of her nakedness. Lighting a cigarette, she emptied the ashes from the ashtray and returned to the phone booth. Leafing through her phone book, Sylvia considered going back home, knowing full well her stubborn pride would not permit her to.

CHAPTER 10

Terrance Daniels didn't usually entertain on school nights. In fact, he rarely entertained at all anymore. Most, if not all of the women he dated in the last year or so left something to be desired. He hated to generalize, but the fact of the matter was, the attractive women rarely worked on anything besides being attractive and the ones he could hold meaningful conversations with did little or nothing for his libido. He was still wondering what it took to get the whole package. Countless dates later he'd given up trying to answer that question altogether.

And the only reason Laura Harrington gained entrance on this rainy night was that his neighbor Marcy who lived in the townhouse a few doors down called to ask if he had today's newspaper and not wanting to see her walking at night he'd met her halfway. Standing outside watching to make sure she got home safely he noticed a car pulling up in his guest parking spot and as soon as he saw those legs that seemed to never stop getting out of the car he knew that it could only be one person and one person only with legs so long and so shapely as those now striding towards him.

Laura Harrington was a dancer he'd met several years ago. Voluptuous and yet still cute, Laura Harrington had a pleasant, if not pretty face and oh yes, legs for days. Close to six feet tall, shapely was neither the appropriate word nor best suited word when one took the liberty of describing her.

When they'd first met and she informed Terrance that she was a dancer, he could for the first time in his life understand why men would go to a club and pay to see a woman dance. He still wouldn't pay but he could at least understand and it wasn't long before he found himself picking her up in front of the swanky club after the show.

She, with fists full of dollars soldiers had stuffed in her G-string, would saunter through the parking lot, grinning, grinding, for her adoring fans, open the car door and slide in. Before Terrance could exit the parking lot good, Laura would burst into tears.

In the beginning, Terrance had tried to soothe her bruised ego. But after two or three of these episodes, Terrance stopped buying tissues for the car opting instead to just let Laura direct him to her favorite motel where she could use all the tissue she wanted. The first few minutes there, Laura wanted to do little more than cuddle. The crying would subside after a few minutes and then she would be on him like a fly on slop, passionately trying to exorcise her demons. Still, with all the intimacy they'd never really gotten to know each other. Terrance knew he was partially to blame for this, for wanting nothing more than being this close to a beautiful woman. But after no more than a month he came to the ugly realization that their relationship was nothing more than one of lust and passion. No more than just a physical thing. And for a while it didn't seem to matter.

Laura Harrington, or 'Candy', as she was more commonly referred to on stage, with those long slender legs was a cult figure among strip club patrons but Terrance soon realized after having dinner with Laura and some of her friends that he really didn't want to be among her circle of friends. To make matters worse the girl was unparalleled in bed. And this was not a good thing.

On stage, Laura could make things move and jiggle that Terrance hardly knew existed. Under the spotlight at the club she undulated like mad bringing the crowd of both men and women to their feet with each performance.

Always the last to go on stage, Candy knew how to work the crowd and was the clubs top attraction. The men would literally fight to be able to shove a twenty in her G-string. But, as talented as 'Candy' was on stage, Laura was just that bad in bed.

Their relationship lasted a few months, ending after Terrance grew weary of the relationship which had now become nothing more than a series of half hour stops at the city's cheapest motels. Tired of the whole charade, one day he simply stopped calling.

Laura hardly took the break-up in stride. And although she must have certainly seen it coming she enjoyed the little time they shared. And yet, the more Terrance tried to distance himself, the more adamant Laura became about keeping their relationship together. It was certainly obvious that she hadn't experienced anything remotely close to the time and love Terrance had shown her and was content with the way things were. And it was soon pretty obvious that Laura was not going to let go or simply walk away without the situation getting ugly.

Terrance, desperate now for his former lifestyle and some peace of mind, was forced to confess his disappointment in their relationship. When this had no effect, Terrance simply alluded to the fact that he did not find her compatible in the bedroom. Devastated by this revelation, Laura not only left the relationship, she left town.

Most recently, Terrance had the occasion to bump into her at Designer Shoes in the mall. It had to have been at least three or four years since the break up but it was easy to see what had attracted him to her in the first place. Laura had gained a pound or two but was still as gorgeous as ever. Men's heads turned constantly as they hugged and made small talk outside of the shoe store. There were even a few women who found themselves forced to turn and look at Laura. Seems Laura had done quite well for herself since their last meeting, opening a chain of spas and tanning salons. She was in Atlanta promoting the chain and would be here until she found a relatively inexpensive piece of real estate in which to open another.

Exchanging numbers, as people do who haven't seen each other and who have shared something intimate and special at one time or another in their lives, Terrance never but never expected Laura to show up at the front door of his townhouse out of the clear blue and without phoning first. After all, years had passed. And although he was still mesmerized by those long, slender legs and more than ample thighs, which Terrance believed, had grown even longer and more firm, it was the same ol' Laura. Buffed and polished on the outside. On the inside, Laura was still a gem in the rough.

Inviting her in, seated on the pastel loveseat in front of the fire place, Terrance and Laura reminisced while they sipped glass after glass of some Merlot he had tucked away for just such an occasion as this. Two and a half carafes of wine later, Terrance learned more of her travels and business ventures than he cared to know. She was still single; still looking for a meaningful long-term relationship but had stopped dating since most of the men she'd met in the last year and a half or so left so much to be desired. Terrence wondered if this last statement about long-term relationship was an attempt to try to work things out after so many years. Glancing down at her shapely legs and thighs, Terrance wondered what else she'd learned since she'd been away.

Before he could venture to find out, the phone rang. Excusing himself, Terrance caught another glance at Laura's fine brown frame and at that moment was glad she'd found the courage to stop by. He was almost sure it was his mother who had been calling quite regularly as of late, hoping to get him to commit to attending this years' family reunion. He hadn't been to one since he could remember and had no intentions of attending this one either. Both knew it but still she called. *Damn, she was persistent* Checking the caller I.D. and not recognizing the number, Terrance picked up the receiver in the bedroom. "Hello. Terrance Daniels, please." The voice on the other end was not one he recognized.

"Speaking."

"Mr. Daniels, this is Sylvia Stanton," she said. Nervous, she had had mixed emotions about making the call but it was too late now. Embarrassed for having had to make the phone call at all, she was relieved that Terrance had answered the phone instead of a female. She knew she had no right to feel this way. Nevertheless, she did. With nowhere to go, she quickly vetoed her pride.

"Just called to see if your offer still stands," She was on a roll now. She'd best continue before she lost her nerve. "I was thinking that if you're not busy then maybe you'd like to meet me at Dante's for a drink? Say in half-an-hour? That is if your offer still stands."

Stunned, Terrance was breathless. He hadn't had a date in more than six months. Now just like that here was Laura looking absolutely delicious almost edible sitting in the living room and Sylvia on the phone requesting they meet for a drink. When it rains it pours. The gods were obviously smiling on him tonight, he thought smiling to himself. Yet, something was amiss.

"Mr. Daniels, are you there?"

"Why, yes, Mrs. Stanton, I'm still here. Are you okay?"

"Couldn't be better," Sill lied, masking her voice, pretending to be upbeat, in an attempt to save face.

Terrance was tempted to comment on the fact that it had been quite some time since the offer had been extended making him a wee bit curious to know what had prompted her to call now. No sooner than he thought to ask he heard the toilet flush and remembered that Laura was waiting on him and decided to curtail the conversation. 'A bird in the hand is worth two in the bush', Terrance thought to himself as he pictured Laura patiently awaiting his return in the living room.

And then almost as if someone had taken control of his vocal capacities he heard himself ask. "Dante's on Fifth and Lansing?" knowing full well where it was.

"That's the one," Sill replied.

"Give me about forty-five minutes," he said. "I need to make a stop first. And though there was no longer anyone on the other end, Terrance sat there on the edge of the bed stunned, still clutching the receiver, wondering what had just transpired. Much as he hated to admit it, Laura's visit was a pleasant surprise. Their past made him comfortable in her presence. And then out of the blue enters a woman he hardly knows and...

Terrance lit a cigarette, took a swallow of wine, lay back on the bed and tried to put everything in proper perspective. His days, which only this morning appeared relatively simple had suddenly become rather complex. Reaching over the side of the bed, Terrance felt around for the bottle of Seagram's he kept on hand purely for medicinal purposes such as this and poured himself a shot to calm his nerves. The whiskey sent shivers through him.

What could be he possibly tell Laura? He'd waited for Sylvia's call for months. As sensational as Laura looked tonight, he had no choice but to excuse himself. The only thing that really mattered tonight though was that he be dressed to the nines and on top of his game. The shot of Seagram's relaxed him somewhat but there was still the matter of Laura.

"Everything alright, Terrance?" Laura asked as she stuck her head in the doorway "Mind if I come in?"

"'No, not at all, come on in," Terrance tried to remain cool, somber, unchanged. Lord knows he wanted her to come in. Or did he? A half an hour or so ago, he would have begged her to come in. Now he was torn between meeting Mrs. Stanton and just leaning back enjoying the pleasant glow of the fireplace and Laura in all her splendor.

Laura made her way to the easy chair opposite him. "Is everything okay, Terrance?" repeated Laura. She knew him well enough to know when something was troubling him and this certainly seemed to be one of those times. "Laura, a situation's come up. I'm afraid I'm going to have to leave for awhile." Terrance wondered if he was doing the right thing.

"I understand, Terrance. Is there anything that I can do?" She was visibly upset. She obviously had plans too. Plans that included him. "Want me to stick around until you get back? We can order out. Have you eaten? Or I could run out and get us some Chinese, another bottle of Chardonnay some candles while you go out. We could make a night of it. I don't meet my lawyer until nine a.m. and I've got so much to show you, darling,"

"You don't know how badly I want to say yes, Laura. But with students you never know how long these things will take," Terrance lied.

"I understand." Laura drank the last of her wine, fumbled in her purse, kissed Terrance on the cheek and headed for the door. Staggering slightly, Laura smoothed her dress and pulled her pantyhose up just enough to let Terrance know what he was missing. "You owe me, Terrance Daniels."

"I'm already paying," Terrance replied, sarcastically.

"Dearly and with interest." Laura smiled, closing the door behind her.

"Need for me to walk you out?"

"No thanks, babe, I'm parked right in front. Call me when you're free. I should be finished by noon tomorrow. I'll be looking forward to hearing from you."

Terrance walked her to the car despite her objections then watched Laura walk the final few feet to her car, thought of the great future she had behind her and cursed himself for letting her walk away. Lord, she was built but Sylvia Stanton was—well—Sylvia. And whereas he knew Laura would be there, Sylvia was unchartered territory. A whole new world just waiting to be explored. He just wished he hadn't had to accept her one and only offer. Not that he wanted so much to be with Laura though she certainly had matured from her days as a dancer. He just didn't want to seem too anxious.

Terrance selected a pair of charcoal gray trousers, a black mock turtleneck and a pair of burgundy penny loafers with tassels. By the time he got in the shower it was seven thirty. He took another swig from the bottle of Seagram's and was gone. Less than five minutes later, he arrived at the ATM machine. He would be late he knew but it would be good to keep the ever so punctual Mrs. Stanton waiting a few minutes. Terrance hoped this would bring her down a peg or two, let her know that she just wasn't that important in the whole scheme of things. He hoped it would knock her off her high horse and put them on the same plane. After all, she had a lot of nerve calling him after this long.

Easing into the parking space in back of Dante's, Terrance got out, checked his profile in the side view mirror and headed for the back door. He'd hoped to go in the back and steal a quick glimpse of Sylvia before she had a chance to see him. He was trying to get the drop, size up her mood, atmosphere, and anything else he could use to his advantage. As soon as he spotted her, he was glad he'd done just that. Awestruck, to say the least, he had to admit he'd never seen her with her hair down or in such provocative attire. He stepped into the men's room to gather himself. '*Here goes nothing,*' he told himself before making his way to her table directly in front of the three piece ensemble. The trio consisted of a bass player, pianist and drummer, playing Duke Ellington's, *In a Sentimen-*

tal Mood. The mellow music mixed with the Seagram's and the fine assed woman in front of him made him quickly forget Laura and had him thinking he'd died and gone to heaven.

Sylvia Stanton, on the other hand, sat there drink in one hand, cigarette in the other, nodding her head ever so gently to the music hoping to forget her evening and that simple husband of hers, as Terrance made his way to the table.

"Evening, Mrs. Stanton."

"Mr. Daniels."

"I was wondering if you were going to show," she confessed, self-consciously. "Do you know how difficult it is for a middle-aged married woman to get a date on a Thursday night?"

Now, why did she have to throw the married bit in there?, he asked himself. Was she setting up parameters for the evening? If she thought this little *tête-à-tête* was going to be purely platonic, she's sadly mistaken. *Hell, he could have stayed home.* He was in no mood for games. Animosity and anger had been building since he'd asked her for a date months ago and she hadn't had the common decency to respond and the alcohol made his patience shorter than usual.

"Let's not play games, Mrs. Stanton. You're neither middle-aged nor *very* married, if you're here with me."

"Sylvia Stanton was chilled to the bone by this observation, but maintained her composure by sipping her drink and staring at the band. Terrance knew what he'd said was risky, but he was not starving having just left a beautiful woman who wanted to be with him for one who was yet unsure of herself.

"Come here often, Mr. Daniels?"

"Not as often as I'd like, and please call me Terrance."

"Likewise. Call me Sylvia."

"Nice to finally meet you, Sylvia. Very nice, indeed."

As they shook hands mockingly, the waiter approached.

"You okay 'ma'am? Can I get you another of the same?"

Sylvia, already tipsy didn't want to appear too cordial. "I think I'll wait. I'm still feeling the last one."

Turning to Terrance, the waiter's expression took on a completely different cast.

"What's up, Tee? Haven't seen you in a month of Sundays. Where you been keeping yourself?"

"Working man, working. How you been. Jazz?"

"Coolin', you know, just takin' it easy," Jazz said. "I called you a couple of weeks ago to see if you wanted to fly down to New Orleans to see Roy Ayers and Boney James. Man, the card was jam-packed and I had two free tickets and the rooms were paid for."

The club was starting to fill up, now. Young men in suits and sport coats, women in pretty floral dresses and Jones of New York suits paraded through the doors. Young Black professionals streaming in like so many rays of sunshine. Good lookin' Black people parading in looking like The Ebony Fashion Fair. The little trio was in a groove now; playing a piece by James Moody that sounded almost too good and the noise level was rising.

"Let me get to work, Terrance. People are spendin' and I need to be earnin'. Whatcha gonna have? The usual? Killians with a twist of lemon and a double Jack on the side?"

"You got it, Tee," Jazzy responded.

Sylvia looked hard at Terrance as Jazzy turned to leave.

"My fault, Sylvia. Jazzy, this is Mrs. Sylvia Stanton. Sylvia this is my good friend, Jazzy. I've got to be careful introducing beautiful women to Jazzy. He has a way with women, you know." Sylvia smiled, her eyes never leaving Terrance.

Jazzy blushed. "He taught me everything I know," replied Jazzy now on his way back to the bar.

"You know, for some reason that does not sound surprising. Sylvia smiled. Jazzy returned to the table in a matter of seconds. "It's getting a little busy in here T. Don't know if I'm gonna get a chance to get back here but if I don't, just tell the waiter that Jazz's got it. "Are you ready for that drink now, Ms. Stanton?"

"I believe I am. I'll have the same as Mr. Daniels, uh, Terrance. Hold the Killians." Turning to Terrance, she commented, "It must be nice to have friends in high places."

"That's why I'm trying to get on your good side. Rumor has it that you have clout in the school system." Terrance smiled broadly.

"Let's not talk about school tonight, Terrance."

"Not a problem, Sylvia."

"Care to dance?"

"I thought you'd never ask."

When she stood up, all Terrance could do was gasp.

"Mrs. Stanton? Are you the same Ms. Stanton who teaches at West Lansing?"

She smiled, acknowledging his feeble attempts to cover his surprise.

"I do let my hair down on occasion, Mr. Daniels."

"It's not your hair I was referring to, Sylvia."

They both laughed as they moved through the crowd and onto the dance floor. The music was hot now as several other musicians stepped up to the bandstand.

Midway through the set, the band, which now numbered eight or nine members with Jazzy accompanying on sax, broke into the very up-tempo *Mister Magic*. Moving self-consciously, Sylvia tugged on Terrance's sleeve in a feeble effort to get off the dance floor. Terrance pulled her gently back on and she responded nicely.

One by one, the crowd of dancers gave way giving them the entire dance floor.

The usually reserved Mrs. Stanton was almost in full swing now. Terrance followed her lead as she broke into one smooth jazz step after another. Terrance tried to keep up but it was clear that the ever so reserved Mrs. Stanton was no novice on the dance floor. The band members, now numbering nine or ten noticed the couple drawing so much attention and picked up the rhythm. The crowd suddenly broke into chants of, "Go girl, go boy, go girl…" When the tempo slowed, Terrance didn't have to be pulled off the floor this time, he led the way, the crowd clapping in appreciation. Jazzy had ordered another round in their absence. Terrance smiled. *Good ol' Jazz. Always on time.*

Terrance, perspiring profusely after the workout, excused himself and headed for the john to freshen up, making it a point to thank Jazzy along the way. "Good lookin' out, Jazz."

Jazz nodded. "You've really got something on your hands this time, Tee. Just hope you can handle it, baby." He'd known Jazzy almost as long as he'd known himself and immediately knew Jazz was referring to Sylvia. This was Jazz's way of complimenting him.

"I'll do my part, if you do yours," Terrence replied.

"Don't worry drinks are on the house, but it's gonna take more than a few drinks to get next to that. You got cash? Here, take this Benjamin just in case you hit pay dirt. When you gonna get a real job anyway? Everybody knows teachin' don't pay nothin' and from the little I've seen of Ms. Stanton, you're gonna need all the Benjamins you can lay your hands on. That right there is high maintenance, my brotha."

Terrance brushed him off. "I'm straight. All I have to give is me and if she wants more than that she's playin' in the wrong ballpark. Know what I'm sayin'? I sure as hell ain't trying to buy no woman. Too many of them out there for free. By the way, guess who just got in town and stopped by the house?"

"Who's that?"

"Laura. Remember the dancer?"

"How can I forget? She was as fine as they come."

"And trust me, Jazz, ain't a whole lot changed in that regard. But anyway, let me get back to her before she thinks I'm missin' in action."

"Yeah okay but let me say this before you go. You know we've been friends a long time, Tee, and I've always tried to be on the level with you, dog. And from what I see, she's either gonna be the best thing that's ever happened to you or the worst. That right there is serious. I don't think that's anything to play with. I've seen men literally kill over women like that. So, go slow and be careful."

Returning to the table as composed as ever, Terrance wondered how prophetic Jazzy was. He'd had those same thoughts when he first considered talking to Sylvia, but right now he was just glad to be in her company.

"Didn't know you were such a good dancer, lady."

"There are a lot of things you don't know, Terrance."

"Hopefully, you'll give me the opportunity to answer some of my questions."

Before she could answer, he noticed someone approaching rapidly from through the crowd. The sight sent chills through him. From the midst of a rather large entourage of women, looking even more ravishing than when he'd last seen her, in a gold and white tunic, white slacks and gold sandals, standing all of six feet was Laura.

Terrance swallowed the remainder of his drink, watching her intently as she approached the table. He could feel the beads of perspiration gathering on the bridge of his nose. At the table now, Terrance introduced the two women, took a swallow of beer and waited for the onslaught.

For Laura it was a Catch-22. If this woman meant anything to Terrance it wouldn't pay to cause a scene. If she made no comment he'd figured her to be at his beck and call. That was certainly not the way for her to renew a relationship. She'd let him slip away once. But Lord knows if she had anything to do with it it wasn't going to happen again,

"Will you join us, Laura?"

"No thanks, Terrance. I'm with some friends." Laura smiled graciously knowing her mere presence was making him uncomfortable, but decided to make him suffer just a little while longer.

"Terrance honey, I didn't know you were working with graduate students now." Laura smiled, excused herself, and said, "Nice meeting you, Sylvia. You must call and tell me all about it sometime, Terrence. I may want to pick up a few credits." She laughed before walking away, knowing full well that her attempt at sarcasm had hit home.

All Sylvia could do at this point was lower her head and grin.

"Moonlighting, Terrance?" she asked. "I didn't know you taught grad school either. She's a very attractive woman, Terrance. I wish I had her height. Another member of your fan club?"

"She used to be," Terrance replied matter-of-factly. "Are you ready to get out of here?"

"Whenever you are," she replied still smiling.

Sill slid out of her seat and Terrance escorted her out of the back door, nodding to Jazzy on the way, and making sure to circumvent Laura and her welcoming home party.

"What about the bill, Terrance?"

"It's been taken care of," he replied. "My place for a nightcap?"

Shortly thereafter, Terrance pulled into a group of moderately priced townhouses off of Village Drive. Sill had always wondered what they were like inside. Now she would have the chance to see first-hand.

CHAPTER 11

❀

Entering the townhouse, Sylvia's heels sank deep into the plush, cream-colored carpeting causing her to lose her balance. Terrance caught her before she fell completely. Righting herself by grabbing a bookcase, she found herself face-to-face with Terrance. Facing him, she looked deeply into his eyes and felt a stirring for the first time in quite some time. There was little doubt that she found him physically attractive but…there were just so many *buts*. Terrance feeling no resistance to their closeness took this as a positive sign. Moving forward to kiss her, Sylvia suddenly turned away.

"Nice, very nice, Terrance," she commented purposely ignoring his advances. Terrance turned the light switch on. Along with the lights came an almost ephemeral sound. No doubt music, but like nothing she'd ever heard before. Dimming the lights, he excused himself.

"Fix yourself a drink, Sylvia. The bar's right through the door on the left. I'll be there momentarily. You can change the music if you like. The remote's on the coffee table."

"No, I like it. What is it anyway?"

"His name is Andreas Vollenweider. He's a German guy. Plays what they call New Age. It's sort of a mixture of jazz and classical. I don't know too much about it. I just know it's relaxing. I can read with it on and it allows me to unwind after a rough day," he said winking at her.

"Well. It's quite nice. Kind of melodic. Sort of puts you in the mood." Sylvia stopped realizing that it was more than just the music that had her going now. Not much of a liquor drinker the Jack Daniels mixed with the music was beginning to have its effect. That and the fact that she found Terrance to be more than a little attractive. He stirred something in her than hadn't been stirred since her final night with Peter and that had been years ago.

Always observant, Sill noticed the two wine glasses on the living room table. One still had the remnants of woman's lipstick on it and she quickly realized that she must have interrupted him earlier with her call since nothing else seemed out of place.

Fixing herself a drink, things started to come together and it dawned on her that Terrance must have been entertaining when she called and probably none other than the tall, shapely woman in the club. What was her name? Oh yeah, Laura.

Terrance had made light of his relationship with the tall, sultry woman in the club when she inquired, but there was obviously something there and Sylvia was certainly going to find out what and how much before she even considered getting involved...*Involved?* What was she thinking? She was still for all intents and purposes, a married woman.

Looking around the spacious home she couldn't get over how tastefully decorated the townhouse was. What impressed her more than anything else were the rows and rows of books, which lined all of one wall. Almost all of the authors were African-American, except for a small segment of westerns by Louis L'Amour.

"You like to read, Sylvia?" Terrance asked, entering the room, catching her off-guard and deep in thought

"Oh, Terrance, you frightened me," she answered, startled by his entrance. "Why, yes, I love to read, I just can't find the time."

"Same here, but I keep collecting with the hopes that one day I'll find the time. I've got good intentions."

As he dimmed the lights, the music seemed to increase in volume. The accumulation of drinks were definitely starting to take their toll on Sylvia, who sank down into the cream-colored leather sofa and nestled her head on the arm. Terrance cleared the wine glasses and went over the glass cocktail table with a damp rag, dried it, then offered her a coaster to put her drink on.

"Company?" she asked. Terrance reluctantly told her of his brief stint with Laura.

In spite of his confession, the atmosphere mellowed with the evening. Sylvia seemed relieved when the story was finally told. She could breathe deeper now and nestle into the sofa even more now than before.

"This has got to be one of the nicest townhouses I've ever been in. So tastefully decorated. I guess...well, I guess I underestimated you, Terrance. You know how some women are. One brother treats us badly and we're skeptical of 'em all. You certainly don't fit the mold, though. I may have to give Miss Laura a run for her money." The alcohol was definitely taking effect now and Sylvia knew it. "No, you're definitely not typical by any stretch of the imagination," she added, "but that's not to say given an opportunity you wouldn't try…God, that music sounds *good*. Tell me who it is again?" She was rambling badly now.

"You're wrong, Sylvia," Terrance owned up, "when I was a kid fresh out of the service, I might have tried to seduce you, but I'm thirty-four years old now. I'd like to think my priorities have changed some. Not to sound tactless, but I've been with enough women in my life to know that it takes more than looks to spur my interest over the long haul. However, in your case…"

Going over to the sofa and sitting beside her he took the drink from her hand and placed it on the coaster. Turning towards her, his palms sweaty, he grabbed the back of her neck gently, and pulled her head forward ever so slowly and kissed her teasingly—then passionately.

"In your case I wanted you from the first—the very first—moment I laid eyes on you and talking to you only enhanced your beauty in my eyes."

Sylvia's hands moved against his chest, fighting, struggling to push him away. Respecting her wishes, Terrance retreated and reached for his glass. Before he knew it Sylvia stunned him, reaching for him hungrily. Terrance wondered who was in charge now, but it mattered little as Sylvia pulled him down onto the sofa. Suddenly, he felt a sharp pain, tasted blood, and realized she'd bitten his lip. Freeing himself from her clutches, he scowled at her angrily before heading to the bathroom for a tissue and a condom. She'd pay for that he thought to himself as he wiped the blood away, smiled and then eased the condom on.

When he returned, Terrance found Sylvia Stanton stretched out and sleeping soundly. He sighed, smiling. How long had he waited for this moment, for this opportunity, for this woman? What was it his daddy used to say? '*If it wasn't for bad luck he'd have no luck at all.*' Terrance smiled on as he took off her shoes, jewelry and loosened her belt. In the linen closet he found a clean sheet and pillowcase and remade his guest bed. After considerable effort, he finally tucked her in and then made a fresh pot of *Folgers* and called Jazzy:

"Jazz, I need you to do me a favor. Sylvia left her car there and she's asleep and I need to get it here, so that she has it when she wakes up."

"No problem, my brotha. Hurry up, though. The longer I'm gone, the more money I lose." Jazz replied.

Terrance checked her purse for her keys and headed for the door. He thought about Jazzy for a minute. He'd known him close to—well, at least as long as he could remember, and in all that time Jazz had only one pursuit—*money*. And he made it, lots of it, hand over fist and in a variety of ways. He was the sole owner of Dante's where he had no real responsibilities, except to sign checks and sign the latest talent, but Jazzy figured if he had to be there he might as well mingle and make a little money too. So, he waitered, bartended and even parked cars if he thought he could bring in another dollar. He could make a hundred and a half easily on a good night and seemed to grab almost as many numbers. The women loved him. He could work a ten dollar table and get a ten dollar tip. And nothing upset him, nothing, except someone messin' with his money.

Terrance pulled up in front of Dante's and handed Jazzy the keys. "I love you, Tee, but you're messin' with my livelihood now," Jazzy said

Terrance chuckled. "Couldn't be helped, baby," he confessed.

By the time the whole affair was over, it was close to twelve-thirty and he was beat. Pouring himself a cup of coffee, he marked a few papers, checked his lesson plans for the up coming day, and went to bed.

No sooner than he closed his eyes he was aware of Sylvia's presence in the house. Making his way to the guest bedroom he found her sitting on the edge of the bed. Terrance reached over and touched her hand, stroking it gently.

"Having second thoughts, Mrs. Stanton?" Terrance shot at her.

"No, no at all, I just wish our planning had been better. I wish it hadn't been a school night."

No sooner had she made the comment than the phone rang. As Terrance reached to turn the volume on the answering machine down, Sylvia grabbed his hand. A woman's voice came on.

"Terrance, if you're home, please answer the phone. Please!" Terrance tried to free himself from Sylvia's grasp and was surprised at her strength, as he waited with some apprehension for the rest of the recorder's message:

ॐ

"I hope I didn't embarrass you tonight. Funny thing though, Terrance, I liked her. Sylvia, is it? A bit old, but, well, we can't fault her for trying to have one last fling before she collects her pension, now can we? If she's there I suppose there is no better time than now to ask yourself if she can move you like I can. Did she make your toes curl or did you simply go through the motions? I'll give you a little time to think about it before you answer and then I'm quite sure I'll be hearing from you. Don't take too long though; you know there's a waiting list on this end

too. None of them compare to you though, sweetie pie. Well, I gotta go. I love you Mr. T. Oh, and—"

The answering machine cut her off at this point. Terrance, who had been listening intently, shot a glance at Sylvia.

"On second thought Terrance, maybe this wasn't such a good idea. Would you please take me to get my car? Got to get up in the morning and it's getting kind of late. He started to explain, and then decided against it.

"Your car is out front. I had Jazzy bring it over."

Sylvia smiled. "The moment I start to think something negative about you, you go and do something like this. I can see why Laura is so hung up on you." Sylvia kissed him on the cheek and was out the door before Terrance could get his pajama bottoms on.

William stood waiting at the door when Sylvia pulled into the driveway. It was one thirty-five. William waited only as long as it took Sill to get in the door, before the barrage of profanity and insults started.

"Do you know what time it is? Where the hell have you been, Sylvia?"

"'Not now, William, I'm not in the mood."

"That's half the problem. You're never in the mood. You know I'm leaving tomorrow. You could have at least have had the common decency to call. You still haven't told me where you've been." William was livid.

"Tell you where I've been," she answered, resentment surging up in her. "I'm twenty one and then some. And I told you when I left that I'm not one of your possessions. I don't have to tell you a damn thing, William Stanton. My mother lives in North Carolina and my daddy's twice the man you'll ever be and I don't have to tell him…

William's fist caught her flush on the side of her head and Sylvia crumpled to the floor in a heap, sobbing convulsively.

"Out there whorin' around. You'd better get yourself together, Sill. You'd damn well better. I leave tomorrow morning and when I get back things are gonna change. Best believe, things are gonna change."

Still sobbing, Sill attempted to get up. William slapped her this time. Sill fell back against the loveseat, crying hysterically and holding her face, which was quickly swelling. William stalked out of the room. Slowly, Sylvia pulled herself up onto the couch, took a deep breath before filling a plastic bag with ice and using it as a cold compress before crying herself to sleep.

William was still asleep when she strode into their bedroom the next morning. If he had known what she felt that morning, he would never have slept. Placing the meat cleaver down next to William's pillow she let him know in no uncertain terms that the next time he thought to lay his hands on her would be the death of him.

On her way to work Sylvia Stanton had only one thought. She prayed that William would not be home when she returned from work. She was exhausted, her head ached and all she knew was that she didn't need another bout with this cowardly lightweight. Life was just too short. William awoke much in the same frame of mind. He was exhausted. Between the office and Sill's selfishness he was at his wit's end and although he was truly sorry for his actions the problem remained. It was then that he saw the meat cleaver. The message clear, William lay back down—stunned.

Thinking about the events of the night before, hot tears flowed like so many rivers down his cheeks. He hadn't meant to put his hands on her. He vowed to make it up to her, but right now he had work to do, bags to pack and a plane to catch.

CHAPTER 12

✿

"Hello, Jazzy. This is Sylvia. I don't know if you remember me. I'm a friend of Terrance's."

"Sure. Sure, I remember you. What can I do for you this evening, Sylvia?"

"I was wondering if you'd happened to see Terrance." Sylvia wondered if she was being too forward. After all, this was all new to her and she didn't want him to think she was just another of Terrance's hungry, love-struck fans. Realizing that this just might be the case and desperate to talk to him, to anyone at this moment, she lost her reserve.

"No, not lately," Jazzy replied.

"Well, should you see him, would you ask him to give me a call at 632-1436. Tell him to ask for Room 213." As soon as she gave him the room number, she was sorry she had. She could just as well have told him to ask for her by name. How stupid. Jazzy was no dummy though, and would probably assume that Terrance had her so strung out that she was lying in bed, in some cheap fleabag motel, passion driving her out of her mind, while Terrance was out with Laura or some other heifer, not giving her a second thought. She was sorry at once for having made the call at all. Yet, even if Jazzy was thinking this, he gave no sign whatsoever and she was grateful for that. Instead, he seemed to read something altogether different in her phone call.

"You sound a little uptight, Sylvia. Is everything okay?" the concern obvious in his voice.

"Oh, I'm fine. Thanks for asking. If you do see him would you tell him that I'll be here for the remainder of the evening?" Again she felt that she'd let the cat out of the bag, intimating perhaps a bit too much. It was too late now she concluded, but she really did need to speak with him.

She'd made it a point to call Edwin earlier that evening and this time she was fortunate enough to reach him. She realized it was a bit late to be conducting business. Edwin was sympathetic and said, under the circumstances, she should have never remained in the house, but should have called her last night, so he could have made sure she was tucked away safely in a hotel. Still bristling with anger she was giving serious consideration to putting the house on the market, then wondered if she were not being too vengeful.

The following day, Sylvia met with Mr. Langdon, the principal at West Lansing, for about forty-five minutes, explaining the situation at home as best she could under the circumstances. Sylvia was quite fond of her supervisor. He had given her the opportunity to teach when no one else had. And, although her resignation was abrupt and without notice, she knew if anyone would understand, he would. Tears streamed down her face as she cleared out her desk.

It was a little after four and the school was usually deserted by this time of day and she preferred it that way. There was no way she could have faced her students. Often times when she grew lonely and despondent and questioned her purpose in the grand scheme of things, her only consolation were those innocent, sweet uplifted faces before her. Oh God, how she would miss them. How rewarding it was to watch them grow from nervous freshman to young adult's right before her very eyes.

As she continued to empty the last few remnants from her desk, her thoughts turned to William. Maybe he was right. Maybe she didn't have the kind of help they needed. Whatever! She cursed William for taking away the one thing she truly loved, her profession. A tearful soul, Mr. Langdon, helped her carry out the last of her boxes and bid her farewell.

"You will be missed, Sylvia," was the best he could do. "Make sure you keep in touch with me, and if you change your mind, remember that there's always a position open for you here at West Lansing." He hugged her again before bidding her farewell. "Keep in touch, Sylvia," he yelled as she exited the parking lot.

"I will," she shouted back, knowing full well that she wouldn't, that she couldn't. She couldn't...

Arriving back at the motel at a little after five, Sylvia checked the front desk for messages and was informed that there weren't any. Then, just as she put the key in the door, she heard the phone ringing. Racing to open the door, Sill burst into the room, threw herself across the bed and grabbed the phone. All attempts at regaining her composure were gone. "Hello!"

"Yes, Mrs. Stanton, this is Beverly at the front desk. I'm sorry I did have a message for you to call a Mr. Edwin Davis. Shall I give you the number?"

"No, thank you, that's quite alright. I have his number." Disappointed that it wasn't Terrance, Sill hung up the phone. She wondered what the devil Edwin wanted. Dinner perhaps. She smiled, and thought of Edwin doing his best to try to stay focused, professional and avert his eyes from her rather ample chest at dinner last week. She had purposely pushed her bra up with the hopes of showing a little more cleavage when she went to the ladies room just to mess with the very astute, very professional Mr. Davis. She really didn't know why she was messing with him except that she could and she liked the idea of having men fawn over her now that she was, in her eyes, once again single. Perhaps, she was just happy to be able to flirt, to be playful—to let her hair down. Perhaps, the thought of some male attention after being taken for granted for so long, appealed to her. But he had resisted. And though she tried to purposely entice him, she appreciated the fact that he hadn't hit on her. Now, he probably was having second thoughts and wanted to do dinner.

In the midst of her ego trip it dawned on her as to why he was calling. She had forgotten to stop by the bank. She had given Edwin the power of attorney and forgotten to transfer the funds into her private account. 'Probably thinks I got cold feet. Let me call him now,' Sill muttered to herself. No sooner had she said this the phone rang. It was Edwin and sure enough he wanted to know if she had changed her mind. There was no reference of last night's meeting or the idea of dinner in the future. He was strictly business.

Terrance hadn't bothered to call either and she had left messages several places for him to get in contact with her. Perhaps she was getting a bit heavy around the love handles. In any case, no one was busting the door down to get in. The hotel phone rang again, shattering Sill's idle ramblings.

"Hello," Sill answered softly, humbly.

"Sylvia, this is Terrance. What happened to you, today? This is the first time in I don't know how long, that I rushed to work and you decide to play hooky. When I found that you weren't there, I can honestly say that it was the longest day I've ever had since I started teaching. What have you done to me?"

Terrance was bubbly and genuinely happy. No, he was thrilled to be talking to her and didn't try to be cool or coy or mask the way he was feeling and she liked that. And to a great extent, Sill felt the same way. His call dispelled all of those notions, those demons she'd been wrestling with a few minutes prior to his call.

If a handsome, young man like Terrance was interested in her, even if it were simply on a physical level, then she couldn't possibly be over the hill. Hell, the ratio of women to men in Atlanta was eight-to-one. And Laura Harrington or whatever her name was living proof that he didn't mess with any scrubs. No, as attractive and sexy as Laura was, he'd chosen her…Still, now was not the time to ponder middle age, menopause and mid-life crisis. The fact of the matter was that Terrance Daniels, who had to be at least five or six years her junior, wanted her, when he could have had his choice of…

"Terrance, are you still there? I'm sorry. My mind's in a million different places. Listen, I know you're wondering why I wasn't at work and why I'm at a motel but trust me, I'll explain everything later. But right now I need you to do me a favor or two. Are you free for, say, an hour or two?"

"Sure, Sylvia. Whaddaya need?"

"First of all, I need for you to call your landlord. See if he has a two-bed-room townhouse for rent. Then rent a U-Haul truck, the largest they have, and meet me at 6909 Wickersham Drive in the Lake Brandt district in an hour. Did you get that?"

Terrance repeated the address and assured her that he'd be there within the hour. Sylvia then called Edwin for the second time to make sure that every-thing was in order, the paperwork completed and then headed for the bank, which had been closed for hours. It felt good to have friends in high places. Edwin greeted her at the door and then led her into his office in the rear of the bank. Pulling up the Princess Anne chair so close to her that their knees touched, he faced her. Grabbing both her hands in his, Edwin looked into her eyes as if trying to probe the very depths of her soul for answers.

"Sylvia, are you absolutely sure you're doing the right thing?" he asked wea-rily. "I understand your feelings and I know it's really none of my business but I just want to make sure you've thought the whole thing through and aren't just acting out of anger and vengeance."

There he'd said it. Edwin knew from the moment the words left his lips that he had stepped outside of his professional boundaries. He'd crossed the line but, for some reason, he was genuinely concerned for her welfare and the repercussions for what she was about to do could not only be devastating but dangerous for everyone involved.

Nodding her head, Edwin handed her paperwork, which was legal and binding and only wished he hadn't known the details. He then handed her the check, which required her signature, then went up front to an empty cashier's window and opened the drawer to cash the check. When they were finished, she thanked Edwin and promised to call him as soon as she was settled.

All in all, things were running as smoothly as they possibly could up to this point and she couldn't see how anything could possibly disrupt the flow. Terrance was at the house when she got there, punctual as usual. The truck was even bigger than she had expected. "You owe me, Sylvia! You owe me a lot!" Terrance was ecstatic. "Listen! Jazzy has a three-bedroom townhouse that's gorgeous. It's ready and waiting and only seven fifty a month. I looked at it and thought it was a steal, so I put a deposit down to hold it 'til you got a chance to see it. I got him to waive the security deposit, so all you're looking at is the first month's rent."

Sill was not impressed. In fact, it was obvious that she was quite disappointed although Terrance had no idea why? She beckoned and he followed her inside the small estate all the while marveling at the spaciousness of the rooms and the décor. There was no doubt that this was her home. She said nothing as she gave him a tour of each room. And then she turned to face him. Her eyes blazed with a fury he had never known and didn't care to come to know. Of that he was certain.

"Did you think that my moving into your little community would bring the neighborhood down a peg or two, Terrance?" she shot at him. "Or did you think that my being in such close proximity would disrupt you getting your groove on with your fan club? What did you think, Terrance? Did you think you could take the ol' woman out one night, buy her a few drinks, and screw her to add another notch to your belt and parade around with that smug look of yours like you do at school with the knowledge that you fucked the ever so prim and proper Sylvia Stanton. If you were truly a man, you might have told me that you were only interested in how I was in bed and you never know, I might have accommodated you. But, no! One night and no conquest and you don't have the time or the common decency to even do a follow-up phone call to say thanks or I enjoyed your company. No you just pass me off. What am I supposed to do? Am I supposed to just pick up and go with your friend, Jazz, 'cause you're not interested. What? Tell me, Terrance. I knew the moment I called Jazz and informed him that I was in a motel room and was looking for you that someone was going to get the wrong impression. Was knowing that I was in a motel room, waiting for your call enough for you to pass me on to your friend. Damn you, Terrance Daniels! Whatever makes you think that you can place me in Jazzy's apartment complex, without even bothering to consult me and—you know you've got a lot of nerve. Because I'm attracted to you doesn't make me a—?"

Terrance, at first shocked by the verbal onslaught, was grinning from ear to ear now. Seeing this, Sill grabbed the first thing she could get her hands on which just happened to be a crystal vase and threw it as hard as she could in his direction. The vase shattered a few feet from Terrance's feet sending chips of glass everywhere. Angered by her miss, Sill searched the room for another projectile. Terrance was laughing out loud now and this only enraged her more. Before she could find another weapon, he grabbed her, pulling her to him; crushing her against his chest, he pinned her arms behind her back and was amazed at her strength. She struggled to free herself but to no avail. And then, he kissed her softly, softly and then madly, passionately. Her struggles ceased as she met him halfway. She crushed her mouth into his, hungrily, as if she were starved for affection. He felt her tongue down his throat and gagged. He tried to push her away but couldn't escape her grasp. He felt himself falling but caught his balance at the last minute. At least she hadn't drawn blood this time. He continued to hold her arms, hoping if nothing more than to comfort her. She did not resist. He looked at her now. She was someone different now. Her tirade had exposed another side of her; a side he would have never dreamed existed in someone so normally docile, so sweet. And it wasn't a side that he wanted to see again. Yet, if anything, it made her more attractive, more enticing.

"A kiss is not an apology, Terrance," Sill observed, her anger diffused.

Terrance studied her face for some clue as to why she thought he owed her an apology and found none. "Why am I apologizing? For what? You asked me to do something and I did it. Now I should be sorry? Lord, please help me to understand."

Pushing herself away from him, Sylvia repeated her earlier position. "When I called you earlier I asked you to do two things. First, I asked you to find a truck and, secondly, I asked you to ask your landlord if he had any two-bedroom townhouses for rent. I had specific reasons for wanting to move into your complex, not any of them being you. And I don't know too many grown men that might pretend to be interested in a woman that would dare to put that woman in close proximity to a friend, who happens to be a single man, a bachelor, a playa', such as Jazzy, unless he just didn't care for that woman."

Terrance began grinning again. "Well, I'm glad that at least the U-Haul suited your needs. I thought I was in compliance with your requests. You asked me to speak to my landlord and I did."

"Well, Terrance, if he didn't have any townhouses available then why would you take it upon yourself to look somewhere else without consulting me?"

"But he did have something available," Terrance replied, still grinning.

"Then, why in God's name are you trying to place me in Jazzy's complex, Terrance?"

"Because you asked me to, Sylvia."

"At no time did I ask you to…Are you playing with me, Terrance Daniels? And why are you standing there with that silly grin on your face. What's so damn funny? What did I ask you to do?"

"You asked me to find you a two bedroom townhouse in *my* complex. You asked me to speak to my landlord. And I did. You see, Jazzy happens to be my landlord. Not only do I secure you an apartment but I took the liberty of putting a deposit on it and having the security deposit waived and this is the thanks I get."

Sylvia was flabbergasted. "Do you mean to tell me that Jazzy runs Lake Spring Village?"

"No, baby, Jazzy *owns* Lake Spring Village but he doesn't live there. He has a home a block or so from here right on the lake and another up on the Upper East Side in Manhattan. And for your information, a playa' he is not. He never has been. In fact, the only love he has aside from his wife, Michelle and four beautiful daughters is music, jazz. Ask me, I'm the godfather for all four girls. And to be perfectly honest with you, I have never met a more devoted family man. Michelle and he have been going together since grammar school and he married her straight out of high school. And I guess they've been married close to fifteen or sixteen years now. Sylvia was stuttering, searching for words to exonerate herself but found none. The best she could come up with was, "I'm sorry, Terrance. I never would have imagined."

"Don't worry about it. You'll pay, Mrs. Stanton."

"I'm already paying for my ignorance and quick temper. As far as your pay, what can I say, the banks are closed but I'm pretty sure I can find some way to reimburse you. Has anyone ever made your toes curl?" she laughed, her anger all but gone now as she recalled Laura's message from the night before.

Terrance smiled, swept up the shards of glass, remnants of the broken vase but never once did he ask what was going on or why her sudden haste to vacate the spacious estate. She liked that about him. With all of her idiosyncrasies and insecurities, he still respected her judgment. Besides, he was sure she'd tell him when the time was right. Right now, there was too much going on and he knew that now was not the time.

Sylvia changed into some old gray sweat pants and a sweatshirt, and then put some Miles Davis on the CD player and poured herself a large drink. She proceeded to wrap her fine china in newspaper.

"What stays and what goes, Sylvia?"

"Oh, I'm sorry, Terrance. Pour yourself a drink. Everything goes but the T.V."

"In that case, I'm calling for some help."

Sylvia, still in another world, never heard him. Terrance called Jazz and a number of other friends, but being that it was Friday night, no one was available. Terrance resigned himself to the task at hand. Surprisingly, Sylvia worked as hard as any man. And not before long the truck was full. Terrance found two wine glasses among the many boxes and a bottle of expensive *Chardonnay*.

"Gonna leave your car here or are you gonna follow me?"

Sill smiled. "I'll follow you wherever you lead me." It was obvious that a load had been lifted from her shoulders. She kissed Terrance, appreciatively, jumped into the car and tooted the horn as if to say, farewell mission accomplished.

"Come on, slowpoke," she yelled, good-naturedly.

Terrance rubbed the spot where she had kissed and replied, "I'll never wash that spot again." They both laughed. Forty-five minutes later, Sylvia pulled into the Lake Spring Village parking lot, took the plants out of the back seat and followed Terrance to the door. Putting the plants down, Sylvia walked back to the car, pulled out her overnight bag, the portable CD player, and the remainder of the wine and glasses.

Terrance gave Sill the key and stood back to watch as she opened the door to splendor. The apartment had everything she could ever have dreamed of. "You have such wonderful taste, Mr. Daniels."

"I thought you'd like it, so I took the liberty of having the lights turned on. I've got a friend that works down at the power company. You'll have to get it done officially on Monday though." He was as proud of the townhouse he'd selected for Sill as he was of his own. And though they'd only really just been introduced as friends he felt as if he'd known her for years.

"You are wonderful. Simply wonderful, Terrance," she said. "Turn the stereo on will you, while I find the bathroom."

Soon Terrance heard the shower running. "Damn that woman. I wonder if we'll ever be on the same page," he muttered to himself.

Just as quickly, the shower stopped. Terrance brought the stereo in, hooked it up, put some Sade on, then lay down on the floor and closed his eyes. The white wine and mellow sounds of the mellow music masked his fatigue. He felt vibrant—alive.

"Oh, Terrance, there's a fireplace. It's so elegant. Hey, Sweetie, do you think you could make a small fire?"

Terrance was sure she'd lost it now. "It must be close to seventy degrees out-side and you're talking about making a fire," he said softly.

"And, if it's not too much trouble would you, bring the box of dishes in first so I can fix us a little something to eat?"

"Sure, Sylvia. Anything else?" Terrance was worn out but saw all the effort as simply a means to an end. And after all he'd done for her today, she would certainly be his in the end.

"Yeah, sweetie pie, do me a favor and call me Sill." She was really feeling her oats now.

"Terrance thought of his father and chuckled aloud. He remembered his father telling him that his mother never called him by his proper name, but nicknamed him, 'Honeydew', which stood for 'Honey, do this and Honey, do that.' Now for the first time, he understood and could relate.

"Hey, Sill, I'm going to stop by the office and let security know you're here, then stop by the house and grab a quick shower. How do you feel about Chi-nese?"

"Sounds good to me, though I could whip up something. Maybe another time. Just don't take forever. I've been waiting a long time to spend some time alone with you."

When he returned not more than an hour later, Sylvia had just about fin-ished unloading the truck. Not only had she managed to empty the truck with no assistance, she had arranged her living room and somehow managed to get the full sized mattress and box spring upstairs and into the master bedroom.

"You couldn't wait?"

"You've done more than enough for one day, hon. Besides, I need you to rest up. There's more tomorrow," Sill shouted from the bedroom

"What are you doing, Sill? You were showering when I left. Hope you like beef lo-mein."

"I kinda' got antsy waiting for you and worked up a sweat. Now what was it that you asked me? *Lo-mein?* Yeah, sure I like lo-mein but what I really like is your thoughtfulness. But right now there's another business that I need to tend to before I even think about stuffing my face."

"What now?" Terrance always thought he had an inordinate amount of patience but she was certainly starting to test it now. They had already eaten and danced together. Worked and almost slept together but they had yet to talk. Really sit down and have a serious conversation. His thoughts were suddenly interrupted by the nearly naked silhouette, which adorned the bathroom doorway. Terrance was aghast. Hell, the talk could wait. What was one more day? Conversation wasn't all it was chalked up to be anyway.

Terrance's gaze was fixed on Sill who stood before him in the laciest cream-colored camisole he had ever had the occasion to see. Black garter belts grabbed her black, fishnet stockings and pulled them ever so tightly over her chocolate thighs. If that wasn't enough, Sylvia Stanton complimented her outfit with a pair of six inch cream-colored high heels.

"My momma always told me that every man wants an intelligent, sophisticated woman in the living room and a call girl in the bedroom. 'Cept momma didn't exactly refer to them as call girls. You think that's true, Mr. Daniels? Can we make an exception tonight and let the call girl come out into the living room?"

Terrance, unable to speak, managed to mumble something unintelligible. Very much in control, Sylvia handed Terrance a glass of wine, then led him to the patio, slid open the glass doors and pulled him, quivering and quaking, through.

"Sylvia, sweetheart what about the neighbors?"

Sylvia fell to her knees and unbuckled his pants and slid his pants to the ground. The neighbors were no longer a concern. They made love not once—not twice—but three times. Once on the living room floor, once on the stairs and once on the bathroom floor.

As a weary Terrance stepped out of the shower, she attacked him once more, emitting guttural sounds, which in all candor, made Terrance quite, nervous and a bit uneasy. Sylvia had looked sinister, almost possessed when he opened the door of the shower. He wondered how long it had been since she had last made love. The last time *they* made love, Sylvia started laughing hysterically for no apparent reason, then stopped abruptly and, without a word, got up and simply left the room. She returned with a lit cigarette in her hand, mounted Terrance, cigarette still in hand and rode him until, drenched and spent, he pushed her away. She fought him this time, swinging wildly in an attempt to keep him in her.

"No! No! You mustn't stop! Not yet! No, you mustn't," she screamed as if someone were tormenting or beating her. She had a distant look in her eyes. Terrance quickly realized that wherever she was at that moment, one thing was certain and that was that she wasn't there with him. It was almost as if she was trying to purge herself of some inner demon. An hour later, with Sylvia sitting totally nude, a glass of wine in her hand staring out the living room window, Terrance gathered his clothes and headed for the stairs.

"Where are you going, hon?" she asked, incredulously.

"I thought you might want to spend your first night in your new place alone," he replied. The truth of the matter was he was spent, drained of all emotion, confused. He never slept with anyone so hell-bent on—he didn't know what. He couldn't exactly put his finger on it but she definitely had some issues, which needed to be resolved in her attempts at lovemaking if you could even call it that.

"Look, Terrance, I realize that we've just met and don't know each other all that well, but I'm sure you've gathered that I usually say what's on my mind. If I wanted to be alone, I would've said so. Shit, I've been alone for the past six years and the last thing I want is to be alone tonight."

"Could have fooled me," Terrance muttered under his breath but loud enough for her to hear.

"And what exactly is *that* supposed to mean? I did my damnedest to try and please you, to show you that Laura and the rest of your little yuppie girlfriends had nothing on this middle-aged sista. Perhaps you're just not accustomed to being with a woman."

Terrance was sure she had issues now and they were obviously too deep for him to work out. Whatever trauma she had been through or was going through of one thing he was sure. She needed professional help and counseling—and time. And he had neither the time, nor the experience to aid in what appeared some rather deep-seated emotional problems. Not wanting to argue, Terrance gathered his belongings and continued dressing.

"What you did was show me," he found himself saying. "What I wanted was for you to share with me. I'm not interested in a live sex show. I'm interested in you and what makes you tick. I wanted to make love, Sill, and you weren't even in the same room with me, let alone on the same page."

Sylvia lit another cigarette, found the ashtray, grabbed the wine and sat up crossing her legs Indian-like on the sofa. "I suppose, you're right, at least to some degree, Terrance. I guess I'm so afraid of growing old alone that I feel I have to prove myself, to perform just to keep a man. I am so very fond of you, Terrance but I keep thinking of the difference in age. And your friend Laura, so young and vibrant and beautiful scares the hell out of me. I kinda feel like she's got a head start and I'm trying to play catch up. I'm not even sure of how to play the game anymore or if I can even compete with someone so young and so beautiful. I can't ask you to forget about her and just run off with me, though I wish I could. But seriously, you don't know how long I avoided you just so I wouldn't have to feel like this.

I know every woman that you dated at West Lansing and prayed that they wouldn't work. You see, Terrance, I did my homework too. And now that I have you and think that this may be what I want, I know deep down in my heart that I don't have a chance in hell of keeping you and it's eating me up."

Sylvia crushed the cigarette butt out in the ashtray and dropped the loose-fitting camisole over her head to cover herself. And then everything seemed to sag at once. Her shoulders rose, and then fell rhythmically, keeping time to the Coltrane playing on the stereo in the next room. Sylvia sobbed softly in despair. She sobbed for the lost loves and turbulent relationships, for the loss of her marriage, for the loss of William, but most of all she sobbed for the loss of hope, and, therefore, for the loss of herself

In an attempt to comfort her, Terrance wrapped his arms around her, and squeezed her gently. Sylvia's startling revelation did Terrance a world of good. Perhaps they were in the same book, if not on the same page after all. Not sure of his own emotions, which only a moment ago seemed so clear, he again submitted to her requests.

"Take me, Terrance. Oh, darling, please take me now! Show me that you want me, that you love me. Please darling! Just take me now." As requested Terrance lifted the camisole and entered her and though he was sore and spent he rode her, trying to soothe her and bring some solace to a woman much more complex than he could have ever imagined. There was so much beneath the surface that he didn't know but even as he lay on top of her he could hear Jazzy's voice telling him to be careful and thought about getting up at that very moment but she was relaxed now and seemed to be one with him. Still sobbing, she met each gentle thrust with one of her own. Slowly, passionately, she rose, and then fell at his command. And then she rose again to meet him, praying that their union would never end. She bit her lip and recognized the salty taste of her own blood. Ignoring this Sylvia fought back the impending climax that would surely mark the end and leave her craving for more. *How long had it been?* And then, when she could not hold it back any longer, she dug the spikes of her heels deep into his buttocks as if she could hold on forever and to make him feel her pain.

A warm wave swept through her. And then another. Screaming his name, she lifted her legs up and wrapped them around tightly around his back to keep him in her. Orgasm after orgasm fell into place as if they had been ever so perfectly choreographed. *Damn, he was good!* Oh, how she wanted to please him, to keep him forever, right here, between her thighs, in her heart. But would he allow her. Still moving beneath him, Sylvia continued to meet his gentle thrusts with those of her own. She felt the soreness between her thighs now and was sure she could not go another minute and then the floodgates opened up and another warm rush of orgasms rained down upon her. She had never before known that such pleasure existed but was sure she could stand no more. Reaching for the headboard, she attempted to pull herself free but found she could not move him. His gentle thrusts were no longer and he seemed to have lost all sight of their coupling. He was coming and she was not going to stop him. Sill felt the pain of his pounding creep from her thighs to the small of her back. Her legs were cramping and her efforts to free herself were in vain. Frightened by his violent thrusts, she screamed for him to stop, and then demanded him to. Her demands fell on deaf ears, as he too, was swept up in a wave of orgasms. It would all be over soon. But when? God! She prayed it would be soon. And then when the pain and pleasure became one, and more than she could bear, Sylvia, tears flowing freely, raw and cut up inside, shrieked from the pain, had a moment of madness and begged him for more, before passing out beneath him.

Terrance untangled himself, dressed quickly, and exited through the back door. He now knew that any man involved with Sylvia Stanton could not simply walk away. He also knew that there would ultimately be a price to pay and right now he wasn't quite sure that he could afford to or had the desire to pay.

The cold night air felt good to him. The seasons were changing but there was still a bitter nip in the air. It was no more than a five minute walk to his own townhouse. And before he knew it he was there. Entering the foyer, he kicked off his shoes and fell into his easy chair. Tapping his answering machine resulted in a slew of messages. There were three from Laura who appeared adamant about seeing him tonight.

Ignoring them all, he ran a tub of hot water, added some Epsom salt and then poured himself a glass of *Chivas* on the rocks before submerging himself. The phone rang and someone knocked simultaneously. On any other night he wouldn't have minded but tonight he was beat. And yet, the night was young. It couldn't have been later than nine or nine-thirty. Stepping out of the tub and reaching for a towel, he realized he didn't care how young the night was. Sore from head to toe, he was finished for the night. And whatever they were selling, he wasn't buying. He smiled; he knew Sill was sleeping soundly. Aside from her, no one else was welcomed. In fact, he wondered if he would have opened the door even if it had been Sill. He tried to ignore the phone but it continued to ring. Whoever was calling was, if nothing else, persistent. Terrance rinsed off the beads of soap and water, and dried himself off before reaching for the phone. A familiar voice greeted him on the other end.

"Why, hello, lover and where the hell have you been? I've been waiting all night for you to fill my rain check," Laura chirped merrily along. "Now, do me and you a favor and go look through your peephole. Hurry up now. I'm waiting."

Tired from the move, spent from Sill's insatiable appetite, the last thing he felt like doing was playing games. He placed the receiver down next to the phone, picked up what was left of his drink and dragged himself to the peephole. There stood Laura in a brand new full-length fur and heels. When she realized that Terrance was looking through the peephole she opened the coat wide revealing everything. There stood Laura, buck naked except for the fur, which she let drape off her shoulder and those heels, which made her appear ten feet tall. Terrance swung the door open, grabbed Laura by the arm and yanked her into the apartment by the arm, looking around frantically.

"My goodness! You are glad to see me, aren't you?" Laura laughed, heartily. She let the fur fall from her shoulders and Terrance watched speechless as it crumpled to the floor in a heap around her ankles.

"Someone else is glad to see me too, I see."

The towel Terrance wrapped around himself had fallen in his haste to get Laura's naked body in the house and out of plain view of the neighbors. And as sore as he was her nakedness had sparked a flame. Following her mischievous gaze, he quickly noticed that his manhood was standing at full attention. He reached for the towel to mask his embarrassment.

"No need for that, Terrance." Laura grabbed his arm and led him to the sofa. "Mind if I fix myself a drink?"

"Not tonight, Laura. Please, baby, not tonight. Believe you me, I had a rough day, today."

"Don't worry, Tee. I'll make whatever's ailing you go away, baby. *Damn,* how I missed you Terrance. And I apologize for making you spend time with your mother while I was gone. What's her name? You know—the grad student?" Laura was in rare form tonight. And, when she was like this, Terrance loved being with her. She could be both witty and charming but tonight was not the night.

Emotionally and physically spent, he couldn't respond if he wanted to. His thoughts turned to Sill. She'd been asleep when he left her but what if she were to awaken and find him gone. She didn't have a phone yet and she'd asked him to stay. If she were to awaken and find him gone she would surely stop by and here they were sitting, he in a towel and she nude. Lord knows what conclusion she'd arrive at. He thought about taking Laura out to dinner, maybe a flick. He had promised her an evening. He knew Laura, knew her strengths and her shortcomings. The jury was still out on Sill. In fact, there had been several times during the course of the day when he questioned her mental stability or as his daddy used to put it—he wondered—'*if all the bricks were in the wagon*'.

Now, here was Laura, intent on cashing in on a debt owed. She was certainly not going to make it easy for him to wriggle out of his promise this time and especially after having been stood up for another woman. In retrospect, their first affair had been nothing short of extraordinary as long as they were not in the prone position. They were the best of friends and she was certainly worth the effort but with Sill in walking distance, there were just too many complications at this point.

"Be a sweetheart, Laura and let an old man get some rest. I'll meet you at Dante's tomorrow at eight. We'll grab a bite, take in the show, you know, make a night of it."

Laura sighed. Her disappointment showed but she agreed. What could she do? "Eight o'clock it is then. Don't be late. You know Jazzy's starting to get better looking each time I see him."

In no mood for her teasing, he was tempted to tell her to go for it but knew that at any other time he would have been glad to see her. But tonight he was truly exhausted. First the move and then all the extra-curricular activities had worn him out, but it was more than that. Closing the door behind her, he let the stopper out of the now cold bath water and sprawled out across his bed. His thoughts returned to Sylvia.

A strange bird, he couldn't exactly put his finger on it but there was something amiss. Again he thought about Jazzy's warning. He'd known quite a few women but there was something unnerving and unsettling about Sylvia though he couldn't nail it down. Like when she was on top of him, making love and had a faraway look in her eyes or the piercing laugh each time she orgasmed. Then there was the fighting and screaming that seemed to be a part of the act that let him know that she wasn't all there. At least that's how it appeared and as beautiful as she was it did little to enhance the lovemaking. Instead, it frightened him and made him wonder what was truly going on. There had been that one girl several years ago when everything came down to the sex partner of the week when it just seemed like he was collecting notches on his belt or trophies as far as how many women he could sleep with. It had been a stage and he had to admit looking back on it now that it had been fun at the time—or at least -up until he met that one girl who was everything he could have imagined in and out of the bedroom, except for one serious flaw. Each time she would near orgasm she would start singing the Star Spangled Banner. He'd waited months for the opportunity for them to have sex and the only thing he could remember was being at her place when it finally occurred and her singing or screaming that god awful version as she climaxed. He'd dressed quickly and gotten the hell out of there as it didn't take a rocket scientist to know that something was wrong. And for months after he made sure to check the caller I.D. and he'd been right to. She started showing up at his job and everywhere else as well. She eventually told him that he was in love with her and she'd kill him if he thought about seeing anybody else. For awhile he couldn't bring anyone home because she'd follow them and threaten them when she caught up with them. The whole affair had lasted months and been nerve wracking and yet he'd felt that same uneasy feeling when he was with Sylvia although he wasn't exactly sure why.

Turning over on the bed, he reached for the remote to turn the television on took a swig from the bottle of Seagram's, thought of how good Laura looked with and without the fur before eventually dozing off. He didn't know how long he'd been sleeping when he heard the phone ring. It couldn't have been long though since he found himself still clutching the bottle of Seagram's. He was tempted not to answer the phone before tiptoeing to the front door to check the peephole. Laura definitely had him spooked. Rushing back to the phone and picking up the receiver Terrance was surprised to hear Sill who he'd left sound asleep only a few minutes ago. She was hardly asleep now and sounded as chipper as he'd ever heard her.

"Hey baby, it's me, Sill. I just called to let you know that you left your cell here."

There was more on her mind than his leaving the cell but he wasn't inclined to engage her in conversation at this hour.

"Thanks for letting me know. I'll pick it up on my way to work in the morning, babe," Terrance replied, hoping to end the conversation at this point.

"Well, it's been ringing off the hook. I tried to ignore it the first couple of times but whoever it is keeps calling. I figured it must be important. Want me to run it over to you?"

Terrance wanted to tell her to just turn the damn thing off but remained polite. "I don't know why they just don't call me here," he muttered. Then he remembered that he'd turned the ringer off at home when Laura left so he could get some sleep. "Oh hell, I turned the ringer off. Whoever it is probably tried to reach me here and couldn't."

"It must be important, Terrance. They had to have called at least five or six times. I would have answered it but I wasn't sure you wanted me to."

Terrance ignored her remark. She was fishing to see how far they'd come and how much leeway she had. It was obvious she wanted to know just how much progress she had made in a night. She was moving entirely too fast now and again it frightened him. He'd always liked the hunt, the intrigue of the pursuit. Once he snared his prey however, he always found himself wanting. If he did commit to pursuing a relationship with Sill he wanted it to be his decision. One thing was for sure. He'd be damned if he would just let her come in and run roughshod over the peaceful little existence he had fought so hard to establish.

"Would you like for me to check your caller I.D. to see who it is?" Sill asked being a bit more than helpful than was required. In actuality, what she was being was too damn nosy and Terrance didn't like it. He didn't like it one bit.

"Don't worry about the phone, Sill. Whoever called can call back tomorrow. I'm sure that whatever it is, it can wait." And without another word he placed the receiver back on the hook.

Sill was shocked. "No, he didn't! No he didn't just hang up on me. That mother—."

What he didn't realize was that Sill had already checked the caller I.D. The first time it rang and when only a number appeared and no name she felt a twinge of guilt and did her best to reassure herself that after all Terrance had done for her that day he must have some type of feeling for her. And she was content knowing this. When they called, a second and third time she ignored it. But when they called a fourth time she had to know who could possibly be that persistent and had answered it. She recognized Laura's voice right away and was at once sorry she'd answered it. She knew she was stirring up a can of worms but it was too late to do anything about it now.

When she called Terrance she was merely looking for an opening so she could tell him of her blunder but he had not allowed her to. Now she'd lied and Laura was certainly going to ask Terrance why he'd hung up on her. *Damn!* She hadn't been involved in such pettiness since she was in college and wondered why she was allowing herself to be caught up in the drama now. Was he worth it? Was any man really worth the trials and tribulations they made women go through? Sill smiled. *Hell, yeah!* Putting her hand between her legs she felt the moistness along with soreness. *Damn*, that man was good. Fuck Laura Harrington! *Baby girl*, she thought, *you're in for the fight of your life.*

Though exhausted, his conscious got the best of him. He considered walking back to Sill's then decided against the idea. The phone rang again. Recognizing his own cell number he picked it up. He felt guilty for having walked out on her and then ending the conversation so abruptly.

"You know, I didn't get a chance to pay you or to even tell you thanks. How much was the rental and the deposit for the townhouse? Did I tell you how much I love it? It's absolutely gorgeous. I especially love the skylight and the fireplace."

"The stairs and the patio aren't bad either," Terrance chuckled, muttering to himself.

"I heard that, Terrance. Don't be fresh. Seriously speaking though, will two hundred cover it?"

"It should," Terrance replied.

"Shall I bring it with breakfast or would you like for me to bring it by now?"

"The money can wait, Sylvia. Ya know, I've been waiting for this night for an eternity and I must admit that you made it better than I could ever have imagined in my wildest dreams." Sylvia knew there was more to come. She cringed at the thought of his impending thoughts. Was this the brush-off?

Terrance continued. "There are just too many unanswered questions. Until I get some answers, I don't think our seeing each other is such a good idea. You've got to communicate more than you're doing. You've got to talk. Talk to me, baby. You've got to help me understand. I mean, just think about it, Sill. You're a beautiful, intelligent sister. More importantly, however, you're a married woman. And the truth of the matter is that some man is coming home to an empty house. His wife's gone and who knows what other pieces are missing from the puzzle."

Terrance could hear Sylvia sobbing softly in the background despite attempts to muffle her crying. There was an uncomfortable silence before she gathered herself

"Goddamn, Terrance! He *beat* me. I gave him six of the best years of my life. For six years I put up with his ignorance. For six years, I was little more than a hood ornament, a showpiece, and his goddamn whore. I begged him to grow, to realize his potential to become his own man. I waited and waited. I supported him in every way I could until I finally realized that he didn't have the capacity to grow. And when I couldn't support his quest for fame and fortune, he beat me. *HE BEAT ME, TERRANCE. Beat me to the ground.*" There were no longer any attempts to muffle her sobs. She was crying openly now. Terrance only wished he'd let sleeping dogs lie. The situation was becoming even more complex and certainly more than he'd bargained for. At first, the thought of a jealous husband and a not so stable woman were his concern. Now, the husband had taken on another quality that made him fear not only for this woman but also for his own safety. She made it seem like the cat was an impulsive gorilla.

"Meet me halfway, Sill," he heard himself say, before he could manage to stop the flow of words.

Her crying ceased almost immediately. "I'm on my way, Terrance."

Terrance hated his student's use of profanity and abhorred hip-hop music because of the derogatory references made to women but he had to admit: *'This bitch was crazy.'* And somehow, someway, he was being lured into her madness. She was like quicksand, the more he tried to wriggle free, the deeper he sank. Never, not in a month of Sundays, would he have imagined that someone so seemingly unassuming could carry so much baggage. Of course, it was her choice to carry this load silently and he had certainly not volunteered to be her personal valet. He had always promised himself that he would never let anyone bring drama into his life. Never would he allow anyone to live rent free in his head for more than five minutes. Yet, here he was at eleven-thirty at night sitting, arm draped around Mrs. Sylvia Stanton, on a park bench by the very, vacant tennis courts of the Lake Spring Village apartment complex.

"My living room sofa is so much more comfortable. We could finish where we left off. I know a virile young man like you couldn't have possibly been finished." Sill's mood was suddenly upbeat. Terrance wondered if the sobbing on the phone was just a ploy to get him over to her place. Now, he was sure it was just that, a ploy. Here he was coming out to supposedly console her and she was just as chipper as could be. Ignoring his somber mood, Sill continued, "Tell the truth, Terrance. Did you leave because you were upset with me passing out on you? I should have told you. I'm not really a drinker and I guess the combination of alcohol, the moving and you, darling, proved just a bit much for me," nibbling his earlobe, Sill crooned. "Can we go back to my place and christen the stairs again, lover?"

Terrance ignored the remark. "What are your plans, Sylvia?"

"Whatever do you mean, lover?"

Tired of the games, his agitation growing, Terrance snapped: "What the hell are you doing, Sylvia? I don't know if you're risking your life but you're certainly putting mine in jeopardy."

Sylvia saw a side of Terrance she had never seen before. Sensing the gravity of the situation, all sense of frivolity was quickly erased. It was obvious that, despite her attempts at denial, the repercussions of her actions weighed heavily on her mind. Sill became fixated, resolute in thought. It was apparent when she did reply that she had given the matter considerable thought before acting. This made Terrance feel a little more at ease but there was still a plethora of unanswered questions.

"What am I going to do? That's the million-dollar question. I wish I knew. I really don't know, Terrance. I consolidated our accounts, today, and, as you know, I resigned. Mr. Langdon was very understanding. And I'm seriously considering putting the house on the market but I don't want any repercussions. William's a schemer and pretty methodical. I doubt that he'll do anything rash. But what do I know? I never thought he'd raise his hand to me because we had a difference of opinion. He was always the one telling me that it's Okay to disagree. I just don't want to be around a man that's going to put his hands on me, or any woman for that matter. I refuse to be beaten. My father never laid a hand on me and no other man will either. I won't allow for it. I thought about pressing charges but I have faith in the Lord. If there is to be vengeance, it will be His. Right now, I'm just tired. I figure I'll take a leave of absence, maybe a sabbatical, go back to school, finish up work on my masters and then begin on my doctorate and learn to love Sylvia Stanton again. It's the first bit of freedom I've had in I can't remember how long and it feels good. Still, I'm not really used to it and, to tell you the truth, it's a little bit frightening. Such a hodgepodge of emotions all trying to find their only little niche. Perhaps, that's why I wasn't as attentive to your needs as I should have been earlier. I do so apologize. Can you forgive me?

Funny thing, though, Terrance, I spent the better part of the school year trying my damndest not to look in your direction, not to respond to your advances because I knew just how easy it would be for me to fall for you. I honored my marriage vows. I honored them not because I so loved my husband. I didn't honor them for the sake of our marriage. I honored them because of the pact I made with the Lord. Now, I'm trying to pick up the pieces but I'm so afraid, Terrance. I'm afraid of intimacy, of getting close, surrendering myself again. I'm afraid of truly loving someone else, of losing them and the hurt that follows the loss. I'm just so afraid. Can you understand my fear, Terrance, darling? Can you understand me wanting to love you, wanting to share a part of my life, my soul with you and yet afraid of being involved at the same time? Hell, it's crazy, I know. Most of the time, I don't even understand. All I'm asking is that you be patient with me. Just give me some time. Can you do that for me, lover?

Terrance still wasn't sure if he was making the right decision but answered 'yes', and felt himself sinking even deeper into this unknown abyss he was coming to know as Sylvia Stanton. "I'm here for you, Sill. Let's go home."

"Your place or mine?" responded Sill as subtle as was possible.

"Does it matter?" Terrance answered dryly.

"Not as long as I'm with you."

Sill put her head on Terrance's shoulder, grabbed his hand, interlocking her fingers with his as if she were a high school junior on her first date with the captain of the football team. She was happy he understood. Happy to be with him and she would make sure that he too would be happy with her. She was running out of chances and it was up to her to make it work and she would or she would die trying.

CHAPTER 13

❀

Stopping by the bank, William Stanton picked up three thousand dollars in travelers' checks, then made his way to the office to pick up his itinerary from Melinda who had been with him since he joined Hill and Morris six years ago. The very loyal and very efficient Melinda handed him his itinerary as he entered the outer office.

"Good mornin', Mr. Stanton. All set and ready to go? Here's your itinerary for the first week. I'll fax you your schedule for next week and I should be joinin' you in Lagos for three or four days to help you tie up any loose ends or administrative problems shortly after that. You'll be stayin' at the Conrad Hilton in downtown Lagos and a car will pick you up at the airport. Your portfolio's on your desk and I've made the necessary changes and made sure all the account information's been updated. If there's anything I've failed to cover, just e-mail me and I'll take care of it."

Eddie Ames from Budget and Finance had objected vehemently to his taking Melinda with him but after some minor finagling and a few promises, Eddie had agreed. Following Sill's refusal, and the okay from Eddie, he called Melinda.

"Africa? You jokin'. Ain't you, Mr. Stanton? Good God! This is an opportunity of a lifetime. What can I say? I'm packing now," Melinda said, trembling with excitement. She hung up without asking when, where, or what country. This was the reaction he had hoped for from Sill. Instead it led to the worst fight they'd had in their six year marriage. A marriage he'd thought was getting better with the years. Sill, had been so anxious to get married and when he asked her on that day in June six years ago without hardly knowing her it had seemed like a no-brainer at the time. And for the first couple of years he couldn't have asked for any more but there were some deep seated problems he hadn't counted on and being such a cautious soul when it came to matters of the heart she had never let on that something was troubling her until last night and oh, how he regretted last night. He'd never put his hands on anyone before but to do that to a woman was the epitome of cowardliness. At least he'd always believed it to be. But he'd been worried sick the whole time she was gone and then for her to just come back in with that flippant attitude—well—it had all been just a bit too much for him to stand. Now he regretted it but what was he to do.

"Mr. Stanton you're daydreaming. Get it together, your flight into Charlotte leaves at nine-twenty and it's eight-thirty now!"

William's first stop was Charlotte, North Carolina, where he had a business luncheon with one of his very first clients, Mr. Flynn, who then put him on board British Airway Flight 754 to London.

He hated flying. The rash of recent plane crashes did little to placate his fears but after a double Scotch on the rocks, William felt fine. Sleeping fitfully, he awoke briefly, ordered another double, relieved himself in the closet like John and slept soundly for another six hours.

This time he awoke to the sound of the captain's voice requesting seats be placed in an upright position. The no-smoking sign was on and a few minutes later, he was sitting in London's Heathrow Airport. It was 7:25 in the morning. He still had three hours between the next leg of his journey and knowing that he would not be able to sleep, decided to get some breakfast.

There were several rather quaint little English restaurants in and around the airport. He chose McDonald's, ordering an egg McMuffin instead. Sylvia would have been outraged. Each time they had gone on vacation Sylvia commented on Americans traveling thousands of miles to eat fast-food. What would she say if she saw him now? He didn't care but he would have preferred one of Sill's home cooked breakfasts. Some grits, eggs, bacon and homemade biscuits the way only Sill could make it would certainly have hit the spot. Instead, there was this slop. William was a firm believer that good food couldn't be prepared quickly. No, sir. Therefore, there was no such thing as 'fast-food'. He thought about all of this as he grabbed the *London Times* and bit down into his Egg McMuffin. Sure tasted good to be processed. William glanced the front page. The headlines read, <u>Yeltsin Wins Election by Narrow Margin</u>. William read on. It seemed that progress and economic growth hadn't come as quickly as the Russian people had come to expect so now they were contemplating throwing out the baby with the bathwater. The Communist candidate had given Yeltsin a run for his money. A run-off was predicted. William thought this was akin to Blacks asking for a return to slavery but then what did he know about politics?

The layover between flights seemed to drag on forever.

Sill would have had him out wandering around London taking in the sights, souvenir hunting. For this reason he was glad Sill had chosen to remain home but this was the only reason. He missed her already and vowed to correct the situation as soon as he returned.

"British Airways Flight 603 now boarding." William jumped up, grabbed his overnight bag and headed down the long hallway.

"Flight 603 to Lagos?" he asked.

"Yes, sir," replied the rather cordial young flight attendant

"If I were ten years younger."

The flight attendant smiled her flight-attendant smile.

"3-C right side. You've got a window seat. Have a good flight, Mr. Stanton."

"If you're on this flight it can't help but be a good flight," he replied with a wink.

Anita, the petite stewardess who had given him his boarding pass, also gave him her name and her hotel room number just in case he needed a guide his first couple of days in Lagos. But after the first three days of board meetings and introductions along with a visit to the U.S. Embassy William was too exhausted to do anything but eat a light dinner in his suite and fall fast asleep. And so tight was his schedule that the only parts of Lagos William was really able to see were from the deeply tinted windows of his limousine.

Lagos was a bustling metropolis, which reminded him more of New York than any place he'd been, except Tokyo. There were Black people everywhere. Everywhere. But not only were they driving cabs and buses and picking up garbage, they were behind the scenes, in board rooms and in the banks. Black people were running things.

William Stanton was energized by a new self-awareness, a new pride. These were his people. He could now understand why his old college roomie constantly talked about his country?

The only Whites he came into contact were somehow attached to the U.S. Embassy. The anti-American sentiment was rampant but he didn't feel it. In fact, the only thing William Stanton felt was warmth. Those that spoke English and spoke to him about the United States inquired about Michael Jordan and Will Smith, who had recently conducted a tour of several African countries. They wanted to know about the plight of their Black brothers in America. Had it gotten any better since the Sixties? All those he met made him feel welcome and after the first week he knew the city well enough to walk to most of his meetings.

The last several mornings, a nine year old, Nigerian boy would greet him in the hotel lobby where they would have breakfast together. This was no mere coincidence or act of goodwill on William's part but was the result of an encounter William witnessed upon his arrival.

The youngster, William later came to know as Alex had been pestering a foreign couple for change in front of the hotel while the doorman was busy hailing them a cab. Alex in his haste to get the woman's attention accidentally touched her arm. The military police heard the woman's screams and immediately grabbed the youngster by the scruff of his neck and threw him up against the wall.

William, having witnessed the whole affair left his breakfast where it stood and spent the next twenty minutes attempting to explain the whole affair from his point of view. The big, burly Black cop who held Alex, released the boy to William, shouted a warning at the boy and left. Alex followed William everywhere after that and was the first person William saw each morning when he entered the hotel lobby. There standing smiling broadly would be Alex peering through the large double doors. William would beckon and after getting the doorman's attention, Alex was permitted to join him for breakfast.

The doorman, however, made it quite clear in his broken English that little Alex's attire was not suitable for the hotel restaurant so in between meetings William Stanton bought young Alex a small wardrobe. The boy was ecstatic, but continued to wear the same outfit over and over.

The meetings took up most of his day and were as a whole not fruitful. The military regime had installed a Minister of the Interior, who had imposed both a ban on the killing of elephants and the sale of ivory. The amendment met with widespread opposition but was tightly enforced causing the price of ivory to skyrocket. Poachers had a field day. Nevertheless, the U.S. supported the ban. There was therefore little for William to accomplish. Ivory was the agency's largest import. Next to ivory everything else was trivial in comparison. Mr. Morris must have known all this. It made little sense and forced William to think about some of the things Sill had said. His hands tied by the ban he had to ask himself why the old man sent him. Ol' Man Morris kept abreast of everything that concerned Hill and Morris, and William was certain the old man was aware of the country's policy concerning ivory. It just didn't make any sense.

Despite his uneasiness William enjoyed the city and became acutely in touch with himself. Never had he seen such pride among a people? Sure, there was poverty. Where wasn't there? But there was a wealth of pride, of values. Many of the brothers he knew at home who had the big cars, and fancy houses didn't possess what these people possessed. Even little Alex in his tattered bits of clothing possessed it and it was beautiful to see. They had a sense of pride, a sense of dignity. Walking down the streets of Lagos, watching the men and women in their multi-colored garments and *kofus,* William also felt a sense of pride, of dignity, of belonging for the first time in his life.

He tried to call Sill to apologize, to tell her he finally understood but as before there was no answer.

At least Melinda would have a chance to see it first-hand. Black people runnin' things. William waited until he knew she was on her way before faxing the minutes of the Ivory Meetings back to Morris and spent the day with little Alex who now acted as his tour guide. There was no question Alex could better use the money he would have paid a guide but Alex was by no means a charity case. In actuality, he had a better command of the English language than most and took him to places no guide would have never considered taking him. He ate Nigerian delicacies in little out of the way shanties where the food was delectable and the conversation better. Thanks to little Alex he learned of tribal politics first-hand and was given an historical perspective of the Civil War between the Ibos and Yorubas.

Melinda arrived the following day and like William, fell in love with little Alex immediately and the country. She kept saying she was 'home.' The Nigerian men took a liking to the little plump, brown-skin woman and made her feel a feeling like she had never known in the States and given half-a-chance or a simple proposal, William felt there was a good chance Melinda would have made Lagos her home.

The day before they were to return home, Alex took them into shanty town. Here, all the homes or huts were bunched together in rows, some made of wood, some sheets of metal just leaning on each other serving as makeshift walls with a piece of sheet metal placed on top to serve as a roof. Chickens, goats and children roamed everywhere.

Alex threaded his way through the throngs of people followed by the two Americans until they reached a hut no different from the rest. Three small children played in front of the shanty. Upon seeing Alex, they ran to him each grabbing a leg and shouting his name, "Alex! Alex!" He hugged them and gave them each something from his pocket. It was then that William noticed that the children's outfits closely resembled the ones he'd bought for Alex. One of the youngster went inside and out poured at least nine children, all of whom resembled Alex and all wore some item of clothing resembling that which William had bought for Alex a week or so earlier. Along with the children came two adults whom Alex introduced as his mother and father. They welcomed Melinda and William warmly. A huge feast had been prepared in a show of appreciation for the American who had helped one of their own. The food plentiful, Alex made sure they tasted every dish and that every comfort was made available to them. His brothers and sisters no less appreciative of their new finery were just as accommodating.

A festive spirit like William had never known filled the air. Someone brought a cassette player out and African rhythms soon filled the air. People sang, and Melinda, never the shy one, danced and shook till William was sure something was going to fall off. All in all, William couldn't remember ever having a better time. Melinda reckoned it to one big block party.

It was two-thirty in the morning before the village began to disperse and an old beat up jeep was brought around to take William and Melinda back to their hotel. Before leaving they thanked everyone, promised to stay in touch and gave three crisp one hundred dollar bills to Alex's parents for their son's services. They politely refused and seemed taken aback by the gesture. William couldn't understand how people as poor as these could be so proud. After all three hundred dollars was three hundred dollars and quite possibly more than their income for a year. Still they refused.

As usual, Melinda came to the rescue proposing a trust fund for Alex's education. On this they agreed and Melinda promised to meet with Alex's father the following day in Lagos to finalize the paperwork. Everyone cried when they departed but no one more than Alex and Melinda. Even William was touched by this scene and had to step away for a few minutes.

When they returned to the hotel, they found a ton of messages. William leafed through the messages but there was still no word from Sill. Melinda said goodnight, thanked William for a wonderful week and headed for her room Sure, Sill was a friend of hers or at least she liked to think so and she had always been appropriate and never anything but professional when it came down to William but she'd begun to feel differently lately. Much differently. She didn't know if it was out of gratitude and respect or….

But what boss would have taken his secretary to Africa with no ulterior motives in mind?

CHAPTER 14

❀

After saying goodnight, Melinda closed the door and threw herself across the bed in a fit of fury and cursed herself. Picking up the phone she called the front desk and ordered a bottle of Dom Perignon before stepping into the shower to calm the heat rising from between her thighs. Stepping into the shower she cursed herself and then William for making her feel this way.

The water from the shower was both warm and soothing. Melinda let the warm jet spray rush over her plump but firm body placing both arms on the shower walls content if only for a minute to let all thought of William and her needs flow from her. Remembering the champagne she'd ordered, she grabbed the soap and lathered quickly making sure not to miss a spot. A good night's rest was sorely needed after all the festivities and she hadn't known just how tired she was until she'd gotten into the shower.

She'd always hated being in the shower knowing that she was expecting someone but continued showering since there would be little time in the morning. Bending over to soap her thighs, she felt the tingling again, began to massage her self vigorously, and was glad for the knock at the door. She was beginning to hate herself for having so little self-control. A good bottle of champagne was just what the doctor ordered. A glass or two and she'd be fast asleep.

Grabbing her sheer see-through cami, she headed for the door, then realized the camisole revealed far too much and was hardly appropriate to answer the door in but in her haste she could find nothing else and at that moment she really could have cared less. Searching for her purse she grabbed a five-dollar bill to tip the bellhop and made sure she stood behind the door so as not to reveal too much.

Melinda was shocked to find William standing there instead of the bellhop, a bottle of champagne and two glasses in his hand.

"Thought I'd drop by and celebrate our trip. I don't honestly know how successful we were but the experience in itself was certainly an eye opening experience for me. Sill tried to tell me, but I guess I just didn't understand. *I couldn't understand.* I never would have imagined Black people living like this, so beautifully, so regally. Did you get that same feeling? You don't know how glad I am that you came. You really don't. At least I have you to share this experience. I don't think it's one I'll ever forget. I tried to get Sill to join us but she believes that the old man is doing no more than using me to be a liaison or better yet, his flunky so she was adamant about not being a party to any of this but I am certainly glad that I had the good sense in spite of the Ol' Man's hidden agenda to get a chance to see the homeland. Shall we have a toast?"

Melinda was still shocked that it was William instead of room service but before she had a chance to answer, the bellhop who also doubled as the waiter and the bartender was standing behind William. And here she was for the entire world to see in a see through nightie. William seemed oblivious, so high was he on his recent revelation that he might be Black after all and more importantly a descendant of kings that he hardly noticed what she was wearing or the fact that what she was wearing revealed everything. The attendant, on the other hand, who doubled as everything from waiter to bellhop and bartender and who had been more overly gracious and more than just a little friendly whether he was serving her a midday snack or a drink at the bar seemed to notice everything. And seemed hell bent on driving the damn-serving cart over William if it meant he could get a better look at her. It aggravated Melinda that the bellhop could see the opportunities even with the few extra pounds she'd gained and this fool was standing here talking about his wife who didn't have enough love to support him in the lily-White world of corporate America. Better yet, she didn't have the brains or the foresight to see a missed opportunity such as a trip to Africa, the Motherland. So wrapped up was she in herself, in her own little world that she would send her husband—a Black man—a most intelligent Black man—with a few rough edges no doubt, but nonetheless a good, strong, intelligent, hard working Black man. How naïve could, she be to send a brotha who was attentive, caring and climbing the corporate ladder faster than any man she knew White or Black off with his secretary who was craving just such a man.

'Either she lacks women's intuition, common sense or she gives me no credit for either being able to get a man or hold a man. Whatever it is, one thing's for sure. You never ever send your man off with his secretary to stay together in the same hotel for two weeks. I don't care how good a friend she is.' There it was. That thought again. But what perturbed Melinda more was that this silly fool was standing in the doorway to her hotel room while she stood virtually naked talking about how he wished his wife had come. For a brief moment she thought about letting the bellboy in to service all of her needs but decided against it.

Seeing the bellhop, William moved aside ever so slowly and allowed the young man to approach the door where Melinda stopped him, held out the five spot and pulled the tray in herself before dismissing the young man.

William hardly noticed.

"I see you had similar thoughts," he said." Hoped you had intentions of including me. You know they say it's not good to drink alone."

Attempting to be humorous, Melinda had difficulty breaking a smile but remained cordial despite the animosity she was beginning to feel inside.

"William, do you realize what time our flight leaves? I don't know about you but I'm exhausted. Exhausted. And I still have to pack. Thanks for offering though and you'll never know what this trip has meant to me. I will be forever grateful." And with that said Melinda closed the door slowly revealing a wisp of the see through camisole and what could have been. "Maybe next lifetime", she muttered as she closed the door.

She was still having mixed emotions but maintained that she had done the right thing under the circumstances and quickly busied herself with tidying up her room packing souvenirs and other miscellaneous items she'd picked up here and there during her stay while sipping champagne and continually patting herself on the back for her sudden display of will-power, discipline and moral turpitude although she had no idea where they originated.

The champagne had had the desired effect and before she knew it, she was fast asleep, her dreams taking her back to the wonderful festivities of Alex's village where she danced the night away.

The following day, their last, William went one way, Melinda the other, trying to tie up any loose ends they may have left dangling. Mr. Davenport, one of William's primary customers, an exporter of African artwork, made it a point to see William personally, to assure him that his cargo of artwork would clear customs despite a few pieces tinged with ivory. He was also sending a small gift for Mr. Morris. This point he made quite clear, much to William's surprise. He wondered how Davenport, a foreigner, had amassed such wealth in a country populated and dominated by Blacks. Sill would have called it 'exploitation.'

William attributed it to savvy business acumen. This done, William met Melinda back at the hotel at three o'clock, packed their bags and readied themselves for the flight home. Close to a day later after several adjoining flights, they arrived at Jackson International back in Atlanta.

Melinda and William were still reminiscing as they walked down the long runway leading from the plane. "Sill's certainly gonna' be tickled when she sees all the goodies I brought her," William said aloud. He couldn't wait to get home to apologize to her and tell her just how right she'd been. Making their way to the baggage claim there appeared to be some type of commotion.

"Probably just some new security precaution," William assured Melinda. "911's still got everyone uptight."

William wanted no delay. All he wanted was to grab his luggage and head home. All he could think about was getting home to Sill. The trip to Africa made him feel as if he'd been born again. Africa in all her splendor and glory had been nothing short of a renaissance for him.

There was a long line of arriving passengers standing before him. Customs officials were everywhere and he hadn't even reached the baggage claim area when a gentleman man of about forty approached him.

"Passport and ticket, sir."

William passed the customs inspector the documents requested. Waiting impatiently, he thought of how unusual it was to be asked for his passport on his return, then let the matter drop. His thoughts returned to Sill. He really was fortunate to have married a woman of Sylvia Stanton's stature. After all, take away the college degrees, he was, in all essence, nothing more than the son of a no-account, backwoods, dirt farmer. He sighed. And as much as he hated to admit it, Sill with her upper middle-class values and liberal ideas had been right about so many things.

There was no question, though; a change in their marriage was sorely needed. Being at fault, he would have to initiate the change. He might even consider opening his own agency as she had suggested. After all, the monies were available. He had the contacts. And with Sill and Melinda's support how could he possibly fail? He'd make them shareholders—no—equal partners and deal strictly with Third World countries. The resources were abundant and there was so much to do in the way of philanthropy. He hoped he wasn't being smug or pretending to be bourgeoisie. He just wanted to do his part. Besides that, he was thoroughly disenchanted with Hill and Morris.

During his stay in Lagos, they hadn't responded to any of his inquiries or correspondences, oftentimes leaving him to ad lib and make ad hoc policy decisions, which were well out of his jurisdiction. They hadn't even bothered to respond to Melinda's faxes for petty cash. When it became obvious after several faxes that a response was not forthcoming, Melinda joked about the Enron scandal and the possibility that Ol' Man Morris may have flown the coup, 401K in one hand and their worthless shares in the other. William saw little humor in Melinda's remarks but smiled cordially just the same. It was now quite clear that there was something amiss. Furthermore, everyone in corporate affairs at Hill and Morris was aware of the political climate and the ban on ivory, which existed so why in heaven's name had they sent him?

At that moment, lost in thought, William became acutely aware of two rather nattily-attired gentlemen approaching him rapidly from his left. Only a few feet from him, William identified them as customs agents from their badges. Out of all the people in line waiting to claim their baggage, why had they chosen to pick him from the crowd? Sill would have called it 'racial profiling.' William smiled at the thought knowing full well he'd done nothing wrong.

"William Stanton?"

William turned to find the taller of the two gentlemen standing just to the right of him. The shorter red-faced agent moved to his left almost strategically.

"Yes, I'm William Stanton. Is there a problem gentlemen?"

William at six foot five towered over both men and could have easily made short work of them but after their initial charge he hardly gave their approach a second thought. Probably just some minor misunderstanding, he thought. With all the threats of terrorism, he told himself, one couldn't be too careful.

"I'm sure it's nothing we can't work out, Mr. Stanton. Would you please come with us? Our Chief Inspector would like a few words with you, if you don't mind."

The shorter man then picked up William's overnight bag assuring William that despite their politeness he had little option but to follow. Melinda was aghast.

"Want me to grab your bags, Mr. Stanton?"

The same fellow then turned to Melinda. "That won't be necessary, ma'am. We already have them."

William followed the two men into an out of the way cubicle which someone had done their best to turn into an office but which in reality was little more than a holding tank and a room for questioning. Entering the room, William found a roundish rather balding gentleman of about fifty, waiting. Burly, with a thick red mustache, he was every bit as polite as his subordinates. Yet he also possessed a no-nonsense quality that made William just a wee bit leery. He was now quite sure despite his earlier dismissal that whatever the problem was it was much more serious than what he'd initially thought. The man rose from behind the desk with a good deal of labor, extending his sweaty palm to William and introduced himself.

"Mr. Stanton. I'm Terry Shannon. I guess you're curious as to why I've asked you to take a few minutes out of your travels to speak to me."

"Frankly, I am, sir." William was just that now. His anxiety gave way to sudden curiosity of knowing there was a crisis at hand but had no clue as to what it pertained to.

"Well, so as not to delay you any further or keep you in suspense since you obviously do not know why you are here, let me get right to the point. The reason I've asked you here, Mr. Stanton, is that from all our surveillance, we are quite sure, better yet we strongly believe that you are carrying contraband."

William blinked in bafflement. He was so utterly appalled by the allegations that he felt the hair tingle on the nape of his neck. Angry, seething, he stared at the little Irishman. '*Fat, little bastard. I ought to level him*', he thought to himself. The last time he had been this angry was when Sill left that damn meat cleaver on his pillow. He was sure these three pugs would do more than just threaten him. Who the hell do they think they are?

Slowly composing himself, William said, "Mr. Shannon is it? Mr. Shannon, I had the pleasure of meeting with the U.S. Ambassador to Nigeria and Mr. C.J. Davenport. I'm sure you're familiar with Davenport Enterprises. Both of whom assured me that the small quantities of ivory that I would be transporting into the U.S. were within the legal parameters." Still, he wondered, '*What kind of games are they playing?*' He was once again on the defensive almost hostile.

The thought of these toy cops pulling him out of thousands of commuters to question him about a few ounces of ivory was for lack of a better word, absurd. This was a complete waste of time. He could be spending this time with Sill, making amends, relaxing.

"You mentioned a Mr. Davenport. By the way, is this you first trip to Nigeria, Mr. Stanton?"

"Yes, sir. Yes, it is."

"And you're aware that Mr. Davenport and your boss, Mr. Morris, if I'm correct have been doing business for many years." Mr. Shannon was alluding to something or another, trying to establish some causal-effect type of relationship. But what? Where the hell was he attempting to go with all this conjecture?

Why didn't he just ask what it was that he wanted to know instead of beating around the damn mulberry bush?

"Yes, I'm aware that Mr. Davenport and Mr. Morris conducted business prior to my joining the agency. Now, would you be so kind as to tell me what this is really all about? I know it's not about the ivory because the ivory is legal. Aside from that, I've been living in hotels for three weeks and am a bit anxious to get on home to my wife and my own bed." There! No more bullshit, he'd said what he had to say and in a way as to not enrage these stupid wanna-be cops.

"All in due time, Mr. Stanton. All in due time. Please try to bear with us. I assure you this won't take much longer. Now, did you by any chance get a chance to check your cargo prior to leaving Lagos, Mr. Stanton?"

"No, I did not." William slumped down in the worn-out leather chair resigning himself to the fact that he wouldn't be going anywhere, anytime soon.

"Mr. Stanton, everything you've told us corresponds to what the Nigerian authorities have told us. We are also aware of a network that has been in operation for many years now and, yes, long before your arrival at Hill and Morris. This network was set up between Davenport and your supervisor in the late Seventies and has flourished under the guise of importing ivory. Now that there is no trade in ivory, their interest in Nigeria became more and more suspicious. Certain members of the Justice Department became increasingly concerned since both men were welcomed and openly embraced by a military regime openly hostile to foreigners and Americans in particular. The country was under martial law. There was a new government in power, a power that emanated almost out of the blue. So, secret was the coup that our intelligence wasn't even aware of them until they were firmly entrenched. Yet, both Davenport and Morris, seemed abreast of everything.

At first, it was thought that they were supplying the new regime with weapons. You know gun running and we have not ruled this out entirely. However, we've no concrete evidence to support our allegations on this theory. Of one thing we are certain, however, and that is that they have been using the export of ivory as a cover-up for the smuggling of narcotics into the U.S. and other countries. Heroin, to be more specific."

William was visibly shaken.

"Can you tell us who it was that approached you concerning the trip to Lagos? Did Morris come to you, personally?" Shannon questioned.

"Yes, sir. Do I need to call my lawyer?" William asked nervously.

"We are not charging you with anything, Mr. Stanton. We're pretty sure that the old man was simply using you as a mule, a courier. He's done it before. We've just never had enough evidence for an indictment. We're hoping that with your cooperation, we'll finally get enough evidence to make for an air-tight case."

"And if I decide not to cooperate with customs?" William inquired, although he knew his options were few. The only reason they were being so cordial was that a cooperative witness could only be a boon to their efforts for an indictment.

"Well, the choice is yours, Mr. Stanton. The way it stands now, I think the DEA would be somewhat interested in the final destination of your cargo. Let's see, we have three cartons containing a little more than thirty-five pounds of high-grade heroin with your name attached. That's enough in itself to send you away for how long, Pete?"

The shorter of the two men standing was from DEA. He seemed to relish this part of the inquiry and didn't hesitate to throw the book at him.

"Do you believe in reincarnation, Mr. Stanton? Throw in concealment, conspiracy, attempting to distribute, international trafficking and that kind of weight. Well, let me put it this way, Stanton: If you died and came back you'd still be facing a life sentence or two."

Shannon spoke up again.

"We're not even considering that as an option, Mr. Stanton. We've taken the liberty to check your background. We know you're not a player. From all accounts, our records indicate that you've never had so much as a traffic violation let alone a trafficking conviction. Your boss is the one we're really after, Stanton. Say, you don't mind if I call you William, do you?"

William nodded, giving his consent to the feeble attempts at familiarity and friendship.

"Call me Terry. I don't think there's a need for all the formality being that we're going to be working with each other for the next few months. Do you agree?"

Again William consented. He had no desire to fight some long, drawn out legal battle with the Government with the odds clearly stacked against him.

"William, do you have any idea what two hundred pounds of pure heroin can do to a city the size of say New York or better yet right here in Fulton County? I've seen it. Trust me. It's not a pretty sight. Just think of the kids. Isn't your wife a teacher? Think of little Alex and his brothers and sisters on that shit. C'mon, Stanton, think!"

William was doing just that. He was thinking of Sylvia. She had begged him not to go and he had ignored her pleas, her remarks, and her better judgment until he could bear it no more. Then he'd done something he'd seen his father do so many times to his mother. He slapped her. And for what? At the time, he thought Sill was like every other no-account sister, grateful to be wherever, with whomever, doing whatever with no more sense of purpose than a man on the moon. Criticizing Mr. Morris because to fathom a trip to Africa was beyond her comprehension. She, who was so in touch with her Blackness…How could she possibly turn down a trip to the Motherland? The thoughts of his last encounter with Sylvia swirled around in his head until he found himself becoming lightheaded. How could he possibly face her? She with her holier-than-thou attitude? Shannon was still speaking to him but little mattered now. William felt betrayed and then Shannon said something that pierced the sea of self-pity he found himself adrift in.

"By the way, if it's any consolation, the Nigerian people were extremely pleased with the way you carried yourself while you were there and the way you befriended young Alex. Everyone to the person, from the doorman at the hotel, to the U.S. ambassador told us the story of Alex and the trust fund. By the time I reached the airport, I knew I had the wrong guy. Did a world of good for our diplomatic relations over there. Might wanna pass on a tip or two to some of our ambassadors about conducting foreign policy."

William smiled sheepishly. After all he'd just been through; it felt good to know that his entire trip had not been in vain. Despite appearing to be a notorious international drug lord, his trip thanks to a nine year old boy, did have some redeeming value.

"Listen William, I can see you're exhausted. Take your time. Call your lawyer. See what he advises. Get reacquainted with the wife. Then give me a call. Here's my card. I must ask that you stay in the country for the time being, however. If for any reason you're compelled to leave the county, all I ask is that you contact me first."

Shannon stood to take William's hand in his own. Grasping it tightly, he warned William to stay on his p's and q's and be cognizant of any peculiarities at work. William thought of the times when he was a small boy not much bigger than Alex when he fashioned himself to be a junior G-man. Now, here he was playing the role in real life.

Shannon assured him before his leaving that the confiscated drugs would be allowed to continue on their journey so as not to affect the sting operation. However, William's thoughts returned to Shannon. 'Get acquainted with the wife' he'd said. William's thought of Sill. She had warned him about going in the first place. If he had only listened. What was it they said about a woman's intuition?

Terry was still talking when William's focus returned.

"You know, William, most of the people affected by that shit would be little African-American boys and girls. Not to say that they'll necessarily be the one's shooting it into their veins. It's the trickle-down effect that really eats at me. Anyway, it was nice to meet you. Wish it could have been under different circumstances. And don't worry. There's no need to look over your shoulder. There won't be anyone following you. What we'll be following are the drugs. And from our reports they've already left the airport. You have a good day, sir. We'll be in touch."

A good day! How the hell could anyone in their right mind have a good day after being informed that they were for all intensive purposes a drug courier? By the time William left the airport, he was exhausted. Drained both mentally and physically. He was glad Melinda hadn't waited. He could have taken the airport shuttle but felt the long walk in the brisk, night air might help clear his head. He cursed Ol' Man Morris, sometimes aloud, calling him among other things, 'A dirty bastard.'

An hour or so later, William turned the nose of the Mercedes into the long driveway. Opening the trunk, he arranged the many gifts and souvenirs in the order he wanted Sill to open them. Then he rang the doorbell. He was sure that in spite of everything she would be glad to see him. With all the adversity befalling him, she was still the one constant in his life. He rang the doorbell again. Still, there was no answer. He had no idea where she could be. It was well past five o'clock. Too late for her to still be at school and too early for Bible study. She hadn't been home when he'd called each evening either. His mind began to race. And after a day like today, he refused to think the worst. No, Sill had to be home. Maybe she'd gone out to grab a bite to eat. William put the packages down, rummaged through his trouser pockets, found his keys and opened the front door. And there he stood, frozen in his tracks.

"What the hell!" he yelled.

His initial thoughts were that they'd been robbed. There was nothing there except for the big-screen TV. And then it dawned on him. No wonder she hadn't answered the phone. Dropping the packages, he ran from room to room, screaming Sill's name, half expecting to find her in a crumpled up heap, blood everywhere in the corner of some room. Or maybe he'd find her, clothes ripped and torn, sprawled across their bed, a victim of rape. Gruesome images hurled their way through the muck and mire, which clouded his mind. And then in the middle of the empty room, where their bed once stood, sat a bottle of cognac with a note attached. He caught his breath, bent down, picked up the empty bottle and read the note:

∾

"Thought it best that you go your way and I go mine. I gave all that I could give and now I'm taking a little something back. You've always had a liking for nice cars, good food and good liquor so I'm leaving you a sandwich in the fridge, a bottle of good whiskey and you'll find your car outside. Good luck!"

Sill

Devastated and on the verge of tears, William uncorked the bottle. An hour later, he was still sitting there in middle of the now empty room, Sill's note in one hand and an almost empty bottle of *Courvosier* in the other. In a drunken stupor, William Stanton did something that day, which he hadn't done in years. He cried. Cried like a baby.

The following day was Thursday. William's head was still buzzing when he came to the sudden realization that he was alone, had always been alone and more than likely always would be. But for William this was by no means the end. Thanks, in large part to Sill and his recent fiasco abroad, he had to force himself to gather himself together and take a new lease on life.

He wouldn't forget, however and in time there were those that would be held accountable for the grief and heartache, which he was forced to endure. Sylvia and Ol' Man Morris were at the top of his list. They would pay. They had to pay.

He called West Lansing later that day only to find that Mrs. Stanton was no longer employed there. He then called Terry Shannon at DEA to offer his assistance. Not due to return to the office until the following day, William—a bundle of nerves—was perpetual motion. Several times while wandering around the house, he caught himself muttering to himself and wondered if he were on the verge of a nervous breakdown.

The DEA promised to contact him should they need his assistance. In the meantime, he was instructed to just 'hang loose' and report any unusual happenings at the agency. In a way, he was relieved. This would give him the time to investigate a few things on his own.

Melinda called to see how things were going and to thank him for the trip. In the midst of the conversation, he mentioned Sill's leaving. Melinda's shock mirrored his own initial reaction but she regrouped rather quickly almost too quickly. William was suspicious of everyone at this point. He wondered if Sill had given Melinda any inclination that she was about to walk out on him. Too proud to ask, William didn't understand, couldn't fathom Melinda's cheeky attitude when Sill's departure was brought up. Several times during the conversation, she had intentionally brushed off the topic of Sill's leaving. This aroused his curiosity even more. After all, they had been friends. Or so he thought.

"If you need anything, anything at all, William, be sure to call me. You know the number," Melinda offered.

William stopped her. "Well, actually I do need a few things, now that you mention it, Melinda. I could use some groceries and maybe something to drink, you know, purely for medicinal purposes to kind of get me through these next couple of weeks. I've got to do some furniture shopping also. Sill cleaned me out."

"You po' thang. Look, give me about fifteen or twenty minutes and I'll see what I can do. Lord knows we can't have you pickin' out any furniture. If your taste in furniture is anything like your taste in clothes, it'll be stars and stripes forever. Remember that green plaid jacket you tried to match with the lime green paisley tie in Lagos?" They both laughed out loud.

"Hurry up, Melinda. I'm gonna grab a quick shower so I'll leave the front door open for you."

Melinda pulled up in the long driveway right as William stepped into the shower. Hearing the screen door slam, he shouted. "Melinda, is that you?" When she affirmed that it was he continued. "I'm in the shower. Come on in and make yourself comfortable. You noticed that I didn't say, 'Have a seat.' Sill took the chairs. There's a bottle of *Courvosier* on the dresser in the bedroom. I would tell you to get a glass but Sill took them too.

"I must admit, girlfriend didn't leave much, at least she left your bed. A man don't need much more than that, makes for a simple life. Go to work, come home and go to bed."

William finished showering and stepped from the bathroom just in time to see Melinda peering in empty room after empty room as if by some divine intervention they were suddenly going to be refurnished. Shaking her head, she turned and faced a partially dressed William Stanton. William finished buttoning his shirt and bent over to tie his shoes. Feeling the intensity of

Melinda's gaze, he looked up only to confirm his feeling. She was staring—staring at him like he'd just committed a cardinal sin. She was mystified.

"What?" William was at a loss.

"And what masquerade party you plan on attendin' on a Thursday afternoon, William Stanton? Did Sill take your clothes, too? Lord knows you need someone. If no more than to help you get dressed. Maybe undress too. Whatcha' think? But seriously, William, just tell me this. Was one of your parents color blind?"

He scarcely heard the last remark. He was used to her subtle little innuendoes about needing help getting undressed. This was not the first time she had made remarks with sexual connotations. It happened from time to time at the office. And he had joked about her sexually harassing him in the workplace.

In Lagos, it had become almost a daily occurrence with him dismissing it in the course of the conversation. But there was no dismissing her remarks now. Still, everything needed to be put in proper perspective. There was a time and place for everything. Now was neither the time nor the place. Not ignoring the remark William replied, "I've come to accept the fact that I may need help getting dressed but I wasn't under the impression that I needed help getting undressed too. Maybe when I get this mess sorted out you can give me some pointers in that area too."

William's attempt to waylay her advances did just that. Without discouraging Melinda or hurting her feelings with a cold rebuff, he let her know that her timing was all wrong. Yet, he left her hopeful. And with Sill gone and winter rapidly approaching, her tight young body might be just what the doctor ordered.

Melinda grinned from ear to ear.

"Goodness gracious William, that's the closest thing to an *almost* I've heard from you in six years. You must be slippin'. C'mon, let's go shoppin'. Oh, I almost forgot. Please change those clothes."

William and Melinda chose a charcoal leather sofa and loveseat for the living room, a couple of stylish glass end tables and a gorgeous, mahogany, dining room set. Melinda was ecstatic. For the first time in her life, she could actually shop without having to worry about how much she had to spend or what something cost. Of course, it wasn't for her but it sure as hell felt good to be able to spend freely regardless of whose money it was. She'd been obnoxious through the entire shopping spree, knowing that whatever furniture she suggested, William would gladly go along with.

During the course of the day, she had driven the salesgirl up the wall with unnecessary queries about this wood and that, simply because, for the first time in her life, she could. William's Gold Card gave her the right. By the time she finally made her final choice, she was so exhausted that she came close to dozing off on the loveseat while they waited for the salesgirl to run William's *Visa* card through. Minutes later the salesgirl returned, her walk punctuated with a new rhythm.

"I'm sorry, Mr. Stanton, but your credit card's been denied. I'm afraid I'm going to have to hang on to it"

"Not a problem." William searched through the bevy of cards before handing the girl his *American Express* card.

"Good as gold," Melinda said to no one in particular. The salesgirl assumed the remark was intended for her.

When the *American Express* card met with the same fate, the sales clerk made sure she handed the card to Melinda.

"Sorry," she then smiled before attending to another couple who had been waiting patiently for some time.

William and Melinda left the store in silence, puzzled to say the least. William drove to the nearest ATM where he was again notified that there were insufficient funds for him to withdraw any amount of money from his savings. The results were the same when he tried his checking account. He was livid now.

"There's close to a hundred grand alone just in the savings and I can't get a damn dime out of the machine. Will you please tell what's happening, Melinda?"

Clearly shaken by this latest turn of events, William was sure that Terry Shannon had frozen his accounts without telling him. He pulled the Mercedes into a 7-Eleven, found the DEA agent's business card in his wallet in between the worthless credit cards, grabbed his cell from the glove compartment and dialed Agent Shannon.

"Terry Shannon, please."

"Mr. Shannon's in a meeting. May I ask who's calling?"

"Tell Shannon it's William Stanton. Tell him it's important that I speak to him *now*."

"Shannon here. What can I do for you, William?"

"Shannon, let me ask you a question. I need you to be perfectly frank with me. Do you have any earthly idea of what's been going on since I got back? No credit cards, no savings or checking accounts. Tell me, honestly. Do you know anything at all about this?"

"William, right now I need you as much as you need me. DEA and customs are doing their best to do absolutely nothing to disrupt any of the lives of the people involved in this case. This is a very delicate situation, and a very sensitive case, William. Our best chance for an airtight case and perhaps a conviction is to make sure that everything runs smoothly and according to plan. If it does, then we can better observe the players in their natural environment. If they're comfortable they may slip up and make a mistake. Then we've got 'em. If, on the other hand, we disrupt the normal flow of things, we'll set off a widespread panic. With the money and resources those two fellows have it's very, very possible that they'll seek refuge in a foreign country in some hidden villa where we'll never find them. And, even if we were to find them, they'd probably be dead and gone by the time extradition proceedings took effect.

Furthermore, you're our only link to the inside, our ace in the hole. What sense would it do for us to make problems for you when you hold the key to our success? I'm sorry, William but you're barking up the wrong tree this time, my friend."

Terry Shannon seemed to be speaking in earnest. But he was not above suspicion. And even after the long spiel, William was not convinced.

"Tell me again, Shannon. Make me understand." An exasperated William confessed he couldn't even buy gas at the 7-Eleven.

"Look, William. Believe it or not, but it's in your best interest as well as ours that you maintain the same lifestyle that you had before any of this madness took place. In Morris' case, the slightest change could raise suspicion. We don't want that at all, believe me. If there's the slightest change in your financial situation, it's not us. What we need is for you to maintain everything as it's always been. Are you followin' me, William? I know you don't know me very well, but try to trust me. Ask around. Find out about me. Trust me, William. If all goes according to plan and it should and we bring Morris down, you won't have to worry too much about the balance in your savings. Just be patient and stay in touch. Now, if you like I can check into your account history and find out what the problem is."

"No, no that's okay," William replied.

Terry Shannon hung up the phone. And for some reason, William believed the dumpy, little Irishman on the other end. And since he believed him, William threw the Mercedes in gear, made a U-turn and headed for First Union Bank on the corner of East Lansing and Bessemer. Entering the bank, it became obvious to the tellers and bank manager that William Stanton was not about to wait in line. A shapely brunette with far too much mascara and too little personality cut William off before he could enter the branch manager's office.

"May I help you, sir?" she asked.

"I really don't think so. That is unless you're the branch manager. Now, if you'll excuse me."

Unaware of the slight, she led him to the branch manager's office, showed him in, did the introductions and closed the door behind her. When he exited twenty minutes later all anger had dissipated and in its place was a firm resolve. The shapely brunette smiled apologetically or at least that's the way William took it. It seemed like everyone knew that Sill had taken him to the cleaners yet no one was talking. And there were no leads. It was almost as though Sylvia Stanton had simply vanished into thin air. He thought about placing a missing persons report and then decided against it. If he found her at this juncture in his life, he couldn't be responsible for his actions. Besides, Sill could wait for now. There were more pressing matters to be addressed.

"Are you OK, William?" Melinda asked, concerned.

"Fine, Melinda. I guess I just have a lot on my mind," he lied.

"I can imagine. Why don't you stop by the supermarket? I'll grab a couple of steaks, throw them on the grill and we'll see what happens."

"See what happens?" William laughed aloud. "If anything else happens they'll be carrying me off to the funny farm."

"That's what happens when people get *too* attached to the almighty dollar. That's why all those fools went jumpin' out windows back in the late twenties. Didn't see no black folks jumpin' though, did you? Black folks are useta' not havin' nothin'." Melinda laughed a big hearty laugh that made William chuckle, too.

They stopped off at the Super K and Melinda was in and out within minutes."Where to?" William asked.

"Well, I don't have a big fancy house like yours, William, but I think my furniture may be a tad bit more comfortable." William chuckled; made a right at the light, then drove down Decatur to Coolspring Street.

Despite having driven Melinda home on several occasions, he had never been in. Always in a hurry to get home to Sill. Perhaps, if he had stopped in earlier the loss of Sill wouldn't have been quite so hard to take now. In any case, he was here now and was pleasantly surprised at how charming and tastefully decorated Melinda's home was. But then, why should he have been? She was meticulous and an impeccable dresser.

"Pour yourself a drink while I get comfortable. Might wanna grab a couple of glasses too, you know, to take with you."

She flicked on the stereo. Aretha Franklin lit up the room with *Natural Woman*. William made himself a gin and juice and flipped through the *Essence Magazine* on the coffee table. Making his way to the étagère, he leafed through the albums, recognizing artists like King Curtis, Jimmy McGriff and a few others when Melinda returned wearing only a faded blue terrycloth robe.

"William, I was goin' to go in and put on somethin' sexy and try to seduce you after you'd had a couple of drinks but I don't know what I'd of done if I'd gone through all that trouble and you'd rejected me. I'd really have felt bad if I couldn't turn your head, bad as you're feelin' right now."

William didn't respond right away. He noticed Melinda's head drop but was at a total loss for words. After some time he spoke. "Melinda, what I need more than anything else at this point in my life is a friend not a bed partner but a friend."

He held Melinda's hands in his own, gently.

"I'm sure you've known how I've felt about you for a while, William. I appreciate the fact that you were sensitive enough not to laugh in my face. I had the hardest time sittin' in the next office, just achin' to seduce you. Those nights we stayed late finishin' this project or that, tryin' to beat a deadline were the roughest. I tried my best to respect your marriage—to respect Sylvia. I knew I wasn't in the runnin' but that doesn't stop me from wantin' you. Some nights I would come home and just fantasize about you having romantic candlelight dinners. But you know what I admired most about you, William? I admired the fact that in spite of my little snide remarks you always remained so faithful and so true to Sill. I guess it's every woman's dream to have a man's undying devotion. And you were never short, William. You never brushed me aside. My little sly innuendos were like so many countless teardrops that you simply let roll off.

At one time, I promised myself that if I ever had the opportunity to get my foot in the door, I would do everything in my power to hold you, to keep you. But, I didn't fool myself. I knew. At least I thought I knew that you and Sylvia would somehow always be the perfect couple. Not for a minute was I so naïve as to believe that should something come between you and Sylvia that I would be the natural successor, so I resigned myself to bein' the best secretary, friend and confidante a man could hope for. So, William, if it's friendship you desire, you'll be hard pressed to find a better one."

When Melinda finished purging her soul, it was apparent that they had happened upon a new found respect for each other. They talked some more at length during dinner. The conversation eventually making its way to the ordeal at the airport. William, despite Shannon's instructions, told Melinda everything. As he told her the details of the fiasco, Melinda's eyes welled with tears. When she closed them it was as like floodgates had opened. It was several minutes before she spoke. The words she now spoke were slow, deliberate. It was apparent, she was angry and hurt. William realized at that very moment that he hardly knew her. This was the first time in the six years that he'd known her to be visibly upset.

"I knew something was wrong when the faxes from Davenport mentioned shipments being in route. Yet they never confirmed their arrival. When I questioned Mr. Morris' secretary, Mia, she told me she knew of no shipments arrivin' from Davenport Enterprises but promised she would check with Mr. Morris. A little later, say about a week, I received a memo, which said, in fact, that the Davenport account would be handled by Morris, personally, and I should no longer concern myself with this matter. I kept the memo and I kept tabs on all the Davenport accounts the same way I kept a file on every other account to cover myself in case there were any discrepancies later."

"You may have just saved my life, Melinda." William jumped up from the dining room table knocking over his glass of *Zinfandel* in the process. "Tell me more, Melinda. Tell me about the memos! Please tell me that you didn't make a copy and leave them in the office files." William was ecstatic.

For the first time since his meeting with Terry Shannon and DEA, did he even have a glimmer of hope?

"No, silly. I told you they took the handlin' of the account out of my hands even though I handle all of your other accounts. That's why, when Mia sent me the memo statin' that Mr. Morris was going to handle the Davenport account personally, I knew there was something else stirrin'. Then about a month ago when the old man flew down from Boston to see you and tell you of the Lagos venture; he brought his secretary, Mia. Well, I hadn't seen her since she transferred to corporate headquarters in Boston, so we decided to make a night of it. In any case, we went out had a couple of drinks and started talkin' about the good ol' days. You know Mia and I go back to Fulton County Community College."

William was becoming impatient. "Melinda, get back to the files."

"In any case, Mia and I started talkin' about all the inconsistencies at H and M when she brings up the mystery account. Now, Mia ain't never been able to drink and I guess we're on our fourth of fifth, *Long Island Iced Tea* when she starts tellin' me about this mystery account. Seems Morris told Mia that any correspondence relatin' to the Davenport account should go directly to him. Mia's is strugglin' with the fact that she's held accountable for every Hill and Morris account Yet, Morris never returns any paperwork, nor any correspondence, billin' statement, invoice from the biggest account that Hill and Morris handles. And, then, when I mention the tact that I'm missin' information from the Davenport file, Mia says that the Ol' Man flew off the handle. She said she'd been with him for close to ten years and she'd never seen him get so angry over something so petty. That's when I received the memo about Morris handlin' the Davenport account. Mia lost a lot of respect for the Ol' Man after that and I think that she forwarded me every single correspondence concernin' the account just to spite him, I even have requisitions for toilet paper. If it's got the Davenport *logo* on it, then I've got a copy."

William couldn't believe that he was hearing. "Melinda, I've got one question and one question only. Where are the files? Please tell me you didn't leave them in the office."

"Of course not, silly. No one leaves a paper trail anymore. That's so 'Seventies'." Melinda was teasing him. She enjoyed watching William squirm.

"Funny thing about the Davenport account—"

William had had enough. "Melinda, please, spare me the details. Where are the files?"

"Relax, William. I've got every Davenport correspondence for the last two-and-a-half year's right here. I downloaded them onto this floppy disc. All you have to do is insert the floppy, wait for the Davenport icon to appear and double click on the mouse." Melinda, recognizing the fact that William refused to become computer literate, went through the whole procedure just as she had each day in the office. It was all to no avail. William ignored the procedure, content instead to stare at the computer screen until *Voila*! The Davenport *logo* appeared.

Three hours later, William rose from the easy chair, smiled, yawned, then turned and, without a word, gave Melinda the biggest, tightest, bear hug she had ever received. He then grabbed Melinda's phone and placed a call to Chief Customs Inspector, Mr. Terry Shannon, to inform him. Terry was almost as elated as William was and they spent the better part of the next hour plotting the best possible course of action. In the end, they decided not to run their plan past Terry's superiors. Instead, they decided to let nature run its course, letting the chips fall where they may. And then as if by some chance of fate the following day William received a call summoning him to the corporate headquarters in Boston. It was only the third time he'd been summoned to the headquarters since he'd joined Hill and Morris.

CHAPTER 15

❀

The following Thursday, William flew to Boston to corporate headquarters and met with Ol' Man Morris in person. Leery, William had no idea what Morris had up his sleeve this time. The word was he was certain to be offered a senior accounting position; the highest position one could attain outside of being named a junior partner. There was no doubt that the board members, were in direct opposition to having an African-American in the position but that was the word along the grapevine.

Little did Morris know, William wasn't the least bit concerned about being named senior accountant or partner. If Melinda's plan worked and Agent Shannon received the OK, there was a good chance Hill and Morris wouldn't even be in existence a year from now. And even if it was, William was sure he wouldn't want to be connected with it, let alone have his name associated with a firm that was sure to be under indictment for narcotics trafficking, laundering money as well as numerous other improprieties. William put the final changes on his proposal and walked into his outer office where Melinda was busy putting the final touches on some of William's more recent proposals.

"Ain't worked this hard in my entire life," Melinda commented mostly to herself.

"It'll all pay off in the end, Melinda. If everything goes according to plan, it will all pay off in the end. Matter-of-fact, I have a meeting with *the* Man now. I should be back in an hour or so." Melinda knew who *the* Man was. She smiled hoping not to show her concern.

"Hold all my calls and see if you can get any more information on the Davenport account. We should be hearing something any day now. Make sure everything's in order."

"Everything's in order," Melinda said. The proposal for your two o'clock is right here." She held up a large manila envelope. "Packets are displayed in the second conference room, the door is locked and, except for Mr. Rivera the janitor, no one else has a key. Mr. Aiello is printin' your schemata as we speak. He's already printed a black and white card as you ordered. However, he and I both thought that blue and gold would be much more spectacular a bit more stylish, more in keepin' with their company *logo*—so much more impressive.

Aside from that, I edited your speech and don't see any problem with your proposal or presentation. The people from Apple should be ecstatic that they will be able to sell that many personal computers and software to match. They stand to make a bundle. With only a two and a half percent mark up, the Nigerians may name you their next Minister of Education or at the very least, Secretary of Commerce," Melinda forecasted. "As far as any new developments concernin' our little problem, I'll talk to you about that over dinner, if we're still on for tonight."

The Wednesday dinners began as a simple meeting to discuss any changes in the Davenport account but had now become a weekly ritual often ending in their retiring to Melinda's where they'd work until the wee hours of the morning on one proposal or another. William had come to enjoy the routine almost as much as Melinda. Both knew, however, that William, despite his recent success at work, was still very much in love with Sylvia.

Melinda, would all too often, catch him staring off into space or seemingly in deep thought and knew that it was more than simply business which kept him so utterly absorbed in his work and his mind so preoccupied.

William met Terry Shannon at the Lone Star Cafe for lunch. The meeting was brief. Shannon opted to go with Melinda's plan without authorization, wanting Morris almost as badly as William. Though neither man showed it, Shannon confessed that he hadn't been this close in years and wasn't about to be denied due to some bureaucratic red tape. Shannon recognized Melinda's plan as simple and as a winner. If it unfolded, as he was sure it would, it would do wonders for his career. If it backfired and Morris somehow got wind of the plan or something went awry, there would be hell to pay. With Morris' connections and political influence, not only would his career with the government be over, but chances were good that he probably wouldn't be able to get a job shoveling shit

"Anything new on your end, William?" Shannon inquired.

"Not a damn thing, Terry. Melinda keeps telling me it's time but so far there haven't been any faxes from Davenport or Morris. It's almost as if they've been tipped and have decided to go on a hiatus. It's not as if they're pressed for cash and have to make a move so we're just waiting.

There is some good news though. I'm preparing to fly over in a couple of weeks. I have a major software package the Nigerian government seems interested in. And as soon as I receive confirmation, I'll be on my way. I'm hoping that my trip will sort of force their hand. Other than that, the only thing I can come up with is that Morris is waiting on me, so he doesn't have to use any potentially, incriminating correspondence."

"He's a shrewd one, that Morris. He didn't get where he is making mistakes. The D.E.A.'s had knowledge of Morris' involvement in the drug trade for close to twenty-three years and has never been able to lay a finger on him. This is the closest we have ever been and we're still light years away.

I feel confident about it this time, though, William. I really do. Hell, I've been on this case for close to twelve years and for the first time I see the possibility of him going down. For years, I've had to sit by and watch our kids shoot each other and turn into zombies before my very eyes while fat cats like Morris get rich selling our kids poison. I'm not naïve, William. Morris' arrest may not make a dent in the amount of drugs entering the country but if not part of the solution, well, you know the rest."

"How'd you ever get involved in drug enforcement, Terry?" William asked. "Dangerous business, isn't it? Can't see why anyone would wanna put themselves in the line of fire. It doesn't make any sense to me."

"It's a long story, William. I'll tell you about it sometime. Right now's not the time, though. I've gotta head back to the office. Phone me when you get the go ahead And tell Melinda I said hello."

Both men were on edge but firm in their beliefs. And neither too confident about tackling someone of Morris' stature. None but Melinda who could barely contain herself.

"Is it a go?" she asked as William entered the conference room at one forty five. William gave her the thumbs up. Melinda grinned like a teenager about to go on her first date. Tem minutes later, she escorted the six Apple representatives and trustees into Conference Room 2B and began taking notes.

William had never been more eloquent in his delivery or clearer with his proposal. After thirty minutes and what seemed like a lifetime of questions from the various reps and board members present, Melinda returned the thumbs up.

Minutes of the meeting were faxed to the Ol' Man at corporate. Now, was the hardest part, Waiting. Melinda met William later that evening at the Tavern for dinner, and even he had to admit, he had never seen her more glowing or more radiant.

Dressed in a black evening gown showing her dwindling cleavage and a split the length of the San Andreas Fault, William was suddenly aware of just how long it had been since he'd been with a woman.

"Melinda, what can I say? You look fabulous," he blurted out

No longer was she the pleasantly plump little girl with the great typing skills and Dolly Parton cleavage he'd hired at twenty-one. She was not even the robust twenty-eight year old he watched dance the night away under the moonlight in that tiny African village twenty miles outside of Lagos. Not at all, she had suddenly come of age. Melinda Bailey had become, not in a Piaget stage, but rather all at once—a woman

She, on the other hand, was focused and had one goal in mind. That goal was to escort William Stanton to the top of the corporate ladder, then, God willing, to the altar. The first part was easy. The second part presented one obstacle and her name was none other than Sylvia Stanton. She would, however, cross that bridge when she came to it.

Tonight was the first night she had even considered the latter. Down from a size fourteen to a size six, the girls at the gym applauded her graduation and loss of twenty-nine pounds. She was a real inspiration to all of them. Trainers who couldn't find the time to speak to her three months ago were pushin' up, and sweatin' her for dates. She would smile cordially and then ask: "Where were you, sweetie, when 1 couldn't bend over to tie my shoes? Lord knows, I needed someone then, sugar."

She continued to wear her same baggy, loose-fitting garb she used to wear to hide her excess baggage. Now she wore it for another reason. William was adamant about her banking her bonus money as well as every penny in excess of her real need in case the bottom fell out. Tonight was special, though. After months of denial, painful exercises and sore muscles, she was going to do something for herself. After work, she stopped by the mall, picked up a black evening gown with gold embroidery she only dreamed about getting into a couple of months ago, and a sexy pair of pair of black leather pumps. Then on a whim she stopped by Trés Chic to see if Kim could squeeze her in without an appointment. Her doo needed major work but if Kim could just…

Everything had gone as well as could be expected. When William's eyes locked onto Melinda's as she came sashaying, sultry like, through the door, Melinda knew all the aches and pains, giggles, snide remarks and cravings were well worth her efforts. It was at that very moment; Melinda came to the realization that if they survived the DEA ordeal, William would be hers to lose. But tonight, she was a winner. *Sylvia Stanton, eat your heart out,* she whispered to herself.

"A celebration is in order," Melinda proposed. "After hearing your presentation today, Mr. Stanton, I would have to say a celebration is *definitely* in order. You were too smooth. You were even color coordinated. Right down to the socks. Sill must have come back home."

William smiled. It was the first time he hadn't winced and retreated into his little cocoon at the mention of her name.

"There's a lot riding on this account," he said. "Matter of fact, there's a lot riding on all of these accounts we pick up from here on out. Gotta make sure I come correct. I met this little gay fella at this men's store on Fifth Avenue and he put me down for an outfit a week and I bless him with an extra fifty under the table."

"Thank goodness," Melinda said, emitting a sigh of relief at William's admission.

"I really thought Sill had come home," Melinda repeated the statement so she could get a feel for his present sentiments since William seldom but ever mentioned her any more. It was almost as if Sylvia Stanton had never existed at all.

"Melinda!"

"Yes, William?"

"As good as you look tonight, baby, if I were married and I mean happily married, you'd sure as hell would make me consider leaving home. Damn, you look good!" Melinda blushed.

"Be careful, Mr. Stanton. Your comments are bordering on sexual harassment and you really don't need any more legal headaches, now do you?"

William grinned.

"Anyway, we don't have time for that now, William, although I can hardly believe I'm saying this but there are other issues that I think are far more important than my appearance.

You know I seriously believe that Terry Shannon is both honorable and very dedicated in his endeavors but if something should go wrong this whole damn thing's gonna fall on you. I guess you're aware of that and so I guess I'm not really telling you anything you don't already know. And trust me I'm not trying to put any undue pressure on your shoulders but I think it best you concentrate on what's going on so we can both keep our jobs and save our necks at the same time."

"I suppose you're right," William said somewhat dejectedly. "But in all the time we've worked together I must admit I've never seen you so alive, so vibrant, so absolutely stunning as I have since we returned from Lagos. I don't know if I was blind, so infatuated by Sill, so absorbed in trying to climb the corporate ladder and doing the Ol' Man's bidding that I didn't take the time to notice but you are one attractive woman, Melinda. And I am certainly not trying to cross the line but I gotta admit I have become quite attracted to you.

I hope I'm not coming on too strong or too forceful but I don't know what else to say. I've been harboring these feeling since Lagos when every one from the bellboy to the U.S. ambassador was trying to pick you up. I guess I felt a little tinge of jealousy."

"You certainly have a strange way of showing it." Melinda interrupted, smiling at this latest admission.

"Well, I still had hopes of working things out with Sill but it didn't mean I didn't notice. I thought I was going to die that last night in Lagos, when you came to the door in whatever that was you had on. My God! I'm gonna tell you the truth. That was the first time since Sill and I met some seven years ago that I really truly felt my marriage was in jeopardy. Thank God you didn't let me in. That's not to say that you would have necessary let me have my way but Lord knows I would have been compelled to at least try and seduce you. And that's like I said, that's at the very least. I didn't sleep a wink that night. In fact, I ended up down in the lounge with your friend the bellhop, bartender waiter or whatever the hell he was. I never did figure that one out.

All he did was ask me questions about you. Were you married? Did you have a male friend? How did you like Lagos? You know questions of that nature. When he told me how fortunate I was to have a secretary and a friend as lovely as you are it was the first time I truly saw you from a man's perspective. But at that moment I knew exactly what he was talking about. You certainly were something, quite special that night. And tonight you have surpassed that a thousand times over. So, Ms. Bailey, you'll have to excuse me if I put Hill and Morris and Terry Shannon on the backburner and turn my undivided attention to you."

"That's very sweet, William," Melinda replied but before she could finish he interrupted.

"The hell with being sweet, Melinda. Every Wednesday for the past month in a half, since this whole charade with Shannon started we've had dinner together like business partners. Which in itself is fine. It's obvious we're comfortable and enjoy each other's company but Lord knows it's becoming more and more difficult to sit across from you and keep things on a purely platonic basis. I guess what I'm trying to say is that not only am I attracted to you but I seriously believe that I am fallin' in..."

Melinda interrupted this time.

"Don't even say it, William. It's not that I'm tryin' to dispel what you're sayin' or make light of your feelings. I know with Sill leaving and all it must have been a pretty rough ordeal. But in all fairness to both of you, I think you need to give yourself a little more time."

Melinda didn't believe she was saying these things and she knew that if William demanded she be his at that very moment then all she was saying would be out the door but she was counting on his being his usual unassertive self. So she could play the whole scenario out. It was important that he was sure of his actions and that they weren't merely a reaction to her being there in his time of need.

"You know a lot of times when someone is faced with the kind of adversity that you've faced in the last couple of months, William, with Sill leaving you and the trouble with DEA and all the uncertainty surrounding your future employment with Hill and Morris you might be at the most vulnerable point since I've met you. And my support may be being misconstrued at this point. I don't want you to think that the world's abandoned you and I am the only support, the only crutch you have because that's not true. This is just a small segment in your life. It's just a small segment of the greater whole, William and shortly, very shortly, I promise you that all this will be nothing but a bad memory and no more. Before the end of the year you won't remember any of this. I promise you."

"So what are you telling me, Melinda? What are you sayin'? Is this a polite way of tellin' your boss that you're not interested in the way he feels about you with an idea that if you make sure that your presentation, your brush off is politically correct then you can hold onto your job? Is that what this is, Melinda?"

"Not at all, William. If you were to ask me the same thing tomorrow or a week from now I might not utter a word and let you lead me wherever but that's not how I'm feelin' today? I'm not only tryin' to look at the long haul but I'm doing my best to make a good decision so neither of us have any regrets in the long run," Melinda said as she felt the moistness between her thighs.

William had no idea how badly she wanted him at that very moment. It had been weeks since she'd even considered relieving herself of any tension. Evenings in the gym had substituted nicely for her evening works at home but she was terribly, horny and feeling very sexy tonight. And after touching herself several times during the course of dinner she realized that it had been quite some time since she had even entertained the idea of sex let alone sexing herself.

Most of the time, she was too exhausted after her workouts to even think about anything besides a hot bath and her bed but with William sitting in front of her offering himself to her in that charcoal gray pinstriped suit looking better than a hot fudge sundae on a sweltering August afternoon she could do little about the way her body responded now and almost wished she had kept her mouth shut.

Yet, she knew that everything she was saying held an element of truth in it. Besides that, she knew she'd appeared anxious even if she hadn't thought she appeared that way. He had alluded to the fact that he'd known her intentions far before she thought about letting the cat out of the bag. When he'd told her this some weeks ago she'd been thoroughly embarrassed. The last thing she ever wanted to do was tread on another woman's turf but what was it he said about her snide remarks? Well, this was chance, her last chance to attempt a reprieve and whether she had to sit alone at home for one more night or not one thing was for sure. She would not submit to his or her desires tonight. And before he could answer or sway her decision she ignored his remarks and brought the conversation back to where they both felt most comfortable. Hill and Morris.

"So, Ol' Man Morris has scheduled a meeting for tomorrow after the internet presentation. I have a few minor things to wrap up but after reading your presentation I see of no reason he shouldn't be considering you for a promotion of some sort especially after the way you had those Apple representatives eating out of your hand. You were sensational to say the least. I was so proud of you. And from what I can see tomorrow's presentation should be equally as good. After all you've already sold the Nigerians on the idea of the pc's and Apple is selling so many units that they could care less about how little the markup is since they stand to make a fortune just in volume. And what's a pc without access to the net so tomorrow should be a mere formality if you ask me.

But tell me something? Do you have any idea what Morris is calling a meeting about? Has he alluded to anything concerning the nature of this one? For him to have you flying up there and then for him to be flying back down here and requesting that all board members be present, I would have to believe that it must be pretty important. Do you think he got wind of Shannon and might be thinking about bowing out? You know, retiring?"

William laughed, good naturedly.

"I'm aware of how you changed the subject from us to Hill and Morris. Don't think I didn't notice. But your transition left a lot to be desired. But trust me, I haven't forgotten the topic and despite your misgivings I am quite aware of my feelings and the situation I find myself in. Not only that, I have never felt more in control and sure of myself than I do at this very moment. In addition, Ms. Bailey it has always been my motto that hard work and perseverance can overcome almost any obstacle and unless there is someone else in the picture I intend on pursuing your elusive ass until one you concede. What is it they say? Persistence overcomes resistance. Well, let me assure you of one thing. I plan on being quite persistent."

"Shoot your best shot, Mr. Stanton," Melinda said smiling "Every great work of art is not meant to be owned," Melinda laughed.

William ignored her. She was playing hard to get and it only made him desire her that much more but pushing her at this time might not only alienate her but could ultimately cause him to lose his most essential asset. And after all, he was a businessman before all else and he could hardly afford to lose her at this juncture in time with all that he had going on. He needed her but more so he appreciated and valued her efficiency. In actuality, she was more of a partner than an assistant. How many times had she junked one of his hair-brained schemes replacing it with one of her own and how many times had he reaped the benefits of her good judgment. To be perfectly honest the whole idea for the Apple presentation had been hers and he was really counting on her with the whole DEA affair, which was also her brainchild.

It was funny but on the few times she'd been out sick or on vacation in their six or seven years they'd been together he'd had the occasion to use the various temp services during her absences and was always but always disappointed. Not once did he have a temp that came close to Melinda's overall efficiency, let alone her attention to detail and penchant for punctuality.

Oh, there had been some beautiful girls. There had been the pretty redhead with the enormous boobs that she'd insisted on keeping in his face almost the entire week she was there. And he'd been mesmerized like some kid playing Simon Says. But after a couple of days he grew tired of fantasizing and her freakish offers for him to feel them and bury his head between them. And when it came down to typing and handling the essentials around the office the girl didn't know the difference between a pencil sharpener and a paper shredder.

Of course, it took him several days to find this out since he had difficulty seeing past her chest and in the end it had been Sill who after joining him for lunch one day and cleaning up her mess fired her so that Melinda wouldn't notice the utter disarray this chile had made and quit on her return. William watched contritely as the buxom redhead packed her belongings and headed for the lobby door, which Sill held open. The one's that followed her were even less descript. And after awhile he stopped using the temp agencies altogether and simply waited for Melinda to return to work.

In Lagos he had felt a bond, a closeness that often happens when Americans are in a foreign land but now something was different. In fact things seemed to have changed in the last week alone. To William it seemed like the metamorphosis was overnight. She was certainly dressing better and he really began to wonder if she was seeing someone.

In any case, he thought it best to keep the conversation on a level playing field if that's what she really wanted. So, he continued with the conversation that made them both feel at ease.

"I'm not sure what Morris' intentions are. What I am sure of is that no matter what offer he intends to throw my way at the end of the meeting and in all likelihood he'll pull me around some little dark out of the way corner and make his pitch or tell me he's throwing me a few more dollars. But whatever it is he's selling, at this juncture, I'm not buying. He won't use this little Uncle Tom again. That's for damn sure."

Melinda wiped the corners of her mouth with her napkin before she spoke, quiet and deliberately.

"I don't know what the meetings about either, William. What I do know is that whatever dark, musty corner the old man pulls you into after the meeting, 'you will go', and without hesitation. Do you understand? That's what you've always done and that's what you'll do now. Any offer he makes you, you'll gladly accept because that's what you've always done. This isn't about you or your ego William Stanton. This is about putting an end to all the tragedy that this man has created right here in our own backyard. Now if you don't believe that you can't handle whatever it is that he may throw your way for one reason or another then you let him know that very apologetically and very contritely so that he doesn't get an inkling that you may be trying to undermine him in any way. After all, this is not about William Stanton anymore. There is a panoramic view that looms so much larger and is not quite so scenic as it was and you and I and a host of other people are in the midst. Excuse me, William, I got so caught up in our little chat that I totally forgot the time. Do you have any idea what time it is?"

William glanced at the Rolex donning his left wrist and replied, "It's a little after nine. Why?"

"Oh, well I have another engagement and am supposed to be there at nine. It totally slipped my mind," she lied, "and you know how I hate to keep people waiting." And with that said Melinda slipped out of the booth revealing the split and those legs William so desperately wanted to get to know and headed for the door.

"See you Monday and call me if anything breaks," she said in her haste to meet whoever it was she meeting. "Oh, and thanks for dinner William. It was lovely."

William pulled out his wallet placed a Benjamin under the tray of peppermints and almost broke his neck trying to follow her to the door.

"Guess I'm gonna miss my nightcap. I'd gotten kind of use to stopping by," he admitted.

William had a hard time understanding this woman he thought he'd come to know so well. Couldn't understand her coldness. Just when he thought they had broken down all the barriers…Pulling her car around to the front of the restaurant, William opened the car door for Melinda and though angry he knew he had know right to be.

He had ample time in the years that he'd known her to properly assess this woman and hadn't. Even in the weeks after Sill left he had failed to appreciate her in any more than in a professional sense until a bellhop in a foreign country made him aware of the treasure that stood before him. He'd always felt awkward approaching women. Even when they threw themselves at him he was at a loss as to how to respond.

Now standing here watching Melinda, looking better than she had ever looked and knowing that in all likelihood she was on her way to meet another man was more than just disheartening. It was excruciating.

Melinda, hoping that he would object to her leaving, waited patiently. The silence was positively deafening.

Opening the car door, he knew he had no right to be angry, although he was. William was at a loss for words.

Finally, she spoke. "Your presentation was sensational, William. You're a shoo-in for the computer contract." With that said, she closed the door, started her car and was quickly swallowed up in the throng of early evening traffic before he had a chance to reply.

He'd barely gotten over Sylvia's leaving. Now, Melinda seemed to be moving on, too. How could Melinda leave at a time like this, when everything was in such a state of turmoil? This was certainly no time to abandon ship. It wasn't that long ago when he told her the one thing he needed most was a friend and hadn't she agreed to be there for him? He was irate but in his heart, he knew Melinda was not the reason. She had offered herself to him in every conceivable way.

It was he that had chosen to live in the past, to dwell on Sill. And he'd only recently come to the realization though that it no longer mattered that Sill was gone. What mattered was the fact that she'd left him, rejected him. And not for the abuse. She rejected him because he did not meet her standards. His inadequacy drove him now as it had in college, as it had his entire life. He had felt inferior as a Black man in a White world and tried hard to emulate the norms and nuances of White America in order to be accepted. Despite finishing at the top of his class and his efficiency and productivity work, he remained an outsider. Hoping he would fare better at a Black institution, he'd been rejected for being 'too White'. Certain that his economic status and right wing politics would be a true indicator in defining his role, his niche he'd married an elegant Black woman, hoping to improve his status, his lot in life and, still, he was met with rejection. He'd treated her like a queen, placing her in a castle overlooking the whole of Atlanta and still the rejection.

It was the rejection, the idea that he wasn't good enough, that he didn't fit, which bothered him most and above all. It drove him, obsessed him, overwhelmed him.

Only recently had he'd been able to see, to feel, to know, to come to terms with his own frailties, his feelings of inferiority. He could do this now. He could do it because he had found his inner peace, his so-called comfort zone. He had found it, thanks to Melinda, the small town, little country girl, who had no formal education in the way of a college degree, nor what William considered enough drive and desire. But she, more than anyone else, convinced him that it was just as important "to be good at what you're good at" and not continually try to chase the genie in the bottle with the idea of making every dream come true when one would certainly do.

It was her loyalty, her support, more than anything else, which was responsible for his turnaround and his recent success. Now, it seemed, she too was leaving. She was the sole reason he wasn't behind bars at this very moment. It was, after all, her idea to open the trust fund for Alex when his parents rejected the money. It was this act of goodwill, which led the Nigerian government and the D.E.A. to examine, William Stanton, a little more closely, convincing them, that he may be more than just another money hungry, foreign power broker out to siphon millions from poor Nigerians, and deal a little yayo on the side to boot.

William turned the Mercedes around in the middle of Maine and headed north. Fifteen minutes later, he pulled up in front of Melinda's tiny home and sat wondering what he could say that he hadn't already said. Not more than five minutes later, a dark blue sedan pulled up. William witnessed an elderly man leaning over and kissing Melinda. Out of the car, before Melinda's foot could hit the curb, William grabbed her by the arm swung her around and escorted her at the quick step to his car and opened the door...The man, in the long blue Lincoln Town car hurried to her side. "You alright, pumpkin?" the elderly man asked,

"Couldn't be better, Uncle Dennis. Just a friend who wasn't sure about what he wanted until he saw someone else with it." Melinda smiled.

"Why you scoundrel. You played me, didn't you? Played me for the fool that I am." William said while Melinda grinned broadly.

"You're no fool, William. A bit slow but you're nobody's fool. Where are we going?"

"Your choice, Melinda. I could care less as long as I'm with you."

"William. William Stanton. Don't tell me you're tryin' to be affectionate?" Melinda smiled.

"Better late than never, wouldn't you say?" William remarked. "Damn, you look good tonight. Wonder why I never noticed?"

"I'm just grateful you did. I was gettin' a little tired of having to scratch my own itch."

"How's the Tavern sound? We've still got a bottle of champagne on ice."

"Tonight's kind of special for me, William. I've waited close to six years to gain some kind of foothold in your life. I'd like to remember it even if it's only for one night Make a left at the light. There's some place I've always wanted to take you."

William made the left at the traffic signal. On the right was the ever-so popular night spot William had heard so much about. Parking the Benz behind the club, William was somewhat apprehensive at first. He seldom frequented bars or clubs. He always felt out of place but tonight he felt a little more comfortable, a little more at ease, when he saw several well dressed couples, some

Black, some White, waiting in line. The headliner was up and coming jazz vocalist, Cassandra Wilson.

Once inside William was pleasantly surprised. The décor was exquisite. The petite young hostess who greeted them led them to a table up front. William had to admit he was quite impressed. There were Hispanic couples, White couples and even an Asian couple or two but the overwhelming majority were Black.

Melinda ordered a bottle of *Moet* and smiled at William's reaction, his surprise.

"Thought you were the only Black professional in Fulton County didn't you, William? Are you surprised? See the gentlemen over there. That's Jazzy Monroe. He's the owner of this little juke joint. He knows every great jazzman from Florida to Maine. He probably did more to keep American jazz alive in the last twenty years than anyone else on the East Coast.

When jazz musicians were forced to go overseas to find work to take care of their homes and families, Jazzy paid their plane fares and did all he could to keep them afloat. Most of 'em, you know, the older ones like Ray Brown and Count Basie, you know, the biggies, simply adore Jazzy. Most of them perform for free when they're in town 'cause they know Jazzy and they know Jazz ain't tryin' to exploit 'em, bein' that he ain't nothin' more than one of them himself. Jazzy, ain't nothin' but a strugglin' musician who got tired of strugglin'. He plays a sweet horn himself but couldn't make enough just playin' so he started buyin' and sellin' real estate to augment his income. With four daughters, he had to do something,

After his real estate business took off, he opened this place and set up a pension plan for those musicians who didn't or wouldn't necessarily have anything to fall back on. Now; he's in the process of tryin' to set up an insurance fund so they're covered in case they need medical attention, you know, medical insurance.

"You probably wouldn't know it, to see him but Jazzy's a millionaire several times over. Would you like to meet him?"

"Sure, Melinda, but not right now. Let's enjoy the set right now. I believe Kirk Whalum's up next," William said, "I, too, respect a good horn."

Melinda continued pointing out the faces. It read like a <u>Who's Who of Fulton County</u>. "See the gentleman on the olive suit at the table to your right? That's Edwin Davis. He's the vice president of one of the largest Black banks in Fulton County. He's a good man to know, William."

"Sounds like a <u>Who's Who of Black America</u>. How can you possibly know all of these people?"

"Jazzy's my uncle. I've spent every summer working here since I was in high school. Now, I work when I want to, usually on weekends when there's a big name in town or whenever he calls and says he needs me. He supported my mom and my sister when my father passed so I owe him a lot I even worked some weekends with Jazzy's accountant, Mr. Davis when I was junior in high school on an intern basis. He was fresh out of college. Talk about a shrewd cookie. The brother taught me everything I know about bookeepin' He taught me how to balance the books, where to look for tax write-offs, everything. It was like doin' an internship at Howard. That's where Mr. Davis went, you know, Howard.

Tried to get me in there on a partial scholarship. He and Uncle Jazz were goin' to foot the remainder of my tuition but when things broke down at home, I thought it best that I stick around and help out with my baby sister while my mom worked and went to school."

"You certainly seem to know a lot of people." William remarked almost with a tinge of envy.

"The number of people a person knows is irrelevant. What's important is the *type* of people one knows. These are some of Atlanta's best and brightest, the elite of the Black community, the movers and shakers. This is where you'll come to rub elbows when you get the confidence to open your own agency. This is the Augusta National Golf Club of the Black community. This is the unofficial boardroom where the really big deals are made. This is where the power lunches are held, the bids are submitted and the contracts signed."

Just then Jazzy arrived at the table, beaming. "I saw you come in. How's my favorite niece?" he said bending over and kissing her on her cheek. "Good. Good. I must say you're looking rather elegant this evening. Your Uncle Dennis told me you were coming. He made sure I held a table up front for you. Told me what he'd do to me if I didn't. So you make sure you tell him you were almost on stage you were so close. Have you eaten?"

"I'm comin' from dinner but some seafood would hit the spot. Uncle Jon, I'd like for you to meet William Stanton. William, this is my Uncle Jon better known as Jazzy."

"Nice to meet you, William. Stanton did you say? Boy that name sounds familiar. Any relation to a Sylvia Stanton?"

William's mouth dropped open. He could feel the blood rush to his cheeks. "Why, yes." Caught totally off guard, he glanced at Melinda who was equally stunned. Just when Melinda thought that Sylvia was out of the picture, she'd once again managed to creep back into their lives. "Sylvia's my ex. We're separated."

"I'm sorry to hear that. I had the opportunity to meet her a couple of weeks ago. She came here. Danced beautifully and Took the place by storm. She's one helluva dancer. Well, it was nice to meet you, William. Now that you know we're here, don't be a stranger. As for you, young lady, I could certainly use you over the next couple of weeks. I've got some business to take care of and will be out of town until the first of the month. If you could sort of hang around and keep an eye on things and look over the books until I get back, I'd appreciate it."

"No problem, just call me and let me know when you're leavin', Uncle Jon." Melinda said. Jazzy hugged her and was soon engulfed in the ever-growing crowd.

Melinda sighed, almost wishing she hadn't introduced William. William, on the other hand, hadn't even considered the fact that Sylvia was still in Fulton County. Knowing that she was, only tended to peak his curiosity. If she was still there, what the devil was she doing at Dante's and with whom? A mutual friend of Jazzy's? It had to be. Otherwise, how would he have come to meet her? Jazzy obviously knew something and, being that he was Melinda's uncle, she could surely give him the 411 on Sill's whereabouts. But then what? His lawyer had already advised him on the improbability of his recovering the money and it was comparatively inexpensive in comparison to the alimony he would be forced to pay. So, what was the use?

William shrugged and before he knew it, he found himself tapping his foot lightly, actually groovin' right along with the saxophonist and the tiny brown songstress, crooning on stage. Melinda smiled a nervous smile, wondering if she'd lost everything she'd recently gained. William shot her a reassuring glance, then moved his chair next to hers in what Melinda thought, was an attempt to better see the stage.

Looking at William, Melinda considered the months she spent at the gym, the late nights spent at the office, filing, editing. For what? Had she really been trying to better herself or had she been trying to lure William. Now this. A mention of her name and all her efforts were in vain. It was then that she felt something under the table: William's hand was gently massaging her thigh and moving upwards! She gasped. His eyes never left the bandstand though his hand had made plenty of progress as he now caressed her inner thigh making her sing a song all her own. *Oh my God! Oh, my God!* She grabbed her drink with both hands while William parted her thighs and kissed away her tears of joy.

Feeling his warm breath on her earlobe, she could only imagine what William had to say. Hand still caressing her inner thigh, she moved closer. How long she had waited. Ready to sing song *aloud*, Melinda was certain William was ready to leave when he whispered something to her. Kirk Whalum was wailin' on his sax,

"Melinda, would you mind introducing me to Mr. Davis when you get a chance?" he asked her finally, surprisingly.

Melinda shoved William's hand from her thigh, angrily. Business, always business. Fixing her hair and gown, she got up from the table and made her way to Mr. Davis' table. The two hugged as old friends who haven't seen each other in some time often do. Edwin introduced Melinda to the members in his party. Melinda waited a few minutes inquiring about the family before relaying William's message. She returned to the table a few moments later. "Edwin knows more than you think, William, but he can be trusted so whatever it is, don't worry. Just remember that. Don't be arrogant, though. He despises that

In the meantime, I'm gonna take a look at Jazzy's books and see what kind of shape they're in. Let you men talk. Just remember to go slow and be easy. Don't be pretentious."

Presently, Edwin Davis made his way to William's table. Half an hour later Melinda watched as the two men raised their glasses and made a toast. A deal of some sort of had been consummated and Melinda's intuition told her that a major transaction was in the works.

William looked around for Melinda and eventually noticed her standing idly by the bar. He beckoned her, ordered another bottle of champagne, filled both glasses, then leaned over and kissed her gently. All of Melinda's fears and trepidations faded with the kiss.

"If you have a mind to," he said, "you may want to start looking for a two bedroom condominium. Something in the low 90's that we can both be comfortable with. I'm seriously considering putting the Greenwich Hill house on the market sometime in the next couple of weeks with the help of Mr. Davis or should we keep it in the family and let your uncle have the commish?"

Staggered by the news, Melinda Bailey found herself speechless for the first time in her life. As much as she wanted to scream and tell him yes, yes, yes she could not utter a word. Only a few minutes ago, when Jazzy mentioned Sylvia, she wondered if she had lost him, again. Now, he was asking her to pick out a home in which they would be comfortable. She figured there had to be more to it than that but tickled by the news she didn't inquire further.

The William Stanton she thought she knew so well was chock full of surprises but she never expected this. Not wanting to appear too anxious or too easy, she chose her words carefully.

"Don't you think it would be better if we waited, William, and looked together?" she inquired politely.

CHAPTER 16

❀

Mondays always arrived in the office of Hill and Morris with a gloomy vengeance and though not readily welcomed by most, Melinda's cheery presence usually brightened even the gloomiest of her co-workers. For Melinda, the weekends were the time she dreaded the most. Home alone again she began to feel more and more like a Black female version of McCauley Culkin. She hated the fact that she was on a first name basis with the manager of Blockbuster's and the idea that after weighing all of her weekend options, she found herself on aisle seven once again, trying to choose between Blockbuster's new arrivals and the five movies for five nights special At least in the movie *Home Alone*, McCauley had an intruder to occupy his time. She didn't even have that. Oh, how she abhorred the weekends.

Every weekend, it seemed that the whole world was moving—doing something. And, of course, everyone had a mate. Everyone that is but her. How nice it would be, to be off somewhere, snuggled up with William. And it didn't have to be in an exclusive hotel like the Marriott or the Hilton on some exotic beach in Tahiti or San Tropea. No, in all actuality a Motel 6 on the outskirts of town would suffice nicely right through here. The idea of her finding a place for them was nice but hey that had been a while ago and he hadn't mentioned it since. And Lord knows her moods swings were in a frenzy teetering back and forth between horny and lonely. If she wasn't one she could count on being the other.

If William had, time constraints, and he always did and he couldn't spend as much time as she needed or wanted, then she guessed she'd just have to adjust. Hell, if she was nothing else, she was flexible. If he couldn't spend the night because he was preoccupied with work and business and making a dollar, then fine. Better they didn't go to Tahiti or San Tropea. If he couldn't spend a weekend, then, a night would do. If he couldn't spend a night then—. Oh hell, that's what made Motel 6, Motel 6. It was one of the few motels that had hourly rates and hell an hour with William was a month of memories. She could at least use those memories to carry her through those next few lonely weekends and Lord knows her memories beat the 5 for 5 Blockbuster specials hands down. Now those dreams of spending quality time that she had coveted over the years, like so many Afghans in a spinster's hope chest were fast becoming a reality. And she had to commend herself on playing her cards close to the vest.

Yet, she couldn't believe how stupid she'd been. She had actually dissuaded him from spending time alone with her.

She tried to rationalize her mistake by remembering her mother's advice when it came to sex and men.

"Why should they buy the cow, when they can get the milk free?" And then telling herself that she'd waited this long she might as well stick to her guns and let the whole scenario play out. After all, at this juncture in their relationship she still had virtually nothing more than a promise and good intentions. Therefore, she had nothing to lose. She believed him to be sincere and William had assured her that their union was inevitable but until she heard the words, 'I do', she would take nothing for granted and would remain alone on the weekends.

The waiting had become even more painstaking since they'd begun seeing each other and by the time Monday morning rolled around, she could hardly wait to get to the office to tackle the memos and files, which she knew awaited her.

Arriving earlier than usual, Melinda found the fax machine already purring. And after putting the coffee on, rearranging her desk and prioritizing her workload, she somehow found her way over to the fax and tore the long sheet off. Another memo from corporate, no doubt, probably suggesting they limit the use of toilet paper to cut down on rising costs. This would, in turn, heighten the chances of the clerical staff getting a cost of living raise in the upcoming fiscal year. Hell, Melinda thought aloud, if they just cut down on the number of ridiculous faxes, which in itself would be a start.

She put the fax on her desk and checked the coffee maker. She poured herself a cup and checked her watch. Five minutes to nine, William should be walking through the door momentarily. She then poured his coffee, added two spoonfuls of sugar and that horrible French Vanilla creamer he so adored. It was God-awful but he loved it and refused to drink his coffee without it. Putting the mug on his desk, she returned to her own and picked up the fax to see what those brainless twits in corporate had come up with now. But her thoughts retreated to Friday night at Jazzy's and the way William had looked at her. Smiling now, she could almost feel William's hand parting her thighs. She thought about her mother's advice and wondered just how strong her convictions would have been of William had decided to grab her suddenly and take her back to his home or even the nearest hotel room.

She was still smiling and holding the fax when William burst into the office, looking almost as fine as he had on Friday night. Good God Almighty, she thought to herself! She couldn't wait to get a hold of that man. Attempting to regain her composure, she dropped her head and mumbled, "Good morning, Mr. Stanton".

"Mornin', Melinda." He was strictly business now and Melinda wondered if he was having the same problem she was having in trying to maintain proper office decorum after all the time they'd spent together lately. But William didn't seem to be having any problem and seemed to barely notice her at all after taking the fax from her hand. He read it quickly and then placed it back on her desk. There was no mention of the weekend, no reference to her appearance, not even a thank you for his coffee which he always thanked her for before even entering his office. Had she done something to annoy him? She wondered. What?

"Melinda."

"Yes, William?"

"Would you arrange my itinerary and get Terry Shannon on the phone for me. I think it's a go," he said the anxiety now obvious in his voice.

Melinda was shocked. "When? What, William?"

"Didn't you read the fax? Morris has me scheduled to leave on Wednesday and I'm only to be there until Sunday, supposedly just to tie up any loose ends from the previous trip and to make sure that everything is being set up according to our specs and guidelines with no penny pinching by the crew that's over there but you and I both know the skinny."

Melinda placed her finger to her lips in an effort to shush him, summoned him close enough so only he could hear then whispered.

"Be careful William. You know Morris has his own division of Homeland Security and I wouldn't be too surprised if he's not sittin', listenin' to every word," she whispered, slowly regaining her composure.

"Don't worry. This is the last run through and everything's gonna work out just fine. Trust me you're gonna be happier than a pig in slop when this whole mess blows over. But you're right I do need to be more careful." William admitted.

"Absolutely. Now pick up the phone, Terry Shannon's on line one. Better yet, I'm gonna disconnect him and you call him back on your cell. Apologize to him for me cuttin' him off but I should have never called from this phone."

William smiled, walked into his office, then turned, and stuck his head out of the door as he hung his suit jacket on the coat rack behind the door.

"Melinda?"

"Yes, William?"

"Did I mention how utterly desirable you look this morning?"

"No, you didn't," she said, smiling.

"And I didn't thank you for my coffee either, did I?"

"No, you didn't," she repeated.

"I didn't think so," he said, grinning right along with her like a couple of teenaged pranksters. He then closed the door to his office picked up his coffee in one hand and his cell in the other and called Terry Shannon.

"Terry? William here. Looks like everything's a go. Can't really talk now but just keeping you posted."

The usually tight-lipped D.E.A agent was elated about this latest turn of events and insisted, despite William objecting vehemently that he take William out to dinner sometime before William's departure on Wednesday. That left only two days and William, still exhausted from the weekend, hardly wanted to sit in some crowded restaurant with the very bland and morose D.E.A agent when he could be wining and dining his very sexy, very voluptuous secretary who seemed to be getting better looking everyday. Yet, he agreed to meet him that night and get it over with once and for all. After all, they were finally coming to the finish line of what had become a very nerve wracking and grueling marathon between good and evil and, frankly, he was ready for the whole damn thing to be behind him once and for all.

"Do you know where Li'l Paisano's is down on Mulberry and West 4th?" Shannon asked

William affirmed.

"How 'bout we meet there. Say, about eight?"

"Eight o'clock is fine. I'll see you then."

The rest of the day went off without a hitch. William confirmed the upcoming trip with the Ol' Man that afternoon, helped Melinda shape his itinerary, which he purposely left loosely scheduled so as to afford him some time with

Alex and his family and to give himself some much needed rest and, other than that, it was a typical lackluster Monday.

At seven thirty that evening William found a parking spot on the corner of West 4th and Mulberry and waited patiently until he saw the rather stout, stoop shouldered DEA agent cross the street in front of the little Italian restaurant. Locking the car and activating the alarm, he rushed to meet Terry Shannon before he could enter the restaurant. He'd heard of Paisano's but had never ventured to frequent the well-renowned restaurant.

William had always felt somewhat uncomfortable entering an all—White or all—anything establishment without knowing what awaited him on the other side. He hated being in the spotlight and hated it even more when he was alone and the only Black. On several occasions, he'd been forced into this predicament and the results were always, but always, the same.

As soon as he entered, all eyes would turn in his direction and, then, there would be the muffled sounds of muttering. And he assumed they were saying something to the effect of, 'what's this nigga doin' in here or isn't there anywhere left that we can go that's off limits to *them*'. Sill used to tell him he was paranoid and even though he was usually the only Black at business luncheons and seminars, he'd never grown accustomed to the feeling.

Sill, on the other hand, had been pretty adamant about his moving in mixed circles and was always trying to encourage him to be more outgoing. She forced him to attend a good deal of Hill and Morris' little social gatherings no matter how boring. When they did attend, despite his objections, she was not only the focal point but seemed to relish the spotlight, mingling and laughing and always surrounded by a crowd, who seemed to savor her every word. But not him. He would find a corner and, with a drink in his hand, simply pine away, checking his watch at regular intervals waiting for the crowd of ogling fans to dissipate, so he could snatch her up and head home but they seldom did.

When he could stand it no more and he'd gained some courage from the drink in hand, he would somehow find the inner strength to make his way through the crowds and suggest, almost apologetically, that it was getting late and they needed to be getting home. Sill would almost always be vehemently opposed but after a fair amount of prodding he'd finally drag her away. He wondered if he was the only Black that felt this sort of discomfort, being the only Black and all, but there really wasn't anyone to ask.

Moments later, he caught up with Terry Shannon. They entered the restaurant together and just as he suspected all eyes fell upon him, or so he thought.

He imagined how he would have felt if he hadn't waited for Terry, and glancing quickly around the restaurant and not seeing another Black he immediately regretted accepting the invitation. Terry, on the other hand, did not so much as notice the other patrons or the attention they received so elated was he in meeting William.

"Thought you weren't going to make it when I didn't see your car," he said trying to curb his enthusiasm.

"I parked down on the corner," William said nervously, as they waited to be seated.

There was no hostess, but a burly gentleman, who substituted between waiter and cook, soon greeted them. The hospitality and the gracious smile William was so used to when he dined out was nowhere to be found and William wondered if it ever had been. The man was obviously not happy in his work and the long hours and shuttling back and forth between the kitchen and dining room had clearly taken its toll over the years, William assumed. The fact that the restaurant was packed seemed to do little to improve the man's temperament and William could hardly understand why anyone would encourage such rude behavior by frequenting the place. The look of disapproval must have been apparent. Terry dropped his head, a smiled etched on his tired face.

"You need a table for two?" the waiter asked as he wiped his greasy hands on a dirty towel that hung from his apron, which was equally as dirty.

"Yes, sir," Terry answered, trying to be as cordial as possible.

"This way," he grunted.

The two men followed and William prayed that he wasn't being led to some table by the service entrance or near the bathrooms. But, instead, the waiter found an empty table in the center of the restaurant and in the same gruff manner that he had greeted Terry and him with, asked the young White couple seated next to them to move over so there would be more room. He then turned to William and informed him that he'd send the bartender over to take their drink orders but if they knew what they wanted then they could order now and save him a trip.

"The veal parmegiana is the best this side of Sicily," Terry said in an obvious effort to take William's mind off the waiter whom William was staring at with the most guarded of looks.

"Give me two veal parmegiana dinners, a bottle of your best red wine, a couple of salads and lots of bread."

"Dressing for your salads?"

"Uh, yeah. I'll have the Blue Cheese and you, William?"

William snapped back from his thoughts. "I'll have the wine and vinegar."

And without another word, the waiter turned and walked away. Terry Shannon looked at William and smiled. "Don't even think about it. The first time my wife brought me here, I wondered if it was me. But he's been the same ever since I've known him. Gruff. I guess that's just his disposition. But the food's hard to beat. I've traveled a little, thanks to my wife, and she's always been the one to want to try something new and I'll tell you, honestly, that in all our ventures, I've yet to find a better Italian restaurant. That man right there has a gift. He can really cook. So, I guess we have to put up with his shortcomings. In any case, let's talk about Morris. So, he finally gave you the green light? I'll tell you the truth, William, I was starting to have my druthers. You know, I don't know if I told you but I've been on Morris and Davenport's case for close to twelve years and this is the closest we've ever been to getting to him. Actually, we've been close a few times but that Morris is a shrewd one. Anytime, we started to make any headway, he'd shut down for a while until we were forced to abandon our surveillance. You know the bureau's not going to continually fund an operation with no results and Morris is well aware of this, so he'd stop trafficking for just long enough that we'd have to disband and then he'd pick up right where he'd left off and never miss a beat. It was almost as if he had someone on the inside. And to tell you the truth, I don't know that he didn't. What I do know is that with you, we have the best chance we've had in some time to finally nail this cat and, William, you don't know how badly I want him," Shannon said.

"Can I ask you something, Terry?" William asked.

"No doubt, William. Ask away."

The bartender brought a basket of Italian bread and both men jumped on it like it was the last supper,

"Tell me something. With all the traffickers, and I'm sure with one of the major airports in the country and easy access to 95, why such a hard on for the Ol' Man," he asked between mouthfuls of the crusty bread.

"I want them all, William, and believe you me you're right about Atlanta being a major city for the drug trade but I guess after you've stalked someone for as long as I have you kind of take it personal.

I don't know if you recall asking me some time ago about why I became a DEA agent to begin with. Anyway, I was running short on time then and I couldn't really explain but if you can bear with me, I'll do my best so that maybe you can get a better understanding and see the whole picture."

As he began to explain, the cook returned pushing a little tray, with their dinners that resembled a snack tray on wheels. He was having hard time getting through with the young couple's chairs in his way. After he left they had moved their chairs back together the way young lovers do when in love and sat holding hands and nibbling at each other's earlobes.

So occupied were they with each other that neither saw the cook as he tried to maneuver past their chairs, which were directly in the aisle and in his path. He may have been an outstanding cook but he was certainly no navigator and before either of them could make a move to save the couple the humiliation and embarrassment that was to follow the carafe of red wine was on the floor and the cook in an unmitigated rage.

"I told you before to move your fuckin' chairs to make room. Now look what you have done with your stupidity. Take you kissin' and touchin' somewhere's else. This is a restaurant! This is not the place for that! Now get out! Leave my restaurant and don't come back until you can behave betta'!" He shouted, arms flailing in anger. "Tonight, your dinner is on me. And may you make a thousand babies." He then waved, summoning the bartender who was there within seconds.

"Yes poppa?"

"Clean this mess up for me, Guido, and bring these men a bottle of our best wine," he commanded.

"Yes, poppa."

The waiter and cook, who William now gathered was the owner, too, then turned to William. "I am sorry about your wine. I hope I did not get any on you. Please forgive my rudeness. It has been a long day."

Placing the food in front of the two men, he took the bottle of wine form his son and poured each of them half a glass before leaving the table.

"You were saying," William said, ignoring the fiasco that had occurred only moments earlier.

"Oh, yeah, I was saying that of all the cases that I've worked on during my twenty or so years with the bureau, Ol' Man Morris has been the most elusive."

"No, Terry. What I'm curious to know about is the driving force, the motivation that makes this particular case so much more enticing, so much more alluring than the rest of these assholes selling poison out here in the streets."

"I think you and I both know what motivates me, William, but if I understand your question correctly as to what drives me or as you so aptly put it why I have a hard on for Morris in particular, I guess it's because Morris had no need for the money. Hill and Morris are one of the top firms in the country, no, the world. It's listed in Forbes and Fortune 500, as one of the top grossing companies in the world, making Morris a millionaire many times over. So there's no reason, not that there's ever a legitimate reason, but there's absolutely no reason Morris should be peddling that shit on the street. Maybe, if he had kids he'd have a better grasp of the pain and suffering he's causing. But then again I don't know. It's obvious there's something other than greed that's driving him but I'll be damned if I know what it is. I'm no closer to understanding his motivation than you are mine. Funny thing I've learned about people though, William. Just because they've mastered one aspect of life, doesn't mean they have a grasp on other aspects. Take your cook here. Tell me that's not the best veal you've ever tasted."

William, his mouth full, nodded in agreement.

"I thought you'd like it. I think he's one of the best chef's, Italian that is, what I've ever had the occasion to sample. But he's a complete asshole. Doesn't know what people skills are. Doesn't know that when you're in business, your livelihood depends on your customers. And to be honest, I don't think he cares. Anyway, my point is that we all have certain gifts or blessings and, because we have those, we're sort of expected to have common sense and everything else that goes along with possessing those gifts. But that is a supposition that doesn't carry much weight. You know I've seen *Ben Hur*, you know the movie, a dozen or so times. Loved it. All the critics deem it a classic and I was inclined to agree with them. And you know what made *Ben Hur?* Charlton Heston—. Charlton Heston was Ben Hur. He made the movie! Excellent actor—. Every year the movie would come on right before Easter and every year I found myself glued to the T.V., watching Charlton Heston playing Ben Hur and say, '*Wow*', now that man's an actor. He's mastered his craft.

Then, a couple of years ago I was working a stakeout on the Eastside. We ran up on a couple of teenagers trying to get into the game as they call it. I think it was their first buy. And we had this sting operation in effect. We were going to bust them with a little over three kilos of some low grade coke. It would have been the first bust for most of them. With the legal system set up the way it is, the most they would have done was a couple of years of probation but they panicked and started firing. Bullets were flying everywhere. It remained me of my second tour in 'Nam. I kid you not. It reminded me of the time my unit was ambushed along the DMZ. Anyway, in all the chaos and mayhem, I ended up shooting a seventeen-year-old kid that day. I don't know how long it took me to get over that. To be honest, I don't know if I'm over it yet and that was thirteen years ago.

Sometimes, I wake up in a cold sweat and see that boy's face as clear as day. Sometime after that, I picked up a newspaper and saw Charlton Heston in front of this huge poster, lauding the NRA and it's opposition to tighter gun controls. I couldn't believe that Ben Hur was the president of the NRA. I couldn't believe that Charlton Heston, a man who had the opportunity to travel the world ten times over, could be oblivious to the pain and devastation that guns are causing right here at home. But he was and he is. I never watched Ben Hur again. My point is that it took some time before it dawned on me that because a man was good at one thing, didn't necessarily make him cognizant of other facets of his life and those around him.

Still, that didn't make me want Morris any less. But of course there was more than one or two motivating factors that caused me to join the bureau and if you've got a few more minutes we can order dessert. I'd like to tell you a story that I think will help you to understand even more.

CHAPTER 17

※

At nineteen years of age, Mary Ann, a promising young medical student in her senior year at New York University, crossed the busy Manhattan Street and entered Washington Square Park. Once in the park, she hoped to purchase just enough, China White, to take the edge off and help her relax before she started studying for her midterm exams later that evening.

A day earlier, the very same, Mary Ann, who also carried the needless burden of being senior class president, had enclosed a New York University application in a large manila envelope and mailed it to her younger brother. Two years older than he, Mary Ann adored her only brother. She was truly hoping that he would join her the following semester. She knew he would love the Ivy League school, known to be one of the best in the country and New York as well.

After all, how could anyone from the little hick town of French Lick, Indiana not love New York City? Oh, how she hoped he would make N.Y.U. his choice after graduation. She would take him to the East Village to see the Bohemians and the artists. She would take him to the coffeehouses where famous writers met. She had written him about it all but there was nothing like being there. How could she write about John Coltrane's horn? Like Coltrane's horn, New York, all too often, defied words. She'd written him several times, in the past week alone, hoping to sway his opinion but had yet to get a response. So, she'd sent him the application, with the hope that he would see just how badly she wanted him to join her. She loved the city but it was easy to get lost and, more often than not, she felt alone. She was treasurer for the young Communist Party, a member of the 52nd Street Jazz Ensemble, played volleyball at the YWCA on Tuesday nights and basketball at the YMCA on Thursdays. On Friday nights, she would go barhopping, with her sorority sisters on Bleecker Street and she was constantly trying out for a role in *some off-Broadway play. Then there was the matter of being senior class president while maintaining a 3.75 grade point average. All this she could handle. What she could not handle was her constant fear of being alone, a loner in a strange place—an outsider.*

The same day her brother received the application, he boarded a flight for New York's LaGuardia Airport. Upon his arrival, he took a cab into Manhattan with all intentions of surprising Mary Ann. He'd finished high school a semester earlier and had already been accepted at N.Y.U., where he planned to study law.

After a good deal of exasperation, supplemented by a twenty dollar bill, he was finally able to convince the Resident Advisor in Mary Ann's dorm, that he was indeed her brother and that his intentions were honorable. Entering his sister's dorm room that day would impact his life forever. Sitting with her head resting on her chest, thick white globs of saliva from the corners of her mouth, a bloody needle still dangling from her arm, her body still warm, sat Mary Ann Shannon, medical student, senior class president, her future now behind her, dead at nineteen years of age, a victim of a heroin overdose.

"It was at that moment, that very day, that my life changed," Terry Shannon said. "I dedicated my life to my sister's memory and to all the Mary Anns of the world. That was twenty-four years ago. And since then little has changed."

The evening, which had begun so optimistically for William, had suddenly taken on a grave overtone and the darkening skies peering through the worn, red and white curtains of the little Italian restaurant did little to lift the somberness.

"I'm sorry to hear about your sister," was all William could muster. Pushing his dessert aside and sipping the last of his wine, William sighed and thought for a moment of all the Mary Anns that he had contributed to since his trip to Lagos.

"Tell me something, Terry. Why does your department allow this shit to hit the streets? You told me yourself that DEA has known about Morris and these shipments for years. How many innocent kids just like Mary Ann have to die before anything is done?"

"William, understand something," Shannon confided. "Simply because I'm a contingent of DEA, does not mean that I either condone or understand their practices. In the case of your boss, who has political ties with both parties, all the way up to the oval office, it's imperative that this thing be done correctly. If he had any knowledge of you or I sitting here discussing his foreign affairs, chances are we'd be dead by morning. Are you getting the gist of the gravity of the problem? If our case isn't airtight, he could bring the DEA to its knees.

That's how much power he wields. But this time I think we have him. I know the plan seems a little unorthodox, and it probably is, but it's the only plan we've got. All I can suggest from my vantage point is to say a lot of Novenas, William."

Terry Shannon paid the waiter, tipping him handsomely. Still, his demeanor did not change.

"Thank you and come again," the waiter said beneath a heavy Sicilian accent.

"You think he means that?" Shannon said.

Both men chuckled as they headed for their respective cars.

A week later, William had Melinda drive him to Fulton County Airport. Several hours later, William arrived at Heathrow in London. To William it seemed like an eternity. He hadn't had any hard liquor since that night at Dante's and was determined not to drink now despite his fear of flying. Once in London, he decided to take advantage of the sights and see as much of London as he possibly could. He had become since his dinner with Terry Shannon cognizant of how precious life really was.

In between flights, he was able to visit Buckingham Palace, Trafalgar Square and Westminster Abbey. Not knowing what tomorrow would bring, he strolled the streets thinking of Oliver Twist's London and how much the city had actually changed from the dank, damp and cold of Dicken's time. Five hours later, William Shannon boarded a British Airways flight on the last leg of his journey bound for Lagos, Nigeria.

On his arrival, Nigerian customs officials welcomed his return and quickly escorted him to a waiting limousine almost as if he were some foreign dignitary. Someone in government scrapped his hotel reservations and he was driven to a tiny villa overlooking Lagos. The panoramic view of the bustling city of Lagos was magnificent. That evening an entourage of smiling black waiters brought in tray after tray of Nigerian delicacies. He wondered if such a grandiose reception was the result of his last visit and his treatment of young Alex or was this just the government's way of insuring that they receive a fair market value in the upcoming negotiations? If it were, they certainly had endeared themselves in his eyes. Unsure of how to handle such fanfare, William offered the headwaiter a hundred dollar tip at the end of the evening to split among his entourage. His refusal to accept it, left William with a plethora of questions he simply could not answer.

On his second day in Lagos, William was picked up at eight o'clock in the morning in a black chauffeured limousine and driven at his requests to the outskirts of town, then transported by land Rover to Alex's village in the country. Everyone was busy with their daily chores when he arrived. Dismissed as another stalwart government official with another new decree, William found the village atmosphere in sharp contrast to the very festive mood he'd experienced only six months before. In the broad daylight, the stench of abject poverty filled his nostrils much the same way it had on his first trip to the back streets of Harlem in the early Nineties.

He found his way to the one-room hut Alex's family occupied only to find it abandoned now. After a good deal of inquiry, which consumed the better part of the morning, an elderly woman who remembered the American from his last visit, approached him. From what he was able to gather from the bits and pieces of broken English, government officials, tired of complaints from hotel management, conducted a citywide crackdown on panhandling. Alex and one of his younger siblings were arrested. When their father tried to intervene, he was beaten, thrown into the back of a paddy wagon and hauled off along with his children.

Alex's mother, after searching for months to no avail for her husband and children, was also threatened with incarceration if she continued to annoy the authorities. Unable to locate her family and unable to pay the rent, the property owner evicted what was left of the family. Heartbroken, she packed up the few belongings she could carry and walked the twenty some odd miles with her six remaining children in tow to her sister's village.

"She went to the bank where you set up trust fund for Alex's education in hopes of contacting you but the bank people would not help her. We tell her to take money out to pay officials for her rent. She say, this money for Alex education. I tell her, 'Education hell, pay rent. Get you husband and children from the jail,' I say to her. 'What do we know of education? I tell her she a fool. The educated ones are the ones, which cause so much hardship. I tell her: 'Pay the rent.' But all she say is, 'Money is for Alex to go to school.' All she keeps telling me is that my Alex will go to college. I tell her: 'He is in only college the authorities will allow him to go to; but she just keep shaking her head saying, 'No.'"

William and the old woman hugged, tears streaming down both of their dark cheeks.

"I will do all I can, I promise. And, you in return, must promise me that you will not allow anyone to move into their home. When you see the landlord, tell him I, William Stanton, would like to speak to him. Tell him I will make it worth his while," William said.

He gave the old woman his business card and scribbled a number on the back where he could be contacted then hugged her again, tightly.

"You are good man, Mr. William," said the old woman. "The village has given up hope but as long as there are men like you, my friend, there is reason to live; there is still reason to hope. I know you will bring our Alex back to us. I know you will make it right, Mr. William."

Climbing back into the Land Rover, William picked up the cell phone and called Davenport Enterprises.

"I'm sorry, Mr. Davenport's in a very important meeting and does not wished to be disturbed," the secretary informed him.

"Tell him it's William Stanton from..." before William could telling the voice on the other end the agency he was from, Davenport was on the line.

"Davenport here. That you, Stanton? Good to have you on board, son. Morris tells me you've got one helluva proposal for the government. Tells me the yield over the long term could very easily run into the hundreds of millions. Funny thing, though, he wouldn't elaborate. Just kept telling me, 'It's your baby.' First time I've ever known him to be that close-mouthed about anything and I've known Jonathan going on close to thirty-five years. He's taken a real likin' to you, son, and I think it goes beyond the dollars you're bringing in. Tells me you've got some head on your shoulders and could come back a partner, despite what that crazy board says. That's some kind of an accomplishment for a young man after only a couple of years with the firm," Davenport said, pausing before continuing. "You know, William, Jonathan and I have been around for awhile. I guess we'll both be bowing out in the next couple of years and let you young Turks run things. But from what I hear, you look to be that son he never had. The way it looks right now, you may just inherit the whole shebang, if you play your cards right. He told me to look after you while you were here. 'Nothing but the best is the way he put it.'"

William was almost back within the city limits and Davenport was still yakking. "Are the hotel arrangements to your liking?" Davenport inquired.

"Fine sir, and thank you," William responded, surprised. So it was Davenport and not the government who was responsible for all the hoopla. Now it all made sense. After all, why would the government go through all this trouble to make sure he was comfortable and then negate it all by locking Alex up?

"But the government vehicles, sir?" William said in amazement.

Davenport chuckled.

"It's good to have friends in high places sometimes. The government is somewhat suspicious of foreign investors and their investments so I thought it best that they be a party to this. Anyway, what is it that I can do for you?"

"Well, sir, a friend of mine, a nine year old boy, who I had the opportunity to meet and who acted as my tour guide and interpreter on my last visit has been jailed for panhandling, along with his father and some of his siblings. Is there any chance I can have them released into my custody?"

"I'm well aware of the situation, William. I contacted Jonathan as soon as I heard. It appears you were working on two new rather lucrative accounts and I don't think he wanted to disturb you at the time. He knew how you felt about the boy and didn't know how much influence or bargaining power you would had in getting him released so he asked me to look into the matter but I must confess I haven't been able to make any headway with the current regime's Minister of Defense. He's quite a character. So I turned to the Minister of the Interior, who appears to be a somewhat more reasonable fellow but he's also having trouble. Seems Alex and his family are being used as examples. You've probably noticed that panhandling outside the villa is almost nonexistent. Wasn't like that when you were here before. Petty theft and street crimes are down in general so there have been some benefits to the crackdown. Still, I know how you must feel and it certainly doesn't warrant the time they've been locked up. Believe me, William, I know how you feel."

"Do you, Mr. Davenport? Do you really?"

"I know that it happens everyday, son, but let's not forget why you're here, William. With power comes change. Make your play, present your proposal and when you come to an impasse, then discuss the boy. That's how business is done, my boy."

"I guess you're right, sir," William had to concede even though he detested Davenport calling him *boy*, that he was right.

"Are we still on for lunch on Thursday?"

"Yes, sir."

"Good! Let my secretary know if any changes arise."

"I certainly will, sir."

"And if you need anything, anything at all, just let me know. Your flight leaves on Friday?"

"Yes, sir. Nine forty-five a.m."

"Well, it's been good chatting with you, William, and remember to proceed slowly and cautiously with government around the boy's situation. They don't want to feel pressured or threatened from outsiders, concerning internal affairs."

"I understand, sir."

William was to meet that very afternoon to present his proposal for the computer contract but cancelled at the last minute. Disregarding Davenport's advice completely, William telephoned the Secretary of Commerce, Mr. Oluwola to offer his apologies for the cancellation.

"Is there anything wrong, Mr. Stanton?" he asked.

"I'm not sure, sir. I'm sure it's just a mix up. You see I've spent the better part of my day trying to locate the little boy I set up the trust fund for on my last visit to your beautiful country. Now, I'm quite distressed. So far, I've had no luck in trying to locate him. I've heard such far-fetched stories that he may have been incarcerated. I assured those that told these wild tables that my friends in government would never allow a nine year old boy, and a friend of mine, to be jailed. Perhaps you can help me locate him, Mr. Oluwola."

"I will certainly do all that I can do help you locate your friend. I can assure you that my government would never lock up a child so young. But first, let us discuss your proposal. Shall we say tomorrow at ten o'clock in the morning?"

"That will be fine, sir." William hung up the phone and called Melinda at home."Hey, sweetheart, how are you?" It was the first time he'd spoken to Melinda in two days and as much as he hated to admit it, he really wished she had come along.

"William? William, is it really you? It's about time you called. You think you would have at least had the decency to call and let me know you arrived safely. Boy, do I miss you."

"I'm sorry, sweetheart. I should have called but it's been hectic. It's been one thing right after another. Melinda, you wouldn't believe the accommodations. It makes the Hilton we stayed at look like Motel 6. Davenport arranged the whole thing. Talk about rolling out the red carpet, it would have made the perfect honeymoon suite. Now, all I need to do is find a bride," he joked.

"You might want to think about taking out an ad in the personals. I'm sure you'll find something," she snapped back.

"Or catch something," he quipped. "No, I've got a little filly in mind. She just needs a little training. Gotta break her in right, you know. She's pretty spirited but with the right trainer and handler she's gonna do fine over the long run."

Melinda laughed. "You are so corny, William. But I do miss you. Tell me, did you get a chance to visit Alex?"

"It's a long story that hasn't completely finished unfolding. I'll tell you more about it when I see you."

"And your presentation? I know you knocked 'em dead."

"I had to postpone my presentation until tomorrow," William said rather nonchalantly as not to arouse her suspicions. It did little good, though.

"William are you okay?" It was evident that she was concerned, if not a tad worried.

William did his best to console her.

"I'm fine, sweetheart. Look, I'll be home on Saturday, if all goes well and I won't be taking no for an answer this time."

"The way I've been missing you the past two days, you may not have to by the time Saturday rolls around. I may just jump your bones," she said, adding: "Do you need anything?"

"Come to think of it, I need you to do a couple of things for me, babe. First of all, I need you to redo the proposal. Raise the bid to four and a half percent above cost instead of the original two per-cent. Morris has given me complete authorization, his signature isn't required but don't fax it from the office. He doesn't need to know. I need the new figures by eight a.m. tomorrow morning. My meeting's at nine. Can you handle it?"

"There's nothing you have that I can't handle, William. Expect the revised copy somewhere between eight and eight thirty. By the way, William, I don't know if you're aware of this or not but I think I'm falling for you so you be safe and hurry home." Melinda hung up the phone before he had a chance to tell her he loved her but he was guessing she already knew.

He hung up the phone and leaned back on the bed. He reread the proposal for what seemed like the millionth time only to find himself still making changes here and there, as he saw fit. And when he got to the point where there was absolutely no way to improve it any further, he'd find something else that required revision until he finally drifted off to sleep.

The next thing William heard was the phone ringing and the steady drone and click of the fax machine. Checking his watch, he noticed that it was already eight thirty and he had yet to shower and he still had to rehearse his presentation and grab some breakfast. He checked the fax for errors and rechecked Melinda's calculations. Everything was in perfect order. Five to ten percent was the usual mark up over cost but in actuality, there was no limit. William knew the next closest bid was somewhere around five per-cent. If he could supply the technology along with training at four per-cent no one would come close. He knew it. The government knew it. What they didn't know was that William's original proposal promised a mark up of only two percent. Why then the sudden change, which could result in several millions more in revenue for Hill and Morris?

At ten o'clock sharp, William Stanton walked into the conference room wearing his olive green suit, white shirt, green and burgundy paisley tie and burgundy penny loafers. The Secretary of Commerce, Mr. Oluwola, who William had spoken to only yesterday, was there with a bevy of system analysts and other computer consultants.

"Gentlemen, my name is William Stanton and I represent the Hill and Morris Agency of Boston Massachusetts. I am sure that you have all been familiarized with our computer hardware, which just so happens to be the most current and innovative in the world today. Since you have all been familiarized with the product, let's cut to the chase and get down to the meat and potatoes of the package. I'm talking cost. The normal cost for a package of this size and magnitude would run somewhere in the neighborhood of one hundred and seventy-five to two hundred million per year, depending on the agency marketing the product. That does not include software or training. What I am offering is one year of free computer training for you programmers and analysts as well as one year of software free. We can send representatives or you have the option of training abroad The cost to your country, Mr. Secretary, will be one hundred and eighty six million dollars. This represents a four percent mark up over cost. It is a package with a figure you will find difficult to beat Now, Mr. Secretary, gentlemen, please excuse me I have some rather pressing business to attend to."

And with that, William Stanton rose, shook each gentleman's hand and left the conference room,

William had difficulty sleeping that night. He thought of Alex and the old woman in the village, and wondered if they weren't better off living as they always had. He wondered about the risk he was taking. He thought that Morris and Davenport who seemed to know everything as soon as it happened. Did Davenport know that he had not followed his advice and was using the Apple proposal as leverage to free Alex? He wondered if they knew of the sting operation, he and Shannon had put in place. William tossed and turned most of the night. He was used to having Melinda around to talk to. He now wished he hadn't insisted on her staying home, despite the danger.

He awoke at around eleven the next day, bathed in a cold sweat. Hard pressed to reach the Office of Commerce where he was to meet him Secretary Oluwola, William skipped breakfast and ordered a bottle of *Chivas Regal* in its stead The trip he had so looked forward to was fast becoming as stressful as any he'd made in his tenure with Hill and Morris. What was he thinking? Risking a two hundred million dollar contract on a little African boy he hardly knew. This was something Sill would do. He was playing a dangerous game. No one made demands on a military regime. If the gamble didn't pay off, he wouldn't even know where the hit was coming from. Morris would never excuse him for losing this one or the reason behind it. And the Nigerian government could not allow an American to just waltz right in and embarrass them by forcing them to release Alex. William prayed that the economic side would soften the blow. More than that, he wished he had contacted Melinda before giving the Secretary an ultimatum. One thing was for sure. It was too late to worry about it now.

The more William thought about the brash move he'd made the more he became convinced that he'd made another blatant blunder in judgment. Too late for that now he turned the shower on and heard the slow steady drone of the water beating against the shower wall. An error in judgment was certainly something he could hardly afford at this point. Yet, knowing there was little to do at this point but wait he showered quickly and promised himself to be a little less brash and a little more congenial in his meeting with Secretary Oluwola.

Stepping from the shower, William heard the phone ring and a steady knock at the door. Choosing to answer the door, William was surprised to see Mr. Oluwola's driver standing before him.

"Afternoon, Mr. Stanton. Secretary Oluwola awaits you downstairs and requests your presence promptly sir," the young man stated rather matter-of-factly.

"But our meeting isn't for another hour," William replied checking his watch to make sure.

"That is true sir but I believe Mr. Oluwola has some very pressing news that he would like to share with you and is requesting your attention at this time sir."

William, shaken and apprehensive dressed quickly and followed the limousine driver downstairs and out to the Mercedes limo where he half expected to be shot upon sight. Instead he found a rather jovial, Secretary Oluwola smiling from ear-to-ear.

William bent his large frame into the backseat of the car, exchanged pleasantries and waited patiently for the Secretary to make known his intentions.

The secretary recognizing William's uneasiness seemed content to let him agonize in apparent discomfort before speaking.

"That was quite a ballsy play you instituted yesterday, Mr. Stanton. Quite a coup if I must say so myself. I don't know that I would have attempted such a nervy display as to not only double the original bid you put on the table but to walk out of the meeting with a take it or leave it offer for the sake of principle. You certainly dispelled my idea of money hungry Americans. So tell me Mr. Stanton. You would risk a six figure commission for the Sake of one little Nigerian boy and his family that you hardly know," the secretary inquired. William, sweating profusely now, nodded affirmatively.

"Then I am afraid that you are not truly cognizant of the way things work here, my good man. This is not a democracy, as you know it. And many a good man has been dealt a severe hand for far less. Murder is a common solution for many problems and is most definitely more than just a consideration when we are talking of usurping the government of millions of dollars simply because you can. Diplomatic immunity means little here. And it means even less when one believes he can hold the government at ransom and dictate to them appropriate means of governing. That is out of the question.

Yet, I believe you have done something that I have yet to see happen since our government has come to power. You have raised a consciousness where I believed there was none. When you so naïvely placed your own life at-risk to come to the aid of one of our very own at an enormous financial cost to yourself as well, I believe you endeared yourself to a great many people in and out of government circles. I, for one am extremely grateful to you and must say that I applaud your efforts on behalf of the boy and his family.

Still, I would suggest that when you are finished conducting your business you make haste in returning to America. Our government works from a position of strength and cannot show any weakness and maintain a strong face when it is made to acquiesce to a single individual and a foreigner at that. I reiterate that I would not have made the same play but then I know things that you could not even conceive. Still, I applaud your efforts and you will be glad to know that your offer was accepted and that both the boy and his father have been located.

I am glad to say that Alex is in fine health and is being transported as we speak. I apologize, however, for the grief and the tragedy that the family has had to endure. I, am aware of many of the cruelties and inhumanities that have been imposed on many of our own but we are a new government and as in every new government there are a certain amount of growing pains associated with maintaining order. You have only to look at the plight of African-Americans in your own country to realize the struggles one must endure in the birthing of a nation. We too have our problems and although I don't condone all of the methods and techniques; some are quite necessary in restoring order and creating a society where everyone can have a suitable quality of life over the long haul. Would you not agree?"

William was so relieved by this time he would have agreed to anything short of being drawn and quartered and nodded in agreement.

The secretary continued.

"Again I apologize for the hardships the family has suffered at the expense of our military which sometimes becomes a bit extreme in its dealings with our people. I have, however, been up the greater part of the night placing calls and doing my best to arrange a reunion of sorts and to make sure that everyone involved is somehow compensated for their pain and suffering. I am not sure how can you can compensate for the tragedies these poor people have endured but I have thanks to you been made aware of this atrocity and done my able bodied best. Before you are reunited with your friends I must confess that although Alex is in extremely good health and spirits and is dying to see you and Melinda, his poor father has lost both an eye and his right arm, but is otherwise in fairly good health overall.

I've sent a truck to the mother's village to pick the rest of the family up. They will be reunited tonight at your villa if that is all right with you, my friend. We will sign the contract then, if all is in order. On behalf of my country, and myself, I thank you, Mr. Stanton."

William was so relieved, he dismissed the limo driver for the day, choosing to walk the twenty or so blocks back to the villa. Yet, despite the morning's success, William knew that his ordeal was no closer to being over than when he arrived. Making his way through the crowded streets of downtown Lagos, he noticed a familiar structure towering above the rest. He entered the Hilton and headed straight to the bar. Before he could reach the lobby, he could hear a voice summoning him."Mr. Stanton. Mr. Stanton." It was the bartender from his previous visit "How did it go, my friend?"

He told the bartender of the day's proceedings, as a host of hotel employees obviously familiar with the plight of young Alex gathered around to hear the story. When he finished, they cheered him and hugged him as if he'd just finished pitching the seventh and deciding game of the World Series. Drinks were on the house and after several gin and tonics, he staggered his way back to the villa, which now seemed miles away and collapsed on his bed. Fatigue from anxiety was setting in but before it had a chance to truly manifest itself, the phone rang.

"William, it's me, Melinda. Whatcha' doin', baby? How did the presentation go?"

William replayed the day's events with little emotion this time.

"I'm so proud of you, William. I knew you could do it. By the way, Mr. Davis called. He thinks he has a buyer for the house. If you agree on the price, we can close tomorrow. The only problem he foresees is that the buyer wants to move in immediately. Should I hire a mover or wait until you get back?"

"By all means, hire a mover. Hell, put the furniture in storage. I guess 1 can find a room or stay at the Radisson until we or better yet, *I* find a place." William hoped Melinda would offer her home until he found a place of his own. He was surprised when she didn't acknowledge or offer to let him stay with her.

There was a knock at the door."Gotta go, Melinda. Handle things, baby. See you soon."

"Good night, William." Melinda said, hanging up the phone.

William couldn't figure it out Melinda was still as efficient as ever. Yet there were no more sexual innuendos. She hadn't even mentioned the fact that she loved him or missed him for that matter. Something was definitely amiss. The last time he'd left a woman alone he'd been robbed blind. And now he'd given Melinda the power-of-attorney and she was acting strange and out of sorts. He had little time to dwell on the sudden change in Melinda's attitude. Whoever was knocking at the door was not taking no for an answer. William crawled out of the bed and hurried to the door.

At the door stood Alex's mother and six of her eight children. All were teary-eyed. "Tell me it is true, Mr. William. Tell me you have arranged for my husband and my children to come home. Tell me, it is true, Mr. William. Tell me they are coming home."

Alex's mother was accompanied by the old woman from the village, the bartender and a host of other people until it appeared that the whole village had descended upon William's villa. There were many tears and as many hugs but not quite so many as when the Secretary entered followed by Alex, his father and little sister. Alex's mother held William's hand, thanking him over and over again.

Alex's gratitude was unquestionable but talking with Alex, one thing was immediately apparent; the nine-year-old's innocence was gone. In its place had grown hatred and bitterness. The laughter in his eyes was gone. Unlike the tears of joy, which flooded William's suite, Alex cried out in anger. The nine-year-old little boy William had become so enamored of, the little boy he had fought so hard to have freed, was no more. The rite of passage paved with hardship and injustice had forced nine year old Alex into manhood. Gone was the easy smile. Gone was the quick wit and bubbling spontaneity. He now appeared burdened, mired in deep thought no nine year old should be saddled with.

"May I leave with you, Mr. William?" Alex inquired when he finally got the chance to talk to William alone.

"Why, Alex? What about you family?" William asked, nonplussed.

"I can no longer help my family. The government says I can no longer work. Now, I am but another mouth to feed," Alex said sadly.

"Let's enjoy the evening, Alex. We can talk about this some more tomorrow. I think you may change your mind," William said, feigning a smile when he thought of what was in store for the youngster.

After speaking for a good part of the evening with Alex's family and the old woman, William excused himself from the homecoming celebration. He ordered enough blankets and pillows for everyone there instead of having them take the twenty mile trek so late at night. He then retired to his bedroom where he found Alex already asleep in his bed.

Early the next morning, William put Alex and his family into the limousine. He then piled into a government truck with what seemed like half the village now and headed for the hills. An hour later, they arrived at the home of a former government official who had been kidnapped and later killed in a failed *coup*. The nine-bedroom home was beautiful. Maintained by the government, it was now used mainly for retreats or a hideaway for top government officials and their mistresses.

The family, who had no idea that William had arranged the purchase of the home as part of a business deal, were thrilled beyond belief No longer would they have to go to the river of water or worry about flooding during the season of the heavy rains. Now those that could read would have more time to teach those who could not. No longer would they have to cook their food over an open pit. Neither would they have to worry if there was food enough for all. And although it was not a part of the village, they were close enough to visit when they saw it safe to. Not once that day did Alex ask about leaving. The smile William had grown so accustomed to returned to Alex's face as he ran from room to room with His brothers and sisters, flicking light switches off and on. When they grew tried of that, they played with the faucets, flushed the toilets and did all of the things children given a free rein will do. Again, they embraced William, thanking him, repeatedly for all he'd done and begged him to stay. Unable to, he promised to return the following day to help them get settled into their new home.

Once back at the villa, William signed the contract and sent it by courier to the office of the Secretary. He called William upon receipt. He then taxed a copy of the signed contract to Ol' Man Morris and one to Melinda to be put in the files. Later that afternoon, William met with both Secretary and the Prime Minister, General Mfume to discuss a particular clause in the contract. William and Secretary Oluwola had already discussed the escape clause, William had only recently begun adding to His contracts over the past six months.

Oluwola thought it best to inform the General. This done, William added fifty thousand to Alex's trust fund in the name of Hill and Morris as Mr. Morris had instructed him to do in their last meeting. This would only allow Alex but several of his brothers and sister to attend school. William made it a point to let both of Alex's parents know that should a crisis ever occur like the one that just transpired the money was to be used to alleviate any suffering. The money, William explained, could be replaced. Their lives, however, couldn't be.

Now that it was not imperative that the children work, he sought their parents' permission to enroll them in school. William had some difficulty understanding Alex's mother's reluctance but after a good deal of pressure from all sides, she finally relented and agreed to send all but the two youngest who were needed to aid her in the upkeep of this big house.

With that in order, William paid the tuition for seven students for the next two years, including their uniforms at a Catholic school, which was recommended by Mr. Oluwola, and run by Jesuit priests. When that was completed, William met with officials from the U.S. Embassy, under the guise of being an American businessman in a foreign country concerned with the exorbitant tariffs on imports. He then conducted the final and perhaps most important meeting of his five day trip.

Davenport met William at three o'clock at one of Lagos' swankier downtown restaurants. Only this time, two strong-arm men accompanied him. William started nervously as they escorted Davenport into the restaurant.

"Hello, William. It's good to see you, son. You're looking well."

"Good to see you also, Mr. Davenport. Bodyguards?" William said, gesturing to the two thugs now waiting at different ends of the restaurant.

"Can't be two careful, son. The world is becoming more and more violent every day. There have always been poor people. Now, where there is poverty there is also desperation. But you know, William there's a difference. When I was coming up, there were poor people but they were rich in values. And they seemed to have had hope. Nowadays, values have deteriorated, and poverty and despair have increased. Frustration and desperation are commonplace. It makes leaving your home a risk Throw in Robin Leach, with his "Lifestyle's of the Rich and Famous," and now I have to be escorted by these two goons when I go to feed the 'damn dog'."

William laughed. Davenport didn't seem quite so smug, so self-assured this time around. In fact, he seemed vulnerable, human—almost likeable.

"I hear the big boys loved your proposal. You've made quite a name for yourself, since you arrived. I hear they're naming the library after you over at St. Martin de Porres Elementary School I also hear they're talking about bestowing an Honorary Doctorate of Education from the university on you. Quite impressive, William. It must have been some package you dropped on them. The Ol' Man will be quite proud, I'm sure. Congratulations, once again, William. Anytime you want to jump ship and make some real dough though, you come and see me. Tell Morris I said that." Both men laughed.

"Thank you, sir," William said.

"Oh, and by the way, I have a few packages I'm sending along with you to Morris. Nothing out of the ordinary, just a little something for he and the misses."

"No problem, Mr. Davenport. Just send it with the rest of the merchandise. Everything goes straight through to corporate headquarters in Boston. They'll see that he gets it."

"Fine, William! Now if you'll excuse me, I must make certain everything is ready to be shipped. It's been good seeing you again. Have a good flight."

He *had* him. He *had* Davenport cold. And for that matter, Morris too. Now all he had to do was get out of Lagos. *Alive.*

"Thank you, sir."

Davenport rose from the table, shook William's hand and left. William wondered if Davenport had noticed how clammy his hands were. Beads of per-spiration were forming on his brow. He was sweating profusely. Clicking off the tape recorder, he wondered if the two goons were waiting outside to check him for a wire or maybe to off him.

He left the restaurant and headed back to the villa to call Melinda."Hey, baby. Just called to remind you to pick me up at the airport." This was the code; William had devised to let Melinda know that everything was running according to plan.

"Will do." It was now Melinda's job to contact Terry Shannon and let him know that everything was on schedule.

Back in the villa William filled the Jacuzzi, poured himself another shot of Chivas Regal from the half empty bottle and laid back sipping the twelve year old scotch while doing his best to clear his mind and think of absolutely nothing. Over the past day or so, the thought of Melinda in her black evening gown kept recurring and was driving him absolutely crazy. It had gotten to the point that he could hardly keep his mind on the business at hand. There were Secretary Oluwola's words about embarrassing a government that used brute force to quell dissension or anyone posing a threat. Now the thoughts of government officials with a signed contract in hand knocking at his door loomed large.

The combination of the warm water, and Chivas soon dispelled these thoughts and he soon found himself nodding in the warm water. Dragging himself from the relaxing, cocoon he now found himself swathed in William wrapped the long, thick, terrycloth robe around him and made his way over to the king-sized bed, bottle of Chivas and glass still in hand.

In a matter of minutes he was half asleep with not a care in the world when from somewhere distant he heard knocking. Thinking he was dreaming he ignored the tapping but growing in persistence William could hardly ignore it and after he gathered that who ever it was had no intention of going away decided to answer it. Walking to the door his thoughts suddenly returned to the secretaries' words warning him to leave the country with haste.

But by this time the whole ordeal with Alex had taken a heavy toll on William. And in conjunction with the bath and the Chivas he would have hardly cared if the whole Nigerian Army were lined up at the door.

Just the same, William checked the peephole and was shocked to see a stunning, young woman of about thirty years of age, with skin black as the sky at midnight standing there in front of him a bottle of very expensive champagne in one hand a bucket of ice and two glasses in the other. Her hair was closely cropped appearing as though she had none at all and when William opened the door to inquire as to who she may be looking for he found himself at six foot five staring directly into her eyes. He had to admit that at that moment he had never in his life and fairly extensive travels met anyone of such rare and exquisite beauty.

At any other time he would have been tongue tied in the presence of such physical beauty but the combination of the scotch and his own exhausted ness allowed him to speak freely.

"I'm sorry, I didn't offer any champagne. I believe you have the wrong room, my dear."

It then dawned on him that she would have told him that upon seeing him and he not being whom she was expecting. And since there were no other rooms in the villa she was either way off course or there to see him. Perhaps she was just another of the grateful well-wishers from Alex's village he thought. But then she looked like no one he'd seen in Alex's village. The clothes she wore were of the finest material and suggested either New York or Paris. At a loss and tired of the suppositions William, did what most logical people would do in a similar situation after getting over the initial shock of having someone so striking calling on them.

"Hello. Is there something I can do for you miss?"

Replying in a voice as sultry as any William had to admit that if ever a face went with a body it was hers and he was at once enamored.

"No, there is nothing you can do for me, Mr. Stanton. It is what I can do for you. You see, my name is Naomi and I am here to simply make your last night here as pleasurable as you can ever wish for."

"It is my privilege to meet you, Naomi. You are very, very beautiful. May I ask you a rather personal question, Naomi?"

"As long as it is not *too* personal," she smiled and handed William a glass of champagne, which he placed on the cocktail table.

"I'd like to know why having never met me, you are interested in making my last night in Lagos so pleasurable. You are an extremely beautiful woman and I am sure that the men here must find you utterly irresistible so why the interest in someone you've never met before when you can have your pick of the litter?"

"I am here because you are a very bright and a very handsome man. And you are special in other ways too. I have heard how you took the time to help my people out so I was glad to make your last night here a special one. Many times I have done this what I am doing tonight. Sometimes, I choose to. Other times I do not wish to. Tonight I volunteered to be with the man that was willing to give up his life for one of my people. It is the least I can do."

"Well, I'm quite sure that no one in Alex's village could afford you or would consider sending you and I know the government frowns upon such things."

"Unless it is for the government," Naomi interrupted, smiling.

William continued.

"So if it isn't the village or the government who then sent you to me, Naomi?"

Naomi eyed the floor warily, shamefully and mumbled,"Mr. Davenport pays me."

William smiled at his own ingenious.

"I kind of figured as much, Naomi. And if you don't mind me prying again may I ask how much Mr. Davenport pays you, Naomi."

She smiled. "That is not personal. I am paid five hundred dollars for the night, Mr. William. It is a lot of money. You must be very special. Usually we are not paid quite so much but he asked for the best and the most, so it is five hundred."

"Well, Naomi, this will be the easiest five hundred dollars you will ever earn." William filled Naomi's glass, watched her drink it, then grabbed her hand, and led her to the door, saying: "You are truly a beautiful woman, Naomi. Good night." Puzzled to no end, she kissed his cheek and left.

Moments later, William, glass in hand, fell fast asleep.

The flight home held little intrigue. His thoughts repeatedly returning to Alex and his family, who had met him at the airport and showered him with an array of Nigerian gifts. He thought of Alex who, despite being reunited with his family in their new home, had pleaded with him to let him go. After talking at length to him, and his parents, it was decided that William would send for him when the school year was over. And still Alex cried.

William slept most of the flight. Then slept some more after picking up the connecting flight into Atlanta. Melinda was there to meet him, looking even better than when he'd last seen her. Casually dressed in red flats, red shorts and a red t-shirt, she was stunning. William couldn't wait to—She kissed him quickly, but passionately as they waited in line for the customs officials. Passing through, William saw no sign of D.E.A Agent, Terry Shannon.

"Good, trip?" Melinda questioned.

William told her of Alex and his family's new home as they made their way through the crowded airport to the baggage claim. Melinda offered little to the conversation until William had his bags and they were in the parking lot.

"William, I'm pretty sure someone is tappin' my phone, which is why I couldn't really talk after our first conversation." This latest bit of information, though disturbing, brought a smile to William's face, which hardly went unnoticed. "You're involved in international drug smuggling. My phone is being tapped and you're smilin'. William Stanton, I don't believe all your bricks are in the wagon."

"And all the while I'm thinking you've found another man and didn't like me anymore.

They both laughed.

"Shannon thinks it's the Ol' Man's keeping an eye on the Nigerian Holdings, so I think it is in your best interest to explain your sudden decision to increase the profit margin. He may think your tryin' to skim off the top. You know a liar and a cheat can never trust anyone. You need to explain it to him ASAP. He must have gotten wind of it somehow."

"When did you notice your phone was being tapped?"

"Well, I kept hearin' noises in the background and growing up around Jazzy and all his shady dealings, you learn these things. Shannon was nice enough to send a team over to check it out. They confirmed it but couldn't trace it. I guess that was Wednesday evening."

"It's nobody but the Ol' Man trying to keep abreast." I mailed him the contract with the two percent increase you calculated for me Wednesday afternoon. That's his way of staying on top of the situation after he's given you the freedom to run it your way. He still wants to know what's going on."

"Why did you increase the amount, William? You could have lost the account."

"I'll tell you about it when this whole thing blows over." Melinda knew better than to ask anymore.

"Where to, Mr. Stanton?"

"A bed and to sleep," William replied.

"How 'bout to my house and we find you some place tomorrow?"

"I don't think that I'll look to good should we end up in divorce court. Husband caught sleeping with his secretary. By the way, when you get the chance get in touch with your uncle. See if you can't get Sill's address. Contact my lawyer as soon as possible; ask him to file for divorce stating irreconcilable differences. Then I want you to find the prettiest white dress you can find that is if you'll marry his Ol' Man nine years your senior."

William pulled out the largest diamond ring Melinda had ever laid her eyes on.

"Oh, William!" Tears rolled down her cheeks as she stared first at William, then at the ring.

"I'll call Jazzy, tonight." Melinda giggled."Oh, William, I'm *so* happy."

She dropped William at the Radisson Hotel, then made a beeline to Dante's. Given Sylvia Stanton's address, she only wished tomorrow wasn't Sunday.

On Thursday evening of the same week, Sylvia Stanton returned from her run, picked up her mail, dropped it on the living room table and made her way to the shower. She had finally convinced Terrance to move in with her, although it had not been an easy sell. She had appealed to him in every conceivable way but was convinced that his final decision to sublet his own townhouse and move in with her, was not solely because he loved her but for economic reasons. Talk about stubborn. Still, she enjoyed his just being there for her, and was sure she would eventually win him over and make him see the light. No longer did he have to cook or clean for himself. She was at the same time learning to listen and, at least, sound concerned about his day at work, though most of the time she didn't give a damn. She was there for him, physically, whenever he desired to have her. She tried to keep the relationship new and fresh and made a concerted effort not to wear the same negligee and heels more than once a week. How often had he come home and found her naked, except for the heels he so adored. In addition to taking care of his physical needs, she would run him a hot bath and serve him the dinner of his choice. She transformed the guest room into a study for him and had a carpenter build shelves on three of the four walls. When she found that he didn't have quite enough books to stock the shelves, she went on-line and purchased fifteen hundreds dollars worth of books by famous Black authors not in his collection. He had been at his family reunion when she'd come up with the idea and when he returned, she had everything in place. She had even gone so far as to find those God-awful Louis L'Amour westerns he so adored and ordered the leather bound editions that were missing from his set. She had never seen him so happy. And on those days that he retreated into his study, she made it a point, as much as she hated to give him his space and leave him alone. He had been good to her, too. He was finally starting to adjust to the fact that he'd given up his independence and the space that he seemed to value above all else. The only gripe was sexually. It was never enough. Sure, he took care of her in the evenings but when he first moved in that was all they did. Often times she had to—as much as she hated to—tell him no, so bruised was she from their last tryst. It had been wonderful. She had even gotten to the point where she stopped wearing clothes in the house because all she found herself doing was taking them off, then there was the week when she was glad he'd gone to work, so sore was she. But that didn't work either. Terrance started popping up on his planning periods for a quickie and then rush back to school for his next class. Sill smiled just thinking about it. *Damn, that man is good.* Now only a month or so later, she thought about making a sign the way the homeless, do, saying: 'Will Work for Sex.' Well, at least, with his being there, she didn't have to worry about Laura sneaking around. Besides, Laura was out traipsing across the country, promoting her chain of health spas. By the time she returned, Sill was confident that she'd have Terrance in check.

Terrance wasn't home from work yet and it had been a good three days since he'd given her any. She thought about making the sign as a joke and greeting him at the door with just the sign and some heels on but thought that, as prudish as he was, he would probably be offended. Since she'd stopped teaching, she had little to do but live for him. Due to walk in the door any minute, Sill wanted to be dressed when he got home. Thursday night was the night they usually went out to dinner.

Sill hated getting in the shower when she was expecting someone. Too many Stephen King movies, she suspected. She grinned at the thought. She had not been this happy in a long time. Peeling off her sweats, she grabbed a towel all in the same motion, pulled back the shower curtain and stepped in. The water was warm and oh, so soothing.

"Terrance, is that you?"

"Yeah, sweetheart. Are you ready to go? I thought we'd do Chinese tonight," she yelled over the flow of the shower.

"Sounds good to me," he replied.

"How was your day? The kids didn't beat my baby up too badly, did they?" she asked, doing her best to sound concerned. There was no reply. Perhaps he didn't hear me. Before she could repeat the question, the shower curtain flew back. Terrance grabbed her, lifted her dripping body from the shower with one hand, and with the other unbuckled his trousers, letting them fall to his ankles. This was even more than she had bargained for. Picking up her cue, she ripped the buttons from his shirt. Knocking her to the floor, Terrance entered her warm chasm, as he never had before, first plunging, then rising each time with more force than the time before. Digging deeper with each pounding thrust, he heard her head bang against the porcelain tub. Time and time again, her head bounced off the tub. Ignoring this and feeling the shudder of her body as she climaxed, he grabbed her legs and raised them until her knees touched her face then entered her again, driving himself deeper and deeper inside her now dry canal. God how it hurt, Sylvia thought but that's what she was there for, to please him. Besides, it'll be over soon, after the third time, her insides were a mass of mushy, bleeding pulp. She bit her lip to try to conceal the pain. She finally prayed that he would stop.

Alarmed and frightened by this sudden onslaught, her body scarred and torn from the force and roughness of his assault, she couldn't—wouldn't endure another second. She screamed: "Stop, Terrance! You're hurting me!"

She was crying now. "Stop it! Terrance Daniels, you're hurting me. Oh, God! Please make him stop! Dear, God! Please make him stop!"

Then there were the flashes of that horrible night back at Bennett College. "You're *raping* me, Terrance. You stop it this instant! This is rape! Stop, Terrance! Oh, my God, please make him stop!"

Terrance ignored her cries. And after wrestling with her, for what seemed like an eternity, he was finally able to turn her over, onto her stomach. At which time he entered her again, this time he entered her from behind, until her screams became little more than sobs and her rigid body went limp. When he was finished, he left her like that, her buttocks pointing skyward, her head resting on the bathroom rug, one arm on the tub, the other by her side.

It was some time before he heard the shower waters beating against the bathroom tiles and an even longer time before she was able to limp down the stairs. For the second time in her life, she knew what it was to be forced—*to be raped.* Is this what she'd done to him? Ashamed, she blamed herself. She tried to rationalize his assault. What could she have done to warrant such anger, such hostility? This is how he must have felt our first night together, she surmised. She was confused. How could this be love? Mixed emotions filled her head, clouded her thinking and her judgment. Wrapping a towel around herself, she felt her insides throb in pain. It resembled nothing, she had ever felt before. What she could have possibly done to warrant this? Was he still angry? Whatever it was, she would make up for it. After all, she was trying. She really was trying to be compatible.

Unable to speak, she gazed at the fireplace as if it held the secret to her gaffe. When no revelation descended upon her, she somehow found the strength, despite the pain, to walk into the study. There, Terrance sat in the Lazy Boy she had purchased for him just last week so he would be more comfortable reading or watching the ballgame on television. Distant and detached, he sat, scanning the latest issue of *Newsweek* magazine. She knew she was on hallowed ground and really hated to disturb him by entering his inner sanctum but she was curious to know what she had done to merit such enmity. Afraid to speak, she stood there. Even with the towel draped around her she felt, for the first time, since she had known him, completely exposed—*naked.* Embarrassed and humiliated, she turned, prepared to run if she could just bear the sharp, piercing pain long enough to make it out of the room before he could see her naked, vulnerable. But she wasn't naked. And how could she be vulnerable with a man who loved her, a man she loved and cherished. Still, she would dress. She would feel better then but the throbbing between her legs and down her back was too great and she was reluctant to move. Without so much as looking up to acknowledge her presence, he asked rather nonchalantly: "Are you ready to go?"

In her best effort to ignore the callousness of the remark, she tired to sound indifferent as well. "Ready to go? Why, Terrance Daniels, what do you think I'm made of? Five minutes ago, you tried to go through me. I honestly thought you were digging for gold. Now, you want me to jump up, get my groove on, look good and be good company. I'm sorry, hon, but my recuperative powers are not that great. I'm hurting. All I'm looking for now is a double shot of Jack and a Tylenol or two, and some sympathy from you." There she'd done it. She'd played the whole incident off nicely. She could handle it. She had screamed rape but it wasn't, really. She was probably just having flashbacks.

She knew that, despite all the time she'd spent in therapy after the *incident*, as she liked to call it, that she wasn't in denial any longer. She had only slept with two men since the incident, one being William and the other, Terrance. In fact, she could count the times she'd slept with William in the six years of marriage on both hands and still have fingers left over. And Terrance was the only other man and he was too good to her in bed for this to be rape. She didn't know enough about sex to know the difference between rough sex and rape anyway. Truthfully speaking, the only real knowledge she had on the subject was from the dirty movies she and her sorority used to watch in the dorms late at night, back when she was in college. And aside from tonight and up until this point, Terrance was, undoubtedly, the sweetest, most gentle man she'd ever know. No, it wasn't rape at all, just her silly inadequacies raising its ugly head again. She just hoped he wouldn't be angry with her and the way she had reacted. It was after all, new to her.

It had taken her some time to get dressed and it really was too late to go anywhere, being that it was a school night and Terrance usually reviewed his lesson plans each evening in preparation for the upcoming day.

At dinner, there was little conversation. Terrance seemed to be in another world. Sill noticed that he didn't appear to be in the best of moods. In fact, he seemed almost morose. In an attempt to raise his spirits and, for the sake of conversation, she asked:

"What possessed you to be so damn aggressive, tonight?" She promised herself, while she struggled to get dressed, that she would let the whole affair drop but as she squirmed in the dining room chair, pain shooting up one side of her body and down the other, she couldn't help but ask. When he finally answered, she was sorry she had.

"You're not serious. You can't possibly be. I though I was bringing something new to the table. Thought you liked it rough. Thought you had some date rape fantasy or something. That's how you introduced me to lovemaking. I just naturally thought—."

Sill began weeping, gently.

"Damn, I'm tired of you walking around here sniffling and crying all the goddamn time. The only time you're happy is when I'm—. Oh, to hell with you. I knew I should have never given up my house and moved in with you. What was I thinkin'?"

And then just like that he changed the subject. "Did you get the mail today?" he asked.

Sighing, she answered: "It's on the table in the living room."

Terrance divided the mail, handing, Sill hers.

"Oh, Lord, no!" Sill screamed in a moment.

"What's wrong?"

"William's located me which means he knows I'm living with you," she said.

"So, what's the problem?" Terrance was having difficulty understanding.

"He's asking for a divorce."

"And? I'm still trying to understand." Terrance was truly at a loss. "I thought you'd be happy. You made it seem like that was all that was standing between us."

"Don't you see, Terrance, I can't contest the divorce if he has evidence that I'm living with someone."

"Why in God's name would you want to contest it, if he abused you? Please, make me understand. The man beat you and you want more. I guess I wasn't entirely out of line. Come on, let's go back to the bathroom so I can finish what I started. Is that it, Sill? You haven't had enough. You want more?" Terrance was visibly upset and it showed.

"William was good to me, Terrance. He was very good to me. I attacked his inner person, his ego. I tried to force his hand. I got bored with the daily routine, tired of marriage, afraid of commitment. The night he hit me, I was out with another man. I'd never gone anywhere without his knowing it and especially at night. He was crazy with worry that something had happened to me and when I got home I was pretty flippant and, well, I guess I brought it on myself."

"You need to take your little raggedy ass right back on upstairs to the bathroom. Sill, women, abused women, make excuses everyday for their being beaten when there's no excuse. Truth is, he's less than a man if he puts his hands on you. That's the bottom line."

"And what if I thought that of you, Terrance? Trust me, he's a good man. The last two years of your marriage, I can count the times I slept with him on two fingers and still have one left over. And not once, not one single time did he try to force his hand. I sleep with you on a regular basis and, for all intents and purposes, you raped me. William has never beaten me the way you beat me tonight. *Never*! My butt feels like it's on fire and I can barely walk."

"Tell me you're not going there, Sylvia. What occurred between you and me has nothing to do with any of this. What's happening here is that the last little puppy you had running around, chasing your apron strings has probably found someone else to spend his time and money on. Someone, I am willing to bet, is more loving, more appreciative, more giving, than you will ever be. And you, Miss Thang, who's always been afraid of giving of yourself, now finds herself with someone who is equally as selfish. You see, I'm not one that likes to give up my time or my space and if you didn't know before tonight I was tired of you taking up my time, my freedom and my independence so I treated you like you do me on a regular basis and took something back. Doesn't feel too good does it, when someone takes something from you that's very close to you. You didn't even have the guts to say you were raped until now. You would've denied it just to keep me around just to ward off that one thing you fear more than anything else, more than being raped or beaten. You'll suffer abuse at a man's hands any day just as long as he doesn't abandon you. Your greatest fear, Sill, is of being alone. You've got issues that are far too complex for me. I don't know what to tell you or how to resolve them but I'm used to a peaceful existence and being involved with you is far too much drama for me. I'm outta here."

"And where will you be? Shacked up with Laura, I suppose."

He ignored her remarks, choosing not to get into another spat if he could avoid it.

"If you need to reach me, leave a message at Jazzy's." he said. "You can't have your cake and eat it too, Sill. I love you. I always will. But you've never learned to love. When you do, you'll learn that you can't buy or own people and when you get tired of them, trade them in like a used car."

"Don't do this," Sill implored. "There's no need for you to do this, Terrance. We've come too far, made too many strides. You know I'm good for you. And it's just a waste of time. You'll only be back tomorrow. Look, I'm signing the papers. I'm consenting to the divorce." Tears rolled down her cheeks as she signed the divorce papers, sealed the envelope and handed them to Terrance. "Does this confirm my commitment to you?"

"I'm sorry, Sylvia. I saw your reaction when you opened the letter. The only reason you want me to stay is that your pride won't allow you to be walked out on—abandoned. But you're just not ready for a relationship, Sill, and I guess I'm not either."

Terrance gathered his suitcase from the storage and packed a week's worth of clothes.

"I'm ready, Terrance. **Please** don't leave," she begged on her knees. Ignoring her pleas, Terrance made his way to the study, Sylvia rose and still limping in a great deal of pain grabbed his arm. "Terrance, I'm asking you *not* to do this," she cried.

As far as he was concerned, the conversation, like the relationship was over. Grabbing his attaché case and his lesson plans from the desk in the study, he made his way to the door. Outside he threw the briefcase in the front seat of the Volkswagen and returned for the suitcase. Sylvia, still pleading, started emptying the suitcase. She was desperate now and on the verge of breaking down again. Tears welled up and spilled out of the corners of her eyes.

"Terrance, please don't leave me. What do you want, baby? Just tell me what you want, baby, and I'll get it for you. I know I can make you happy, baby. Just tell me what it is that you want. Do you want me in the bathroom, baby? Do you want to rape me again, baby? Just tell me what you want."

And then, right there in the doorway, Sylvia began stripping, tearing at her clothes with both hands until she was naked. Terrance pushed her into the hallway and grabbed his bag, pushing the clothes back as quickly as he could while Sylvia grabbed and pawed in attempts to first kiss him and then hold him there. "Look, baby, I'm nude and I'm yours. Do whatever you like."

There was a steady flow of tears now and Terrance couldn't help feeling sorry for her. Middle age was taking its toll on her and she was scared stiff of it—of growing old alone but this reckoning did little to dispel what he'd believed since their first encounter. Sylvia Stanton, behind the facade of sophisticated beauty and elegance, had some real, deep-seated emotional problems that were beyond his knowledge and his comprehension. Of one thing, he was certain of now, though: she was, if she hadn't already had one, was in the midst of having a nervous breakdown. Terrance was quick to notice that faraway look in her eyes she had when they had first made love. It was back now and she didn't seem cognizant. Again, there were the unintelligible mutterings and incoherent sounds. She slumped to the floor and then rose just as quickly and picked up the *Essence* magazine that was amongst the mail on the table and began leafing through it like a woman possessed, when she finished, she began again. Terrance was frightened now. From time to time, she would look up and stare at him as if she were trying to figure out why this strange man was in her home. It was almost as if she were trying to place this face, to recognize him. At other times, she would stare directly at him but it was obvious that she didn't or couldn't see him. And then as if nothing had happened, she jumped as if a pot were burning on the kitchen stove, grabbed her robe from the hall closet and wrapped it around her.

"Terrance, darling, would you be so kind as to pour me a stiff drink, please. I'm not sure if there's any *Chivas* Regal left. If not the *Glenfiddich* will suffice."

She seemed to have no recollection of the events, which had transpired over the course of the past hour.

"Did I give you the letter from William's lawyer?"

"Yes, Sill," Terrance replied, softening a bit.

"Please, make sure that it's mailed at your earliest convenience? I would hate to stand in the way of progress."

Terrance put down the suitcase and headed for the kitchen to find that there was no *Chivas* or *Glenfiddich*. Pouring her a glass of *Courvoisier,* he wondered why he hadn't noticed that there was something wrong before. Or had he, and simply chosen to overlook it? His mind raced. Returning with the glass of brandy, he handed it to her. There was no glazed look now.

"Terrance was I supposed to be getting dressed for dinner?" she asked.

"No, Sill. I think it's a little too late. I've got school tomorrow," he replied.

"Then why is your car running?" she asked.

Terrance forgot that he'd started the car in his haste to get away before there was a scene.

"Trying to sneak out on me, are you? I knew it wouldn't be easy trying to keep a good lookin' young man like you down. But tell the truth, babe, there aren't too many women out there that work as hard as I do to keep their man happy, are there?" Terrance didn't know how much more he could take. On the verge of tears, he wondered if he were responsible for her erratic behavior. She continued leafing through the pages of the *Essence* magazine.

"Are there, Terrance?" she asked again.

"Are there what, Sill?" he asked forgetting her question. His mind was a thousand miles away.

"Are you listening to me, Terrance Daniels? I said, 'There aren't many women out there that take care of their men as well as I do.' Is this true or isn't it?"

Terrance wasn't sure whether Sill was playing him or not. Was she simply baiting him out of guilt to answer appropriately or was she truly sincere in her questioning with no idea of what had just occurred. William chose his words carefully. "I don't know too many women who cater to a man's need the way you do, Sill," Terrance replied, carefully.

Sylvia placed the *Essence* back on the living room table, took off her reading glasses and walked to the hall closet. Reaching down, she picked up a brown shoebox and opened it to reveal some gold high heels with laves for days. She then proceeded to wrap the laces around her calves, tying them in bows right below the knee.

"Don't move a muscle, Terrance, darling, I've got something to show you." Sylvia walked up the stairs. Reaching the landing, she paused, and commented,"My God, I'm sore today. Guess I shouldn't have run that extra mile."

Terrance's head dropped to his hands and tears flowed freely. He couldn't stay here. There was no way he could face Sylvia after what he'd done. He felt an overwhelming sense of guilt and shame. All he wanted to do was extricate himself from the feelings burgeoning inside of him. But *how?* If he walked out on her now, he'd never be able to look himself in the mirror. And if he stayed, he was only fostering her hope and her denial. What she needed was help. Professional help. He felt that he owed her that much. Still she was so proud. What if she rejected his attempts to seek help? Perhaps he would suggest that they seek counseling together. A professional would certainly be able to recognize the signs of schizophrenia, as he surmised was what ailed her. He had never been this close to anything of this nature and truly believed that he had somehow triggered it. Now what?

Sylvia Stanton approached each step as if she were a supermodel on a Gucci runway. She sported a gold wreath atop her hair, which was now in a bun. Sheathed in a gold and white print, she flaunted a Roman toga with deep, revealing slits on each side. When she hit the landing and was in full view, she raised her arhis, letting the toga fall gently to the floor. And though he'd seen her in the nude before, he gasped. *Good God*! Underneath, she wore a two-piece ensemble, consisting of little more than a gold halter with gold sequins and fringes and a thong to match. The laces, which caressed her thick brown calves almost made Terrance, forget the ills and misfortunes, which had befallen them. There wasn't an Egyptian queen or Roman goddess who could

hold a candle to Sylvia Stanton. She was simply gorgeous. And then for no reason, he searched her eyes, the eyes which only hours earlier were so animated,
so full of life were once again oddly vacant, empty, devoid of life.

"I've been saving this for you, Terrance. How do you like it?" she asked. She
made her way to the sofa where Terrance sat. Nuzzling his ear, she started to
unbutton his shirt. Grabbing her hands, he spoke to her, gently but firmly!
"You are amazingly beautiful, Sylvia, even more beautiful without the outfit.
There's a beauty inside of you that makes you the person you are, the person
that made your students adore you so. That inner beauty is what attracted me
to you, from the very beginning. But there's also something else—something
wrong, Sill. There's something eating you up inside, something has deeply hurt
you, maybe even traumatized you and it's eaten away at you so long that it's
making you, well—ill. Let's you and I go and talk to someone that knows about
these things, maybe get to the bottom of all this, find out what's wrong so we
can make it right."

"Oh, so now you're my therapist? Did you think I put this outfit on so I can
receive bargain basement counseling at a discount price? Tell you what, Mr.
Daniels, I'll get help when you get help. Ask yourself why you need the approval
of more than one woman to consider yourself a man. Are you that insecure? All
I'm trying to do is hold on to the one man that I love and after months of baiting,
then luring me to the point where he can screw me he decides he doesn't want to
play anymore. Now, you need your space, your independence, as you call it.
You're nothing but a cold, calloused, insensitive dog."

Terrance gasped. "Sill, I'm leaving. I've had enough for one day." He pushed
her off him and went for the suitcase, which was still sitting at the door. "When
you decide to get some help, call me. You know that I love you and will be glad to
go with you. That's the only way I'd be willing to continue in this relationship."

"Let me ask you one thing before you step out that door, Terrance Daniels,"
she said. "How is it that you can speak your mind and no matter how angry I
get, I listen to you and try to work things out but when I disagree with what
you say, there's no debate? You just get angry and leave, case closed. My way or
the highway. Explain that to me."

Terrance ignored her. "Like I said before, when you decide to get help call
me," Terrance said picking up the suitcase.

"Terrance Daniels you need to bring your little scrawny ass back in here.
You already know that you're not leaving me. Terrance, please don't make me
cry again."

"I love you, Sylvia." Terrance closed the door behind him.

Sylvia still attired in halter top, thong and heels opened the front door for all to see. Neighbors stared in disbelief but she saw no one but Terrance."Damn you, Terrance. OK, I was wrong. I was wrong about everything. Damn, what more do you want. What? You want to rape me again? *Here,* rape me, then."

With the front door wide open, Sylvia Stanton pulled off the thong retreated to the living room and bent, spread eagle over the sofa. "Go ahead, Terrance, you can have me. C'mon, rape me again, if it's good for you, baby, then just keep raping me. I can take it. Just don't leave me." When she heard the Volkswagen roar out of the parking space, she grabbed her toga and ran back to the door where the neighbors still stood, watching in amazement. Embarrassed, she yelled: "Get that license plate number. That man just raped me." Dressed in her six-inch heels, thong and halter-top, Sylvia Stanton was somehow less than convincing.

CHAPTER 18

During the next two months, William immersed himself in his work, refining his oral presentation for prospective clients and took courses in assertiveness training and public speaking both of which of which were recommended, somewhat ironically by Melinda.

In the month since the trip, William grabbed three new accounts and was on the verge of closing on a fourth. He had been named, 'Employee of the Month,' for the third consecutive month, and was a shoo-in to receive the award again this month. To say he was hot was an understatement. He was in the zone.

And Ol' Man Morris, who always kept abreast, was well aware of William's recent success and was quick to offer him a small bonus for each of the new accounts. William, however, adhering to Melinda's plan declined the bonuses in favor of a lump sum stock option. Morris, quick to realize a gold mine, not only agreed to William's request but restructured his contract for the second time in a manner of months, giving him a thirteen per-cent share of the company making William the largest minority shareholder.

Morris knew the incentive would have a dual effect. First, it would keep William productive. After all, the more the agency brought in, the higher the shares; thus making William's holdings even more valuable.

The move also eliminated Morris having to consider making William a partner in the very near future. And although he'd consider making the move over the past few months, there were already rumors about preferential treatment among some of his other employees and a few of the board members who were in league with Jack Thomas coup to be the next senior partner based solely on seniority.

Aware of the politics, which sought to disclaim William's recent success, Melinda had suggested letting an article leak to her good friend Val who just happened to be the financial editor for the Atlanta Constitution, Atlanta's largest daily newspaper. That way William's success would be known throughout the Atlanta business community and any thought of moving someone ahead of him could very well shine a negative light on the firm as well as result in a possible discrimination suit and the last thing a firm with billions of dollars in holdings in Third World countries needed was a lawsuit screaming discrimination. But that was not the only reason Melinda deemed the leak important. William's name needed to become a household name in the days ahead if there was any chance of success for her plan. These days she was so overwhelmed with implementing her strategy, taking care of the usual day-to-day routines that made the Atlanta branch of Hill and Morris run smoothly that she had little time for herself let alone anything else including herself. Still, she maintained her regular routine at the gym. By the time she reached home at night she was so exhausted that she could do little but crawl in the bed and call it a day. She saw little of William these days outside of the office and even less of him in the office as he was constantly on the go, driven by a passion to be the best in his field despite the grumbling from Jack Thomas who viewed William as little more than a token nigga and the recipient of affirmative action on the corporate level.

Still, he was content to keep this to himself and a few of the board members who agreed but the anonymosity was there. And when the Ol' Man made it a point to fly down shortly after William picked up his fourth consecutive, 'Employee-of-the-Month Award', and give it to him in person at the quarterly meeting, Jack Thomas was fuming. After all, he'd been with Hill and Morris for twenty-five years and Morris had never given him anything resembling an award and he'd led the company in sales almost from it's inception. What was more, was that during the meeting and in spite of the impending flak sure to come, the Ol' Man went so far as to offer William Stanton a full partnership in the firm of Hill and Morris, effective immediately.

Upon hearing this, a few of the board gasped but only because it had come as such a complete surprise. Overall, most of them that had come to know him over the years were well aware of his achievements and had grown to respect William. And were as a whole happy for him.

Jack Thomas, on the other hand, was outraged and let it be known in no uncertain terms that the whole thing was nothing but a goddamn charade.

And well that he'd earned that position and, 'would never, not in this lifetime, ever work for a nigga'.

In spite of the whole drug trafficking affair that consumed William whenever he thought of the Ol' Man he'd never felt closer to Mr. Morris than he did that day in the board room of Hill and Morris when the Ol' Man visibly shaken by Jack Thomas', outburst as anyone in the room took a minute before replying.

"Well, Jack, what can I say? As long as I've known you you've been a loyal and valuable employee of Hill and Morris. You've always been a top-flight account representative. If you had only been as good a man as you were a rep then I may have been faced with a dilemma in naming a partner but as your discourteous manner has shown you still have a ways to go. Since you've decided that you can't work for the man I've chosen to succeed me I again thank you for your loyal service over the years and will make sure that you receive a first class recommendation."

William smiled appreciatively and shook Morris' hand before addressing the board members.

"First of all, I'd like to show my gratitude to Mr. Morris, my mentor, for taking a chance on me and then having the patience to show me the ropes during my tenure. He has always been there when I needed the support. In many ways he has been more than a mentor. He has also been somewhat of a father figure to me. Again, I appreciate his offer and I know some others would leap at this opportunity, (although I won't mention any names), but I must admit that…well, it comes somewhat of as a shock and although I would love to have the opportunity to take over the reigns when Mr. Morris chooses to retire it's not a decision that I can just say yes to that easily. I currently have twenty some odd accounts open and I would like to think that my clients have their faith not just in Hill and Morris but also in me. I, would therefore hate to abandon them when they have put their trust in me. Please give me a few days to see if I can't reassign some of my more tedious accounts and let me get back to you," William said turning to Mr. Morris who seemed more shocked by this display of uncertainty on William's part than he had by Jack Thomas' theatrics.

Morris returned to the podium.

"Always so deliberate, so methodical," he smiled at William and then the board members. "I'm sure we'll be receiving William's assent within the next day or two," he smiled, returning his gaze to William.

"Now, if there are no further questions then please excuse me. I have a flight to catch." And with that the Ol' Man shook William's hand, then leaned over and whispered into William's ear. "I hope you don't think I'm taking no for an answer," and William noticed that he wasn't smiling now. Call me on Wednesday and give me your decision.

No sooner than Morris left, William realized the embarrassment his indecisiveness caused the Ol' Man and though he hadn't meant to, he could hardly accept the position and still be in accordance with Melinda's plan. Oh God, how he hoped she knew what she was doing. If she didn't the whole damn thing was liable to blow up in their faces.

Anxiety was beginning to play a large part in his attitude and on returning to the office he hardly heard the congratulations or felt the countless pats on the back. His thoughts were somewhere else completely. And Melinda bore the brunt of his angst.

By the time Wednesday rolled around he had received word that Morris wanted to see him in person and not knowing what the gist of the meeting was he was even more nervous than he'd been when he'd been offered the partnership. Entering his office Wednesday morning there were no cordial greetings or attention given to Melinda's attire. It was just as it had been for the past two days and was a side Melinda had never seen before. She wondered if this was the same man that had placed his hand on her thigh ever so gently, told her he loved her and proposed to her all in the same evening. Stepping into the office on Wednesday morning William Stanton threw his London Fog over the chair in the outer office and barked at his assistant.

"Get in touch with Valerie at the paper! Ask her to let you have a copy of the article before it goes to print," he proceeded almost breathlessly.

"Anything else, Mr. Stanton?" William not used to being referred to so formally by Melinda, suddenly realized the solemn nature of his own tone and demands and started to apologize when Melinda stopped him.

"Forgive me, Melinda, I don't know what's gotten into—"

"No need to explain, William, I understand. I'll take care of everything. *Just relax, William. Relax.*"

Melinda hit the trunk release as she pulled up in front of the airport terminal. William jumped out, grabbed his briefcase, leather duffel bag and headed for the entrance.

"William," she cried.

William turned, noticed Melinda for what seemed the first time, so preoccupied, was he. He walked back to where she was standing, put his bags down, hugged her briefly and looked at her as if he'd never seen her before. Afterward, he held her as though their parting was permanent instead of only until evening when she would return to pick him up.

"I'm sorry, I've been sort of preoccupied as of late," William confessed lamely.

"So I've noticed. I guess I should have kept you with me this weekend. I'm sure I could have taken your mind off of all of this," Melinda said.

"It's never too late," William, replied. "What about tonight?"

"We'll see," Melinda said, smiling.

Melinda, now all smiles, waved goodbye as a traffic cop gestured for her to move the BMW. William broke into a quick smile.

"See ya at six."

Forty-five minutes later, Melinda arrived back at the office and checked the voice mail. Full, Melinda returned the ones she deemed important. She then contacted the *Constitution,* the paper, and spoke to Val who assured her she would send a copy of the article by courier as soon as her editor was finished proofing it. She then called the real estate broker and set up the closing for the condominium.

That completed, Melinda checked the mail. One particular letter caught her attention. She dropped the letter opener, tore the letter open, and read it quickly. She threw her hands up in the air in joy, jumped up from her desk and danced the Crip Walk around the office as though Ed McMahan of Publisher's Clearinghouse had just selected her their grand prizewinner. Sylvia Stanton's lawyer stated that the divorce was final. Sylvia would not contest it. *"Glory be!"*

Melinda called Mr. Davis next, who was not in and left word to proceed as planned according to Mr. Stanton's directions. This done, Melinda set out for Dante's for lunch. Once there, Melinda ordered a dry martini, then phoned DEA Agent, Terry Shannon, for an update. "Terry, this is Melinda. William asked me to get in touch with you. Said he hasn't heard from you since he got back and, frankly, he's a little worried."

"I'm sorry I haven't contacted William but things are kind of hectic here. Let me just give you the scoop," he said. "Thanks to William, we've confiscated the largest shipment of heroin ever in the state the Georgia. Not even my immediate supervisor knows. I'm holding the package, now all we can do is sit and wait. It shouldn't be long before there is some backlash. Already we have received a number of correspondences between Davenport and Morris. We have at least three, which implicate Davenport. He's accused Morris of receipt of the package and failure to pay. Each correspondence had become more and more threatening.

I'm sure there will be some type of confirmation sooner or later. I figure the less William knows the better. He's done everything we've asked him to do. The only thing we can do now is sit tight and wait. I can assure you it won't be much longer before a break or a mistake in made.

When you owe someone like Davenport a million and a half, you end up paying one way or another. Davenport wants his money and from what I've seen thus far, Morris has no inclination of paying for services not rendered. I understand William's concern but spare him the details just let him know that everything is going as planned. Like I said the less he knows the better."

"Thank you," Melinda said, "and have a good day, Mr. Shannon."

"You, too, Ms. Bailey," Terry Shannon said.

William entered Morris' office at ten o'clock. Morris shortly thereafter.

"Good flight, William?"

"A little turbulence outside of New York but nothing to speak of," William replied, calmly.

"Sorry I'm late. If you don't mind I'd like to get right down to business," Morris said.

"That's fine, sir."

"I've checked your overseas account and I am quite impressed with the results. However, I'm still puzzled about a number of things. First, what possessed you to increase the bid to four percent? That's double your initial bid. Was it your commission or lack of?"

"Actually, Mr. Morris, I got wind of the competitions' bids and realized ours was much too low so at the last min—"

Morris interrupted, "And to think I thought your disenchantment with the government and the jailing of your friends was the reason. I'm certainly glad to know you didn't let friendship and personalities come into play. After all, business is business. Another point that concerns me in the shipment from Davenport. A package was to have been sent by Davenport. Did he happen to mention it?"

"Yes sir, he did," William replied curtly. "Said he would be shipping it along with everything else some kind of personal gift for you and the missus." William wondered if he had offered too much information. Morris, however, didn't seem overly concerned. After all, William wasn't supposed to know anything. Little did he know that Morris had never trusted Davenport and, business, after all was business.

"Let me ask you another question, William, and I want you to be totally honest with me."

William slid back in his chair, a little apprehensive but refusing to let it show.

"Anytime one of my employees involves himself as avidly as you do in the activities of Hill and Morris, it makes me proud. Anytime one of my employees enters into profit sharing, buying stock options and the like, it let's me know they are interested in the growth of our agency. It's a symbiotic relationship, of course. They work hard, our agency grows, they collect, we collect. It's a concept the Japanese came up with following the Second World War that has worked to perfection, although many American companies are slow to embrace it.

"It has enabled you to become the largest minority stockholder at twelve and a half percent. But what concerns me is your intent. If you had accepted the offer as a partner in the firm, it would have dispelled any thoughts or questions I may have had about your leaving or any other intentions. You could have chosen your accounts, overseen others, shaped the company in your image. It's one hell of an opportunity. I'm curious to know why you turned the offer down. I'm sure you realize that my time with the agency is almost over. I'll be sixty nine in November and Martha's illness demands so much of my time, that it's difficult to oversee the day to day operations of the company. I was kind of hoping—."

"Mr. Morris, I don't mean to cut you off, but I just don't see myself in a managerial position at this point in my career," William said. "I've just sold my home and am in the midst of a divorce. Right now, I'm staying in a hotel. It would be extremely difficult to even attempt to manage a company the size of Hill and Morris, when I can't handle my own domestic affairs."

"I didn't know, William. I think I understand and I'm sorry. I must confess I didn't know. Tell me, though; you have any plans for that huge commission you just picked up? That should ease some of the pain."

"Well, sir, I guess I'll put it back in the company. It certainly beats the 401K plan," William smiled.

"Anything else need my attention?"

"No, sir."

"The offer still stands, William. Anytime you decide you've got your house in order and are ready for a change, just up let me know."

"I certainly will, sir."

Relieved that the meeting was over, William exited Hill and Morris as it was then known for that last time.

Two days later, an article appeared in the *Atlanta Constitution*, featuring William Stanton, senior account representative for the Hill and Morris Agency. Never had Melinda received so many phone calls, telegrams and faxes, applauding his achievements. There were even congratulatory faxes from former Atlanta mayor, Andrew Young as well as the U.S. Secretary of Commerce.

The one from the Secretary of Commerce as symbolic chief of American business was especially gratifying. Then there were the offers. From as far away as Seattle came the offers. There was even one from IBM, asking him to come on as a part-time consultant at twice his current salary. Still, William remained unwavering. He was looking at the bigger picture.

On the other side of town, Sylvia Stanton bent over to pick up the morning newspaper and watched it slide out of the flimsy little plastic bag and into a puddle. "Don't know why he doesn't tie up the damn thing," Sill mused. She had been out-of-sorts ever since Terrance left. Today didn't seem to be any different. It had been three days since he'd left and he hadn't even bothered to call. Not even a phone call, let alone stop by. It was, at that moment, while picking up the paper that Sylvia came across the picture accompanying the article. There in the business section, looking better than he had at anytime in their marriage, was her William Stanton. Gucci'd down to his socks. Seeing his picture was the first time since her leaving, that Sylvia had even remotely considered the notion that she had possibly made a mistake. But, so certain was she of his love and adoration, that she was sure all she had to do was call him and he'd come a-runnin'. The article was great. Sill thought the time apart had really helped William. She especially enjoyed the segment about him setting up a trust fund for a little nine-year-old Nigerian boy. William's increasing financial status situation, never a factor before, suddenly became a factor. Sylvia accustomed to having her way had become increasingly realizing just now difficult it would be to last the better part of the year at the rate she was going. The money she had taken from their savings was over half gone and she was behind in almost all her bills. If she called asking to come home, it would be an admission of guilt, putting her at William's mercy. But to call and congratulate him on the article and his recent success, maybe set up a lunch date, would not be quite so obvious. She'd take him out to Dante's wear something red, low cut and might maybe even give him a taste. He'd have his tongue out, tail wagging, begging her to come home.

Sill called the Greenwich Hill House only to find the number had been disconnected. All that money. Negro still can't pay a simple thing like a phone bill.

She then called the agency. "Melinda, hey girl, how ya doin'. I've been meaning to call you but I couldn't chance William finding me. How have you been?" Sill asked, nonchalantly.

Melinda was stunned. Speechless for a moment. "Sylvia? Why, I'm fine, Sill. How are you?"

"Couldn't be better," she lied.

"I tried calling the house to congratulate, William, on the article in the *Constitution* but the line was disconnected. Know matter how big a man gets, he still needs a good woman to take care of the small things. Maybe he'll appreciate me now. Whatcha think, Melinda? Think he's suffered enough?" Sill chuckled, expecting Melinda to join in as she used to. There was no response this time, however.

"Sill, the phone's disconnected because William's moved."

"Moved? He couldn't have. William loved that house. Are you sure he moved?"

"Closed on a condo just yesterday over on the East Side. Heard it's fabulous. Shall I tell him you called or shall I have him call you?"

"I'd rather he not know where I am as of yet." Sylvia replied, guardedly.

"Sylvia, darling, William has known where you were for months." Melinda lied. "I hardly think he cares."

"Don't be so crass, Melinda. What's wrong? Still can't find a man? Why don't you try losing a little weight, girlfriend. It may help."

"Actually, I've found a man, a rather *good* man, Sill. I really think you'll like him," Melinda smirked.

"Maybe, I'll get the chance to meet him sometime. In the meantime, please let William know I called. Oh, and don't be spiteful. After seven months, I can still wrap William around my little finger and have you fired. So, be a good little girl and give him my message. Thank you, ever so much. Oh, and Melinda? Have a blessed day." Sill hung up with Melinda seething on the other end. What disturbed her more than anything was the possible truth in Sill's words. Sylvia Stanton had that unique ability very few women have: she had that unique quality that caused men to jump through hoops at their command. Most men were at her beck and call and she knew it. Nevertheless, Melinda did what she considered the proper thing and forwarded the message and the gist of the conversation with Sylvia. Oh, what a fool she was. Afterwards, however, she was glad she had done just that. William received the message and smiled.

"Melinda," he confided, "this is a chapter in my life that's over. And there is a chapter that has yet to be written. That chapter includes you and me. Let's write it together." And then he tossed Sylvia's number in the wastebasket and called Edwin.

"How are you doing today, Mr. Davis? William Stanton here."

"Fine, William, just fine. And you?"

"Oh, I can't complain."

"I've been waiting on your call. I've got my man standing by. I'm just waiting on your go ahead."

"That's fabulous. Something should be breaking any day now. Just hang on, I'll be in touch as soon as I hear something."

William leaned back in the black leather swivel chair, content to do nothing but wait. A week later, Terry Shannon burst through the door of William's office accompanied by the sane two DEA agents he had met at the airport. There were no hellos, no greetings of any sort."Ol' Man Morris is dead," he said. "The hit came last night in the parking garage at corporate headquarters at seven-thirty about. Boston, P.D., found the body this morning. Three slugs, from a twenty-two, to the back of the head. We believe it was a professional job but we're questioning everybody there. I don't believe you're in any immediate danger but I'm still assigning detectives, Brown and Perez, to you until we know more."

The old man dead! William was shocked and confused. Stunned, he fell back in his easy chair. He had just spoken to Mr. Morris this week. The Ol' Man called him to see how things were going at home. There was no talk of business. He seemed genuinely concerned about William's private affairs and it had taken William quite some time to assure Mr. Morris that everything was working out fine. Morris had even gone so far as to tell him not to pursue any legal or punitive action against Sylvia.

"A hundred thousand dollars is a small price to pay to get someone out of your life that you didn't see there anyway," Morris had confessed. "I am sure you would gladly pay that to get rid of a life threatening illness, so look at Sylvia as a cancer that you had to have removed."

William thought the old man a bit harsh at the time but he made plenty of sense and William appreciated his concern. Now this. He knew there would be repercussions and was not so naïve as to believe that the effect would stop short of being lethal but he was still shocked. He had never expected this. Never!

After a time, William was finally able to focus. One man's death was certainly a cheap price to pay for all of the children, he'd poisoned. He thought of how Sylvia used to get on her soapbox whenever the topic of drugs was brought up. She called the drug trade, 'A negative by-product of greed that resulted in the genocide of a nation or the Black Death similar to the plague spread by rats in Elizabethan times. And yes, Jonathan Morris III, was a major contributor to this plague, this genocide, this scourge which was devouring inner cities and extending its bloodsucking tentacles into every nook and cranny of America.'

In spite of everything, there was also another side to Jonathan Morris III. There was the man that had flown a bright, yet very naïve Black man to the corporate offices of the Hill and Morris Agency, a Fortune 500 company, six years earlier and hired him on the spot. This was the same Jonathan Morris, who took him under his wing, introduced him to the best and brightest in the field, and despite their objections and protests, demanded that they show him the ropes. Morris didn't know William at the time but, having a keen eye for potential, took him under his tutelage that first year and, although their personal relationship did not have the chance to blossom as both men had hoped, there was a deep and abiding respect between them.

The Ol' Man gave William the opportunity to succeed, to rise to the top of the corporate ladder despite that red necked Jack Thomas who made his feelings quite well-known when it came to skin darkies rising too fast in this White man's world. And it was Morris who made the final decision to promote William, in spite of the board's recommendations to promote Thomas to CEO based on seniority. It was also Morris who bore the brunt of Thomas's wrath about 'never working for a nigger,' when he announced William's promotion. The motives for most of Morris' actions could usually be tied to money, but William knew the guidance and opportunity awarded him by the Ol' Man were invaluable. Whether his actions were sincere or simply out of sense of inexplicable guilt, it hardly overshadowed the deep sense of remorse William now felt for Ol' Man Morris.

At Mrs. Morris' request, the funeral was to be held the following Tuesday in Boston, since she was not in the best of health and could not travel. During the weeks following the Ol' Man's death, Hill and Morris's stock plummeted. When William was sure the stock could fall no lower, he called Edwin Davis."Mr. Davis, this is William Stanton. Have you been following the market." he asked.

"Not doing too good, is it? I guess you know your business, Mr. Stanton."

"Yes, sir. The bottom fell out, so I guess you know what time it is?"

"I guess it's time to dance, Mr. Stanton. What are we looking at?"

"Well, the stock has dropped from fifty-four down to six and a quarter. Let it fall to about six dollars a share. By my calculations, that should come to a little over three hundred thousand dollars with the brokerage fee and all. Are you going in on this one, Davis?"

"I suppose I'll pick up about ten thousand shares. At six dollars you can hardly go wrong and if this thing blows up like you say, don't even consider commission or brokerage fees. I've got a real good feeling about this one, William."

"Oh, by the way, Edwin, if you can put in another ten thousand for Melinda I would appreciate it," William added.

"OK, that's fifty thousand for you and another ten for Melinda. You two are getting pretty serious, aren't you? I should have grabbed her out of college. She's a fine woman, William. Should I put her shares in a separate account?"

"Please! I think it'll make a pretty good wedding gift."

"Well, congratulations. I wish both of you the best of luck. And, William, I appreciate the tip."

"Be careful, though. When white folks don't like you, they call that insider trading." Both men laughed.

"You are aware of the fact that this will give you controlling interest in Hill and Morris," Edwin said.

"Aware? I'm counting on it," William joked.

By the end of the following day, William Stanton was the majority owner of the third largest import-export firm in the country worth close to nothing. Edwin and Melinda concentrated their efforts on the marketing and, by the end of the second day, every major newspaper in the country carried news of the takeover. The stock, which only days before had bottomed out at six dollars a share, was soaring. By the close of the Dow Jones in the third day, the shares had risen to more than sixty dollars a share.

In the past three days, William had cleared close to four million dollars. Edwin Davis, who stood to make close to half a million from the venture was kicking himself for not investing more but was pleased just the same. Melinda had never been so excited. It was two days before she came up for air. She had taken out a thirty thousand dollar loan and invested every penny. The investment netted her close to a hundred and fifty thousand dollars. Funny thing, though, about Melinda's new found wealth was that she had yet to buy anything for herself. In fact, she really hadn't bought anything for William either except for some socks and a couple of suits she'd been eyeing for who know how long. But that was it. The rest of the time she spent selecting furniture and other assorted knickknacks for the condo.

After the third day of sporadic shopping, William forced her to stop. "If any more money is spent on the house, let me be the one to spend it. Put your money in a good investment. You go find yourself the most gorgeous wedding dress you can find and meet me at City Hall at four o'clock. They close at five, so make sure you're on time."

"I guess I can do that," Melinda smiled. *Oh, how she loved that man.*

"Tell your uncle to reserve the best table in the house along with a case of his best champagne for tonight. How's seven thirty sound?"

The money had done little to change William. Edwin no stranger to the transfer of funds, simply let his stock option roll over except for the thirty-five grand he withdrew to purchase Melinda's wedding present with.

Sylvia, having grown more and more disenchanted with her current living situation and the latest turn of events in her life, stood in the middle of her living room alone, muttering to herself. Dressed in a pink terrycloth robe and pink slippers, she looked tired and worn—and wearier. She hadn't combed her hair since Terrance left and that had been four or five days ago and she hadn't bathed in the last two. She'd slept soundly for the first time in days until that good-for-nothing paperboy awakened her, as he did every morning, throwing the paper hard enough to make a thud and dent the screen door and wake up the dead.

Sill finally dozed off sitting up as she had the last three or four nights in a row, a glass of whiskey in one hand. For the first time since she could remember, the whiskey didn't help. She drank anyway and she drank heavily. No longer did it matter what she drank. When she ran out of *Jack Daniels,* she turned to the *Chivas.* When she ran out of the *Chivas* and everything else in the bar, she made her daily run but no longer did she jog around the complex. Now she ran straight to the liquor store, and got her booze and returned to the apartment.

She couldn't understand Terrance not calling her. What was he doing for clothes anyway? Most of what he owned was here. That was—she thought—her insurance.

She picked up the newspaper and after stumbling about, found her reading glasses. The newspapers had piled up next to the door and the house was a wreck. Oddly she hadn't even considered looking at a paper until today. In fact, Sill hadn't thought about much of anything right up until now. The liquor kept her numb. Still she knew it was time to pick herself up and move on. The hell

with Terrance. He was probably shacking up with Laura—somewhere. She
didn't blame Laura, though. She blamed Terrance and all the dogs out there
like him. She blamed herself for allowing him to enter her life, to play with her
emotions. *Trust* was what he told her was the key. *Communication.* Yes, those
were the keys. She had problems with both, she knew. However, she had
bought into it and lowered her guard,—and for what? What had it gotten her?
Nothing! Nothing but a divorce from the only man that had ever truly loved
her...

She poured herself another drink and cursed when she noticed the bottle
was empty. *Damn!* How she hated to go down to that liquor store. The old man
in there had to be forty-five, if he was a day and he was always trying to flirt
with her. Bad as she looked, he was still trying. Hell, he was the owner and he
wasn't all that bad lookin'. I might just have to give him some. She smiled as
she sipped the last of the whiskey. Better not. Old fool might have a heart
attack. Sylvia caught herself laughing aloud and, then, stopped abruptly. Her
thoughts were scattered and she had been having those spells again. She hadn't
had one since she'd been married but ever since Terrance raped her in the
shower, they were coming with increasing frequency. She'd had them after the
incident at Bennett and she was forced to drop out for a time and seek counseling but she hadn't had one in a good ten years until the Thursday before last.
Maybe Terrance was right. Maybe she did need to get some help. No! Hell, no!
The only thing she needed was some good love from that asshole right through
here. Her mind was racing again. *Damn,* she hated when that happened.
Maybe she could call him and have him arrange the appointment with a
shrink. After all, he said he'd go with her. He did tell her that. Said the only way
the relationship could continue is if she sought help. "Well, then, I'll get some
help!" Sill shouted. "Then you'll have to take me back. Let me see. Yeah, I'll call
him at Jazzy's. He told me I could reach him at Jazzy's."

Sill picked up the phone. Her mind was racing again. She thought of William. Was that who she had been meaning to call? God, she hated it when she
couldn't remember anything. It was those damn spells again. Then out of the
clear blue, it dawned in her that William hadn't returned her call. "I know that
fat, jealous, little heifer didn't give William my message. If she had he would
have called me back." she sighed. "Let me get my ass up and get on with my
life."

She stood up, put her glass down on the cocktail table, then leaned over to
put her cigarette out in the ashtray when the headline from one of the rolled

up newspapers caught her attention. Staggering, she bent over, grabbed the paper, pulled the rubber band off and let the paper unfurl.

Could it be true? No, she was imaging things. Had someone actually...? No, they couldn't have. Sylvia reread the headlines. No, there is was, as plain as day in black and white. Someone had actually murdered Mr. Morris. But why? Sill reached into the ashtray, grabbed her cigarette and relit it. After reading, she was still no closer to understanding why someone would murder a seventy-year-old man in cold blood. At least her head was clear now.

Sylvia grabbed a quick shower which helped to rejuvenate her a little, then put on a pair of tight black jeans, over her back sleeveless Danskin, straightened up the house, fixed herself a bacon lettuce and tomato sandwich, then reread the article on Morris' untimely demise. No way.

Leafing through the stack of papers for a follow-up on the Morris murder, Sylvia was stunned to find that *a group of African-American businessmen, led by Senior Vice-President, and recently named Chairman of the board, William Stanton, had affected the buyout of Hill and Morris and renamed it "Stanton and Associates." Sylvia gasped but read on: Mrs. Morris had sanctioned the buyout, telling the press that her late husband had on several occasions asked William to become a partner and run the day-to-day operations of the firm. "William," she explained, had demurred on both occasions but was and had been in reality, the only viable candidate. This, in itself had given credibility to the recent takeover and brought investors back in droves.*

Sylvia was speechless. No wonder William hadn't challenged her leaving, her cleaning out the house and the savings. That son of a bitch had probably been working on a buyout the entire time. Now she'd have to swallow her pride and come a crawlin'. Hell, he'd known this all the time. That's why he laughed at her suggestion to start his own firm. He also probably had money stashed away the whole time. Imagine the gall of that bastard! Sill grabbed the phone and dialed William's office as she had done so often over the years.

"Stanton and Associate," the operator answered.

"Melinda, is that you?" Sylvia asked, excitedly.

"I presume you are looking for Ms. Bailey. She's been promoted to senior account representative," a voice piped.

"No, ma'am, I am actually trying to reach William Stanton," Sylvia said.

"I'm sorry Mr. Stanton is not in his office."

"Look, missy, I *know* that Mr. Stanton is in his office and if you'd like to continue working for Hill and Morris, I suggest you put me through to Mr. Stanton. This is his wife."

"You're a bit out of touch ma'am. First, Hill and Morris is no longer in existence. Secondly, Mr. Stanton is single. Thank you. Please call again." The next sound Sylvia heard was a buzzing dial tone. Sylvia, not to be denied did exactly that "Melinda Bailey, please."

"I can give you her office," the operator reported. "Please hold."

"Ms. Bailey's office," the girlish voice answered. "May I help you?"

"Yes, may I speak to Melinda, please?"

"May I ask who is calling?"

"Sylvia Stanton."

"One minute, Mrs. Stanton." Never in her life would Sylvia have imagined she'd have to go through such bullshit to speak to her own husband. She wished she would have got that first little heifer's name she'd have William fire her right along with Melinda.

"Sylvia, how are you?"

"Fine, Melinda. I'd be better if you'd give my husband my messages when I call."

"Let's clear something up right now, Sylvia. First of all, I gave William your message. I cannot *make* him call you. From my understanding, your divorce was finalized several weeks ago. Therefore, William is no longer your husband. If further clarification is needed, you can see William at Dante's at around eight o'clock tonight. Thank you and have a good day."

At that moment, the receiver went dead. "Why, you fat little…" Sylvia slammed the receiver down. This could not possibly be happening. She'd show the little heifer. Once she had William's little country-ass back in check, she'd clean house.

It was a simple ceremony. Melinda wore a simple two-piece off-white suit, which showed a little more leg than she was accustomed to, but nowadays, she could afford to. She not only looked downright stunning, she was positively elegant.

After a quick dinner at The Tavern, William, grinning from ear-to-ear, drove his new bride to Dante's where they were met by Jazzy and a host of well-wishers at the door. Jazzy reserved almost the entire left side of the club for the newlyweds and their entourage. Edwin Davis and Terry Shannon were there as well as a rather large contingent form Stanton and Associates. Terrance and Laura, appeared as part of Dante's regulars, but were quickly swept up in the celebration, though they kept their distance from the newlyweds. Champagne and caviar flowed as if there were no tomorrow. The band, Pieces of a Dream, never sounded better.

But about eight o'clock, a dark cloud descended in Dante's in the form of Sylvia Stanton. Dressed in the red dress and red heels William liked so much, Sill met Jazzy at the entrance. "What's all the commotion, Jazz?" Sylvia inquired, noticing the parking lot was so much more crowded than usual.

"My niece got married, today. They're having a small reception inside is all? Go ahead in," Jazzy said proudly.

Sill entered immediately, noticing Laura and that no-good Terrance Daniels. Waving at Laura, Sill watched Terrance exit quickly out of the corner of her eye. Some man, I guess he's too embarrassed to even face me. Little does he know I wouldn't degrade myself by confronting him? Scanning the room, Sill first noticed Mr. Davis who nodded cordially, but surprisingly made no further attempt to greet her. Sill hadn't had the chance to digest the slight from him when she noticed William in deep conversation with some White guy about his age. What bothered her more than anything else was the rather attractive young girl at his side? Therefore, William had traded her love handles for this hipless heifer.

"Congratulations, William." Terry said.

"Thanks, Terry."

"William, perhaps I shouldn't tell you this on such a special occasion but we've found Morris' killer. Name's Thompson, Jack Thompson," Terry said. "You know him. Seems he was unhappy about your being promoted or something. He confessed the whole thing. Anyway, congratulations and good luck. You've got a beautiful bride."

Terry Shannon leaned over, kissed Melinda on the cheek and handed William an envelope. "Thanks again for your help. We couldn't have done it without you."

"What's this, Terry?" William asked, pointing to the envelope.

"Just a little wedding gift." he grinned sheepishly.

William gave the envelope to Melinda who gasped when she opened it. "William there must be over a hundred thousand dollars in here. We can't accept this."

"Not now, Melinda, not now. I think we have an unexpected guest. You wanna handle it or you want me to?"

With champagne cocktail in one hand, bottle in the other, Sill made her way through the crowd towards William.

"Long time no see, William. You're looking well. When did you start hanging with the chic and sophisticated?" she asked.

"Oh, I don't know that I can hang with either the chic or the sophisticated. It's more like a few friends just getting together for a small celebration."

"I'm sorry I meant to congratulate you on the buyout. I always knew you could do it. I'd like to think I was the motivating factor."

"Wish I could say that were true, Sill."

"What brings you here anyway?"

Sylvia sipped the champagne coolly. "Actually, I frequent Jazzy's quite a bit. By the way, he mentioned his niece had just gotten married. Where is the lucky girl, William?"

"I'm right here, Sill," Melinda piped up shyly.

Sylvia recognized the voice but couldn't believe it was Melinda.

"My God, girl you look—" Sylvia said. "You're Jazzy's niece? Well, I'll be damned." Sill was shocked. "My God! Look at the size of the diamond! You go, girlfriend! Despite out little telephone conversation, I'm really happy for you. I really am. I can remember my wedding day. It had to be one of the happiest days of my life." And she looked at her ex-husband disdainfully. "Do you remember, William?"

William nodded self-consciously. Sill grabbed Melinda and hugged her ever so tightly. It was not that she was happy for Melinda but simply because it felt so good to be in William's company again. Not even Melinda's new found arrogance could affect her tonight. She was taking her man home in plain view of everyone. Laura could have her Terrance, Melinda with her new hubby. Sill was sure she would be leaving with the Chairman of the Board. But it dawned on Sill that she had yet to meet the groom. After all, it was only appropriate that she meet the groom before leaving.

"You said I'd like him, Melinda. So where is this Mr. Wonderful anyway?"

"He's right here, Sylvia," Melinda said with trepidation.

It was at that moment that William put his arm around Melinda's waist, pulling her to him. Sill gasped. Her world came to an abrupt stop. Dropping both champagne bottle and glass, Sill drew the attention of those not already taking in the whole affair. Finally, able to catch her breath, she spoke, "No you didn't! You wanted a divorce so you could; marry this—this piece of trash. Tell me you didn't. Please tell me you didn't do this, William."

Hearing the commotion, Jazzy sent two of his seldom-used bouncers to William's side. "Piece of trash? Wasn't it you Sill who once told me that one man's garbage is another man's gold." Melinda grinned proudly as she nuzzled up to William.

"Didn't I tell you, you'd like him," Melinda giggled.

Sylvia suddenly felt unstrung and paranoid, as if every eye in the place was now on her. Her observations weren't too far off base. Turning, she noticed Laura looking. She stared at Sill, then flipped open her cellular phone to call someone. Probably calling that chicken-shit, Terrance, Sill thought.

Turning again, she could see Edwin who dropped his gaze when their eyes met. Suddenly the prim and proper, ever so reserved Sylvia Stanton had become the gatecrasher, the evil villain, the ex-wife, and the *other* woman. She glared at Melinda, then William waiting, hoping, praying for one of them to tell her it was all a bad joke but neither ventured a reprieve. The joke was on her. Her, Sylvia Stanton. Sure William had ample cause to pay her back but not like this. Anything but this. This was more than even she could stand. This was simply too much for her to handle.

"Tell me you didn't do this, William. Tell me you didn't…Sill was close to hysterics her head swam and she swooned but couldn't remember Laura walking her to her car or offering her a ride home. She didn't even remember the drive dome. Her only thoughts were of her William being with *that* woman. That goddamned Melinda. How could he? God, how could he?

Melinda was neither college educated or quite trained, sophisticated enough to—. O.K., so she was an attractive girl but, by no means, was she William's type. Melinda would be like a fish out of water at a formal function. She would never be able to mingle with the chic and sophisticated. It just didn't make any sense. Of course, it made dollars for the little gold digger, who stood to become wealthy through this union. How could William be so stupid? Didn't he realize all she wanted was his money? It just didn't make any sense. Sill's mind raced, spinning every which way. First, Terrance and now William. Neither that tall, lanky Laura nor country-assed Melinda could hold a candle to her. Yet, she was the odd man out, the one out in the cold. What was wrong with her? She could get a man. The problem was keeping him. As soon as it seemed that she let her guard down, he was gone. She sighed.

Where the hell was she? Abandoned, once again. Alone. God, how she hated being alone. It was the norm now.

Arriving home, moments later, she opened the door and once inside, fell to her knees. Head in her hands she screamed. Then screamed again. Wailing now. Sill fell face down, tears gushing out she looked around until she saw the note attached to the whiskey bottle.

It was a note from Terrance and practically the only item left in the now vacant apartment. It read:

ॐ

I love you so much Sill that I couldn't bear to face you. I've put the condo in your name and moved my furniture and other belongings out

Good luck and God bless.

Terrance.

Two days later, another note was found at 1604 Havelin Drive, by the authorities when police entered the apartment after the super had made several unsuccessful attempts to have Sylvia sign a temporary lease. Only this time the note spoke of the hurt and the pain that was just too much to deal with anymore

Fifteen minutes away the newlyweds boarded a flight for Freeport, Bahamas, where they would honeymoon for a week. Both were unaware of the tiny article which appeared in the *Constitution*. They sipped huge glasses with orange and pineapple slices and colorful miniature parasols.

978-0-595-36178-6
0-595-36178-1

3/06	DATE DUE		

Printed in the United States
42844LVS00004B/313-315

9 780595 361786